Conviction

BOOK II OF THE MARTYR SERIES

By MC Hunton

DEDICATION

For my family, who had to put up with me while
I obsessively worked on this book during
an unprecedented pandemic.

CONTENTS

ACKNOWLEDGMENTS

To Scott, Becca, and Geoff for patiently dealing
with my nit-picking and insanity.

To Courtney, for caring about commas
as much as I do.

And to Annie, who pestered me for new
chapters so often that I finished writing this
book in record time.

CHAPTER ONE

Clink!

A small, metal slug dropped into the porcelain sink. Thick, red tendrils pooled around it, beneath it, and down the drain. Thorn Rose swore under her breath and pressed her gritty, stained fingers against the gash in her side. Her pulse pounded in them as the blood leaked through. *Ba-bum.* With each passing second, she could feel the flow slowing. *Ba-bum.* Thank god. She didn't have time for this shit.

"Teagan?"

Another knock on the door. Jay Coons had been at it for thirty minutes now, rapping every so often and asking if he needed to call the police. No matter how many times she told him not to, he kept pushing.

"I'm *fine*," she snarled. She felt him hesitate. The cold shape of him, the corrupt energy his humanity gave off, raised an arm as though to knock again, but he paused and dropped it down.

"You're covered in *blood*."

Well, he had her there. "Fuck," Thorn whispered.

"What did you say?" Jay called through the door. Thorn reached up and grabbed a wad of paper towels from the dispenser beside the mirror. She caught a glimpse of herself. A thin, white line above her eye was all that remained of a cut that had dribbled blood along her nose. Her torso was covered in red streaks and fingerprints. She suppressed a bitter laugh.

How was she going to talk her way out of this one?

"Get me a cigarette," she murmured to Sparkie. The lizard dove into her black satchel and emerged a moment later with a lighter and a smoke. Thorn held the paper towels tight against her side. Jay rapped at the door again.

"Who the hell are you talking to?"

"Don't you have customers?" Thorn growled as she propped the cigarette between her lips and lit the tip. Her lungs heaved a deep breath of nicotine. Pain shot through her side as her ribcage widened to make room for the toxic air, and a quick surge of blood soaked the towels. The bleeding would stop soon. Then she could get her drink.

She fucking deserved one after the day she'd had.

"If you don't open that door in half an hour, I'm calling an ambulance," Jay finally said. Thorn took another long puff on her cigarette, feeling his cold energy pause before he walked down the hall and back into the crowded bar. She glanced to Sparkie, and the winged lizard just tilted his head. Half an hour? She could be cleaned up in half an hour.

Two minutes later, with her cigarette nothing but a smoldering butt in the sink beside the bullet and the blood, Thorn pulled the paper towels away to look at the wound again. The damned Puppet had hit her good, right in the rib. It was broken, but it would heal on its own in a few days. The bleeding had subdued to a slow leak, winding its way down her side like a dying creek in a drought. She sopped it up with a few more paper towels before she reached into her satchel for her first-aid kit.

The thing was well-loved, and it showed. Over the decades, Thorn had become an expert at patching up her own injuries on the go. Usually, it was because she was too damned busy to drive the hour back to the Underground or wait for the wounds to heal. Today was a little different.

She had to look put together if she expected Jay to give her an ounce of alcohol.

Poor kid. Thorn was going to be the death of him.

She opened the faded fabric case and dug out some gauze pads and medical tape. As she pressed the gauze against the wound, she pulled a strip of tape with her teeth and held it out to Sparkie. He ripped through it with his tiny fangs to cut a piece big enough to line the bandage. Three more, and the gauze held tight against her skin. In an hour and a half, the bleeding would stop altogether. This thing should last that long.

Being a Forgotten Sin had its perks.

With the bandage in place, Thorn stood in front of the sink and took a good look at herself in the mirror. Her long, black hair was okay. She was lucky she hadn't gotten a cut on her scalp. They always bled so much, and hair was harder to clean. Her lean stomach and arms looked like a child had raked red finger paint across her skin. The line of blood falling down her nose and onto her lips was already dry. She couldn't go out there looking like this.

First, she had to get out of these ruined clothes. Thorn stepped out of her leggings and peeled the blood-soaked, black, fingerless gloves from her elbow and over her hands. A tangled web of deep, thick scars slowly revealed itself on the inside of her left forearm, extending all the way from her elbow to her wrist, where they became heavier and more gnarled. The scars twisted up onto the heel of her palm and wrapped, just barely, around her thumb and onto the back of her hand. Below the wrist, on a small, circular patch of perfectly smooth skin, was the *Peccostium*.

Thorn didn't pay it any attention. Or, at least, she tried not to. This damned thing and the scars it had permitted were just more reminders of everything Wrath had taken from her—and what it had turned her into.

Now that her clothes were out of the way, Thorn set to work on cleaning up. She turned on the sink and splashed water over her face. The fine line from the cut above her eye was already gone. She soaked a couple of paper towels and scrubbed the red, flaky trail off her nose. She mopped up her stomach, swirling the wet blood around with water until it was diluted enough that she could soak it up with a fresh bunch of paper towels.

It was quick work. It usually was.

Moments later, Thorn stood and looked at herself again. If not for the gauze on her side and the collection of bloody clothes and rags discarded in the corner of the room, no one would ever suspect she'd just faced off against a handful of gun-wielding men behind the Pfizer building. She'd come stumbling into this bar looking like she'd lost a fight with a glass door. Now, she seemed no different than she did any other given night. Thorn took in her own reflection, from her strong, porcelain-white legs to her black, half-empty eyes, and she heaved a sigh.

This was all so fucking stupid. It started out as a routine patrol of Pride's biggest asset to determine if other Sins were attempting to safeguard it. Thorn had let herself get caught off guard by the *exact* thing she was supposed to be looking for. If she had been on top of her game, that Puppet never would have landed a bullet into her, and she wouldn't have had to kill him.

A spark surged up in her stomach. It twisted and twirled like bees whose hive had been disturbed. She'd gotten lazy. Complacent. And they'd both paid the price for it.

Jay's cold energy approached the door again. Thorn dipped down to her satchel and pulled out new clothes. She always carried them around with her, just in case the ones she was wearing somehow got covered in blood. It happened more often than she liked to admit. She was pulling on the new black leggings when Jay knocked. "You have five minutes."

"All right," Thorn said.

"Seriously?" There was a dull thunk. From the sound of it, Jay had dropped his head against the door. Thorn threw a red tank top over her head and grabbed a fresh set of gloves out of her bag as he said, "What's going on?"

Thorn pulled them on and made sure her scars and the *Peccostium* were completely covered. The fabric brushed against it, and a chill shot down her spine. Her mangled skin pulsed all the way up to her elbow. She flexed her hand— open, closed, and open again—to ease the sensation. "Nothing's going on."

"Bullshit."

Thorn got to her feet and shoved her old clothes into her satchel. She quickly wiped the blood from the sink, mopped up the ground, and hid the towels in her bag, too. Sparkie jumped in with them, folding his red, leathery wings to his sides. At last, she opened the door.

Jay Coons's mouth dropped open at the sight of her. He ran a hand through his tousled, auburn hair, and his blue eyes narrowed as he looked her up and down. Thorn watched him with her eyebrows raised.

"I'll take a scotch, please."

Thorn swirled her drink, holding the glass inches above the pitted bar. Dim, overhead lights cast dark shadows across the wood. The amber liquid threw bright splotches of golden light into those shadows, the same way stained-glass windows brought the illusion of color into the dark and dismal house of God.

Thorn stared down into the scotch, and Jay stared down at Thorn. She could feel his eyes piercing the top of her head like he was trying to find a bullet hole through her hair.

"What the fuck happened?" he finally asked.

Thorn brought the drink to her lips and downed the rest in one deep, satisfying swallow. "Nothing."

She put the glass back onto the bar, right under Jay's nose. He sighed, refilled it, and shook his head.

"I know what I saw."

Thorn didn't answer him.

"You were bleeding."

"Do I look like I'm bleeding?"

His brows furrowed, and his lips tightened into a fine, pink line.

"You were in the bathroom for an *hour*, Teagan."

"It's just girl stuff," Thorn said with a shrug, and she reached across the bar for her drink again. "Do you want details? I could give you details…"

Jay rubbed his eyes with his fingers and thumb. "You're impossible."

Thorn answered him by taking another sip. The alcohol burned against her tongue and the back of her throat. Jay moved away to serve another customer, but the way he left, without a wink or a word, made it clear that he was exasperated with her. Thorn was good at getting people to that point.

But that was fine. It was easier to keep that level of separation between herself and others—easier for her, at least. In her one-hundred-and-forty-four years on this planet, Thorn had lost a lot of people. All of the losses hurt, but they hurt a little less if she didn't let herself become attached. People died. Thorn didn't.

All the same, she appreciated that he wasn't willing to argue with her right now. It felt like all she did lately was *argue*, thanks to Darius Jones.

A bubble of fury awakened in her stomach and swirled with the scotch. Her fingers tightened on the glass; it groaned beneath the pressure. Thorn stared down into the drink and watched her shallow, shimmering reflection stare back.

Darius Jones—the vagrant, the Virtue, the man whose very presence in the Underground had been nothing short of revolutionary—was stirring shit up in the Martyrs, trying to get himself *killed*, and she didn't like it.

Thorn's grip hardened, and she closed her eyes. The taut muscles in her arm ached to throw the glass, to shatter it into a million pieces against the wall of liquor just three feet in front of her so she could watch the shards and alcohol fall like rain onto the sticky ground beneath her feet. In the last six months, Darius had become more than the first Virtue this generation of Martyrs had ever seen. He'd quickly risen up and gotten a position in their leadership. Now, he was trying to *change* things.

In the ninety years Thorn had been a Martyr, she'd never seen someone so new cause so many waves.

No one else seemed to mind. Even Alan, her own uncle and one of the *founders* of this damned organization, was relaxed about Darius's involvement. It seemed like Thorn was the only one who wanted to slow things down, and she was really sick and tired of being outvoted in almost every single meeting. It was getting to her, and she was having a harder and harder time keeping her temper in check. She wanted to break something, and she was ashamed to admit she had almost been *happy* those Puppets had ambushed her this evening. It had given her an outlet.

But that thought made her angry, too. Was she turning into such a monster that she relished the chance to hurt the innocent people the Sins sent after her?

"You're going to break that."

She opened her eyes again and looked up to Jay. He had his arms crossed over his navy, button-up shirt and was watching her with the same heavy, exhausted eyes he'd had before.

Thorn's fingers were white. The outlines of narrow bones and blue veins cut through the back of her hand like mountains and rivers. She took a deep breath and relaxed. Blood rushed back into her fingertips, giving them color and warmth again. She threw the last mouthful of her scotch to the back of her throat and slammed the glass down in front of Jay. He pulled the bottle off the wall and poured her another.

"Bad day?"

"You have *no* idea."

Jay sighed. "I might."

Thorn couldn't help but give up a soft laugh. That's right. She'd almost forgotten. Jay *had* seen her covered in blood before—just once—when she'd faced off against Pride and his Puppets in an alley to save Eva Torres's life. That time, it had been nothing but a quick glimpse of her through a closing car door. This incident had been a bit bigger. When Thorn had sneaked in through the back to clean herself up—something she'd done hundreds of times before—she hadn't been careful enough. Jay turned the corner and looked down the hall just in time to see Thorn, wounded and angry, opening the bathroom. She might need to do more than distract him with simple lies and incredible sex.

"I can't talk about it," Thorn said at last.

Jay waited for a moment before he laughed. It was a nervous laugh. "I'm starting to think you're not just a journalist."

She only smiled.

"I wish you would open up to me."

Thorn's smile faded. The laughter left Jay's eyes.

She took a drink. Said nothing.

That told Jay all he needed to know. He deflated, his shoulders shrinking down and his body curling to follow them. Without a word, he headed back down the bar to help another regular who was sitting around the corner. She watched his back, and a part of her wondered if this was it—if this was the final straw that would make Jay realize he deserved more.

Part of her hoped so. She'd miss the company and the sex, but it would be easy enough for her to find another willing participant. Jay wasn't the first, and he certainly wouldn't be the last. He was just a small, transient part of Thorn's long life, and she had bigger things to worry about.

Like the Puppets.

Since the showdown at Teresa Solomon's estate, when Envy's host had been killed and Pride had been destroyed for good, the remaining five Sins had gone quiet. Shockingly quiet. Holly and the Gray Unit verified that they were still around, but their activity out and about in the city had fallen to a low murmur. Where the Martyrs usually had at least one skirmish with their Puppets a week, they hadn't had a single incident since that early, January day.

But now, here it was, the first day of July, and Thorn just had to dig a bullet out of her side. She couldn't shake the feeling that something weird was going on. The tide was coming in. Thorn suspected that Wrath and the other Sins were just reorganizing their assets in the wake of losing two of their own. Envy's vast Programmed network would be absolutely disintegrated by now, as well as the power Pride had over Pfizer and various other large corporations in the city. It would take time to recover.

But something about this felt... different. This wasn't the first time more than one Sin had lost its host in the same short period of time, but it was the longest the Martyrs had gone without having a real incident since Donovan's death. Thorn had lost control, killing five of their hosts, and Alan had killed a sixth, leaving Wrath as the lone Sin standing for almost a full year until the others had the chance to repossess.

This wasn't like that time. There were still five Sins active—five Sins who had years of Influence under their belt, sophisticated networks of corruption at their fingertips, and a thirst for Martyr blood. So, why weren't they coming for it?

It didn't feel right.

The door to The Cross swung open. A wave of hot, foul air came in from the night outside, stinking of the pollution and waste that poisoned the Harlem River just across the block. The hairs on the back of Thorn's neck pricked up as she recognized the cold energy pausing at the door.

Speaking of things that didn't feel right...

Sloth made his way into the bar. Thorn reached for the knife clipped to the pocket on her left thigh, wondering if she could grab her handgun out of her satchel without

9

drawing attention, and she waited.

There was no way the Sin wouldn't recognize her, and she wasn't stupid enough to assume this was some kind of coincidence. While Gregory Witham was a regular fixture in these southern Bronx neighborhoods, she was sure he'd followed her here. The Puppets must have been his…

Just *more* evidence Thorn had grown complacent. She should have been more fucking careful.

Witham slithered his way through the crowded room. He moved quietly, quickly. Thorn felt his energy shift and merge with the other patrons as he squeezed his way through the gruff, older group playing pool by the door and those sitting on the grimy tables in the center of the bar. He came straight toward her. No pretense. No hesitation.

But there was fear. There was always fear when the Sins were dealing with Thorn.

She spoke as soon as she knew he was within earshot.

"I'll give you ten seconds to turn around and get the fuck out of here before I kill you."

The energy paused. Then a squirrelly, sticky voice said, "Go ahead and try. I'll kill everyone."

Thorn's thin brows pinched together, and she turned around to see Gregory Witham standing just three feet behind her. Long, greasy hair fell on either side of his pale face, and the pupils of his bright, blue eyes were pin-tight. Every few seconds, his head twitched to the left, but his hands were steady, and with one, he drew back his coat just enough for Thorn to see what he was talking about. Her heart pounded hard against her ribs.

Attached to his skinny hip was a small device. In his hand, Sloth held a detonator.

"You're crazy," she hissed.

"Maybe." He twitched again.

"What the fuck do you want?"

"To talk." Witham spoke quickly. It seemed like he was fighting the urge to look around the room, but he was too afraid to take his attention off Thorn. His eyes darted wildly between her face and the knife in her left hand.

She raised a brow. "We—you and I—" Thorn used the closed blade to gesture between herself and the Sin "—we don't *talk*."

"We do today, or—"

"Or you'll kill everyone," Thorn growled with a sigh.

And he probably would. Of all the Sins, Sloth had lost its host the most. In the time she'd been familiar with the Sins, she'd known him under twenty different identities. Maybe more. She'd lost track. The frequent host loss had scattered his consciousness, and that made him dangerous and unpredictable.

Thorn couldn't think of a way out of this that wouldn't end with dozens of fatalities. Except one.

"Fine, but we talk outside."

"No." His fingers tightened around the detonator, and Thorn raised her hands up—low, at waist level, to avoid making a scene. "We talk here. You can't pull *shit* in here."

Thorn shook her head. "I don't want to—"

"I don't give a fuck what you want." The words rushed out so quickly Thorn had a hard time hearing them. By this point, they were drawing attention. Jay looked their way, a tight frown on his face, and a handful of the men behind Witham watched him with dark, dangerous eyes, waiting for any indication Thorn might need their help to handle him. Most of them knew she probably wouldn't. Thorn put her knife back in her pocket and took a deep breath.

"The back table."

Witham nodded, and Thorn led the way. It went against all her instincts to turn her back on the Sin, and Sparkie risked poking his head out to keep an eye on him as they walked to the corner near the hallway. Thorn slid into the old church bench, and Witham took a seat across from her. They were cast mostly in shadows. The only light was from a dim, tungsten bulb on the wall several feet behind the Sin. The streetlight outside the stained-glass window provided just enough illumination for Thorn to see Witham's face, broken up in grimy, colorful fractals. He had one hand on top of the table, and his fingers tapped erratically on the wood. The other was hidden underneath, clutching the detonator. While Thorn kept her focus on his face, Sparkie watched his thumb hovering just above the button.

Thorn cleared her throat.

"So," she said. "What the fuck do you want to talk about?"

"Dane," Witham said. "Derek Dane. What did you do to him?"

Thorn's brows furrowed over her dark eyes, and her mouth ran dry. She resisted the urge to swallow and said, as evenly as she could, "What do you mean?"

She knew exactly what he meant. Teresa had obliterated Dane just over six months ago. Pride was gone. Forever.

But there was no way the rest of the Sins knew that. Envy had been the only one to witness it, and seeing as it was floating around somewhere as an ethereal being, hunting for a new host, it couldn't have passed on the information.

"I'm not stupid," Witham snarled, and his twitching became wilder. "I'm not *stupid!* He's gone. Isn't he? He's gone. I can feel it. We can *all* feel it."

"I don't know what you're talking about," Thorn said, but something gripped itself around her stomach and didn't let go. It was the way Sloth had said it.

He's gone. I can feel it.

"You're lying."

The color left Witham's face. In the dark, Thorn could see him swallow a mouthful of spit. The thin line of his lips pursed so tightly it went white and cold.

"We know you—you Martyrs—we know you did something to him. You fucking did it."

Thorn didn't know what to say, so she settled for lying again. "All right, fine. You're right. I killed him. I slit his throat and—"

"Don't FUCKING LIE TO ME."

Witham screamed and slammed his fist on the table. Sticky, hot spit bubbled in the corners of his mouth. Thorn reached for her knife, and the bar went silent—except for Jay.

"Hey!" he called out as he drew a long, metal bat from beneath the counter. When he started toward them, Thorn's jaw tightened. The bartender looked at her the same way men always tried to look at women: like she was just some weak girl who needed their protection. She gritted her teeth, and Jay glanced between Witham and Thorn before finally landing on her.

"Is this the guy?" His voice was angry and shaky. He looked over Thorn again, like he was searching for the blood he was so sure he'd seen before. "Is this the guy who hurt you?"

"What the hell do you think you're doing?" Thorn hissed.

"Is this the guy?!"

"Cute fuckin' bat, man," Witham said as he eyed Jay, head to toe. He gave a long, skinny smile that exposed crooked, stained teeth.

Jay turned to the Sin, and his chest swelled. This had to look like an easy win to him. He'd broken up bigger bar fights between burlier men than Gregory Witham, but Witham wasn't just some regular, tweaked-out druggie with a bad attitude. He could tear Jay to shreds in minutes.

"I can show you just how cute this fucking bat is," Jay snarled.

"Wanna go?" Witham got to his feet. His hand had released the detonator. Thorn's heart raced as she stood up, too. Sparkie slipped out of her satchel and carefully made his way to the Sin. Witham didn't notice. He slapped his hands against his chest and came face to face with Jay, glaring up at him. "I'll fuckin' kill you. Turn you inside out."

"Fucking try."

"Back off!" Thorn pushed her way between them and roughly shoved Jay away. He took a step back, shocked, and glared at her, but her glare was harder. Deadlier. "I'm fine."

She was angry—angrier than she'd ever been at Jay before. It laced its way into the core of the words and charged the air between them. His eyes widened, and for a moment, he lost his presence. The bat dropped feebly toward the ground. Jay's posturing was going to get him killed—it could get all of them killed.

"Fine? Are you fu—"

"Did I stutter?" Thorn snarled. "I'm fine, and you need to *back off*."

"Yeah, pretty boy," Witham cackled from over her shoulder. "Back off."

Thorn couldn't help it. The corners of her mouth twisted up into a sinister shadow of a smile. "And *you*..." She turned back to Witham. When he saw the look in her eyes, his teeth gnashed together. "Your ten seconds are up."

The Sin scrambled. He reached into his jacket pocket, but Sparkie had finished chewing through the wire, and instead of a detonator, he found nothing but the loose end. His pale, sick face went even whiter. There was nothing to stop Thorn from making a scene anymore. Nothing to stop her from killing him where he stood.

She grabbed him by the throat. Her fingers dug in so tightly she could feel his flesh give way and bruise beneath her nails. "You're mine now."

Sloth floundered. He twisted and flopped so erratically that Thorn's grip loosened, and he slipped out of her hands. He threw a punch into her jaw, and Thorn roared. She flew forward and crashed into him, sending them both sprawling into the center of a cold, angry crowd. Witham was pinned. Thorn wrapped her hand around the back of his neck, and she pressed her fingernails deep into the *Peccostium* she knew was hiding just under his hairline. He screamed and went limp. Thorn came in close to his face. His breath smelled sour and rotten.

"You tried to *blow me up*," she hissed so quietly that only he could hear her. "You're going to regret that..."

She grabbed her knife and flipped it open.

But before Thorn had the chance to plunge the blade into Sloth's throat, Jay grabbed her arm and pulled her back. The commotion was enough that her hold on Witham's *Peccostium* let up, and he twisted beneath her, worming his way free. Jay pulled Thorn off the ground and threw her backward. He was staring at her with wide, horrified eyes.

"What the fuck is wrong with you?"

She didn't even acknowledge him. Thorn's eyes were glued to Witham's back as he made for the exit. She grabbed her bag and chased after him, but by the time she managed to squeeze her way through the leering, murmuring crowd and out the door, he was already a block down the street. He turned and looked at her.

"Fuck you, Rose!" Sloth screamed into the twilight. Thorn reached into her bag and drew out her pistol. "And fuck your little Virtue! We know what he's after—what he's looking for. It's going to lead him *right to us*, and you won't be there to protect him this time!"

A cold chill ran down her spine, and her breath caught in her throat as she leveled her weapon. It was too late. Sloth slithered down an alley and disappeared into the dark, summer haze.

"God damn it," Thorn whispered, and her heart did an uncomfortable flip inside her ribcage.

She was right. The Sins were back, and they were going after Darius.

Thorn put the weapon away, threw her satchel over her shoulder, and rushed to her car. Sparkie took to the air and chased Sloth. His blue body disappeared against the navy sky so thoroughly that his silhouette hardly blocked out the stars. He was anxious, frustrated—just like Thorn was—and like her, he was determined to hunt down and kill Gregory Witham.

This was worse than Thorn had imagined. The Sins knew more than they let on. They knew Pride had been destroyed. They knew the Martyrs had uncovered the secret to taking them out for good. But worse than that was the last thing Sloth had said:

They knew what Darius was looking for, and Thorn wouldn't be able to protect him…

She had to do more than kill Witham. She had to warn Alan.

Her car was parked down a side street, alone on the corner, glimmering under the moonlight. Its sleek, black finish marked it clearly out of place in this shady neighborhood. Sparkie had found Sloth. He was running down an alley, making his way from Mott Haven toward Hunt's Point. She could head him off, catch him off guard… or maybe she'd just run him over. It didn't matter, as long as he didn't come out of it breathing.

Thorn pulled her phone out and dialed Alan's number as she unlocked the car and grabbed the door handle. It stuck when she tried to pull it open.

That was strange. It had never stuck before.

It fell into place in the back of Thorn's mind. The hairs on the nape of her neck stood on end just as Alan's voice said "Hello" in her ear. She smelled the spark, followed by the sharp stink of propellant. And then—

Click!

Thorn's gut twisted. "Fuck—"

The car exploded. Sparkie screamed in the distance. Roaring, orange flames lit the whole neighborhood in bright, hot light.

CHAPTER TWO

Darius Jones stepped into the courtyard. The cavernous room stretched out for one hundred yards long and wide. Vaulted ceilings housed thin lights, which were programmed to shine down on them in an illusion of sunlight that never actually reached this far underground. Empty tables dotted the courtyard along with barren planters and vacant space. Hundreds of people could easily wander through without ever touching shoulders, though no one had ever seen the place that crowded. Not for a *long* time.

Today, a number of Martyrs gathered at the far end. Tactical members crowded around small tables, laughing as they kicked back and relaxed after a long day on shift. The doctor and his wife, the head nurse, smiled and talked over plates of food. Recon teams, fresh off a mission, told stories of their latest adventures out in the city. Their voices carried over to Darius, echoing off the vast, concrete walls.

It might not have been *hundreds* of people, but still, this was the busiest he'd ever seen the courtyard. When he'd come into the Underground nine months ago, this place had been a ghost town. Martyrs filtered in and out on their way to and from their posts. It had reminded Darius of the abandoned buildings surrounding the Williamsburg Bridge

Street Market. An empty shell—a *house* for people who needed shelter, but not really a *home*. Everything had been gray, quiet, and tense—like the whole place was just biding time until it inevitably grew too old to keep going.

Things were finally changing. Darius smiled.

It had taken months of hard work to get them here. Long nights, planning projects and activities. Longer meetings, working out the logistics of how to make those plans happen. A lot of frustration when they fell through. Darius spent hours awake, late at night, nursing his coffee in the courtyard while he wondered what he'd done wrong.

In the last few weeks, though, he saw the shift beginning: the Martyrs were acting more like a *team* and less like mercenaries for hire waiting to die in a war they never thought they could win.

"Hey, Darius!"

A warm energy came up behind him, a sixth sense Darius's Virtue provided, and he turned to see Abraham Locke coming down the hallway leading back to the west wing of rooms. His hair was damp, and he'd left the top button of his plaid shirt lazily undone.

"Hey," Darius said, holding out a hand that Abraham shook enthusiastically. He turned back to the courtyard and gestured to the Martyrs gathered across it. "Theme nights are picking up, huh? Great job, man."

They'd better be picking up. After the failed attempts at movie nights, board games, and poker tournaments, Abraham had been ready to throw in the towel. Darius convinced him to try *one* more thing—these themed dinners—and then quietly urged everyone to attend. Seeing a dozen people show up for that first event had lit a fire beneath the counselor again, and Abraham was still riding that high.

"They look great, don't they?" he asked. "Taco Tuesday is way more popular than last week's catfish cookout. Leave it to Mackenzie to find some obscure holiday to celebrate…"

Darius laughed. "Why did you let her pick the theme?"

"She was just so excited about it I couldn't say no," Abraham said with a chuckle as he scratched the back of his head. His curly brown hair had sprouted more gray through the spring. "Plus, I want to encourage people to be involved. Tonight's theme was Raquel's idea."

"Oh yeah?" Darius said, and his mouth watered. The last time he'd had a taco had been from a street vendor on the market. He wondered if Kenia, the older woman who worked as the Martyrs' cook, could do them justice. The little family who ran the stand had perfected the technique. Thinking about them sent a pang of loss through Darius's heart. His smile faltered at the edges.

He didn't miss much about the life he had before the Martyrs, but the things he did miss, he missed deeply.

"Yeah," Abraham said. He didn't seem to notice the shift in Darius's mood. A wide smile still stretched across his face. "I'm thinking of putting a sign-up sheet in the kitchen."

"That's a great idea."

"Thanks!" Abraham clapped a hand on the back of Darius's shoulder. "Join me for dinner? I'm starving."

"I can't," Darius said, but all the same, he and Abraham began to walk toward the kitchen. "I have a meeting with Mackenzie."

"Ah," Abraham said. "Getting ready for your trip to Washington?"

"Mmhmm."

"That's exciting," Abraham said. "Well, come back when you're all set up! We have a lot to celebrate. Plus, I think people stick around longer when you're here."

Darius laughed and looked up at the crowd of Martyrs. Many of them had noticed Abraham and Darius making their way across the room. People paid a little extra attention to Darius—tried to catch his eye, waving when he spotted them. It was always a little like this. Ever since Darius had Initiated Kindness and Teresa Solomon had destroyed Pride, Darius had become a celebrity.

Everyone wanted to know the Virtue—the man who turned the tide of the war and gave them hope again.

Abraham wasn't wrong; they *did* have a lot to celebrate.

"Okay, sure," Darius said. "I'll swing by."

"Great," Abraham said. "Say hi to Holly for me." He began to walk through the bustling throng of Martyrs sitting at the cast iron tables right outside the open, industrial kitchen. Kenia was setting up a new platter of fresh tacos, relieved, it seemed, in the relative ease of preparing this meal compared to some of the others she'd been asked to cook. Before he got too far, Abraham threw Darius a smile over his shoulder and added, "Oh! And *don't* let Mackenzie pick your name!"

Darius just laughed and waved as he continued. A few of the edge tables were close enough to Darius's path that Martyrs looked up and said hello or reached out to shake his hand. The warmth of their energy surrounded him like the sun on a summer day.

Then one of those energies stood out. It was familiar, inviting, and it filled Darius's chest with affection.

Eva Torres.

He spotted her toward the fringe of the dining area. Her back was turned to him and the rest of the Martyrs as she ate her meal alone, which she often did if Darius, Raquel, and Elena were busy. While Darius was intentional about becoming as involved with the Martyrs as possible, Eva preferred her space. Perhaps it was because of her upbringing, or maybe because many of the Martyrs were still leery of her. They hadn't forgotten how she'd left the Underground and put all their lives in jeopardy.

Neither had Eva. The whole episode had gotten her stabbed in the stomach. She was lucky to be alive.

Even so, Eva still made a point to attend the themed dinners Darius had worked so hard on, even if she attended them by herself. She'd just bring her work. Tonight, she leaned over a report, her wavy, dark brown hair pulled over one shoulder, revealing the back of her slender neck over the top of her blouse.

And something about that neck was telling. It was tight—shoulders drawn, muscles rigid and unyielding. Darius frowned.

He could take a couple of minutes for this. Mackenzie was probably going to be late, anyway…

So he quietly shifted course and made his way toward Eva. She didn't hear him coming, too absorbed in whatever she was reading. Darius put his hands on either shoulder and kissed the top of her head. She jumped and almost knocked her plate off the table.

"Jesus, Darius," she breathed, but there was a relief in her voice. The tension along her neck and shoulders relaxed under his touch. She turned around and playfully batted at his thigh with the paper in her hands. "Don't sneak up on me like that!"

"Sorry," he said, with a tone that made it clear he was *not* sorry, and he pulled up a chair to sit beside her. "I'm on my way to see Mackenzie, but I wanted to stop and say hi first. You weren't working today, were you?" He gestured to the stack of rolled-up papers, and tension returned to Eva's body. Her spine stiffened, and Darius's smile faded a bit. "What's up?"

"Nothing," she said. She flattened the report on top of the table and rubbed her eyes with her fingertips. When she dropped her hands back down, Darius reached out and grabbed one of them. She relaxed and went on. "I had a lead on Envy I wanted to check in on, so I went into town for a few hours. A couple of jerks harassed me and followed me the whole time… I didn't make much headway."

A tinge of concern made Darius's stomach flip. "You okay?"

"Oh, yeah," Eva said, waving a hand. "I handled it. It's just that working on the streets is a lot different than *living* on them, ya know? Normally I'd avoid neighborhoods like Sugar Hill, but it's part of my route, so…" She finished the sentence with a shrug.

Darius nodded, but the concern didn't really ebb. Five months ago, Thorn had offered Eva a position inside the Gray Unit. Though Eva's disappearing act last year may have made *other* Martyrs nervous, it impressed Thorn. Her skills at moving, unnoticed, in the city were invaluable to the Intelligence Department. Now that the only two Sin hosts who had seen Eva's face were dead, and their Programming dead with them, Thorn wanted to take advantage of those skills. She'd immediately gotten Eva into training and set her off onto New York's streets to gather any intel that could lead them to Envy's new host, whenever it possessed again. Eva was excelling, but the whole situation made Darius nervous.

Other than TAC, the Gray Unit was one of the most high-risk positions in the Underground. Its members spent half their time in the city and worked closely within the Sins' networks. If Eva were discovered, she'd be killed. Darius tried not to think about it. He hated the idea that she could die on the job.

He wondered how she felt, knowing that he *had* to die, and she was searching for the very same Sin he was meant to destroy.

"So, a lead on Envy?" Darius asked.

"It's nothing serious yet," Eva said with a sigh. "Thorn seems confident Envy hasn't already possessed a new host, so I'm tracking suspicious changes in behavior from people in its circles to see if I can narrow down who it might be targeting. Apparently, it usually possesses people it's at least *seen* before—someone it thinks can help it get what it wants."

"What does Envy want?" Darius asked.

Eva shrugged. "Your guess is as good as mine. Right now, I'm just going in blind."

"Eh, how hard can it be?" Darius said with a wry smile. "If anyone can figure it out, it's you."

Eva laughed, and her fingers tightened around Darius's. It made him smile to hear that laugh. "You're sweet," she said, and she leaned toward him. "A little overconfident, but sweet." Then she lightly brushed her lips against his. A warm shiver went down Darius's back.

"Nothing wrong with having a little faith in you, is there?" he said. "Anyway, I gotta go. I'll see you tonight."

"Looking forward to it," Eva said, and she squeezed his fingers one more time before he stood up and walked away. Eva's table was nearest to the elevator. Darius hit the button, and when it opened, Raquel and a few other nurses walked out. He wished them all a good evening as he got onto the lift and turned around. Through the closing doors, he saw Raquel and her group stop at Eva's table. They laughed, and it made Darius's chest swell with pride. Then the doors snapped closed, the elevator began to rise, and the warmth of the Martyrs' energy gathered below him, blending together.

Twelve children. Last year, the Sins slaughtered twelve children Darius had taken in from the street—children he'd loved and cherished. It had felt like having his soul ripped from his body, torn into pieces, and shoved back down his throat. He'd been trapped. Suffocated. Gasping for air and struggling to find a foothold as he dangled, scared, devastated, and so very, very angry.

That's how the Martyrs had found him—a man who had lost everything.

If someone had told him in less than a year, he'd be helping *run* the place, Darius would have laughed.

But being Kindness opened an opportunity for him to quickly rise in the ranks within the Martyrs—more quickly than anyone had expected. Darius's status within the command circle made it possible to do a lot more good than he ever would have been able to do alone.

He also had more freedom—freedom Thorn *hated*.

The elevator hit the uppermost floor, and the metallic

doors slowly slid open to the lobby. Darius stepped out and made his way down the hallway, past the tactical room and small offices, as he headed toward the leadership's alcove in the far western corner.

But he didn't reach it. Instead, he stopped at the first door. This room had been a conference room six months ago, but now it was the new Virtue Research and Discovery headquarters. Darius had become a part of this department when he'd joined the Martyr leadership, alongside Mackenzie McKay and Lina Brooks. When Teresa died and they suddenly inherited her massive collection of research, reports, and paraphernalia, they quickly realized they simply didn't have enough *room*. So, they'd taken over this space and turned it into the primary workstation for all the Martyrs in the R&D department.

Darius paused outside the door. A handful of people were gathered inside the room, but Darius could tell Mackenzie wasn't one of them. He was beginning to recognize individual auras, and Mackenzie's stood out. Where most of the Martyrs had robust energies, with defined boundaries and a strong sense of integrity, Mackenzie's was weak and faltering, like the goodness inside of her was barely managing to hold itself together.

Part of Darius wanted to ask her about it, but how the hell do you enter into *that* conversation? So, he'd settled on trusting Thorn. Mackenzie was one of the only people in the Underground the Forgotten Sin was close to, and that was good enough for him.

Even though he knew Mackenzie wasn't there, Darius walked into the R&D headquarters anyway. Tall shelves lined the left wall, packed with stacks upon stacks of books, binders, and boxes full of artifacts and loose notes. On the other side, a dozen desks buzzed with computers and the rhythmic clicking of people at work. A couple of research teams sat at these desks, and when Darius walked in, their heads turned up. Most of them greeted him with big smiles and happy waves before they turned back to their screens, but one young woman called out.

"Hey, Darius!" Parker said eagerly. She was barely old enough to drink, and like Chris, she was one of the few Martyrs who had been born and raised in the Underground. Her mother had died years ago, and her father, Marcus Boseman, ran the Cleaning Crew. She turned around in her chair and watched Darius with a wide grin. Her curly hair puffed around her head in happy ringlets as she handed him a file folder. "I got another possible lead for you upstate! Think you'll be able to go back to this kind of thing after you've gotten a taste for cross-country trips?"

He laughed. "Oh, I'm sure I'll be out there again when I get back," he said. "Something tells me these 'cross-country trips' won't be happening very often." He raised the folder and nodded in her direction. "Thanks for the great work, Parker."

She beamed at him and turned to get back to her tasks. Darius walked past her, and his smile faltered a bit.

If Thorn had her way, these kinds of trips wouldn't happen at *all*.

Darius's assignment in R&D had been her idea. He figured she was looking for a *safe* spot for him, but it made sense. The only Virtue in the Underground clearly belonged to the department searching for new ones.

Things had been fine… until Darius started insisting that he had to go on away missions.

Thorn detested the idea of Darius being sent out anywhere adjacent to Sin activity. She fought hard against it every time it was proposed, and every time, she was outvoted. While Darius and the rest of the Martyr leadership understood her concern, they also knew they didn't have much of a choice.

Their best shot at discovering a new Virtue rested upon the fact that Darius, and *only* Darius, could find them. Charity, Patience, Diligence, Temperance, and Chastity were out there, somewhere. The only way the Martyrs could be positive their Recon agents weren't wasting their time was to bring Darius along and see if he felt that magnetic *pull*—tugging at his heart, his soul, his inner Virtue.

Even though Thorn was outvoted, she never stopped arguing. Eventually, they'd compromised: he could only join away parties doing recon on nearby assignments with a Tactical team in tow for extra security.

Until now.

Darius walked past the research teams, through two circular tables covered with more books and reports, to a woman sitting at the back of the room. She was hidden behind a stack of binders, tucked away in the corner. Her mousy, brown hair fell in a neat braid down her back, and her button-up blouse was tucked precisely into the waistline of her slacks. Fine lines were beginning to form at the corners of her eyes. When she spotted him approaching, she looked up, and she smiled.

"Good evening, Darius," Lina Brooks said happily, but she quickly turned her focus back onto her reading. One hand played absent-mindedly with a silver pendant around her throat. "Looking for Mackenzie?"

"Yup," Darius said. "But I see she's running late."

Lina laughed. "Yes, well, that *is* her modus operandi."

"Did she go down to Holly's already?"

Lina shook her head. "No, she probably just lost track of time. I'm pretty sure I saw her dragging a box into the garage earlier. Something about some plan…"

Then she waved her hand dismissively, and her voice trailed off as she turned back to her binder. Ever since they'd brought Teresa's research to the Underground, Lina was like an orphan child who'd been plopped down in the middle of an all-you-can-eat buffet. She ravenously read as though starving for information, and she consumed everything. Thirty-page papers discussing how the Sins may have worked through the Protestant Reformation. Short essays outlining the theory behind slavery and racism in regard to Wrath. Notes in the margins of old history books, speculating where the Sins and Virtues may have appeared.

Now that she was sucked back into it, Darius knew there was no point in trying to pull her away. He thanked her and made his way back down the hallway and into the parking garage. Outside the doors to the lobby was a small, well-lit alcove. On the wall to Darius's left, a door led to the elevators. On his right, one to the hospital's triage room. The parking lot stretched out in front of him.

Of all the areas in the Underground, this was the only place Darius had seen that *truly* felt underground. It reached far back, and the edges were dim and dreary. The drive slowly spiraled upward, where it let out at the gas station above from a secret exit inside the car wash. Easily, hundreds of cars could fit in this space, but now only a handful of identical black SUVs and coupes parked along the closest aisles.

"Son of a *bitch*!"

Mackenzie's dull energy and hot voice drew Darius's attention. He walked out from the alcove and looked along the wall to see her standing on a step ladder in the corner of the garage, hidden behind a giant American flag. It flapped around her ankles, and all Darius could see of the Irishwoman was her tattered sneakers.

With a smile, he made his way toward her. Faint aura aside, Mackenzie was one of Darius's favorite people in the Underground. She was one of the brightest, most optimistic lights in this place.

Plus, she was almost always on Darius's side of disagreements with Thorn. It was nice to have support when he faced off against Thorn's rage. Like yesterday. When Darius had proposed his idea to fly out west to follow the most promising lead he'd ever come across, Thorn practically exploded.

But Mackenzie wasn't fazed, and Darius followed her lead. Together, they'd managed to convince the rest of the Martyr leaders to go ahead with the plan, outnumbering Thorn in the vote six to one. He hadn't seen her since.

Darius glanced around the lot. Thorn's motorcycle was

still here, but her car was gone, which meant she planned on staying in the city for a while this time…

He took a deep breath, sighed it out through his nose, and turned back toward Mackenzie. The Irishwoman hadn't noticed him. She was still struggling with the flag. It slipped from her fingers and fluttered to the ground. Mackenzie swore and clicked her tongue piercing impatiently against her teeth before she finally glanced up and caught sight of Darius. Then a wide, mischievous smile broke out across her face.

"Jones! Getcher ass over here and help me. That's an order."

She winked at him. Darius crossed his arms and arched one eyebrow high on his head. His mouth curled up into a smile.

"What are you doing?"

"What the hell's it look like I'm doing?" Mackenzie asked, squatting to pick up the crumpled red, white, and blue fabric. She'd recently dyed her short, pixie cut neon blue, and even in the dim garage, it was loud and distracting. "I'm decorating! Long live America, or whatever it is you people say on the Fourth of July."

"It's upside-down," Darius said as Mackenzie struggled with the flag over her head.

"Of course it is," Mackenzie said. "America's in distress! Now, get your long legs up here and hang this sonnovabitch up."

Mackenzie came down from the step stool and let Darius up. With her direction, he managed to drape the flag across the wall, fastening it to the concrete with hooks Mackenzie had already managed to hammer in. She stood back and watched with a giant grin across her sharp, little face.

"*Excellent*," she said with a smile as Darius came down from the stool. "Now, time to put these on all the tables." She gestured to a giant cardboard box filled with hundreds of little United States banners.

"Don't we have to meet with Holly?" Darius asked.

Mackenzie slapped her hand against her forehead and swore again. "Oh, *bollocks*, you're right! Holly's gonna kill us. How late are we?" She glanced at her watch and swore again. "*Real* late. Okay, okay, let's get going."

She leaned down and heaved the box up. She was comically small beneath it. Her bright hair barely poked over the red, white, and blue rectangles. Darius offered to help, so she shoved it into his arms instead and led the way back to the Underground. He followed behind her, and though the box was lightweight, its size made it awkward to maneuver through the skinny hallways. It was worse in the stairwell.

Holly worked on the lowest level of the Underground, and her office wasn't accessible by elevator. They walked down six flights of narrow, concrete stairs, and their footsteps echoed back at them. Mackenzie bounced ahead as Darius focused on holding the box. He kind of regretted grabbing it now. When they finally reached the bottom, they found a locked door, and Mackenzie punched in a four-digit code. The handle beeped, a light glowed green, and she opened it.

The underbelly of the Martyrs headquarters twisted and churned with moaning water pipes and the stale stench of damp, dirty floors. Beneath the hundreds of bedrooms, the hospital ward, the kitchen, and amenities, this beast ran it all. They stepped into the massive, expansive space, and Darius paused to take it all in.

White paint marked the floor, highlighting a path along the walkway, branching out with dozens of labeled hallways. Thick, concrete support beams held the Underground up above them. The ceiling was a deep, complicated web of pipes, wiring, and ventilation shafts. The whole area hummed and whirred, spilling hot, moist air into the stairwell. Darius whistled in appreciation.

Now *this* felt distinctly "underground."

Mackenzie shut the door behind their backs. "C'mon. The Nerdcave is this way."

She passed him a playful wink and started walking

through the basement. It felt like a maze. The primary walkway they followed was well lit, but each hallway they passed flickered with motion-activated lights. They turned on and off as Darius and Mackenzie walked, and the edges of these halls were so dim Darius couldn't make out much detail where the walls met the floor.

"It would be easy to get lost down here," Darius said. Mackenzie laughed ahead of him, and he turned toward her.

"Just follow the arrows," she said, gesturing to the ground. Darius realized the paint on the floor also indicated direction, pointing them back to the EXIT in giant, white letters.

The walk was longer than Darius expected. On the wall to his right, he spotted a reinforced, steel door with the words "Shooting Range" painted on the front. Every so often, they'd pass underneath a ventilation grate, which forced dank air into Darius's face. The whole place reeked of oil and mold, and he heard the familiar sound of tiny rat claws scurrying along the aluminum shafts above them.

In the rest of the Underground, where the floors were carpeted and the concrete walls papered and painted, he hadn't stopped to consider there must be a place like this keeping it all together.

At last, they turned a corner to a short hallway with a single door. A large window in its face cast a long, slender rectangle of orange light across the floor. Mackenzie started to move forward, but then she snapped and turned on her heels.

"Oh!" She gestured to the box in Darius's hands and flashed him a smile. "Put that down, would'ya? Can't bring in any evidence."

She winked again. Darius frowned but did as she asked.

"Perfect! Now, let's get this over with."

The two of them walked down the length of the hall. Mackenzie opened the door and knocked on the frame at the same time. As it swung open, a rush of cold, dry air slammed into them like a wall and tried to pull the breath from Darius's lungs. Mackenzie poked her head into the room with a theatrical smile. "Holly! Sorry we're late. We were just—"

"I know what you were doing, McKay. *I could see you.*"

Mackenzie pulled the door all the way open and sidled into the room. Her grin extended across her face as Darius followed behind her. The moisture gathered on his neck and arms chilled quickly and made him shiver. The far wall was plastered with dozens of papers, maps, and graphs. A giant, black machine hummed in the corner, flashing with multi-colored lights and supporting hundreds of neatly bundled and organized cords. Five desks were jammed in the tiny space. The four in the back were smaller, occupied by three women and a man. Darius knew all of them with at least a passing familiarity.

The desk to Darius's right was much more prominent. It was set up with a sophisticated, buzzing computer and eight separate screens. Each displayed something different, from lines of multi-colored code to camera footage. Holly Andrews sat here. She wasn't much older than Darius, but he'd heard she was some kind of child prodigy and had gotten her undergraduate degree before she was old enough to drive. Holly turned toward them, pushed her thick-rimmed glasses up the bridge of her nose, and glowered at Mackenzie.

"What d'ya mean?" Mackenzie put on an air of false innocence.

Holly didn't budge. She crossed her arms over her oversized hoodie and raised her eyebrows. Her boyish, brown hair was tousled and casual. "You know damn well what I mean." She turned back to her computer. Two of the screens showed camera feeds. One was a desolate street Darius thought looked familiar, and the other was a dark blur. With a few quick keystrokes, the second screen paused and rewound. Darius watched as the blurry image became clearer. Soon, his own face popped up on the screen, Mackenzie grinning over his shoulder, as he pinned a red, white, and blue flag directly over the camera lens. He laughed.

But Mackenzie frowned and shook her head. "I dunno what you're talking about," she insisted. "Looks like *Jones* is the one sabotaging your cameras."

"I know it was you."

"You have no proof," Mackenzie said.

For a moment, Holly just stared. Then she turned back to her computer, cued up the video, and turned on the audio playback. Mackenzie's voice came out through the speakers on either side of Holly's desk.

"Jones! Getcher ass over here and help me. That's an order."

Mackenzie was inscrutable. "I don't see the problem here."

"Just like you'd didn't see a problem with the balloons in the stairwell? Or the smiley face sticker on the camera lens outside my bedroom?"

Mackenzie barked a laugh. "Oh, man, that one took you *three weeks* to find!"

"And don't get me *started* with the mashed potatoes—"

"Hey," Mackenzie said, pointing at Holly and raising her eyebrows into her bright blue bangs. "*That* was an accident."

Holly passed her a stern but good-natured glare. "Just take the damn flag down, McKay." Then she turned to Darius and acknowledged him with a nod. "Jones."

"Hey, Holly," he said. "Sorry we're late."

"McKay's involved. I knew you'd be late," she said with a half-shrug as she turned back to the computer. Her desk was a blend of immaculately organized yet thoroughly lived in. She had a coaster set up precisely at the front corner for a massive thermos of coffee, a line of small toys laid out beneath her screens, and a set of headphones wrapped around a mounted microphone. Darius figured she spent a lot of time here, which made sense. Holly had one of the most critical jobs in the Underground: maintaining security. She was constantly on the lookout for suspicious behavior, ensuring their in-town units weren't being followed, and keeping tabs on the Sins at all times.

Holly focused on the third screen from the left on the bottom row. Her fingers moved so quickly on the keyboard that Darius couldn't hear when one key was released and another was struck. "I've been busy, anyway," she said. "Thorn got herself tied up with some Puppets today."

Darius's stomach flipped. Eva hadn't mentioned the Gray Unit having any issues with Puppets. "Is she okay?" he asked.

Holly nodded. "Oh, yeah. She was doing surveillance outside the Pfizer building—you know, Pride's old company. Some Puppets jumped her. I wouldn't have even known about it if people hadn't started talking about hearing gunshots on social media. It didn't get called into dispatch. Anyway, I went through the security footage. She got shot, but it looks like she's fine. She always is. She headed to her regular hangout in Mott Haven about an hour ago. If it was serious, I'm sure she'd have come right back here."

Mackenzie frowned. "You've got a camera on Thorn's bar?"

"Hah, yeah." Holly's face broke into a broad smile, and she gestured to the other video feed. It was an empty street outside an old, remodeled church with dark, grimy windows. A neon sign in the shape of a cross glared out the front. Darius recognized the neighborhood now. It was in the Bronx, close to where he and Juniper lived before they migrated down to Alphabet City.

"Most businesses in that area don't have cameras," Holly went on, "so I had to go install one on the power pole across the street. Did it in the middle of the night a couple of years ago. She'd kill me if she knew, so keep it quiet."

"Oh, your secret's safe with me," Mackenzie said with a satisfied, impressed laugh, but her tone shifted pretty rapidly. She frowned and looked down at Holly. "I'm less worried about Thorn than I am about the Puppets. We haven't had any issues in *months*. Something must be up."

"That's my thought, too," Holly agreed.

"What do you think it is?"

Holly shrugged. "It's too early to tell. My team is on high alert for any Sin activity, and I'm writing up a report for Alan, but we knew this was coming. This break in the violence couldn't last forever. Anyway, let's get to work."

She cleared her throat, tapped away at her keyboard, and a form lit up one of the screens. Darius tried to focus, but his mind kept wandering back to Thorn and the last time she'd been shot. Two bullets and a punctured lung had been how Darius discovered she was a Forgotten Sin in the first place. Even though he knew she healed three hundred times faster than a human being, he still couldn't help but worry—probably because he wasn't totally used to the idea that Thorn wasn't really human herself.

All the same, he was unsettled.

Holly's voice brought him back to the present. "First thing's first," she said. Darius blinked and looked down at her as she went on. "If you're going to fly, you need a real ID. The one we put together for you before was fine for most things, but the airport will spot that fake a mile away."

"A real ID?" Darius frowned and crossed his arms. "You can do that?"

Holly flashed him a smile. "Oh, you'd be surprised what I can do. You don't exist in the system, so we're going to add you—at least, add you well enough that no one will realize you're a big fat phony. The big benefit is you don't have any family out there that might be looking for you. Makes my job easy."

She wasn't wrong. Between a drunk driver killing his mom when he was ten and his father drinking himself to death a year later, Darius had been left an orphan. Whatever biological "family" may have existed out there probably thought he died years ago, and the family he built for himself had been reduced to a bloody pile of bodies. Eva was all he had left.

"So," Holly continued. She put her hands back on the keyboard. "Let's get started."

She read out the pieces of information she needed from him in a quick list: height, weight, eye and hair color, birthday, and so on. She typed so fast that she could ask him the next line item as she was entering his answer to the one before it. When she got to the name, she stopped and turned around. "So, Jones, what do you want to be called?"

"I don't know. I don't really care."

"Oooh, let me pick!" Mackenzie clapped her hands together and bounced a little on the balls of her feet. "Not to brag, but I picked Thorn's alias, and it's a real winner."

"She hates it," Holly said.

"Like I said—a winner."

"Go ahead," Darius said with a smile.

Holly sighed and shook her head. "You're going to regret it…"

But Mackenzie's bright blue eyes lit up, and she tapped purple-painted nails against her mouth as she thought. Darius could hear light clicking as her tongue piercing tapped against her teeth behind closed lips. At last, she jumped up. "Got it! Dante Stone."

Darius laughed. Mackenzie laughed. Holly rolled her eyes and typed the name into the form.

"Don't come crying to me when someone asks if you're a porn star. I won't let Thorn change hers, and I'm not letting you, either."

"What *is* Thorn's alias?" Darius asked. He turned to Mackenzie, whose thin brows were raised so high on her head that her eyebrow ring disappeared behind vibrant, blue bangs.

"*Teagan Love.*"

"Wow," Darius said, and he grinned. "That's *bad.*"

"I love it so much."

"All right, *Dante,*" Holly grumbled as she typed in a few more commands and slammed her pinky on the enter button. "Stand in front of the blue sheet."

He shimmied past Mackenzie and stood up against a vinyl drape on the wall behind Holly's desk. She set up a webcam to her center screen and sat down to adjust the zoom. His face stared back at him from one of the screens above her. His dark, brown hair was trimmed short and styled in soft waves on the top of his head, and green eyes shone brightly against his deep, olive skin. There was a healthy glow there he still wasn't used to seeing.

"Say cheese," Holly said.

Darius smiled. A flash blinded him. Mackenzie, who had moved to sit on Holly's desk, popped up a double thumbs up and a wide grin. Holly dragged his picture from the top center screen to the bottom and input it into the form.

"So, how is this different from the ID you already gave me?" Darius asked again.

"Well, for one, it has a stupid name," Holly said as she cast Mackenzie a glare. "But, more seriously, this information is going to be tied to a legit identity in the system. It'll be printed by the New Jersey DMV, not my crappy little desk printer. I'm also going to take the details you provided me and get you a social security card and birth certificate. Those, along with the license, will be ready in a week or two. Congratulations, Jones. You exist again."

"No," Mackenzie corrected. "*Dante Stone* exists."

Holly shook her head and rubbed her eyes under her glasses. "Oh my god—"

The camera footage outside Thorn's favorite bar suddenly shone with such a bright, intense light it snatched the words right out of Holly's mouth. She frowned and turned her attention onto the screen. Then, the tiny, cold room filled with piercing sound.

An alert blared from the speakers on Holly's desk. She immediately called to her team. "Get me a location for all the Sins—*now*." The four other Martyrs sitting in the back of the room were a sudden flurry of quiet activity. One of Holly's screens flashed in bright red, and her phone rang.

"Alan," she said as she put a wireless headset on and answered the call. "No. I don't have eyes on Thorn. Let me trace her."

Darius's stomach churned, and the fun side of Mackenzie evaporated. She furrowed her brows as she came up beside Holly. The security officer tapped away on her keyboard again, and the alarm stopped beeping, but the flashing red screen was still going strong. Holly hit a few more keys and a new application popped up. Darius wasn't paying attention to that. He focused on the camera footage in the top corner. The light had faded, and he could see the street again. The sidewalk was a blur of furious movement—of people running away. A bright, flickering light blew out the details in the background. Was that fire?

"Phone's not sending a signal," Holly said quickly. "Last location was on the corner of Bruckner and Lincoln. There are reports of an explosion…"

"Explosion?" Mackenzie's face went white. She turned to Darius, and they shared a dark look.

Holly turned her attention onto a digital map. Bright green dots moved along several streets. "Silver and Montgomery are nearby. Sending them coordinates."

Another application opened—some kind of messenger. Whatever text Holly sent them was gibberish to Darius with the shorthand she used, but it must have done the trick. The closest green dot started moving—quickly—toward the corner of Bruckner and Lincoln. It slammed to a stop, and Holly froze as she waited for her messaging application to ping again.

When it did, her eyes widened, and her jaw clenched tight. Darius peered over her shoulder. The words "code black" looked back at him from the screen.

Then Holly turned to Mackenzie and Darius. "You gotta go." She got up from her chair, hustled them out the door, and slammed it shut behind them. Darius turned to Mackenzie, but she had already started rushing down the hallway. He caught up to her.

"What's 'code black' mean?" Darius asked.

"Severe casualties," Mackenzie murmured as she brushed quickly around the corner and ran the distance between the hallway and the door. Darius kept close to her heels—his throat tight and his heart pounding hard against his ribs. Sweat beaded at his hairline and dripped down his face. Mackenzie's hands shook so hard she had trouble turning the doorknob.

"She'll be fine," Darius said, but it was mostly to ease his own nerves. "She heals so quickly…"

Mackenzie paused in the stairwell and threw him a dark, terrified look.

"I've been here for seventeen years," she said. "I've seen Thorn shot, sliced up, beaten to hell… I've seen her dragged back into this place with shit that would have killed anyone else—shit that *could* have killed her. But I've never seen her called in as a code black. She may be dead."

The breath was squeezed from Darius's lungs. Despite the hot, humid air closing around him, Darius felt cold.

CHAPTER THREE

Thorn had been brought into the Underground an hour ago. One long, painful hour.

Darius hadn't gotten a good look at her as she was wheeled into the emergency triage station attached to the garage. All he saw was Dr. Harris and a couple of nurses quickly rolling a stretcher through the double doors. One of Thorn's hands—a mangled, bloody mess—reached up and desperately grasped the doctor's shirt. That was it, and it had sent a chill down Darius's spine, so deep into his core that he hadn't been able to shake it.

Now he stood on the far end of the long waiting room. His arms were crossed, his fingers tapping anxiously against his bicep, while he and a handful of others waited to see whether or not she was going to survive.

Mackenzie paced impatiently outside the double doors to the hospital, her tongue piercing clattering against her teeth. Every thirty seconds, she'd stop and crane her neck to peek in the windows. Across the wide, empty ward, the doors to the operating room were firmly shut. A cluster of nurses gathered at the nurses' station, staring at them. Whispering. In the operating room, Darius could feel frantic energies converge. Elijah and more than half of his medical team swarmed over an empty space—a vacuum where Darius could only assume Thorn was laying—doing whatever they could to save her life. He couldn't feel her. He never could, but it had never been so inconvenient before.

Standing, quiet and statuesque, in the center of the waiting room was Alan Blaine. The Martyr Founder was tall and formidable, and his black slacks and deep red button-up did nothing but add to his stature. He stood completely still; the only motion to betray his anxiety was a consistent but light stroking of his goatee as he stared out into nothing. A veil of curtain-like, black hair obscured much of his face, but Darius could see his brows were drawn heavily over dark, half-empty eyes.

The last person in the room was Chris Silver.

She'd walked in and taken a seat along the far wall fifteen minutes ago, and now she was staring forward with a distracted, far-away gaze. She looked better than she had when they'd first gotten back; her beige pants had been so saturated in blood they looked rust-brown. Alan insisted she go clean up, and when Chris tried to refuse, he threatened to have her escorted out, so she'd done a quick, careless job. The low ponytail she usually wore had fallen out. Strands of matted, blonde hair draped around her face. Her black undershirt was mostly clean, but streaks of watered-down crimson smeared across her bare arms and pale face. Two fine, clean lines left behind by silent tears cut through the grime, making her green eyes bright and piercing.

Since coming back to the waiting room, all she'd done was sit in that chair, her hands clasped tightly between her knees. Still. Silent. Scared.

The look on her face—one of fear, pain, and the kind of hollow disgust that only haunted people who witnessed horrendous carnage—sent an aching stab through Darius's chest. He pushed himself off the wall and came to sit on the chair beside her. Chris didn't look at him, but when he reached across her lap and wrapped her hands up in his, she squeezed his fingers with painful, grateful urgency.

A very light, very gentle *ding!* broke the silence. Darius felt a robust, warm energy step off the elevator and make its way down the hall. It moved with purpose. Alan felt it, too—though to Alan, it was cold—and he quietly turned around and looked over his shoulder. The heavy sound of quick, sure footfalls on the tile drew Chris and Mackenzie's attention. Seconds later, the massive, hulking figure of Jeremiah Montgomery strode into the room.

He had been with Chris when they'd found Thorn, but he had taken more time to fix himself up. He wore a fresh uniform, the black turtleneck and cargo pants crisp and clean. The only sign the incident left behind was a few crimson slivers caked into his dark nail beds. He didn't waste time with the rest of them. Jeremiah headed straight to Alan.

"It was the Sins."

His deep voice echoed throughout the room. Mackenzie stopped pacing. Her mouth fell open.

"Oh, good job," she said sarcastically, waving her hands in the air in desperate, angry emphasis. "Spot-on detective work there, Montgomery. 'The Sins did it!' Of course they fucking did!"

"Miss McKay," Alan said, almost snapping. "If you cannot maintain your composure, you will leave."

For a tense moment, Alan and Mackenzie glared at each other, Mackenzie a tightly-wound, blue ball of energy and Alan full of frigid aggravation. It seemed Mackenzie planned on fighting back at first. Her tongue piercing slammed against her teeth in a rattling of irritated clicks. At last, though, she resumed her pacing by the hospital doors without a word.

Darius glanced between Alan and Mackenzie. Chris just watched Jeremiah with the same cold, numb expression. Alan's face was hard to read. His lips had thinned into a fine line as he frowned, and his eyes narrowed almost imperceptibly as he turned to Jeremiah again.

"What evidence do we have?"

"I just spent the last hour with Holly going over her

footage," Jeremiah went on. He ignored Mackenzie as she crossed her arms and glared at them. "Gregory Witham met Thorn at The Cross this evening, just before the explosion. There was some kind of altercation outside, and Witham got away. Thorn went to her car directly afterward. It was destroyed. The bomb was planted there."

Alan took a deep breath and ran his hand over his goatee again. "How do you know Witham planted the bomb?" he pressed. "Do you have footage on the scene?"

Jeremiah shook his head. "No, but Holly and her team tracked his movements for the last few weeks. What they could find, anyway. It looks like he's been gathering materials to make an explosive for a while. He probably had Puppets doing most of the dirty work. She stumbled onto a few of them, and her people are still looking for more."

"It's too much of a fuckin' coincidence," Mackenzie said, but her tone was more controlled now. She stomped over to where the two men stood. They turned to face her. "Thorn ran into a bunch of Puppets today, then Sloth, *and* gets blown to smithereens? No way it was an accident. They planned this."

Alan frowned. "Thorn ran into Puppets, too?" He looked back to Jeremiah. "Why wasn't I informed about this?"

"It's in Holly's daily report, sir," Jeremiah said. "There was no reason to suspect anything bigger than a routine Sin incident. They were outside the Pfizer building, and we assume the remaining Sins have an interest there. It's hard to ignore the possible connection now, but on its own, this hardly seemed to be that far out of the ordinary."

"Well, Thorn did get *shot*," Darius murmured. Alan's eyes widened.

"*What?*"

"She gets shot *all the time*!" Mackenzie threw her arms out and groaned. "She went to the damn *bar* after the fight! We're asking the wrong question. It's not *if* the Sins are involved—since they *obviously* are—it's what they're up to."

Jeremiah crossed his arms over his broad, barrel chest. "Seems pretty clear to me what the Sins are after," he said flatly, his full lips set into a deep frown. "They want Thorn dead."

Alan sighed and dipped his head into one hand as he turned and walked a few steps away. His hair parted around his neck at the base of his skull, and Darius caught a glimpse of the *Peccostium* he kept hidden there. "That doesn't make any sense." He said it quietly—almost to himself—but the words were crystal clear in the silence of the waiting room.

"Sure it fuckin' does," Mackenzie growled. She propped her hands up on her hips. "As far as people go, Thorn's the biggest threat against them."

"She's right," Jeremiah said. "They probably assume Thorn killed Dane and Smith. She's killed more of the Sins' hosts than anyone else here. They may just be sick of it, and you have to admit that the Martyrs will have one hell of a time recovering with Thorn gone. We need her."

"Thorn's *not* gone," Darius interjected, and his hand tightened around Chris's fingers. This time, she squeezed his to comfort him. He took a deep breath and shook his head. Alan considered the two of them for a moment before he turned back to Jeremiah.

"I understand what you're saying," he said. His voice leveled out again, returning to the stoic, cold demeanor Darius had come to expect from him. "And when it comes to most of the Sins, I would agree with you, but *Wrath* does not want Thorn dead. She enjoys nothing more than making Thorn miserable."

"There are five other Sins that don't have her thirst for revenge, especially not revenge against Thorn," Jeremiah pointed out.

"But they all fear Wrath," Alan said. Something in his tone, tight and quick, made Darius think he was speaking more to convince himself than the rest of the room. "I have seen her kill other Sins to preserve Thorn's life. Even Pride wouldn't touch her."

"Hunt has had decades to make Thorn's life miserable," Jeremiah argued. "For god's sake, Alan, she killed her *son*. You don't think she could finally be getting bored with the game?"

"No." The word was firm and unwavering. "I don't. Wrath has had standing orders for the rest of the Sins to leave Thorn alive, no matter what."

"Then how do you explain this?" Jeremiah asked.

"I can't," Alan said quietly, and he turned away from Jeremiah and back toward the hospital doors. "But hopefully, we will have the chance to ask Thorn ourselves."

Darius felt what Alan did. The energies converged around the empty space of Thorn began to dissipate. One of them broke off and made its way toward them. Darius got to his feet—Chris coming up with him, clutching his hand—as Elijah Harris exited the operating room and made his way across the ward. Mackenzie and Jeremiah fell silent and watched as the doctor finally threw open the double doors.

He looked exhausted. Heavy, dark rings puffed up under his steely eyes. Dr. Harris's graying hair was pinned to his head under a green medical cap, and he heaved a sigh as he peeled bloody latex gloves off his fingers and removed his mask. He paused in the doorway and looked around at all of them before he said, "I don't know how, but she's going to be okay."

The tension in the room released like a broken dam. It washed over Darius in a torrent. Chris let go of his hand, collapsing back onto the chair behind her, as Mackenzie pulled her fingers through her bright blue hair and breathed, "Thank fucking god."

Alan stepped forward and held out a hand to the doctor. "Elijah, I can't thank you enough."

Dr. Harris grabbed Alan's palm in his. "I'd love to take all the credit, but I can't," he said. Then he exhaled a deep breath as Darius moved to stand beside Alan. "I have no idea how she managed to survive this. Most of the skin on the lower, right half of her body was blown away. She had shrapnel in almost every one of her major organs. Broken bones. Lacerated muscle. Burns up to her face. All we did was put the pieces back together, and her body took over from there." He frowned and crossed his arms. "If I could tap into whatever keeps that woman fighting, I'd never lose a patient."

"Can we see her?" Darius asked.

Elijah turned to him, and his nose wrinkled, just slightly, as he shook his head. "Weren't you listening? She's barely recognizable right now. It's not pretty. Besides, I pumped her full of enough anesthesia to drop a horse—and it will still probably wear off in an hour." The doctor rubbed his eyes with his thumb and fingers. "No. Get some rest. Check in with me in the morning. Except you, of course," Elijah said, gesturing to Alan. "If you want to go see her—"

"Yes," Alan said quickly. "I would."

So Elijah and Alan headed back into the hospital ward, and the waiting room quietly emptied. Mackenzie disappeared without much fanfare, darting down the hallway as she pulled out her phone and texted furiously. Jeremiah approached Chris. Without saying a word, he grabbed her shoulder in one massive, comforting hand and passed her a warm smile before he, too, made his way toward the elevators. Chris didn't move. Darius sat down beside her.

"You okay?" he asked.

She didn't answer right away. A fresh wave of silent tears had fallen down her face, but they were drying up now. She took a breath, cleared her throat, and said, "It was hard seeing her that way." Her voice was quiet and far away, but the words were sharp. "Thorn's been a part of my life for as long as I can remember—more than my own parents. She's the only family I have left, and I thought I was going to lose her."

Darius didn't know what to say to that, and in situations like this, he found that actions usually were more effective than whatever words he could clumsily put together. He reached out around her and pulled her in close to his side. Chris relaxed a little under his arm. The sickly-sweet smell of Thorn's blood still clung to her.

"You didn't lose her," Darius murmured after a few quiet moments. "None of us did."

"Thank god," Chris said. "Jeremiah's right. The Martyrs need Thorn just as much as she needs the Martyrs. I don't know if either of them could survive without the other."

For two days, Thorn healed alone.

Darius stopped by to visit her the next morning only to find she'd been moved to her private quarters in the middle of the night. Besides Dr. Harris coming to check her dressings and Alan occasionally bringing her food, no one else had seen her.

Naturally, rumors about the whole scenario ran rampant throughout the Underground.

"D'you think what Mackenzie said is true?" Parker asked. She and a handful of other researchers were eating their lunch at one of the tables in the center of the room. She looked around at her colleagues with big, anxious eyes. "That Thorn was basically *scalped*...?"

"Would her hair grow back, you think?" Daniel Park mused as he chewed his food. He was one of the research team leaders, focusing primarily on leads outside of the tri-state area. Daniel had passed off the intel for the trip Darius was taking now. He took another bite of his apple and gave Parker a good-natured, sidelong glance. Parker's eyes only widened.

"I haven't even *thought* of that," she whispered.

Daniel and the other researchers chuckled, and Darius turned around in his chair to face them. Both Lina and Mackenzie were out for the afternoon, so he was technically the most senior official in the room. He cleared his throat.

"Let's not *add* to the stories Mackenzie is trying to

spread," he said with a slightly scolding tone, but he passed the group a half-smile anyway. "I just sent out a few more articles to our high priority list. Parker, can you sort through these when you have a minute?"

"Of course," she said eagerly, and she quickly shoved the last morsel of her sandwich into her mouth and slapped her hands together to get rid of the crumbs. Then she pushed away from the table and took her spot beside Darius. She had been ecstatic when he'd chosen the workstation next to hers today. "Foun' s'more leads?" Parker asked through a full mouth, covering it with the back of her hand.

Darius nodded. "Yep. Mostly around the city."

"Good ones?"

"Pretty good," Darius said. "Not as good as the one in Washington, but promising."

"How do you do it?" Parker asked as she wheeled her chair a little closer to his and looked at his computer. "Like, how does being a Virtue *help* you know if a lead is good or not?"

Darius glanced back at his screen, and the program Teresa Solomon had designed looked back. Thinking about her sent a bittersweet pang through his heart, and he took a deep breath.

The Martyrs used a sophisticated algorithm crafted by the late Humility herself to track down other Virtues. It dug through headlines and keywords from news sources, forums, and social websites to look for stories that might indicate a Virtuous presence in the area—anything from good deeds to standout events, programs, and technologies being developed. And, while all the researchers were experts at the program by now, Darius had something the rest of them didn't...

He had his Virtue.

"It's a gut feeling thing," he told Parker, and he turned back to the screen, indicating the highlighted articles he'd selected. There were only four out of hundreds of results. "When I read these headlines, it just *feels* a little different. I know that sounds weird," he said with a laugh, "but Teresa thought it had to do with our instincts. I think it's more like... like these stories are steps on the path I should be following." He paused and turned to face Parker with a good-humored frown on his face. "Does that make me sound crazy?"

She smiled, and her cheeks flushed a little. "No, not at all!"

Darius laughed. "Good, because sometimes it *feels* like I'm crazy, especially since the leads I've followed in New York haven't led us to anything yet. But I have a good feeling about this upcoming trip."

A *really* good feeling.

This wouldn't be the first time Darius had followed up on a lead that had given him that gut feeling, but it was the first lead he'd ever come across that he felt this strongly about. He couldn't even place why. The article hadn't been anything spectacular—just some charity ball. He'd passed over dozens of more extravagant events in bigger cities all around the country, but for some reason, from the minute he'd seen that headline, he'd known he had to follow it. It was like a little beacon lit up in the back of his head:

Spokane's Largest Charity Gala Sells Out In Six Days.

And he was going to be there.

Suddenly, an alert pinged on Darius's phone, and he jumped. He still wasn't used to carrying one of these things around. When he pulled the device out of his pocket, Thorn's name flashed at the top of his screen. Seeing it made his stomach flip a little. She'd sent a text to all the Martyr leadership, and it just said three words:

"Urgent meeting. Now."

Darius excused himself and walked to the conference room next door. There was no energy on the other side, so he assumed he'd arrived first. He reached out, opened the door...

And he stared.

Thorn stood across the long table. He hardly recognized

her. Dark, loose-fitting clothing obscured much of her body. Her long-sleeved top and baggy lounge pants hung off her strong shoulders and lean hips. She'd pulled her black hair into a messy bun at the back of her head to keep it from touching her fresh, new skin—and her *skin* distracted Darius the most. The right side of her face, from just above her brow line, all the way down her throat and under her swooping neckline, was bright red and shiny smooth. Both of her hands shared the same look of fresh, tender flesh. Her deep, dark eyes glared at him from across the room, as though daring him to comment on it—to tell her she looked like hell.

If things hadn't been so tense between them lately, maybe he would have.

But right now, he just told her a different truth: "I'm glad you're okay. I was really worried about you."

The heaviness between them lightened a bit. Thorn's shoulders relaxed toward the ground as she nodded. The movement made her wince, and she reached her left hand out to grab the back of the chair in front of her. Her forearms were in better shape; the scars winding up from her wrist stood out, and the *Peccostium* was as clear as ever, untouched, it seemed, by the explosion.

As much as he hated seeing the thing, Darius knew Thorn wouldn't be alive without it.

"Me, too," she said. Her voice was still strong. Still focused.

Darius moved around the table toward her and frowned. "How are you feeling?"

Thorn shook her head with the slightest motion she could manage, and it still made the muscles along her jaw tighten in pain. "Not great," she said. "But it could be worse. I could be dead."

"According to Dr. Harris, you *should* be."

She gave a noncommittal kind of huff, and the door to the conference room opened again. "Good morning," Alan said as he walked in, striding to his place beside Thorn with

49

commanding grace. He didn't ask how she was doing; he didn't say anything to acknowledge her condition at all. He just pulled out a chair and sat down, his black trench coat whipping behind him. Darius followed his lead and sat on Thorn's other side. Thorn remained standing. It was probably less painful for her.

Moments later, the rest of the Martyr leadership joined them. Everyone paused to stare at Thorn as they came in. Mackenzie's jaw dropped, and she walked around the table.

"Jeez, Thorn," she said, reaching one finger toward Thorn's face. "I mean, good on you for trying out such a bold new look, but I gotta tell ya, the one eyebrow thing is really throwing me off."

Thorn said nothing as she pushed Mackenzie's hand away. Lina shook her head and quietly said, "Mackenzie…"

"How are you feeling?" Jeremiah asked as he took a seat beside Alan. Abraham Locke joined him on that side of the table. He stared at Thorn with wide eyes and absent-mindedly rolled his shirt sleeves to his elbows.

"I didn't call you all together so we could talk about how I'm feeling," Thorn said as she looked around the room. Mackenzie and Lina sat down on Darius's other side. He felt their warmth tuck in close beside him. Thorn's cold, half-empty eyes passed from one person to the next, starting at Alan, to Jeremiah and Abraham, to Lina and Mackenzie, before they landed on Darius and stayed there. She watched him for a long moment. Darius was uncomfortable. The look of her bright red, healing flesh made a shiver run down his spine, but he respected Thorn too much to let her see how upsetting he found her injuries, so he just stared back. Then she looked away, toward the others, and said, "The Sins know Teresa destroyed Pride."

Those words silenced the room so thoroughly that Darius could hear his own heart beating hard against his eardrums. Jeremiah frowned and leaned back in his chair. It creaked beneath his weight.

"That's impossible."

"It's not," Thorn said. "I spoke with Gregory Witham, and he told me that he could *feel* Pride's absence—that *all* the Sins could feel his absence. I tried to feed him some story, but he didn't buy it. The Sins know we've figured out how to destroy them."

Another round of silence. Darius's tongue darted out over his lips—they were suddenly dry and sticky. Jeremiah sighed and crossed his arms. "Well, that explains why the other five Sins just disappeared back in Wellsboro. They must have felt Pride's loss, and it rattled them so much they pulled back."

Thorn nodded. "We also had Darius with us, and they don't know which Virtue he is. For all they knew, he could have taken any one of them out. It wasn't worth the risk."

"But how could they know? Are they connected?" Darius asked. He turned to Lina. Like Teresa, the Martyrs had paid for Lina to get a Ph.D. in history, and now she was their resident expert in the Sins. She glanced at him, frowning a little as she thought about it.

"There are a few ways it could work, I guess," she said. "There are a lot of implications for this sort of co-existence in texts from cultures all over the world. Look at Christianity, for example. God, Jesus, and the Holy Spirit were considered three parts of the same whole."

"So the Sins are one being?" Abraham asked.

"I have no idea," Lina said. "I can't possibly know what they are, at the root of it, but if they can feel when one of them is destroyed, it stands to reason they have an ethereal connection of some kind."

"Wouldn't Alan and Thorn feel the same loss, then?" Jeremiah asked. "They share a connection to Wrath."

"Our energy has been tainted by Wrath and has a loose connection to her, yes," Alan said, looking between Jeremiah and Lina, "but seeing as the larger whole of Wrath's essence was ripped from us, it isn't surprising we don't have a link to the rest of the Sins."

"I don't give a damn about this bloody link," Mackenzie

blurted out. "All that matters is they know Pride got destroyed. We've lost our upper hand. They haven't been keeping low because they're trying to salvage Pride and Envy's work. They're afraid."

"A frightened enemy is more deadly than an angry one," Jeremiah said, and he cast Alan a look. "They're willing to go a lot further and do much more."

Alan pressed his steepled fingers against his lips and watched Jeremiah for a moment, thinking, before he turned to Thorn and said, "It seems they have already gone further than they would have before."

Thorn looked down at her uncle. She seemed more conscious about appearing strong now that the rest of the group had arrived, but Darius could tell she was hurting. Her fingers gripped the chair in front of her, and her jaw set tight. This close, he could see the details in her new skin as it healed. It was rubbery smooth and seemed almost sticky. Her sleeve clung to it as she shifted her position.

"They're worried," Thorn said. "For the first time in millennia, there seems to be a real threat against them, and that threat is sitting here with us." She glanced at Darius. Her half-empty, black eyes caught his, and she gave him a hard look before she turned back to the room again. "We need to cancel Darius's trip."

"*What?*" Darius's heart skipped a beat, and he leaned forward in his chair. She looked back to him, and he frowned. "Why?"

"The Sins know you're going, and they're coming for you."

Sound erupted in the conference room as Mackenzie, Jeremiah, and Abraham all began to talk simultaneously, asking variations on the same question: how the hell could Thorn possibly know that? Lina, lost in thought, stared at the wall just behind Thorn's hip. Alan simply focused on his niece with tempered patience.

Darius said nothing. He watched Thorn as she held one bright red, withered hand up to quiet the others. The skin was so thin Darius could make out the soft, purple lines of her blood vessels in the light.

"Witham told me they know what Darius is after, and it's going to lead him to them," she said, and she paused as she took them all in. This time, she didn't dwell long on Darius, like she didn't want to see the disappointment spread across his face. "They know about Washington."

"How could they possibly know that?" Jeremiah asked, fixing Thorn with a dark, suspicious expression. "Are you implying we have someone *feeding* the Sins information? That is a heavy accusation."

"That's not what I'm saying," Thorn snapped. Her mouth twitched in a wince of pain, but she pushed through it. "What I *mean* is the Sins have ears and eyes everywhere, and they're primed to listen for intel about us and what we're working on. It's not unreasonable for us to assume they've caught wind of this."

"You're speculating," Jeremiah said, opening a palm toward her and offering a shrug. "Witham's threat could mean any number of things—"

"What *else* is Darius after?" Thorn interrupted, and Darius saw the muscles on the good side of her face tighten. "Nothing. He's hunting the Virtues. Sloth also said I wouldn't be there to protect him. They know Darius is planning a trip so far away from the Underground that there's nothing I could do to stop them from killing him."

"That doesn't make any sense," Lina said. Thorn turned to her with a frown. Lina cleared her throat and leaned forward on the table. "Why try to kill you if they knew Darius was going to be across the country?"

"To guarantee I'm out of the way?"

"They wouldn't need you out of the way if the plan was to get to me while I'm in Washington," Darius said. "You wouldn't be anywhere nearby. Taking you down is a risky move, and the Sins could get themselves killed trying. Plus, if they wanted to get me while I'm away, wouldn't it make more sense for them to lie low until I'm gone? Why risk raising suspicions?"

"Besides that," Lina went on as she gestured to Darius with an open palm. "We only approved Darius's idea to fly to Washington four days ago—the day *before* you were attacked. According to Holly, Sloth has been planning this bombing for at least a month, maybe more, which was well before Darius even had this lead to follow in the first place. Even if information about this trip somehow leaked, they've been planning to kill you for much longer."

Alan crossed his arms as he watched Lina down his long, prominent nose. "What are you proposing, Miss Brooks?"

"I don't think the Sins know about Darius's trip at all," she said. "I think they have another plan to lure him out of the Underground, and they're getting close to putting it into action. Killing Thorn was the first step."

That was a scary thought. The idea they were targeting Darius in Washington, while far-fetched, at least gave them something to prepare against. Thinking the Sins had a different plan in mind—one they'd been working on for months—was terrifying.

Especially if it involved killing Thorn.

"If that's true," Jeremiah said quietly, and Darius saw Thorn turn to watch him—as she had turned to watch each and every one of them when they spoke—with mounting fury. Her thin lips tightened into a hot, fine line, and a wild glint shone behind her dark eyes. "Then sending Darius on this trip may be the best thing we can do. He'll be out of New York for a while."

"Damnit, *no!*"

Thorn slammed her fist down on the conference table so hard that the tight, new skin around her knuckles tore like wet paper. Blood seeped from the wounds. Thorn said, through gritted teeth, "We can't guarantee any of that! What if you're wrong? What if we send Darius right into a trap? I won't let us lose him this way! It's bad enough—"

She winced and stopped talking as she drew herself back to full height. For a moment, they all just watched her. They knew what she was going to say:

It was bad enough they had to lose Darius to destroy Envy.

This topic made them all uncomfortable—the idea that this Virtue who had so recently decided to join their ranks had to give up his life for their war. Thorn seemed to resent their need for Darius to make the ultimate sacrifice more than the others. After Teresa had died, Thorn told him she thought he should leave the Martyrs—to go and experience a long, full life.

"It's easy for us to take life for granted," she'd said as they stood over her son's grave. "We've gotten our fair share of it. You *deserve* more than this."

Darius had stuck around anyway.

"We can't take the risk," Thorn finally finished.

"Thorn has a point," Alan agreed. He'd been watching her with a heavy, mournful expression, but it disappeared as he turned back to the room. Darius looked down at his hands on the table. Droplets of Thorn's blood speckled the wood a foot away from his fingers. Alan went on. "We don't know what the Sins are planning, and we need to prepare for all potential situations."

"Alan, I can't lose this lead," Darius pressed. "We're looking at an event that only happens once a year. If we don't go, the Virtue—"

"You don't even know there's a Virtue there," Thorn snapped. Darius cast her a dark look.

"I know this is important," he pressed, and he looked at Alan again. "Teresa told me to follow my gut. I *know* that I need to do this. I can't explain how—"

"How *convenient.*"

"Damnit, Thorn, let me talk!" Darius got to his feet, too, and stood toe to toe with her. Thorn's eyes darkened. She didn't look away from him as he took a breath, turned to the room, and went on. "Teresa knew more about Virtues than anyone, and this is the system she used to track them down. We know she found a Virtue at least *once*, and I bet she would have found more if she'd had the chance to try. Maybe she'd have found all seven."

"You know," Lina offered thoughtfully. "I looked back at some of the leads you fed to us over the years—leads that, I'm assuming, came from Dr. Solomon?" Alan nodded, and Lina continued. "Well, two of them dealt with Lower Manhattan. Obviously, we didn't find Darius back then, but he *was* living in the area when she found those leads and sent them our way. Maybe he has a point. If Dr. Solomon had been able to show up herself, she'd have sensed him immediately."

Alan nodded, and Thorn watched him with a venomous glare Darius hadn't seen on her face since they'd been living at Teresa Solomon's house together. Her uncle seemed aware of her fury. Darius wondered if that was just intuition or if, on some level, he could feel it.

"Let's take a vote," he said. "Who thinks Mr. Jones should be permitted to continue with his trip to Washington?"

Darius raised his hand and looked around the room. Three others—Jeremiah's, Mackenzie's, and Lina's—joined his. His heart skipped a beat. Thorn swore again.

"This is fucking *unbelievable.*"

"It's settled," Alan said, "but I think Thorn should accompany him."

The rage on her face subsided just a bit. The curled snarl upon her mouth softened.

"The Sins believe you are dead," Alan went on. "If they really are planning to ambush him in Washington State, they won't expect you to be there, and you can handle them. It also gives us a window of time to observe them in New York and see what their next move is. Mr. Jones, I know Miss Silver was originally slated to be your security escort, however…"

"It's no problem," Darius said, and a weight lifted off his chest as he gave a small smile and raised his hands. He hadn't realized how heavily the threat of losing this had been sitting on his shoulders.

"You leave in a week?" Alan asked. Darius nodded. "That will give Thorn plenty of time to heal up and get her affairs in order. Thorn, does this work for you?"

"I want more precautions put in place," she said. Her anger ebbed as she focused on the task at hand. "Contingency plans, escape routes…"

"See that it's done," Alan said with a nod before he addressed the room again. "Now, let's talk about the next steps we need to take when it comes to the other problem here—this other possible plan the Sins have been working on."

The rest of the meeting deviated from Darius's trip. Alan assigned Jeremiah to get his team prepared for more altercations—upping training schedules, performing weapons maintenance, and increasing tactical planning. Abraham left to talk with Holly about how best to organize a digital search of the Sins' activities. Thorn was asked to get her Intelligence operatives looking into Darius's history for *anything* the Sins could possibly use against him.

The peace was finally over.

CHAPTER FOUR

"So, what *exactly* is the Gray Unit doing now?"

Darius and Eva stood side by side in the elevator on their way up to the topmost level of the Underground. Eva was hopping a ride back to New York with Chris and Jeremiah for her first "wide shift" in the city. Over the last seven days, all the Martyrs' responsibilities had drastically expanded. Holly's tech team doubled down on tracking Sin and potential Puppet behavior, TAC was increasing training and extending patrols, and the R&D department was shifting focus from searching for Virtues to helping the security team identify suspicious activity in the city.

As for the Gray Unit, Thorn had them stretching into wider shifts, which essentially meant Eva and the rest of the Gray Agents had to broaden their networks and routes, cover more ground, and take bigger risks to get closer to the Sins than they were usually permitted to do.

"I told you," Eva said, tilting her head and throwing him a soft, compassionate smile. "For *me*, it just means walking larger sections of the city. Envy hasn't repossessed yet, remember? I'm just looking for potential hosts. Don't worry. I won't be getting *anywhere* near the Sins."

Darius took a deep breath. That didn't make him feel

much better. The Sins were at the point where they were willing to blow *Thorn* up, and the whole of New York felt more dangerous for it. He wanted to tell Eva he didn't want her going into the city until the Martyrs had more information on the attack, but he knew it wouldn't do anything. Eva was used to dangerous work, and Darius didn't want to come off like he didn't trust her.

They might have known each other for almost half a decade, but their romance was still fresh. It wasn't worth spoiling.

"Well," Darius said, reaching out to grab Eva's hand. "Just be careful."

She squeezed his fingers. "Always am."

The elevator dinged, and the doors slid open. Darius and Eva walked through the foyer to the parking lot. Chris and Jeremiah were already there. Jeremiah sat behind the wheel of a large, black SUV, tapping his massive fingers on the side of the open window, while Chris quietly spoke to John Waters near the entrance to the waiting room. A weary frown pulled at her mouth, and she shook her head before she spotted Darius near the doors and quickly put on a smile. John glanced over his shoulder, and as soon as he saw Darius, he tried to wipe the frustration off his expression, too.

"Darius!" John said, grabbing Darius's hand in a friendly, familiar shake. "Ready for this meeting? Sara's waiting for us."

"Ready as ever," Darius said, and as John turned to say hi to Eva and give her a hug, Darius glanced at Chris with a questioning look. She just shook her head and rolled her eyes up a little, which he took to mean she and John just had *another* argument about Thorn. He knew better than to bring it up, so instead, he said, "Starting on double shifts here soon?"

"Not double," Chris said. She reached behind her head and pulled her blonde hair into a loose ponytail at the base of her skull. "Not yet, at least. But we'll be out a little longer.

With Gray expanding their work, we want to be able to be on-scene immediately if a situation comes up."

Darius threw Eva another nervous look.

"I'll be *fine*," she said.

"Of course you will," John said, and he wrapped his arm around Chris's shoulders and pulled her to his side in a tight, affectionate embrace. "Chris'll be there. She's got first-hand experience taking the Sins down now. How many other TAC members have killed a host?"

He meant it as a compliment, but Chris's bright green eyes flashed, and her jaw tightened. Six months ago, Envy had torn a knife through her face, and Chris had responded by slitting the Sin's throat. Though Darius had fixed the physical injuries, psychological trauma was much harder to heal.

"We'd better head off," Chris said shortly. She reached up, kissed John on the cheek, and squeezed his hand as she made her way back to the black SUV. "I'll text you," she told him. Then she turned to Darius and waved. "And you, too."

Eva gave Darius a tight hug and light kiss as she followed after Chris. John watched them until Chris closed the door and disappeared behind dark, tinted windows. His ocean blue eyes narrowed, and he pressed his lips together in a frown. As soon as the vehicle was out of sight, he and Darius walked back into the Underground.

They hadn't taken two steps into the building before Darius's phone went off in his pocket. It was a text from Chris:

"Don't let them kill each other. Good luck."

He chuckled, and John let out a groan.

"Man, I was looking forward to taking this trip with Chris," he said as they headed up the hallway toward the R&D headquarters.

"I know it sucks," Darius said, elbowing John in the arm, "but it's not like we're going on vacation."

John laughed and glanced at Darius from over his shoulder, running a hand through his styled, black hair as he did it. "It's the closest thing I'd *have* to a vacation with Chris," he said. "She works *so much*. I thought some space would be good for her. Instead, I get some 'quality time' with *Thorn*…"

There it was. John had never tried to hide how much he didn't like Thorn. He didn't like the way she pushed Chris, the way she trained with Chris when she was so obviously unmatched… and he especially didn't like the way Thorn thought he was not good enough *for* Chris.

Ever since John found out Thorn had taken Chris's spot on this assignment, he'd been sour and moody.

Darius took out his phone and navigated to Chris's chat. He responded with two words:

"No promises."

"Anyway," John said, and he cleared his throat as they reached the R&D department. He stretched his neck from side to side, like he was shaking the bad feelings off and resetting himself. "Let's get to work!"

He threw open the door and led the way into the room. It flowed with hurried, anxious energy. Lina sat in the back, simultaneously pouring over more of Teresa's documents while she guided her team in their updated tasks. Researchers clicked away at their workstations, and Recon units filtered in and out to gather new mission intel before heading back into the city. People glanced up, said hi, or reached out to shake John's hand in a fraternal kind of way as he and Darius made their way to a table at the center of the room.

A woman sat there alone. She was tall, full-bodied, and she'd pulled her dirty blonde hair into a bun on the top of her head. Massive, over-the-ear headphones worked as a barrier between her and the rest of the world as she flipped through documents in a folder on the table in front of her. She adjusted a pair of stylish glasses while she jotted some notes on the paperwork.

John tapped her on the shoulder. "Hey, Sara."

She turned and took her headphones off. As soon as she spotted John—and Darius standing behind him—her blue eyes went wide, and she jumped to her feet. On the way up, she knocked the file off the table, sending papers fluttering to the ground in a grandiose display. Her cheeks went pink.

"Oh, *fuck*!"

Darius laughed as he and John leaned down to help her clean up. John peered at Darius from over Sara's shoulders, throwing him a big, "I told you so" grin.

When they had it all collected and put back into a pile, the three of them sat down at the table again. Sara, her hair messy, her face red, cleared her throat.

"Sorry 'bout that," she said, shuffling the papers and hastily resorting them. She didn't look up at Darius as she did it. "Here's everything I need you guys to go over for the trip."

Sara Park was John's superior officer and the most experienced person on the Recon team other than maybe Mackenzie herself. Where the rest of the Recon units focused on closer, shorter day missions, Sara and John spent two weeks at a time out of the Underground, exploring faraway cities. Where Sara organized things on a big-picture level, John handled the nitty-gritty details.

Darius opened the folder and looked through the pages. "There's a lot in here," he said, impressed. When he'd gone on the one-day missions, there hadn't been nearly this kind of prep.

"Yeah," Sara said. She cleared her throat again, but the color in her face was beginning to fade. "This kind of assignment is a lot more complicated, but even *more* now that we've got you." The color popped up again, and she got to her feet. "Anyway, I have to go meet up with Mackenzie to finalize our travel plan and get the cyber-Intelligence officers a breakdown of our itinerary. John," she looked at him from over Darius's shoulder, and he quickly wiped the self-satisfied look off his face and replaced it with a more serious expression. Sara raised her brows high on her head, as though she knew what he was thinking, but she went on without commenting on it. "Get Darius up to speed with all this stuff. I'll see you guys when we head off in the morning."

Then she smiled at them, pushed herself away from the table, and scurried toward the exit. On the way, she pulled her headphones back over her ears. As soon as the door shut behind her, John chuckled and turned to Darius.

"She's *so* excited to get to work with you," he said. "Just a couple of weeks ago, she was complaining that you hadn't found any leads that would get passed onto us. You should have *seen* her face when Mackenzie told her this was happening."

John laughed again, and Darius just provided a soft smile. Most of the Martyrs still looked at him with that kind of reverence, but not John. Not anymore. There were a few people who had gotten to know Darius on a more personal level over the last few months. The Martyr leadership, for one, but as Darius had gotten close to Chris, he'd started spending more time with her group, too. That included Raquel, who had become one of Eva's close friends, and John.

Ever since the magic of knowing *"The Virtue"* had worn off, John loved watching others get tongue-tied around Darius, forgetting, it seemed, that he'd been one of the tongue-tied ones himself not too long ago. The thought made Darius's smile widen.

"What do we need to cover?" Darius asked, holding the folder out.

"Okay," John said, rubbing his hands together as he grabbed the file, opened it up, and spread the contents across the table. "Here's what we've got."

There was a *lot:* the original article that had drawn Darius's attention, travel itinerary, booking confirmation slips, budget reports, inventory and shopping lists, blueprints of some hotel, a flyer for the event, and printed photographs of the high-end donors sponsoring it. Darius picked up the donor photos and flipped through them, hoping maybe the same Virtue sense that had told him he had to go to this event in the first place would ping again, but it didn't.

"The event is called '*Bleeding Hearts For Fresh Starts*,'" John said, with a humorous wince at the name. He adjusted in his seat and leaned further over the table. "It's a black-tie fundraiser designed to raise money to help recovering convicts get back on their feet."

"Black tie?" Darius asked.

"Fancy as fuck, like top hat and tailcoats kind of thing," John explained. "This is the fourth year the event has been put on, and so far, it's the biggest yet. They sold out tickets within *six days* of opening sales. It's also the biggest charity event Washington State has seen in over a decade, which is shocking since it's in *Spokane* and not *Seattle*. The numbers and weird coincidences alone back up your gut feeling that there's some serious Virtuous shit going on here."

He chuckled and smiled so broadly that his eyes squinted in a way that made them look like they were smiling, too. Like Mackenzie, John was a welcome beacon of positivity in the Underground. Darius wondered if that was just who John was or if it had to do with his position on one of the Recon teams. More than most Martyrs, John got a break from the bleak routine, and he rarely, if ever, had to face the tragedy of their work firsthand.

Darius would bet the closest John ever got to conflict was pacing the waiting room, wondering if Chris was going to be okay after yet another run-in with the Sins and their Puppets.

"Well, good," Darius said. "Because Thorn is gonna be *pissed* if we get there and there *isn't* a Virtue."

John's smile faded a bit, and the good-natured glint in his expression hardened. "Thorn's gonna find a reason to be pissed no matter what we do," he said shortly, and though he tried to keep the joy on his face, it felt plastic.

Damnit, Darius knew better than to bring up Thorn. He cleared his throat.

"So, what's our plan?" he asked. "How do you normally go about finding a Virtue?"

John laughed and sat back in the chair. He crossed his arms over his chest. The deep blue of his t-shirt brought out the same oceanic colors in his eyes. "I'll let you know when we actually find one," he said. "You're the first Virtue any living Martyr has ever met."

"Well, then what did you do *before* you had me?" Darius asked. "How could you ever know?"

John's expression hardened again. "Thorn," he said simply. "Most of the time, our trips are a total bust. We get there and find nothing interesting that merited any more of our time. But, on the few occasions we *did* narrow down a person of interest that fit certain criteria, we'd take Thorn along on a follow-up trip."

"Ah…" Darius nodded. "Because if they're a Virtue, she can't sense their energy…"

John clicked his tongue against the side of his mouth and pointed a finger in Darius's direction. "Bingo. But that never worked out, obviously. Hardly surprising. There are only seven Virtues—or, I guess, six now." He nodded toward Darius. "And thank *god* we have one. After this, I'm hoping I never have to take Thorn on a Recon mission again."

Darius took a deep breath and made a mental note to keep John and Thorn from tearing each other's throats out on the trip. He wondered if Chris had any advice about this…

"Then what's up with *this* mission?" Darius asked. "How's it different now?"

John shrugged and ran his hand through his rich, black hair. It was swiped back in soft waves away from his face— a style that was clearly designed to look good and take as little time as possible. "Not much, honestly," he said, and he came forward again to sort through the papers on the table. He grabbed a few items—the blueprints for the event venue and a shopping list—and pulled them to the front. "The biggest difference is the shit Thorn's putting together in case the Sins actually *do* show up."

"What's she doing?"

"Escape routes," John said, but the way he said it made it clear he thought it was a waste of time. "We have a car, so we can just leave town if the Sins start causing problems. You'd think that would be enough, but she also wants a private jet on standby. Just in case. Seems like a waste of resources to me, but…" He gave a shrug. "Assuming the Sins never show up, though, it's just business as normal. If we find a Virtue, the goal is to identify who it is and create rapport. Until then, *my* job is going to be getting everything in order for the trip."

"Why do we need *tuxedos*?" Darius pulled the shopping list out of John's hands. "Or *dresses*?"

John chuckled. He looked Darius over and gave him a charming half-smile as he gestured toward the shirt and jeans he was wearing. "Remember *black tie?* C'mon, man. You walk in like that, you'll stick out."

"Walk *in*?" Darius said, surprised. "We're not going into the event, are we? Isn't that dangerous?"

John frowned. "Why would it be?"

"Aren't there going to be Sentries?" Darius said, and he felt weird that he even had to point it out. "People the Sins have Programmed to recognize me? Or Thorn?"

John's mouth dropped open a little, as though he suddenly realized what Darius was worried about, and he gave a single, slow nod before he shook his head. "Oh, no. Not at all. They don't have a network of Programmed Sentries that far from the city. That kind of thing would be almost impossible to maintain since Programming disappears within a few months after a host is killed. They couldn't replace their people effectively. Once we're out of the tri-state area, we've *never* had any issues."

Darius nodded slowly. It made sense, but something was still off—something else he couldn't explain. He leaned toward John and crossed his arms. "So how are the Sins such a huge threat, then?" he asked. "If they're trapped in New York, how are they corrupting *the world*?"

"They're not *trapped* in New York."

Darius jumped a little at the suddenness of Thorn's voice and turned around. She had opened the door so quietly he hadn't heard her enter the room—and he hadn't sensed her, either. He had gotten used to being able to feel the people around him that only she and Alan were able to catch him off guard anymore. She closed the door behind her and turned toward John and Darius. "They set themselves up here *intentionally*."

"Why *here*?"

"The Sins don't need an army of Puppets or Sentries to take over," Thorn said. "They just need *people*, and a lot of them. New York is one of the top tourist spots in the world. They come here and get steeped in the Sins' Influence and then carry it with them wherever they go. The Sins have also dipped their hands into every political, religious, and corporate entity in the city. Power isn't just about *spiritual* corruption. It's about *systemic* corruption."

"So, they *are* everywhere," Darius said.

"Yeah," John said, "But not *physically*. You'll be totally safe in Spokane."

Thorn's lip curled into a small, angry frown, but she didn't say anything. Instead, she turned away without excusing herself and headed toward the back of the room. Darius watched after her.

If he hadn't seen Thorn just a few days ago, he never would have known she'd been injured. She was back to her old style—both in dress and demeanor—wearing tight-fitting and quick-moving clothing and a subtle furrow to her serious expression. Her flesh was smooth and fresh, a perfect canvas of flawless, pearl skin. In the warm weather, she'd switched from long-sleeved shirts to tank tops, but her forearms were covered entirely by black, fingerless gloves.

Rumors still circulated wildly through the Underground. Mackenzie enjoyed fanning the flames of these whispers. Darius had overheard her on a few separate occasions giving differing accounts of Thorn's injuries—everything from missing fingers to having all the skin on her body singed off. Since no one other than the doctor, a few nurses, and the Martyr leadership had actually seen Thorn before she had healed, there weren't a lot of rational voices to drown out the craziest of the stories going around.

Thorn did nothing to squash them, either. She had just gone back to work as though nothing had happened. As she stepped up beside Lina's desk and leaned over the edge, her long, black hair poured over her shoulders like a veil of silk. Sparkie clung to her back, and as he was revealed, his head turned and took in the room.

"Where the fuck is McKay?"

Lina glanced up from her reading. "Downstairs," she said with a frown. "Working with Holly to get the plane set up. She said you were meeting her?"

Thorn sighed and rubbed her eyes with the fingers and thumb of her left hand. "I was *just* down there, and she's not answering her phone. If you see her, tell her to use her fucking calendar so she stops *missing meetings*."

"Of course," Lina said.

Thorn nodded and turned to walk away, but before she'd taken three steps, she snapped her fingers and came around again. "Oh," she said, and her tone shifted. It got quieter. More intimate. Darius paid attention as she went in a little closer to Lina. "We found Jacob. He made contact this morning."

Darius hadn't known that Lina was holding onto an ounce of worry until he saw her shoulders melt in visible relief. She let out a quiet "oh!" as she closed her book and put a hand over her chest. "Thank god," she breathed, and she looked up to Thorn's face. Darius couldn't see the expression Thorn was wearing, but he could read her empathy by the way she reached out and gripped her hand tightly on Lina's shoulder. "Where has he *been*?"

Thorn shook her head. The motion made her smooth hair ripple across her shoulder blades. "He wouldn't say, but he's fine. I just wanted to let you know."

"Thank you."

"Jacob?" John's voice called out across the room, and he looked at Thorn and Lina with a frown. "We haven't heard from him in, what, six months?"

"Longer," Thorn said, and she turned and made her way back toward the exit. "I was starting to think he was dead."

Lina sighed and shook her head. "Abraham was, too."

"He'll be here to drive us to the airport," Thorn said as she opened the door to the hallway. John groaned, and Thorn cast him a dark look. Darius thought she was going to reprimand him for a moment, but instead, she dismissed him and turned to Lina again. "If you and Abraham want to see him, I'll tell him to come early."

"I'd like that, yes," Lina said.

Thorn nodded. Then she left the room, as quickly and quietly as she'd come. Sparkie's tiny head shook free from the long strands of Thorn's hair and peered backward until the door closed behind them. Darius's brows pinched together as he turned to John and Lina. He'd *thought* he knew everyone in the Underground, but it looked like he was wrong.

"Who's Jacob?"

"Abraham's brother," Lina said.

"I didn't know Abraham had a brother."

"Because he's crazy," John said with a short laugh, but Lina threw him a hot look, and he responded with a sheepish but kind smile. "Okay, that's not fair. He's just… a little off. But he's a good guy. Totally harmless. Though I wish he weren't driving us to the airport…"

"Why?" Darius asked.

John shrugged. "He's… really careful. Annoyingly careful. Maybe I'll get lucky, and he won't show up."

Lina glowered at John again, but he'd already turned back to the documents on the table and didn't see her.

CHAPTER FIVE

Three days later, with all the essentials for their trip packed and ready to go, Darius found himself in the back of an older but immaculately cared-for hatchback with Jacob Locke behind the wheel. The resemblance between the Locke brothers was uncanny. It was as though someone had taken Abraham and wrung him like a wet rag between their hands to squeeze all the liquid out, and the end result was Jacob. They shared the same brown eyes and long nose, but Jacob's cheeks were hollow and his forehead creased in deep worry lines. His brillo pad hair was graying heavily at the temples and jammed underneath a faded, orange ball cap. Every so often, his tongue darted out to wet his lips.

The introductions had been quick—they met Jacob in the garage, and he was eager to be on his way—so he and Darius did little more than shake hands before he helped the four of them pile their gear into his car. Their loved ones had been there to say goodbye. Eva and Chris waved as Daniel, Sara's husband from the research team, kissed his wife on the cheek and closed the door behind her. No one came to see Thorn off, and she quietly stepped into the front seat.

"It's been a while, Locke," Thorn said as she strapped

herself in. She looked over at Jacob as he drove them up and out of the Underground. He glanced at her shortly as they exited the car wash, and the vehicle was doused in pink, dawn light. "Where the hell have you been?"

"Keeping low," he said. The words came out quickly. "Sins were close. Too close. So I moved again."

"Where'd ya move?" John asked from his spot by the window.

Jacob threw him an annoyed, incredulous look in the rearview mirror. "Can't say."

"Of course not," John muttered. Darius looked across to him and then to Sara. She just shrugged, giving Darius a tight-lipped smile. Thorn glared at John from over the back of her seat before she turned to Jacob again.

"Next time, I need a check-in sooner," she said. "I thought you were dead."

"Nope," he said. He didn't look at her. Now that they were on the road, his wide eyes darted back and forth between everything outside the car—every other vehicle, pedestrian, and building—in rapid, disorienting shifts. "Not dead. Not *yet*, at least."

"Two months," Thorn said. "That's all you get. *Two months* or I'll start searching for you myself, and you *won't* be happy when I find you."

"Two months," he said, but he didn't apologize. "That's fair. I can do that."

Thorn nodded. Her eyebrows were low over her dark eyes. "Good."

Then Jacob went silent and focused again on the road ahead.

The drive from the Underground to the Newark Liberty International Airport took forty minutes. No one tried to make conversation. John rested his head against the window and promptly fell asleep. Little foggy clouds on the glass faded and reappeared with the pattern of his breathing. Sara just watched out the windshield ahead. Thorn was stoic, cold, and unmoving.

But Jacob, for all his silence, was full of motion and activity. His eyes were wide, his pupils pin tight, as they darted around the world outside the car. The slightest movement on the road immediately drew his attention. His focus shifted between dozens of points every minute, but somehow this didn't make his driving erratic or unpredictable. If anything, it was just another facet of this hyper-alert behavior. He didn't go above the speed limit, and he indicated every turn with clockwork consistency.

Darius thought maybe he was just nervous, but part of him knew that wasn't right. Something about him felt... *off*. He remembered what John had said: that Jacob was crazy.

When they finally arrived at the airport, Jacob drove past the curbside drop-off three times. Whenever there were more than a couple cars stopped, letting people out, he went right on through and came around for another pass. John had woken up by this point, and neither he nor Sara seemed put off by this behavior. Neither did Thorn. No one commented on it at all.

When the fourth pass came around, there were no other vehicles. Jacob quickly pulled over, parked, and pushed a button on his dash to open up the back of his car.

"Go on," he said as he jumped out. Darius and the others followed and began to gather their things.

"Take care of yourself," Thorn said as she reached out and shook Jacob's hand. Their eyes met, and Darius saw a similarly dark and driven look in both their expressions. "We'll only be in Spokane for a week. Keep an eye on the Martyrs for me."

"Always," Jacob said. John and Sara closed the back of the car and started toward the automatic doors. Thorn glanced at them, then back to Jacob, and gave him a final nod before she walked off, too. Darius moved to follow her, but Jacob grabbed him by the wrist.

"Hey," he said. Darius turned, surprised. Jacob's voice was low and quiet, and he licked his lips and glanced over Darius's shoulder before he went on. "I heard what you're doing. In the Underground. Good stuff. Good work. Keep it up."

"Oh," Darius said, taken aback. "Well, thanks—"

"And I heard about the lies," Jacob pushed on. He spoke so quickly, so quietly, it was hard for Darius to hear him. He frowned and leaned in, and Jacob continued. "That Blaine didn't tell you who you were. What you were. It's fucked up, man. I'm sorry."

It felt like a stone dropped into Darius's stomach. "I—uh… It's really not that big of a—"

"It is," Jacob said, and he shook his head. "They do good. They want to do good. But they shouldn't lie to you. It would've been better if they didn't lie."

Darius didn't know what to say to that—and he didn't have time to think about it. Thorn's voice cut through the growing clamor of voices at the drop-off line.

"Jones!" Darius looked over his shoulder to see her storming right up to him. She threw her free hand up in the air. "We've got to *go*."

"Right," Darius said, and he turned back even though he knew Jacob would be gone. He'd felt his energy slink away, climb back into his car, and drive off. Darius watched the clean, little hatchback disappear into the traffic with a frown before he turned and followed Thorn into the airport.

They rushed into the building, and Darius was slammed with a hot, intense wall of positive, human energy. Hundreds of people gathered in the corridors. The security line twisted around, over and over, and they stood so far back Darius couldn't see the front. Every few minutes, they'd take one or two steps, only to stop again and wait some more. John groaned impatiently and glanced at his watch for the twelfth time since Darius and Thorn had joined them.

The monotony was foreign. At the street market, there were no real *lines*. Instead, people pushed in beside one another, loud and impatient, fighting for a place to stand. These travelers, packed in tight and organized like glass beads on cotton twine, would've been eaten alive by the Bridge Market crowds. Stepped on. Talked over. Pickpocketed.

The airport felt like a weird blend of Darius's two worlds. It had the same busy atmosphere of the market, but, like the Underground, it felt sterile, clean, and secure in a way the market never could.

The biggest, most striking difference was the *feeling* of the airport. Darius hadn't been anywhere so densely packed with people since he'd Initiated his Virtue, and all of this energy converged in a single location was overwhelming. Maybe it was a *good* kind of overwhelm, but right now, Darius wasn't sure. All he knew was that he was *hot*. As they got through security and moved toward their gate, Darius wiped sweat from his brow. Thorn came up beside him.

"It's a lot, isn't it?"

She looked around the busy terminal. John and Sara walked ahead of them, and people passed by on either side. Thorn didn't seem as bothered by it as he was. Darius wondered if she'd gotten more used to it in her long life or if feeling cold energy was more comfortable than heat.

The thought made him a little sad. The heat may have been a lot to handle, but it still showed Darius there was goodness in the world. All Thorn felt was the cold, stark weight of corruption.

Their plane was a smaller aircraft, with two columns of two chairs each. The Martyrs sat toward the back of the cabin. They squeezed their way through the crowded compartment. In this tight, enclosed space, warm energy smothered in around Darius like he was trapped in a car on a hot summer day. He shoved his things under the seat in front of him and flopped down in his chair with a sigh. His back and chest were so sticky with sweat that his shirt clung to his skin.

Thorn quietly eased herself into the chair beside his.

Thank god. Darius had never been more grateful that he couldn't sense her soul than he was now. It was a welcome break in the overbearing heat around him.

That made Darius realize something.

"Hey," he asked as she put her backpack and satchel under the chair in front of her. Thorn pulled her dark hair behind her ear and turned to look at him. "Where's Sparkie?"

Without a word, she tapped her bag with the side of her foot. Sparkie's little head popped out from under the front flap as though to say hi before it quickly disappeared again. Darius raised his brows.

"How did you get him through security?"

"Carefully," she said.

Then she explained it to him. Sparkie had flown off as soon as they'd gotten out of Jacob's car and circled overhead until they knew their gate. He hung out just outside it until the plane arrived and slipped into the boarding tube as it was extended to the side of the aircraft. He was able to tuck in, unseen, in the seams of the tube, and when Thorn walked by, he'd deftly slid into her bag.

Darius let out a laugh.

"Impressive."

Thorn nodded. "We're good. We've had a lot of practice. Sparkie's not like Rae or Cain's cat. He sticks out, so we've learned to be discreet."

"Why *is* Sparkie so different?" Darius asked. He'd always wondered, but he'd never really thought to ask. "Every other Familiar is a normal animal. Why isn't he?"

"Familiars are a representation of the host's energy *before* possession," Thorn said. "They seem to exhibit personality traits, habits, interests… When Wrath started ripping me apart, my energy was a child, so Sparkie? He's kind of a child himself."

Thorn looked down at the satchel again, and Darius's chest clenched with a painful knot. Thorn's possession had taken seventeen years. Since her aging didn't stop until it was completed, it was easy for him to forget that she hadn't been in her late twenties when Wrath had targeted her.

She was just a kid.

"Anyway." Thorn's tone shifted, like she could sense Darius's pity, and she wanted to get past it as soon as possible. "His form has been a drawback, but it's also forced us to be creative in getting around."

"Why don't you use Influence?" Darius asked. "Couldn't you just, you know, *make* people ignore him?"

Thorn raised one brow and shook her head. "No. I can't just use my Influence like that."

"Yeah, I guess it's not really ethical—"

"It's not that," Thorn dismissed, turning away to latch her lap belt. "When I use Influence, Wrath feels it. I have to be careful."

That caught Darius by surprise. His eyes widened, and he leaned forward. "*What?*"

Thorn nodded. "We're connected—Alan, too. When any one of us uses Direct Influence, the other two can feel it. It's like a damned beacon. Are you hot? You look hot."

Darius hadn't even noticed he was pulling at the neckline of his shirt to try to get some relief. Thorn reached above him and turned a knob on the ceiling. It opened up, and a stream of air rushed out onto Darius's face. He closed his eyes and sighed.

"God, yes. Thanks. So, does that mean Wrath can find you if you use Influence?"

"Yes," Thorn said. "She gets a sense for where we are whenever we use it. Why do you think Alan never Programs any of the Martyrs in the Underground? He takes them out somewhere in the city. That way, Wrath won't get clued into where our headquarters are."

Right. Darius hadn't even wondered about Alan's procedure with Programming. A weight fell into his stomach, and he frowned. Of all the elements of the Martyrs, Darius was most unhappy about this one. Alan Blaine used Programming on every single Martyr in order to keep them safe.

Darius had been resistant to the idea—and furious when

he'd learned that he had been Programmed without his knowledge shortly after he'd been taken in—but the logic made sense. Alan developed a specialized form of Programming where he could make his Martyrs "torture proof." Mackenzie's words. He made it impossible for any Martyr to talk about the Underground and its location. Even if they were having their fingernails ripped off—again, a colorful example provided by Mackenzie—no Martyr was even capable of giving up that information.

Darius had his doubts, so he attempted it for himself. The moment he tried, the words got lost on the route from his brain to his mouth. He couldn't so much as mention the compass direction or the name of the nearest town.

It explained a lot—like why it had been so dangerous when Eva had disappeared last year. She hadn't been Programmed yet, and the Sins could have used her to find the Underground in a way they couldn't use any other Martyr.

"Darius?"

He'd gone quiet, caught up in his thoughts, and hadn't noticed Thorn watching him with firm, dark eyes. Her concern was hard to see—Darius only caught it because he'd spent so much time with her he'd become more tuned-in to her subtlety. The muscles between her eyebrows, just slightly, pinched tighter as she focused on his face.

"Hmm?"

"Thinking about how much you hate Programming?"

Was he that transparent? He supposed he had to be. It was no secret to the rest of the Martyr leadership how much Darius didn't like Programming. He'd spent weeks looking for a better solution and had found none. Eventually, he had to admit it was probably a necessary evil. This Programming meant the Sins had little motivation to capture and torture the Martyrs for information on the location of their hideout. Alan had undoubtedly saved hundreds of people from long, painful deaths over the decades, and the Underground had never been discovered.

So all Darius did was shrug.

"You can hate it all you want," Thorn said. A flight attendant walked down the aisle and checked their lap belts. As she neared, the heat around Darius intensified a bit. He was grateful for the air conditioning overhead. "But Alan's Programming is what allowed him to build the Martyrs in the first place."

Darius looked over to her. "What do you mean?"

"I mean," she said with a frustrated sigh. "The founding Martyrs were all *Oblitus Peccatum*, just like Alan. They had to stay on the move to avoid being caught by the Sins, and they couldn't recruit others to help them. Normal people just can't withstand the torture. It would have gotten them all tracked down and killed.

"Then Cain found Alan. Alan knew they'd never be able to beat the Sins alone, so he figured out how to Program. That's what made it possible for them to set up the Martyrs and build the Underground. Without him and this Programming you hate so much, we'd all be dead. Fuck, I'd probably still be Wrath."

Just saying it brought a bit of that emotion to Thorn's voice. The final word came out deeper, heavier, and the concern in her eyes blinked out. Darius didn't know what to say, so for a few minutes, he just quietly listened to the flight attendant give her safety speech without really hearing it. When the plane jolted to life, the engines roaring and the propellers spinning outside the windows, Darius sighed.

"I get that it's important," he said. Thorn cast him a sideways look. "It just feels like a violation. I should be glad that that's all it is, and nobody gets hurt."

Thorn paused. The way her eyes narrowed and her lips tightened told Darius that he'd hit something, and she was trying to decide whether or not to tell him. Jacob's comments came roaring back. Darius and Thorn made a promise—no more secrets, no more lies. Was she really going to break it after just six months?

She took a deep breath through her nose, watched him for a moment longer, and said, "Programming *does* have some potential side effects, but most of them are temporary, and we've only seen them a handful of times."

Darius's eyes narrowed. "When?"

"Most of them back when I—" she cleared her throat "—before I was a Martyr. They're in the records—memory loss, confusion, things like that. Ask Lina about them if you want more details. As Alan perfected his technique, the side effects disappeared…"

She paused again, but she had the decency not to look away from Darius as she prepared to give him difficult news.

"Then, there was Jacob Locke."

A weight fell into Darius's chest. His eyes widened. "*Jacob?*"

Thorn nodded. "He and Abraham joined the Martyrs almost twenty years ago. Abraham was married to Lina's sister. Lina lived with them. Jacob was… not doing well. Pride had Programmed him as a hitman. He would black out and kill targets without knowing he did it at all. We tracked him down when we got wind of it, but Pride found out and instructed him to kill his wife and kids and then himself. It was brutal." Thorn shook her head, and Darius's stomach churned. "When I got to the scene, Abraham had Jacob pinned, but it was too late for his family."

"Oh my *god*," Darius muttered. He knew what it was like to have Pride murder your family. Sometimes his still visited Darius in his dreams—pale, cold, and bloody. He'd wake up drenched in cold sweat and hot tears, their voices crisp and fresh in his ears.

But to have Pride force *Jacob* to murder his *own* family? Darius couldn't imagine.

"We brought them all into the Underground, but Jacob was still in a blackout rage, trying to complete his Programming and kill himself," Thorn went on. "Harris recommended euthanasia, but Abraham wouldn't have it. So we brought him back to the city, and Alan worked to *undo* what Pride had done to him."

"*Undo* it?" Darius asked. He was trying to stay calm, but

the rising tide of worry was lapping against his lungs. The plane slowly began to turn as it rounded onto the runway. "You can do that?"

Thorn nodded. "It's difficult and risky. One of the biggest dangers of Programming is spending *too much time* inside someone's head, changing too many things. We learned that the hard way with Jacob. Alan spent over two hours trying to find out what was triggering Jacob's violent attacks. By the time he'd broken enough of the Program to make a difference, the damage had been done."

"What kind of damage?"

"Permanent damage," Thorn said shortly. "To his hypothalamus. It's always activated. His body is always flooded with stress hormones. It makes him jumpy. Paranoid. We put him on Tactical for a few years, but he was so convinced that everyone was somehow Programmed by the Sins we were having issues with casualties. It freaked him out, and he asked to undergo another round of Programming to guarantee he never hurt a Martyr, but we still had to remove him from TAC. He was too risky."

"He was just *fired?*"

"No," Thorn said. She threw Darius a harsh look, almost as though she was offended he'd even think that. "He was *reallocated.* I took him on. He's a Gray Unit agent now. One of my best. In the fourteen years he's been Gray, he's helped me gather more intel on the Sins than anyone else. His intel even led to the destruction of Pride's last host, before Derek Dane, about eight years ago. We just have to work with him a little differently. He can't stand living in the Underground. He wants to move constantly and stay off the radar. He's so good at it that even Holly struggles to keep up with him. That's one of the reasons I ask him to help with missions like this."

She gestured around the plane. Darius glanced out the window. The aircraft was slowly rolling along the runway. Then, it suddenly lurched forward. Darius reached out to grab his armrests. He felt like he was being pushed into his chair as the plane ascended, followed by a brief sense of weightlessness when it leveled out. He had the strange, out-of-body realization that, under different circumstances, he would enjoy this experience. But right now, he was too busy worrying about something else entirely. He turned back to Thorn, and his brows drew together.

"Isn't he a liability?" Darius asked.

She shook her head. "No. Jacob is *determined* to keep the Martyrs safe. He also has a 'do no harm' Program. Jacob can't say or do anything he thinks will hurt the Martyrs. Alan added it at the same time he hid all of Jacob's memories of killing his family."

Darius gaped. "Jacob doesn't even *know?*"

"No," Thorn said quietly. "We told him they were murdered by Pride. Because they were. Jacob was just the tool. There is no reason he should carry that burden."

Her voice drifted away from them, and Darius knew the conversation was over. Thorn pulled out a file on their mission in Washington and got to work. Darius heaved a sigh, turned to look out the window again, and thought back to Jacob Locke. His voice rang out in Darius's head:

"They shouldn't lie to you. It would've been better if they didn't lie."

But they *did* lie—to keep Jacob from knowing what had really happened to his family—and Darius couldn't say they were wrong.

CHAPTER SIX

"The plan is to sneak in through the kitchen."

Darius and Sara stood in the guys' room, looking over schematics for the Historic Davenport Hotel. She paced up and down the side of the bed, where the blueprints were laid out, and tapped her lip with a short, bitten nail. Darius stood across from her while Sparkie pressed his tiny nose to the sliding balcony door.

"It looks like there's a separate entrance here for the staff," Sara continued, taking that same nail-bitten finger and pointing it at an unmarked hallway beside the ballroom. "This will lead us right into the kitchen, which is gonna be *full* of people. We might be able to slip in unnoticed, or, if they *do* see us, we'll pretend that we were looking for a bathroom or something… They'll probably just think we're stupid and send us back into the main room."

Sara pulled her lip between her teeth as she thought about it. Darius nodded quietly.

"The big issue *then*," she said, dragging her finger down the schematics to the entrance for the worker's hallway, "is that this door is right next to the coat check, so the line is going to pass right by here. We'll have to go in at least an hour after the event opens. Maybe two. Just to make sure that area is empty. Or, ya know, empty-*ish*."

Darius didn't like the idea of waiting. They'd been in Spokane for a full day now, and he was already frustrated by having to wait for this stupid gala—and frustrated he hadn't sensed a Virtue as soon as their plane landed.

"Is there a fire escape or something?" Darius asked. "A way we can get in where no one is looking?"

Sara shook her head. "Nope. This worker's hallway *is* the fire escape, and it leads out through here, too. We can't go in when it's swarming with people."

Darius sighed.

"We'll just have to be patient," Sara said with a shrug.

"Yeah, that's not *my* Virtue," Darius said, but he chuckled all the same, and Sara gave a quick, chirpy laugh.

"It's not a big deal," she said. "If there's a Virtue there, it won't matter if we're a little late to the party."

A feeling of dread twisted up in Darius's stomach. He hadn't admitted it to anyone else yet, but that was part of his concern. He was starting to worry there *wouldn't* be a Virtue there.

"What's up?"

Sara's voice drew him out of his thoughts, and he looked up to her with a slight frown. "Hmm?"

"You look upset," she said, and her cheeks flushed pink.

He tried to laugh it off, but even he could tell it felt fake. Sara's hand moved back to her mouth, and she bit at her cuticles while she watched him. There wasn't any use in pretending, so Darius shook his head. "It's just that I made a huge scene to be able to be here," he said. "There'd *better* be a Virtue at this stupid event, or the others won't agree to this kind of thing again."

Specifically, *Thorn* wouldn't agree. If he'd dragged her across the country for nothing, she'd never let him live it down.

Sara nodded slowly. "Ah," she said with understanding. "Well, I wouldn't worry about it. We had a track record of *zero* Virtue discoveries until you showed up." She gestured an open palm in his direction and smiled. "Give yourself a break. There are only five left out there. You won't find one every time, right?"

Darius gave a conceding nod. That was certainly true. So far, none of his missions had led to a Virtue.

"I guess not," he said, and the corners of his mouth pulled up. "Thanks."

She smiled just as Sparkie got to his feet and started pacing by the door. A few seconds later, an energy Darius recognized entered his awareness from somewhere below him. He passed Sara a look. "John and Thorn are back," he said as that energy moved toward the elevators. "Maybe they had more luck finding another way in."

While Sara and Darius stayed in the room, John and Thorn headed off to the venue to scope the place out and run some last-minute errands before the big event. Darius tried to join them, but Thorn refused to let him leave the hotel, and she left Sparkie behind to make sure he didn't.

So much for Chris's request. Darius couldn't very well keep Thorn and John from killing one another if he wasn't along for the ride. Their voices carried down the hallway now, loud and angry, as they argued all the way from the elevator.

Darius caught Sara's eye. She shook her head and took a deep breath.

Then the door opened, and shouting filled the room.

"—you come in and take over, like this is *your* mission!"

"I'm the highest-ranking officer in this room, Waters. It *is* my mission. The priority here is keeping the three of you alive."

"Alive?" John barked a laugh and dropped a paper shopping bag on the other bed. It tipped over and spilled its contents all over the duvet. A couple of protein bars dropped to the floor, and Darius quietly squatted down to pick them up. "What the hell do you think's gonna happen? We're over two thousand miles from New York!"

"What's going on?" Darius asked.

Thorn ignored the question. She walked right past him and draped a couple of large, garment bags across the back of a chair. Sparkie bounded across the carpet after her and leapt to her shoulder while John watched her furiously. He crossed his arms and turned toward Darius, but his ocean-blue eyes didn't leave Thorn's face. "She says my security sweep was 'too relaxed,' and she wants to send us into the gala with *these*."

He reached into the other bag he was carrying—a heavy, fabric tote—and pulled out a small pistol.

Darius's eyes widened, and he looked to Thorn, too. "*What?* Why?"

"Because 'something's up with Wrath.'"

"I will hit you straight in the mouth if you don't drop the damned attitude," Thorn snarled, pointing a finger in John's face.

Darius stepped up and grabbed Thorn, putting himself directly between her and John. She turned aggressively, and her eyes darted from Darius's face to his fingers wrapped firmly around her shoulder. "No one's hitting *anyone*," he said, throwing her a dark, reprimanding look. He turned to John and gave him the same glare. "Now, what the *hell* is going on?"

John's jaw tightened as Thorn propped her hands on her hips, but she turned to Darius and said, more calmly, "If we are going to this event, we need to do more than just a walkthrough of the building—"

"It's not just a walkthrough!" John's voice rose again, and he threw his hands into the air. "I've been checking over the guest list, checking out the exit avenues, navigating which streets work best for our *multiple* escape paths, *and* I've even been keeping up with Holly to make sure there isn't anything suspicious going on back home. There's *nothing* sending up red flags about Hunt or any of the other Sins, and *no reason* we should worry about anything going wrong here!"

Thorn threw John another hot look. Sparkie's leathery

wings flared up in a wild arch. The semi-transparent webbing let just enough light through to cast Thorn's head in a crimson halo. Darius's fingers tightened around her arm, and she glanced at him before speaking to John again.

"Holly can't see everything," Thorn said. "*I'm* telling you, something isn't right."

"How can you know?" Darius asked as he finally released her and crossed his arms. Thorn looked at him. Her eyes went dark, serious, and if Darius wasn't mistaken, a little bit afraid.

"I just can."

That was all Thorn said, and Darius believed her. The link between Thorn and Wrath was real enough to let her know when the Sin used Influence. Maybe it was real enough for this, too.

"So, what do you want to do?" Sara asked. She stepped up beside John and looked at Thorn. Thorn glanced down at her, and though her expression softened slightly, Darius still wouldn't have called it relaxed.

"If we did what *I* wanted, we wouldn't go to the gala at all," she said. "We have no evidence of a Virtue here. It's not worth the risk."

The energy in the room shifted awkwardly. Sara threw Darius a look, and he felt his face flush.

"We have to go." Darius knew his arguments were no stronger than Thorn's. In his gut, he still felt that this was *right*, but what evidence did he have to show her? He'd been so sure that he'd sense a Virtue before now—so sure he'd have a more tangible trail to follow. The more on edge Thorn became, the more convinced she was the Sins were planning something, the harder it would be for him to convince her this was important.

Thorn seemed to know that. She took a deep breath and held it for a moment. "Have you felt any sign of a Virtue? At *all*?"

Darius paused. Shook his head. Thorn nodded quietly.

"We'll hold off on making any final decisions until

tomorrow," she said. "But unless something changes, we need to consider going home."

Darius's heart sank. It looked like he really *had* dragged them here for nothing.

Four in the morning.

It was four in the morning, and Darius laid awake, staring at the ceiling, lost in thought.

He'd been tossing and turning for hours. John's energy shifted in the other bed, and Sara lay calm and motionless in the room next door. Darius heaved a sigh and turned toward the sliding glass door. A crescent moon gave barely enough light to see by…

Then something moved—a fluttering of wings. Darius frowned and sat up. A creature paced back and forth on the railing before disappearing into the sky. Darius caught a hint of shining blue and deep red.

He got to his feet, walked to the door, and opened it to the cool, summer air. It rushed into the room, onto Darius's face, and he took a deep breath. His bare feet touched out onto the concrete patio as he stepped into the night and looked up at the sky, but Sparkie had disappeared. The balcony beside his, attached to Thorn's and Sara's room, was empty except for a single ashtray filled with spent cigarette butts.

Darius turned to go back inside when he chanced a look down at the street below, and he saw her.

Thorn.

She was standing in the middle of the bridge that stretched over the Spokane River, staring out across the roaring water. He could hardly see her. Her dark hair and clothing provided camouflage in the night, and it was only when a passing car's headlights highlighted her silhouette that Darius recognized her there.

What was she doing up at this hour?

Only one way to find out.

Darius quickly went back inside. He threw on his shoes and a shirt before grabbing his keycard from the side table and stepping out into the hall. The hotel was eerily quiet this early in the morning. Even the hostess staffing the front desk didn't look up from her phone, too absorbed in whatever game she was playing to notice Darius slip out of the elevator and through the main lobby.

While the hostess wasn't paying attention, someone else was. Darius had no sooner stepped out onto the sidewalk when flapping wings and a rush of cool air greeted him. Sparkie dove down from the sky and landed on Darius's shoulder. So much for the element of surprise.

He walked down the road until he got to the street crossing the river. As soon as they hit a more well-lit area, Sparkie vaulted back into the sky. Darius assumed he was keeping an eye on the hotel, ensuring no one got in or out without Thorn knowing about it.

Which meant she knew Darius was coming.

And though she knew it, she did nothing to show it. Darius started across the bridge. Thorn hadn't moved an inch from where she'd been when he'd first noticed her there. She was leaning against the metal railing, her hands clasped in front of her, as she looked out at the water. A light breeze from the river pulled her loose, long sleeve top in graceful waves around her figure. Darius came up, joined her without a word, and he sighed.

"It's really quiet here," he said at last.

Darius hadn't known real silence until he'd found himself in the Underground. New York was nothing but lights and noise and chaos at any time of the night or day. But Spokane? Spokane slept. Darius watched the soft silhouette of the city against the night sky. Every so often, a car lazily drove through the streets on the other side of the river. Lights flickered on—and then off—in nearby apartment buildings. He could practically feel the city breathing easily, quietly, as it rested.

Thorn simply nodded. She stood up a little straighter, dipped her hand into the pocket of her lounge pants, and pulled out a red pack of cigarettes and a lighter. Darius watched as the flame illuminated her face in warm, orange light. She held the cigarette to her thin lips and drew on it until the tip began to smolder. The sleeve of her shirt slid down just enough for the flame to cast light onto her *Pec-costium*. The scars on her arm left deep, heavy shadows. Then, the light went out, and they were thrown into darkness again. Darius could barely make out the lines of Thorn's features as she took a long draw on her cigarette and breathed a furl of smoke out into the warm summer sky.

"What are you doing awake so early?"

She asked the question through a mouthful of smoke, and her voice came out heavy and thick.

"I could ask you the same thing," Darius said. Thorn glanced at him from over her shoulder, took another drag, and let loose a second stream of gray smoke before she replied.

"I couldn't sleep."

"Me neither."

They went silent again. Thorn slowly breathed her cigarette down, casually flicking ashes over the edge of the bridge and into the river below. The dull roar of the water was hypnotic, and for the first time in hours, Darius found himself being lulled into a state of peace and calm.

When Thorn spoke again, it almost startled him.

"Autumn Hunt hasn't used any Influence in over twenty-four hours," she said. There was a dark concern to her voice, and Darius turned to consider her. "It's rare for her to go so long without it. If she does, it's usually because she's trying to send me a message... or she's doing something she doesn't want me to know about."

Darius frowned and watched the side of Thorn's face for a moment. The crescent moon did little to illuminate her expression. "What kind of message would she be sending?"

"I don't know," Thorn said with a sigh and a shrug. "I never know. That's part of the problem. Sometimes she's up to something. Other times, she just wants to watch me squirm, *thinking* she's up to something. She does it to fuck with me... I hate that it works."

She shook her head and lit another cigarette. Her eyes darkened, and her shoulders drew up.

"The thing that worries me most," she said after a while, "is she thinks I'm dead. Whatever she's hiding, she's not hiding it from me. She's hiding it from Alan."

"Why is that a problem?"

"Because I can't imagine what she would want to hide from him *except* that she had left New York City."

Ah. Darius slowly nodded and turned to look back over the river. It felt as though a rock had fallen into his stomach. "You think she's on her way here."

Thorn nodded. "I could be wrong. God knows I've been wrong about her before. It's cost me a lot." She cleared her throat and raised her cigarette to her lips, but then she paused. "And the only reason it hasn't cost me my life is because she *wanted* me alive. Now that she doesn't..." Thorn shook her head and sighed. She dropped her cigarette back down and looked at Darius for the first time. "Honestly, Darius, I don't know if I can beat her."

The raw openness of the statement caught Darius off guard. He shook his head and leaned in toward her.

"You're probably the *only* one who can beat her," he said quietly.

Thorn scoffed, and a small but somewhat sad smile raised to her lips at the compliment. "I'm not willing to take the chance you're wrong," she said. "I'm sorry. I can't risk this."

He was conflicted. Part of him wanted to agree with her, if only because he saw how earnestly she felt, and he understood where she was coming from. He knew what it was like to have this gut feeling you couldn't shake.

That was part of the problem, too. Darius *couldn't* shake

this feeling. He was about to open his mouth—to argue? To agree? He wasn't even sure.

But then, something in this sleepy city woke up.

The air around Darius—inside him—changed, and he stopped dead. He reached out and grabbed the railing beside him. His hand held onto the metal bar so tightly his knuckles were white and cold. There was something out there. Something distant and faint but very real. It tugged on his chest, on his heart, on his *energy*, from deep within his body, like a powerful magnet drawing at him.

And it was getting closer.

"Darius?"

Thorn's voice hardly broke through. Across from him, another bridge connected the northern part of Spokane with the southern. A solitary, powder-blue coupe sped across it. For a moment, Darius forgot about Wrath and Thorn's anxieties. A wave of relief washed over him, and a smile crept across his face.

Then the coupe hit the other side of the river and disappeared into the city.

And with it, the pull. That incredible, familiar pull.

"Thorn," he breathed. She had turned toward him, and one of her hands was clasped firmly around his shoulder. He hadn't even realized she'd touched him. Her dark, half-empty eyes were wide and worried. "That was the Virtue."

***

Detecting a Virtue in the city significantly complicated matters. Sparkie flew circles around Downtown Spokane, searching for the car, while Darius and Thorn rushed back to the hotel and started to plan.

The first thing they did was call Holly, who collected a list of *anyone* in the area who owned, rented, or leased a powder-blue coupe. The list was long, uninspiring, and provided Darius and the others with no actionable information. They couldn't very well go and *visit* all the people on the list, with the gala just hours away.

Meanwhile, Thorn was still convinced—or, at the very least, paranoid—Autumn Hunt was up to something, but even she could hardly argue against their mission now. It had taken the Martyrs over sixty years to find Darius, and within nine months of bringing him to the Underground, he'd managed to track down *another* Virtue. They couldn't walk away from it, so they prepared to go to the gala, but not without added security measures.

Darius felt weird strapping the small pistol to his chest.

"That's it," he murmured as he buttoned up an emerald green vest over his firearm. "I'm going to take some shooting lessons." He'd only used a gun once before—back at Teresa's estate—and he wasn't any more comfortable with the idea of it now than he was then.

John laughed from across the room as he wrapped a navy tie around his throat. "Chris'll teach you. She's the best shot in the Tactical Unit."

When he got his vest and jacket on, John came over to help with Darius's tie. "How long have you and Chris been together?" Darius asked. John's lips turned up into a soft, happy smile.

"Ten years," he said. "In September. We got together about a year after we graduated high school, after I joined the Martyrs."

Darius frowned. "You met in *high school?*"

"Yep," John said. "I went to a small school in Monroe. That's where Chris's mom decided to send her—you know, the Martyr kids all go to school in small towns around the Underground, once they're Programmed not to talk about what really happens at home. Anyway, she was a loner. Kept to herself. Raquel was determined to make friends. She hates seeing people suffer. It's one of the things that makes her a great nurse."

"And Chris asked you to join the Martyrs?"

"Oh, god no," John said. He chuckled as he finished Darius's tie and stood back to appreciate his work. "No, Chris disappeared as soon as we graduated. Just cut all ties. We didn't see her again until we happened to spot her near the NYU campus, tracking one of the Sins. After that, we kept looking for her. Her assignment was near the school, so we ended up seeing her a few more times before we finally managed to corner her. Then we got caught up in a firefight. I was shot in the leg." John slapped his thigh. "So Chris brought us back to the Underground to get cleaned up. She tried to convince us to leave, but once we learned what was going on, we couldn't."

"What about your families?"

John's smile faded a bit, and he cleared his throat. "They think we're dead. Anyway, speaking of dead, you're going to kill in this suit. You look good."

He thumped Darius on the shoulder and headed back to finish getting ready himself. Darius watched him go, his heart heavy. He had joined the Martyrs with nothing. His family, everything he'd ever worked for, had been shattered. He'd never stopped to think that John—and many others— had probably given up a lot to be here.

Sara's energy moved in the neighboring room. She headed out into the hallway, and soon, there was a knock at their door. Darius opened it.

She looked beautiful. She'd let her dark, blonde hair down and gently curled it around her shoulders. The lilac gown Thorn had selected for her gorgeously complimented Sara's full figure, holding tight to her bosom and flowing out when it hit her hips. John whistled, and Sara rolled her eyes.

"You look amazing," Darius said, and her cheeks flushed a deep shade of pink.

"Yeah," John said with a wide smile, grabbing his phone from his pocket. "We've gotta get a picture for Dan. Has he ever seen you in something like this?"

Sara laughed. "Oh, no. This isn't my style. It's too hard to *move*…"

John raised an eyebrow. "Where the hell are you hiding

your weapon?"

"Right here," Sara said, and she tapped the outside of her right thigh. "It'll be some real sexy stuff if I have to grab it." To demonstrate, she laboriously pulled the hem of her dress up to show off the pistol strapped to her leg. Darius and John both laughed, and John snapped a photo. Sara chuckled as she dropped her dress back to the ground. "You guys ready? Thorn's bringing the car around front."

"Yup," John said. "Let's go get us a Virtue."

The three of them gathered their essentials and made their way down to the lobby to find Thorn standing against the glass doors, waiting for them to arrive. She stuck out like a nice car in a bad part of town, and Darius couldn't help but stare.

If Sara looked elegant, Thorn was stunning. Her long, red dress came up to the base of her throat in the front and plunged down to the small of her back. A slit up the side fluttered, teasing at her long legs when she moved. To hide the *Peccostium* and her scars, she wore full-length crimson gloves that extended to her bicep. Her hair was done up in a messy but formal bun that accentuated the length of her neck. Darius was speechless.

The women in the Underground never dressed like *this*.

Thorn turned as they stepped off the elevator and looked them over. She paused on Darius a little before she said, "Are you all ready?"

"Why the hell would we be down here if we weren't ready?" John asked. Thorn shot him a hard look but said nothing as she led them outside. It was almost eight p.m.— a full hour and a half after the gala had opened—and the sun was starting to dwindle in the sky. Thorn looked around carefully before she approached Darius and unbuttoned the front of his suit jacket. He frowned.

"What're you doing?" he asked, but she said nothing as Sparkie darted into Darius's inner jacket pocket. Darius assumed he'd been hiding under the long hem of her gown— because he couldn't see anywhere *else* on her person the winged reptile would have fit.

"I told you," Thorn said, "We've learned to be discreet. I need a place for him to hide."

And a place, Darius figured, where she could easily keep an eye on him and make sure he was safe if Wrath really did show up.

"There we go," Thorn said, buttoning Darius's jacket up again. Her hand lingered on his chest for a second. Then she turned toward their rental car sitting in front of the hotel. "Let's get this over with."

As soon as they approached the building, Darius felt that *pull*. Stepping in through the front doors, it was stronger than ever. He paused to look around.

He'd never been inside a building as fancy as the Historic Davenport Hotel. It was almost two hundred years old, and it boasted intricate woodwork, plush carpeting, and a rich history that spoke for itself in the multitude of photographs, paintings, and furniture pieces displayed around the main lobby. As they entered, Darius's eyes were drawn up to the second-story banister, where men and women dressed just as elegantly as the four of them passed by on their way to and from the event.

The pull came from somewhere above them, in the general direction the partygoers headed.

"The Virtue is here," Darius said.

"Perfect," John said as he adjusted his vest and smiled. He seemed less impressed with the Davenport than Darius. John probably saw all kinds of beautiful places on his Recon trips. "C'mon. We've got to go upstairs to the Grand Pennington Ballroom. Sara, you know the way." He playfully bowed and swooped an arm out to allow Sara to walk past him. She smiled as she did, and they all fell in line behind her—first John, then Darius, and Thorn taking up the rear. Her black eyes surveyed the hotel cautiously, as though she suspected Wrath to jump out at them from behind a gilded display case.

But Darius wasn't worried about that. He didn't sense any danger—just that pull, drawing him upward.

Even the stairs were carved with impeccable detail. As they ascended onto the second story and followed the signs for the event, the hum of voices and the warmth of human energy assaulted Darius's senses. More than that, the Virtue was now so close the draw was distracting. It took almost all of Darius's willpower to pay attention to what was going on around them. When John and Sara stopped, Darius ran into them.

"Jesus, Jones," Thorn hissed. "Act like you belong here!"

But that was part of the problem. Darius *didn't* belong here. He was used to a different kind of crowd—one that smelled of sweat and dirt instead of thousand-dollar perfume. He straightened his jacket, felt Sparkie wriggle in his pocket, and cleared his throat.

"Damn it," Sara muttered.

They'd reached the coat check, and Darius saw the problem. A tall, armed guard was watching the door through which they planned on sneaking into the event. His arms were crossed over his barrel chest, and he looked quietly over the passing guests as they headed up the stairs and toward the gala. A pistol bulged beneath his jacket at his side. Sara bit her lip.

"That was our way in," she said as she turned to the others. "What do we do now?"

They paused for a moment, and Thorn's dark eyes moved from the guard up to the foyer outside the Grand Pennington Ballroom, where a woman stood at the entrance, taking tickets.

The Virtue was moving inside that ballroom. Darius could feel it shifting, back and forth, further and closer, but without a doubt, at the event.

"I guess we could wait for it to come out here," Darius said, but even as he said it, he didn't like the idea.

"No, we're getting in there," Thorn said shortly. Then she turned back to Darius. "All right, Jones. Time to put some of that Virtue magic to the test."

Darius frowned. "What magic?"

"Your *Influence*," Thorn said.

Influence. Darius felt the color drain from his cheeks. That's right. Teresa Solomon had told him that Virtues could use Influence, too.

"But I don't even know *how* to use Influence."

"Guess it's time to learn. Come here."

Thorn snaked her arm through Darius's and led him into the Hall of the Doges outside of the Pennington wing. Darius was surprised by her behavior—it was very unlike Thorn—until he realized that she was putting on a show for the people around them. Blend in, she seemed to be saying to him, as she cast him a look out of the corner of her eye. Act like you belong here. He felt John and Sara fall into step behind them. By their closeness, they'd linked arms, too.

"Influence is easy," Thorn murmured casually, like they were simply talking about the weather. She threw a warm, seemingly genuine smile to another passing couple. Darius could hardly manage a smirk. "It's just a matter of taking your energy and pushing it into another human being. The one catch is, since you're a Virtue, you've got to touch her."

She jutted her chin out toward the hostess at the door. Darius swallowed a hard lump in his throat.

"That's not how I Influence people. That's how I heal them."

"Good," Thorn said. "Then you get the basics. Now, instead of focusing that energy on healing them, focus it on planting an idea, a behavior, a way of thinking into their head. Focus on what you want them to do and attach that to your energy."

"Thorn, I don't think I can—"

"You want to get in that room?"

"Well, yeah—"

"Then you can." They were standing right outside the

door now, and the hostess looked up at them with a kind, customer-service smile. Thorn's hand found Darius's forearm, and she squeezed it gently. She leaned into him and whispered against his ear, "You've got to want it. Make it *real.*"

Then she withdrew behind him. Darius just stood there, stricken.

"Good evening, sir," the hostess chirped. "Do you have a ticket or a wristband?"

Uh. No.

But he had to want it. Make it real. Whatever the hell that meant.

Darius forced a smile and stepped up closer to the podium. "We already handed in our tickets," Darius said. The woman frowned and glanced down at their wrists, obviously band-free. She pulled out a clipboard and looked down at the sheet.

"That's strange. Did you provide your name to the host who saw you?"

"Uh, yes," Darius said, clearing his throat, and for a moment, he forgot his fake name. It was something weird. Damnit, was he already regretting letting Mackenzie pick it out?

"Teagan Love," Thorn said, stepping up on Darius's side. Her hand found the small of his back, and she softly pushed him forward. "And Dante Stone."

The woman nodded, looking down at her list, and it was clear from the expression on her face she was coming up blank. Thorn pushed Darius forward a little more forcefully this time, and he took a step.

"I'm sorry, I don't see it here."

"It has to be," he said, and he came around the podium. The woman stiffened beside him as he grabbed the clipboard, too, and brought his other arm around her to gently touch his hand to the back of her elbow. He felt energy push at his fingertips, and he forced it forward.

Or tried to.

"Yes, there it is!"

He thought it again and again. He thought it and willed it so badly that his head and stomach felt heavy. He pictured his willpower as a tangible thing, a dense cloud of thought, and he pushed that thought as far into the woman's consciousness as he could imagine it without feeling totally crazy.

"I'm sorry, sir," the woman continued. Her body tensed further, and an awkward flush raised on her cheeks. "I don't think you're—"

Shit. It wasn't working. Darius had to try something new. How did it feel when he was healing another person? Not tense and panicked, that's for damn sure. What was it that Teresa had said?

That to be an effective healer or Influencer, you had to think of it as *giving* part of yourself to them, to give them something they haven't had before.

So he took a deep breath, and he opened himself up. He opened his energy to hers, letting himself be more vulnerable and exposed. Maybe he imagined it, but he thought he felt some of that energy mingle, like they were talking to one another in a more ethereal place. He willed it forward again.

There it is.

Please, god. There it is.

Then the hostess paused. Her muscles relaxed under Darius's fingertips, and her brows furrowed over glassy eyes. She looked back down at the list.

Finally, dreamily, she said, "Oh, *there* it is."

Darius's heart jumped into his throat. He looked over at Thorn. She smiled and offered a very brief, very subtle nod.

"I'm so sorry, Mr. Stone. I see your party now. I-I don't know how I missed this. Here are your wristbands. Please, come on in."

Darius smiled and thanked her, and as he and the others slipped their bands onto their arms, Thorn came up beside him. "Not bad for your first time. Maybe we should teach *you* how to Program the Martyrs."

She threw him a coy look, and he couldn't help it. He gave a nervous laugh. "No, thank you. I'll stick to healing."

Then the conversation faded. They'd done it. They were inside. And they had a job to do.

CHAPTER SEVEN

The four of them walked into the event and paused just inside the doorway. Hundreds of well-dressed, wealthy donors spanned the ballroom from the buffet on the left wall to the silent auction along the right. A live jazz band played music between the doors leading in and out of the banquet kitchen, and couples danced on a wooden floor in the center of the room. Dinner and cocktail tables were filled with patrons, talking and laughing and drinking. Servers wandered between people with trays of delicious appetizers balancing on their hands.

Thorn looked around with a practiced, false interest. She drew attention. Men and women glanced her way, eyes lingering on the finer points of her figure that her red dress highlighted. Thorn was either unaware of the attention, or she simply expected it. "Where is the Virtue?" she asked.

That was a hard question to answer. The Virtue was *moving,* and there were so many people here that Darius couldn't pinpoint it. "Toward the back," he said. "That's all I've got."

Thorn nodded as she turned to Sara. "Park, I want you to stay here. Keep an eye on everyone who comes in and out of this wing. Watch for anything suspicious." Sara nodded. Thorn looked to John. "Waters, you do the same thing, back by the kitchen. The only other way into this room is through there, and I want to have our entrances covered. Jones, let's go find that Virtue."

They split up. Sara found one of the few empty cocktail tables toward the main entrance by the Hall of Doges and sat down. John disappeared through the crowd and wandered toward the kitchen. Darius lost sight of him almost as soon as his energy began to blend into the mass of human heat, becoming indistinguishable. Thorn slipped her arm through Darius's again.

"Lead the way."

The moment they'd walked into the ballroom, the magnetic allure had only gotten stronger. Darius was close enough to feel its every move. It was quick, animated, and much busier than any of the guests in the foyer. It also seemed, somehow, to be more distant than they were. Darius frowned.

"This way."

The Grand Pennington Ballroom outshone the rest of the Davenport by miles. The ceiling stood two stories high, boasting gorgeous cutout balconies where select guests were seated, watching the less-filthy-rich below them hungrily, as though they were betting on dogs in a fighting ring. Six massive chandeliers filled the room with beautiful, golden light. The buffet was full of delicious, savory foods Darius had never seen before. Little cards labeled each delicacy: roast duck, foie gras, caviar, and more. Walking past it made his mouth water.

But there would be time to eat later. He kept following the pull, leading Thorn through the crowd. It was warm in here, and Darius pulled at his collar. He couldn't tell if he was sweating because of nerves or because of the oppressive heat coming off the bodies in the room. They were packed so tightly together Darius couldn't differentiate one person's aura from another until he was almost on top of them.

It didn't matter, though. He wasn't concerned about anyone else. Together, he and Thorn walked past the buffet, past the tables, past the dance floor and the bar, and then he paused.

The pull was coming from further back, but he'd hit a wall.

"It's in the kitchen?"

Darius said it like a question, doubting himself for a moment, but he knew he was right. The Virtue was moving on the other side. He touched the wallpaper, wondering what the hell he was supposed to do next.

Thorn pulled her arm out of Darius's and frowned. "It's not an attendee," she said quietly. "The Virtue *works* here."

Of *course* it did. Darius couldn't believe he hadn't considered that. This event, and others, had become a more regular occurrence in Spokane over the last few years. These donors had come from all over the country, shelling out well over three-thousand dollars a head for tickets. If the Virtue had been an attendee, its Influence would only come here once a year.

Instead, it focused here, and its Influence had spread.

"Well," Thorn said with a sigh. "Go on. I'll be by the bar."

Darius's brows furrowed. "What, you want me to go in alone?"

"You'll draw less attention alone," Thorn said, "and you're the only one who can find him. I'll stand watch out here. Just... be careful."

"What do I even say?" Darius asked.

"Don't say anything," Thorn said. "Find out who it is and then report back. Once we know who we're dealing with, we can plan our next move."

Darius nodded and took a deep breath. "All right. I'll be right back."

Thorn stepped away and headed toward the bar, where she could watch the entrance from a distance. Darius slipped through the swinging door and into the banquet kitchen. It was somehow busier and louder than the ballroom. There were chefs in white aprons working away over hot stoves. Servers came in and out, carrying trays full of food, as busboys hauled huge bins of dirtied dishes toward the back sinks.

Darius paused. The Virtue was moving away from him, toward the far end of the room.

"Hey!" A server caught sight of Darius and frowned. "You lost?"

"No," Darius said, raising his hands and shaking his head. "I'm just looking for someone."

"Who?"

"I've got it," he said, and before the server could argue, Darius took off along the wall and followed the pull. Anxiety started to build up in Darius's gut. Some feeling of foreboding. Sparkie squirmed in his pocket, but Darius ignored him and focused on following the Virtue. Then it stopped, and Darius turned the corner by a large, industrial freezer.

There he was.

"Garmond," the Virtue said, slapping the backs of his fingers on a stack of papers in his hand. He stood out against the head chef's white uniform, the light blue vest underneath his gunmetal suit adding a cold splash of color to the room. His blonde hair was sleekly styled, and the frown on his face set his forehead into hard, deep creases. "The contract clearly outlines a selection of gourmet cheesecake bites for dessert. What the hell are these?"

"Brownies," the head chef said. "Our supplier—"

"I don't need excuses," the Virtue said. "And I *hate* surprises. The last thing I need is for our client to throw a fit because they got a cheaper dessert option when they forked out the cash for the more expensive one. I need to know about these things as soon as possible so that I can sort it out with Jeff, you understand?"

"Yes, Mr. Wolfe."

"Good. Are there any other *complications*?"

"No, sir, everything else is as outlined in the contract."

"Excellent. Hey!"

Wolfe turned around and spotted Darius standing by the

door. He paused, and Darius stood there for a moment, captivated.

He'd done it. He'd found a Virtue.

Wolfe collected himself and gave Darius a pleasant but forced smile. "I'm sorry, sir, only staff is allowed back here."

He came forward, and while he didn't touch Darius, he extended his hands, one behind Darius's back and one gesturing him toward another door out to the ballroom.

"I—sorry," Darius stammered.

"It's no problem, sir," Wolfe said. He led Darius back through the kitchen masterfully, the whole time maintaining order without laying a hand on him while servers and other staff broke around them. He opened the door to the ballroom and ushered Darius through it. "Please, enjoy the rest of the party."

Then the door swung shut. Darius stood there, stunned. He pulled out his phone and started to walk across the room, ignoring Sparkie's wriggling in his pocket. Without looking up from what he was doing, Darius opened the document Holly had sent of all the people who owned powder blue coupes in the area, and he searched it for the name.

One entry popped up. Nicholas Wolfe. Darius did a quick search. He was the Director of Charity Coordination at Cowles Events, the company running the gala.

Darius began to read through Wolfe's profile, but suddenly the hairs on the back of his neck stood up on end. A cold fear washed over him, starting at the top of his head and sinking deep into the soles of his feet. It stopped him dead in his tracks. He felt trapped. Unsafe.

Oh *fuck*.

Darius shoved his phone back into his pocket and rushed toward the bar, but Thorn wasn't waiting there anymore. His stomach dropped. Then slender fingers slipped up the back of his neck and wrapped themselves in his hair. Those fingers tugged—*hard*—and pulled Darius's head down so forcefully he stumbled and slammed to his knees on the carpet. A light, airy voice giggled in his ear and sent a chill down his spine that rattled his bones and sent goose-bumps up his back.

"Gotcha."

Darius's whole body stiffened as Autumn Hunt stood above him. She was out of place here—wearing jeans and a t-shirt—but no one paid any attention to her. No one looked at them at all. It was as though they were ghosts in this place. The rest of the guests continued to laugh and dance and drink. Darius thought he felt the tingle of Wrath's Influence around him, pushing at his temples, and he winced as she yanked his chin upward.

"You're brave to leave your little hideout," Hunt purred. Her rich, brown hair dangled around her face and tickled Darius's forehead as she leaned over him. "I'm surprised Rose let you out to play."

"What do you want?" Darius's throat stuck together. The words were hard to get out. His heart pounded hard and painfully as Hunt's fingers tightened in his hair. Out of the corner of his eye, he saw John and Sara. They were casually making their way toward him. John caught Darius's eye and gave him a dark, quiet nod. They were trying to interfere without raising suspicions—without letting Wrath know they were Martyrs and the Influence hadn't worked.

They wouldn't get there in time.

"Oh, I think you know what I want," Hunt said sweetly. "But we're not going to make it that easy on you... or on *her*. Look."

Wrath thrust Darius's whole body around, and he saw Thorn. She fought toward him in a direct line as the guests who had so readily ignored Darius swarmed around her. They moved to stand in her way, block her path, and slow her down. Thorn shoved through them, her black eyes wide and wild as she pushed people to the side.

"She *knows*," Wrath said. Her steely gaze was set on Thorn with vicious joy. A smile spread from ear to ear, and her face cracked open with a haughty laugh. "She knows I'm going to kill you, but *look* at her fighting anyway. So much *fight* in that one. There always was. But she's too late. She knows that, too."

Then Darius felt it—the point of a knife pressed against the underside of his chin. Thorn continued to move through the crowd like an animal. Then someone else swept in.

Darius had never met him, but he recognized the man's face from the files on the Sins. Carlos Ruiz. Lust. Tall, handsome, and ruthless, he stepped in front of Thorn and grabbed her. She was so focused on getting to Darius that she didn't notice him until it was too late. Her red-painted lips curled up into a snarl as she lashed out at him, but the Sin had already grabbed her left wrist, and his fingers closed tight around it.

Thorn's scream pierced the ballroom, but the music didn't stop. People danced on as Lust dug his fingers into the *Peccostium* on Thorn's wrist and dropped her like a stone. In his pocket, Darius felt Sparkie's whole body go rigid. Of course—the *Peccostium!* Darius tried to remember where Wrath's was. He'd read it in her file and remembered it was on one of her ankles. But which one? Darius thought it was the right—and he *hoped* it was the right since that was the one closest to him...

But could he do anything about it without getting stabbed in the throat?

"God, don't you just *love* watching her?" Wrath asked.

He didn't. Thorn was barely visible to him now. Darius caught her in flashes—in the empty space between dancing bodies, through a tumultuous sea of bright dresses and dark pants. She tried to stand, but she couldn't. Her legs were weak beneath her, and she struggled to hold up her own weight. Ruiz knelt beside her and grabbed her chin with his spare hand. He roughly tilted her face up toward him. The heavy, longing look in his stunning, brown eyes was animalistic and carnal. He kissed her cheek and whispered something against her ear. Seeing the Sin touch Thorn so invasively made Darius's stomach twist. Then Lust yanked her wrist. Thorn screamed again.

"Ruiz is afraid of you," Hunt said. She slowly drew the point of the knife down Darius's throat and twisted it a little. Darius winced as the blade bit into his skin, just barely. Just enough to draw blood. He felt it slowly dribble beneath his collar. "They all are. Fucking *pathetic*." Her sweet tone faltered, and her nose curled up in a sneer. "But I'm not afraid of you, and you know why? Because it doesn't matter which Virtue you are. You're still a scared little boy who was saved by an old lady who got *lucky*. I bet you don't even *know* how to destroy us... do you?"

The blade pressed harder to his throat.

"You want to believe that," Darius said, and he tried to keep his voice as even as he could. He had to buy time— keep her talking. "You want to think you're invincible—"

"I *am* invincible," Wrath snarled, and Darius cried out as she pulled his hair again. It felt like she was yanking it from his scalp. The knife pushed harder. Darius started to think he'd made a mistake—

Then someone punched Lust square in the jaw.

Nicholas Wolfe.

He'd rushed from the kitchen doors in a furious, straight line and come down on Ruiz like a bulldog. The Direct Influence steeped through the room didn't seem to affect him, and he punched the Sin in the face again. Lust's grip on Thorn's wrist broke, and she shot up from the ground. Her sharp elbow caught Ruiz in the throat and sent him reeling backward. His Influence faltered. A handful of the guests in the room seemed to snap out of a trance. Hunt stared at Wolfe, her mouth gaping.

"He's a *Virtue*?"

Her knife moved down. Darius gripped his fists together and quickly slammed them into the outside of Wrath's ankle. She screamed and fell back. Sparkie darted out of Darius's coat pocket, snarling and spitting, as he latched onto Hunt's face. Her Influence dissolved, and the room broke out in chaos. Suddenly aware of the tension, the danger, guests began to panic. Darius scrambled up and pushed his way through them as Thorn pulled the slit of her crimson dress open to reveal a pistol strapped to the inside of her thigh. A few nearby guests screamed. Wolfe watched her with wide-eyed shock, but she ignored him and searched the crowd.

As soon as her eyes landed on Darius, she screamed, "*Run!*"

He darted to Thorn and the Virtue, who just stared incredulously at the scene around him. Ruiz got to his feet, grabbing his throat. Darius barreled into him and sent them both flying backward. Darius stumbled feet over head onto the ballroom and cracked his elbow hard on the wood dance floor. He cried out and gripped it just as Thorn grabbed him by the back of his jacket and hoisted him to his feet with one hand.

"Get him out of here," she snarled. Her gun was in her left hand now, and she used it to gesture to Wolfe. "*Go. Now.*"

A gunshot rang out through the ballroom. More screaming. The security guard held his pistol out at the crowd. The faraway look in his eyes told Darius all he needed to know.

A Puppet.

John ran up beside Darius. A deep cut on his throat poured blood onto his chest. Another gunshot. More screaming. Thorn rushed to meet Wrath halfway across the dance floor. John pushed Darius forward again. His hands were warm and slick.

"Go!"

So Darius took the Virtue by the arm. "We need to get you out of here."

Wolfe looked deep into Darius's eyes, his own dark and calculating. Darius started to pull him toward the front entrance, but he didn't move. Sara ran toward them, and another gunshot cracked. She flew forward, and Darius's world went numb as she collapsed with a bullet in her back. John screamed her name.

Darius shook himself out of it. He tackled John to the

ground just as another gunshot came in their direction. John turned, ready to fight, but Darius hauled him to his feet and turned back to the Virtue.

"We need to go."

Wolfe looked out and around at the room—at the chaos and the bloodshed and the people dropping, left and right, as the guard continued to fire in the crowd. Then he turned to Darius and said, "Follow me."

He led them away... away from Thorn and the Sins and Sara's lifeless body laying in a pool of red on the dance floor. He led them through the service hall to a tiny window on the side of the building. They jumped onto the roof of the parking drive through, scrambled down to the sidewalk, and headed into the garage. Nicholas got them past the valet, grabbed their keys, and they jumped in the car. As they peeled out of the garage, Darius looked over his shoulder to see Lust screaming at them from a second-story window. Then Sparkie latched onto the Sin's face, and they disappeared into Downtown Spokane.

———

Thorn felt Sara disappear. Her cold energy blinked out with the shot of a gun. More of them flickered into nothingness as Wrath's Puppet fired his weapon into the running crowd. Thorn tried to push her Influence out and into him, but Wrath's control was too strong. Men and women collapsed. Their blood stained the carpet. Smeared across the wooden dance floor. Dull eyes stared out at the ornate, golden walls, empty.

Her stomach boiled. Anger ripped up her chest. Into her throat.

But at least she had one sense of satisfaction. Darius, Waters, and the other Virtue escaped, and Autumn Hunt was losing control.

She came at Thorn savagely, slashing left and right with her knife. Thorn kicked off her heels so she could move better. She ducked and dodged. Wrath's blade knocked the side of her wrist—pierced into her skin and sent her handgun spiraling into the air. Thorn swore and rammed Hunt with her shoulder. She sprawled sideways, and Thorn quickly grabbed the knife she had strapped to her other thigh. Ruiz rushed past her, following the path the other Martyrs had taken out of the room, and Sparkie darted after him, but Thorn knew they were in the clear. John's energy was long gone. The Sins couldn't follow them now.

Thank fucking god.

"You'll pay for this!"

Thorn turned around just in time to throw her fist into Hunt's jaw. The Sin flew backward. Thorn ran past her.

The Puppet kept shooting. Sirens wailed in the background. She had to get out before the cops got there—had to leave Spokane before the Sins caught up with them.

Lust screamed in rage and flew out from the service hall. He pulled a gun from a holster at his back. Thorn swore and ran toward the front door. More gunshots. More people blinked out, gone forever.

The Puppet moved in to block her escape. Thorn twisted around him and grabbed his head in her hands.

Snap!

His spine cracked with a quick twist. He collapsed onto the ground. Thorn grabbed the gun. People cried around her as they ran toward the emergency exit.

Thorn shot once. Twice. Three times. The gun clicked—the clip, empty.

She'd hit Ruiz in the thigh. He collapsed, stood up again, and cursed.

God damn it. She'd missed Wrath.

Hunt was closing in. Thorn turned and ran, pushing through guests as she made her way toward the front exit and down the hall. Another emergency door. She opened it and hurried down the stairs. Autumn Hunt barreled in behind her. Thorn could feel her aura and hear her feet slam onto the concrete stairs a floor above her.

Thorn threw herself into the alley behind the hotel, and she stopped. Wrath was just as fast as she was. Probably faster. Thorn didn't stand a chance of outrunning her, and she couldn't risk leading her right to Darius and the others.

So she took a deep breath. Thorn had always known this day would come—the day when she and Wrath fought until one of them quit breathing. She'd always figured it would have been on the streets of New York City, but this would do. Sparkie was halfway to the hotel already. Maybe he would find Darius there. If Wrath came out the victor and Thorn lost her life here in this alleyway, Sparkie would disappear, and Darius would know not to wait for her—to get the fuck out as fast as he could. Thorn's stomach twisted as she turned around and faced the door.

Wrath came roaring out of the building.

The Sin stopped as soon as she saw Thorn. Her shoulders heaved in hard, furious breath. Her nostrils were flared, her pupils pin-tight even in the darkness around them. Thorn stood ready—bare feet planted firmly apart, the knife held up between them. For a moment, they stood off. Thorn was keenly aware of everything around her—of the screams floating down onto the street from the building above. The sirens, closing in. The grit and gravel beneath her toes...

Of Autumn Hunt's rage—palpable, thirsty, as it hung in the air between them. It fanned at the fires of Thorn's anger, tempting them to life. She fought to keep in control.

"It's over," Thorn said.

"Oh, it's not over," Wrath snarled. "It will *never* be over. I'll find them, and I'll rip them to *fucking shreds*."

Hunt attacked. She lunged viciously, grappling with Thorn with her bare hands. Thorn fought back, but her body still ached from Lust's fingernails digging deep into her *Peccostium*, and before long, Wrath had grabbed her by a fistful of hair. Then, she punched Thorn square in the face.

She punched again, and again, over and over into the side of Thorn's head until the bone above her eye fractured.

Pain shot through Thorn's skull. Blood dribbled down from a cut in her eyebrow and onto her cheek. Her knife flew out of her hands and clattered behind her. Somewhere in the distance, Sparkie was screaming, falling, and crashing into a line of bushes on the side of the road.

Thorn swore. He hadn't made it.

"*Fuck!*" Wrath screamed. She threw Thorn onto the ground and kicked her in the ribs. Thorn moved to stand, but Wrath kicked her again.

Thorn coughed and spat a hunk of blood onto the pavement. The sirens sounded closer now. Almost here. "What's wrong," Thorn growled. "Your assassin fucked up, so you're here to finish the job?"

A brief flash crossed Hunt's eyes—something Thorn hadn't seen there in a long time. Panic. Her mouth dropped open, and she managed to spit out one word: "*What?*"

"You never should have sent Witham," Thorn said, and she coughed again. More blood. "He's not *good enough* to kill me."

The panic faded, and it was replaced with heavy, potent rage. Wrath's face contorted into a twisted, ugly form as she lashed out. She kicked Thorn again and again. Enraged. Out of control. Then Wrath grabbed the knife up from the ground and flayed Thorn's back open across her shoulders. Thorn screamed. Hot blood poured into the divot of her spine.

Then Wrath leaned down, grabbed Thorn by the hair again, and tilted her head back. Her voice whispered heavily in Thorn's ear.

"Oh, my sweet little *Jane*. I don't want you to die... but you're going to wish you had."

A hot, putrid swell of rage, of hatred, surged through Thorn. Then Autumn Hunt slammed her face into the concrete, and the night went black.

CHAPTER EIGHT

Sirens blared around her. The whole world rumbled and roared, yanking her to the right and to the left. Thorn opened her eyes blearily to the lights—the whites and grays and flashing movements. Her left eye was swollen, her vision blurry. She couldn't lift her arms. She couldn't move at all. Something held her back. Thorn tried to turn her head, but the motion made her vision spin, so she closed her eyes and groaned.

"Oh, good. You're awake."

That familiar voice pierced into her chest, and an evil energy filled the space around her. Thorn's whole body went cold, and her eyes shot open again.

Autumn Hunt sat beside her in the rear cab of an ambulance. She looked down at Thorn and smiled a vicious, little smile.

"Hello, Rose."

Panic built up in Thorn's throat, threatening to choke her, as she fought against the restraints. She was strapped to a gurney, held so tight against it that she could hardly move. The two EMTs to the side didn't look at her. Their plastic, unreadable faces were far away and distant. Thorn felt Wrath's Influence heavy in the air as she kept them and the driver under control.

"Hush…" Hunt reached out and grabbed Thorn's left arm. Her gloves had been removed and her *Peccostium* exposed. "If you struggle, you're going to *hurt yourself.*"

Wrath wrapped her hand around the mark of the Sins and dug in her nails. Pain shot through Thorn's arm, down the tendrils of her scar, and deep into her bones. It seared within her whole body, from her marrow to her flesh. She screamed. Her back lifted from the table, against the straps that held her down. Hunt laughed and then let go.

"You took quite a beating back there," she purred, leaning in and roughly pushing Thorn's matted, black hair away from her face. "Don't worry. I'll take good care of you. I won't leave your side *ever again*…"

The panic swelled. The two EMTs approached—bracing themselves on the side of the ambulance as it veered from side to side. They were holding syringes filled with something—Thorn was sure it was some kind of sedative. She could feel the energy of the city around them growing fainter. Thinner. They were leaving downtown. They were leaving Spokane.

Her thoughts flew back to the gala—to Darius and the others. The EMTs held her arm down and drew the needle close to her skin…

"No!"

Thorn roared and thrashed. She pushed out with her Influence—furiously, *desperately* trying to sever the connection between Wrath and the medics—but the Sin's control only strengthened. Thorn felt it tighten around the two men like a snake coiled around its prey. Hungry. Constricting. Unbreakable.

Thorn changed tactics—she went for the driver instead.

Wrath's hold on him was weaker. As Thorn violently threw her body from side to side, knocking the EMTs off balance and causing Wrath to lunge for her, she reached out, found the boundary between the driver and the Sin…

And she *pierced it.*

His connection to Wrath severed. The shock of it knocked him out. Thorn felt his cold energy slump forward in the chair and pull the steering wheel to the left—

The ambulance veered sharply. The EMTs and Wrath stumbled to the side. Then, they were weightless—just for a moment—as the ambulance vaulted over some barrier outside and flipped over, onto its side.

It *slammed* down. The back doors flew open. As the vehicle spun, Wrath and the medics were sucked out. Thorn felt one of their energies shatter as she and the table she was strapped to turned and tumbled. She fought against her restraints—pulled at them until she freed her arms—then her legs. As the ambulance rolled to a stop, Thorn jumped out onto the street. She was vaguely aware of the sensation of cars zooming past her. Around her. Her head was dizzy—her vision still a blur—but she could feel Wrath's energy as the Sin came roaring toward her.

"You fucking *bitch*!"

Thorn closed her eyes—relied on nothing but her Sin senses alone as her others were jumbled and confused. As Wrath rushed up to her, Thorn ducked beneath her body, grabbed her arm, and screamed as she threw them both into oncoming traffic.

A car smashed into them. They barreled over the top of its hood and rolled onto the pavement behind it. Autumn Hunt flew far to the side—down a steep drop on the edge of the road—but Thorn landed in the street. She rolled for several yards. Asphalt tore her exposed flesh to ribbons and her shoulder twisted up behind her. It pulled loose in a loud, disorienting pop. A line of cars screeched to a stop; the driver who hit them jumped out of his vehicle, aghast. Wrath's energy started moving, viciously clawing its way back up to the road.

Thorn got up, held her useless left arm to her side, and ran.

The city of Spokane lit up like the sun. Bright red, blue, and white emergency lights flickered between buildings. They reflected off the Davenport and blared brightly into the windows as Darius watched silently. Helplessly.

"What the hell is going on?"

Nicholas Wolfe's voice drew his attention back into the room. For a few moments, Darius stared at him.

What was he supposed to say?

Nicholas had heard them talking about the Sins on the drive back to their hotel. He'd listened as John and Chris argued heatedly on the phone about whether he was expected to leave Sara's body behind. He'd watched, wide-eyed, as Darius healed the open wound in John's neck, turning the deep gash into a fine white scar then to nothing at all.

He knew so much that Darius didn't know where to begin.

"Look," he said, hating the word already—hating the way it felt like he was dismissing Nicholas's concerns with a single syllable. "I'll explain everything. I promise. But right now, we've got to go."

"Go *where*?"

Darius didn't have the chance to answer. The door to the room flew open, and John stomped in. He put his phone back in his pocket and turned to Darius.

"We can't take the car," he said. He rushed past Darius and Nicholas to his bed on the other side of the room and started throwing things into his duffle bag. He was backlit by flickering red and white lights shining through the windows. "The Sins spotted it. There's an APB out with its description to the cops. They'll be looking for us, even across state lines. Holly called the standby plane. They're waiting at Felts Field."

"What about Thorn?" Darius asked, but just saying her name made his chest constrict. John rounded on him.

"We have to assume she's dead," he said. "The Sins were trying to assassinate her back home. We *have* to assume they finished the job."

"Who the fuck are the Sins?"

"Just give it another couple minutes," Darius said. "She's always managed to get away."

"Yeah," John argued, "when Wrath had *standing orders* not to kill her."

"*Who the fuck is Wrath?*"

"We don't have time to talk about this right now!" John roared at Nicholas, running his hands through his black hair and pulling it up into a messy fray. "We need to *leave*."

"We can't *leave*," Nicholas said. His eyebrows furrowed heavily over his bright blue eyes. He appeared much older now than he had back at the Davenport, the dark shadows contrasting the lines around his face. They were smile lines, etched into his cheeks and forehead from years of grinning, but he wasn't grinning now. His nostrils were flared, his mouth a tight, angry curve. "We need to go to the police! Tell them what we know!"

"We can't go to the police," Darius said.

"Why the fuck not? We're witnesses! And it seems like you two *know* the guys behind this. We can't just let them get away with it."

"It's not that simple—"

"It is. It has to be."

"You know it's not," Darius said, and Nicholas paused to consider him for a moment. Darius pressed on. "You've seen shit you never thought was possible tonight. You know it's not simple."

"I don't know what I saw," Nicholas said, the angry edge to his voice flickering. "But I do know we have to help, and running away isn't *helping*."

"Damnit, we *can't* help!" John threw his hands into the air and stopped packing. "Not from here. We need to get out of town. Now."

He was right. Darius knew it. His phone had buzzed like crazy in his pocket until the battery had finally died. Texts from Holly, from Mackenzie, from Alan—all updating him on the situation as they saw it from New York, all saying the same thing.

Get out of there as fast as you can, and leave Thorn behind.

He looked out the window, down at the bridge where he'd found Thorn standing the night before. It was crowded now, full of cars honking and pressing against one another as they tried to escape downtown Spokane while pedestrians forced their way down the sidewalk.

For a moment, he thought he saw something dark among them—his brain trying to give him a desperate sense of hope. Darius swore and shook his head.

"All right," he said. "Let's go." He tore the tie from his neck and threw it into his duffle bag. The gun—unused—pressed against his chest like a guilty weight. What a waste that had been. "How do we get to the airfield?"

"I can't believe this." Nicholas crossed his arms and looked between John and Darius. "People *died* tonight. People are *still dying*."

"You think I don't know that?" John snarled. He came face to face with the new Virtue. He was a couple of inches shorter but much, much angrier. "My *partner* is dead. I've worked with her for *six years*."

Nicholas's lips pursed. "So you're just gonna run away and not do anything to stop the people who killed her? That's some cowardly bullshit!"

Darius saw the signs—the tightening in John's jaw, the clenching of his fists—and he jumped in, pulling his friend back as he took a swing. Nicholas didn't back down. He stepped forward and kept on talking.

"If you want to do right by your partner, you'll go back there and help the police catch these monsters—monsters you *clearly know*." He looked between Darius and John again. "I can't let you leave. I'm calling the cops—"

"No, you fucking aren't."

The door to their room cracked open, and a haggard, angry voice slipped through. A narrow beam of light fell across Darius's face, and his heart caught in his throat as Thorn slinked slowly, tenderly in from the hallway. Her Familiar laid limp across her right shoulder. His head, wings, and tail draped down lifelessly against the raw meat of Thorn's flesh. Darius and the others stared.

Her sleek dress was shredded, her skin peeled in red strips across her arms, back, and long, white legs. The left side of her face was blue and purple—the white of her eye stained violent crimson. Something about the way she moved was wrong. Her left arm dangled at an unnatural angle, lower than the right by several inches, twisted like it had been torn apart and stretched too far.

Darius's stomach churned as he rushed up to her. "Thorn, thank *god…*" He wanted to touch her, to help or reassure her, but all the skin he could see was heavily scraped and weeping, and he didn't want to make it worse— or feel her wounds against his hands. "Are you okay?"

"I'm fine."

Nicholas looked over Thorn in shock. His eyes widened, and his mouth fell slack as he took in her wounds, her scars, and the winged lizard flung across her shoulder. Thorn ignored him as she stepped further into the room, around Darius, and turned to John.

"What's the situation?" she asked.

"Lust spotted the car," he said, and Thorn nodded darkly. "We're headed to Felts Field to take the plane."

"Great," Thorn said. Her voice was gruff, tinted with the slightest shadow of pain. "Get the car ready."

John nodded, grabbed a few items, and rushed into the hallway. Thorn turned to Darius. "Help me in the other room—"

"Hold *up.*"

Nicholas's shock at Thorn's appearance seemed to dissipate, replaced instead with indignation and rage.

"You can't *leave.* You have a job to do."

"I'm doing my job."

"Your job is running away?"

"No—"

"Your job is letting other people die?"

"You don't—"

"Understand?" Nicholas cut her off and cocked a brow. "Yeah. I've heard. You are *pathetic.*"

Thorn's eyes glinted dangerously. Her thin lips pressed into a tight, fine line. "Shut your mouth before I shut it for you."

The words came out in a whisper. Darius took a step forward.

"We need to go to the fucking police! We *have* to help," Nicholas growled. A subtle change flickered through the air. That magnetic pull around Nicholas seemed to be crackling with power. It was so faint, Darius didn't know if he was imaging it or not. Nicholas reached into his pocket and pulled out his phone. "I can't let you leave. It's not right to—"

Nicholas never got to finish that sentence. Thorn pulled back her right fist and popped him in the nose. It broke with a sickening, squelching crack. Nicholas roared and dropped his phone as a scarlet flood poured down his face. It soaked the front of his suit with heavy, red liquid. Darius sucked in a quiet, quick gasp and hurried to the Virtue's side while Thorn leaned down and grabbed Nicholas's cell. She got back to her feet and tucked it into the front of her dress.

"Jesus, Thorn," Darius said.

She ignored him.

"You listen here," Thorn said quietly—so quietly that it forced Nicholas to stop groaning in pain so he could hear her. Thorn raised her good arm and pointed one solid, unwavering finger in his face. "One of my people is dead. The rest of us are being hunted. My job—my *only job*—is to get us out of here alive, and that *includes you.* If you try to stand in my way again, I won't hold back. Do you understand me?"

"*That* was holding back?" Nicholas's words came out stunted and thick, and he moaned.

"Do you understand me?"

Her glare was steadfast. Nicholas just stared at her for a second—hot and venomous—before he nodded. Thorn turned to Darius.

"Heal his fucking face. Then meet me in the next room."

She turned and left the two of them alone. Darius heard the neighboring door open quietly and then slam shut. He heaved a sigh and turned to Nicholas.

"What a *bitch…*"

An angry flare lit up in Darius's chest, but it wasn't worth the fight right now. "Come here," he said as he grabbed Nicholas's hand and pulled it away from his face to see the damage Thorn had done. It wasn't pretty. His nose was swollen and crooked. A crack in the skin along the bridge seeped blood down the sides, and it poured from his nostrils, over his lips. "This may hurt."

Then Darius pressed his fingers against Nicholas's wound. The other Virtue winced at first, but his eyes widened as Darius's skin went hot with power, and that power flowed from his fingertips and into Nicholas's flesh. It stitched together. His nose shaped itself back to its broad, strong outline. The cut sewed shut and disappeared. The blood stopped flowing.

When he was done, Darius drew his hands back and wiped them on his pant legs. Red streaks stained the gray fabric. Nicholas reached up and touched his face, awed. Darius watched him for a moment before he shook his head.

"Look." There he went again, saying that word he hated. "I know this has been crazy. It's been *really* crazy. You have a lot of questions. I know. I had those same questions when I first got involved in all this. All I can say right now is that I *promise* I will tell you everything I know—everything—but you *need* to come with us. They're looking for you now, you *specifically*, and they'll kill you if they catch you."

"Why the fuck would they want to kill me?"

"I'll tell you that, too. Just… trust me."

It was a big ask. Darius knew that. They'd shown up in Nicholas's life less than two hours ago, everything had gone to hell, and now Darius was asking him to abandon his life and follow him across the country. He was desperately hoping Nicholas would make it easy on them; he couldn't imagine how much harder it would be if Thorn had to knock him out and drag him back to the Underground that way. Nicholas just watched Darius for a moment, but his fingers were still exploring his face with rapid, gentle taps. The door to the room opened, and they turned as John stepped over the threshold.

"Let's get moving," he said. He cleared his throat and avoided making eye contact with either of them as he started to throw more things into a bag. If Darius wasn't mistaken, there was a glisten of fresh tears behind his long eyelashes.

"I'll help you," Nicholas said, and John looked up so quickly Darius thought he heard his neck crack. Nicholas cast Darius a dark look and said, "You better keep up your end of the fucking deal."

"I will," Darius said with a quiet nod. Then he excused himself and rushed to the room Thorn and Sara had shared. As soon as he walked in, Darius's gut wrenched.

Sara's things were strewn across one of the double beds. Her wallet was left open. Inside, Darius could see a photograph of Sara and Daniel. Thorn was on the other side of the room, packing her own items with her one good hand. She looked up as he paused and caught him staring at the picture. She sighed. It was deep and painful. "Does he know?" she asked.

"I don't know," Darius said, his voice tight. "Probably. John talked to Mackenzie. I'm sure she told him."

Thorn didn't say anything right away. She just watched Darius with those hard, dark eyes. At last, she shook her head, and her whole attitude shifted back to business.

"Okay." She turned to him and winced. Her shredded dress had been discarded and was lying on the ground. Now, she wore just a pair of leggings and a tight-fitting camisole—

all black, Darius assumed, to hide the blood. How she'd managed to change clothes with her left arm dangling like that, he would never know. "I need you to pop my shoulder back into place."

The blood rushed from Darius's face. His eyes widened, and all he could manage to say was, "W-what?"

"You see this?" Thorn tried to shrug her left side, but pain made her stiff and awkward. "It's dislocated. I need you to put it back."

"But—I don't know how. What about John—"

"No," Thorn snapped. He saw her ego getting in the way. It flashed across her eyes. She didn't want John to see her vulnerable. Not more than he already had. "Please."

He sighed. "Jesus Christ, Thorn. Fine. What do I do?"

She walked him through it. Thorn sat at the end of one of the beds, and Darius stood beside her. With shaky hands, he grabbed Thorn's bicep and tried to ignore the hot, sticky wounds beneath his fingertips. Slowly, deliberately, he turned her arm away from her torso. Sparkie twitched and cried out on Thorn's other shoulder. Thorn just closed her eyes and gritted her teeth.

There was a sickening, dull *"thunk!"* Thorn's whole body relaxed in Darius's hands. He let go of her immediately and wiped his palms on his legs. More smears of blood against his trousers. His heart beat like a drum in his throat, and he swallowed hard against it.

Thorn stretched her shoulder and massaged the muscles with a deep sigh. "Thanks," she said. "How's the Virtue?"

"Not great," Darius said quietly. "Confused. Angry. Scared, probably." Then he looked down at the back of her head. The elegant bun she'd worn for the gala was mostly down—messy black wisps fell in wild loops around her neck and down her back. "It doesn't help that you hit him, even if he deserved it."

She stopped rubbing her shoulder. Thorn turned her head just enough to see him out of the corner of her eye without actually looking him straight in the face. "We didn't have the time to argue."

The tone of her voice was foreign—a strangled mix of anger and disappointment—and Darius suddenly felt bad for bringing it up at all. Thorn got to her feet, and he followed after her.

"I didn't mean—"

"No." Thorn held up a hand to stop him. It was strange to see her without gloves. The *Peccostium* on her arm was always a shock to see—but now, when her rage was so close to the surface, it was hard to forget that Thorn was once Wrath. In many ways, she still was. "Don't. I don't need apologies. I just need to get us the hell out of here."

"The car's ready," Darius said, and, after a pause, "and Nicholas agreed to come with us."

Thorn frowned. "The Virtue?"

"Yeah."

Her thin eyebrows rose. The expression highlighted the blood that had taken over most of her left eye, leaving nothing but a deep, black iris in a heavy crimson pool. "How did you manage that?"

He didn't want to tell her what he promised, so all he said was, "I'm good."

A small smile played at the corner of Thorn's lips, but a darker look quickly extinguished it. "Then we'll have to be extra careful, and don't tell him *anything* you don't have to until we get to the Underground. Alan will want to have that conversation."

Darius's stomach twisted. "Okay," he said. "I understand."

"Good," Thorn said. She quickly gathered all of Sara's personal belongings, abandoning things like clothing and toiletries that didn't matter anymore and instead focusing on those with intrinsic or sentimental value. As she put them in her satchel, her jaw tightened. "Let's go."

Downtown Spokane was a disaster. Thorn drove them on back roads and tried to find a way across the river that didn't drag them through streets teeming with cops on the hunt for their car. Her eyes were narrow, her lips a hot, thin line as she looked through the chaos.

"What do we do if we can't get to the airfield?" Darius asked. Thorn solemnly shook her head. The atmosphere of the car was tense. Though Darius and the others had changed out of their bloodied clothing—and Nicholas had borrowed a shirt from Darius—Thorn's flesh was still tender and weeping. Nicholas stared at her with disgust.

"We're getting out of here tonight," she said. "One way or another."

John pulled up maps of Spokane on his phone—the only one that wasn't dead—while Nicholas tried to guide Thorn through more neighborhoods that were just as hectic as the one they'd left. People crowded the sidewalks while the intersections were a mess of bumper-to-bumper traffic.

"The public airport is easier to get to," Nicholas said after a few more stressful, exasperated minutes. "It's in the *opposite* direction."

"It's also public," Thorn hissed.

Nicholas frowned but didn't argue further as Thorn turned down another road, and another, until—

"*Fuck.*"

Red, white, and blue lights blared to life behind them, and a sinking feeling fell into the pit of Darius's stomach. Thorn slammed onto the gas and peeled off. Their tires screeched on the asphalt. The cops turned to follow after them.

Then they stopped.

Darius gawked through the back window as the police suddenly disengaged, turned off their lights, and turned down another street.

But Thorn didn't slow down. She went pale beneath the dirt and blood that clung to her cheeks and forehead as she turned around and went back the way they'd come, twisting through neighborhoods, away from downtown, and toward the highway.

"What are you doing?" Darius asked.

"Plan C."

"We didn't have a plan C," John said.

"We fucking do now."

Seven minutes later, the four of them were at the Spokane International Airport. Thorn abandoned their car at the drop-off line and ushered the four of them into the building. "Hurry," she said. There was an edge of panic in her voice.

The people around them didn't seem to mind how pushy Thorn was being—sometimes *literally* pushy—as she led the Martyrs past the ticket lines and straight toward security. Though her wounds were starting to heal, she was still covered in deep, red welts and oozing scrapes. No one seemed to mind that, either.

Something wasn't right. It wasn't just that they didn't notice her. They seemed to look right *through* her.

And them. Darius, Nicholas, and John were similarly ignored, which was highly apparent as they went up to the security line. Again, Thorn muscled her way to the front. Again, people acted as though she didn't exist. Darius's heart sank as he realized what was going on. He felt it, pushing at his temples...

"Thorn," Darius started to say, but Thorn cut him off.

"Just go." Her voice was tight, hurried. "We don't have the time to fight about this right now."

John fell into line, following without questioning why. Darius was sure Nicholas would put up a fight, but all he did was rub his head as he followed the three of them through the terminal in silence.

So Thorn forced her way through security. No one argued. No one complained. They squeezed around the metal detectors. The alarms blared, but the security agents simply turned them off without a glance in their direction.

John cast Darius a dark look. The nagging instinct at the

back of Darius's mind told him they needed to move quickly. Something dangerous was coming—and it was coming fast.

The Martyrs and Nicholas arrived at the gates. Thorn rushed down the corridor, looking left and right at all the flights, swearing and becoming more frantic as she went. Darius fed on her anxiety. His heart was thumping hard in his throat.

Finally, toward the end of the passage, she let out a sigh of relief. "Thank god," she said, and Darius looked up at the monitor. A plane was just about to leave for Philadelphia— and the doors were closing. Thorn pushed them through, past the woman at the gate check, down the ramp, and onto the plane. She stopped to let the other three in first, and as soon as Thorn's feet were inside, a stewardess closed the doors behind them.

The passengers ignored them, too. People glanced at them here and there, but no one commented on them—not on the fact that they had come in last second or that there were not enough seats to accommodate them. The flight was full.

"What the hell do we do now?" Nicholas asked.

Thorn didn't even look at him as she said, "Sit on the ground."

They all quietly squatted down between the seats, and soon their plane was moving away from the terminal. Darius's anxiety was mounting; something inside of him was screaming *DANGER!* He peered out a window, looking back at the airport, as they got further and further away. A scene just inside of the large window caught Darius's attention.

Autumn Hunt was watching the plane take off. She screamed, slamming her blood-covered fists against the glass.

Darius's eyes shot wide open.

"Thorn!"

"I know," she said. Her voice was rough, her eyes closed.

She reached out and grabbed the armrests nearest to her, and she gripped them so tightly that her slender fingers were bone white. The muscles along her jaw were so tense and angry that her mouth barely moved as she murmured, "Let me focus."

They were airborne a few minutes later. Thorn kept her eyes closed even when they were in the sky. Her forehead was knitted into tight lines. Darius watched as a single tear fell down her cheek. It left a white trail in the blood caked against her porcelain skin.

Darius looked around the cabin of the aircraft, awed. They'd been in the sky for five hours, and for five hours, every single person in the plane had totally ignored them. As far as Darius could tell, it was business as usual. People chatted with neighbors. Read their books. Glanced around, bored and tired, before they pulled eye masks on and fell quickly to sleep. Even the flight attendants didn't say anything to them. They walked through the aisles with their carts, and when they needed to pass, Darius and the others would stand up and squeeze into the gaps between seated passengers and the chairs in front of them. No one complained.

No one but Nicholas Wolfe.

For the first hour or so, he'd been quiet, but he wasn't stupid. He could see how weird it was here—how they were clearly out of place, and no one seemed to notice them. He'd tried to ask about it, but Darius and John kept their mouths shut. They'd just shared awkward looks and glanced to Thorn while Nicholas glared at her.

This entire time, Thorn remained toward the front of the aircraft, seated with her legs pulled up, her elbows propped on her knees, and her mouth pressed firmly against laced fingers. A tight knit pulled between her brows, drawing them close together in concentration. By now, her wounds had resolved. Her skin was smooth and flawless again, all except the scars stretching down her left arm. The only evidence of her battle was the dried blood giving her black clothing a subtle, splotchy look.

Without getting any answers, Nicholas had angrily huffed off to the back of the plane and hid in the flight attendants' quarters. Darius instructed John to follow him and make sure the new Virtue didn't try anything crazy. They'd quickly fallen asleep, for which Darius was grateful. *Someone* needed to rest, and it sure as hell wouldn't be Thorn.

And if Thorn couldn't rest, neither would he.

With John and Nicholas gone, Darius had come to sit by Thorn's side. He could feel her Influence. It hung about the cabin, itching at his temples with steady pressure, but it wasn't painful. He took her in before he turned and looked at the passengers again.

"Did you Puppet them?"

They didn't *seem* Puppetted. Puppets had a *look* about them. Glassy, disconnected eyes. Plastic expressions. These people didn't act quite like that. If Darius couldn't feel Thorn's Influence, he wouldn't have thought they were under any kind of control at all.

"Thorn?" Darius asked when she hadn't responded, and he turned back to look at her. "Did you—"

"No," she said shortly. Her voice sounded tense and strained, and she didn't open her eyes as she took a deep breath and shook her head. "I can't Puppet."

Darius frowned. "I thought you could do everything the Sins can."

"Not everything," Thorn said. "There are limits, and this is one of them."

"What's the difference?" Darius asked, looking back out at the people around them. "It seems like you can get the same basic effect…"

Thorn took a slow breath and coughed deep in her throat. When Darius turned back, he saw that her hands shook slightly when she pulled her mouth away from them to speak. "Not exactly. My Influence is surface level. I can change thoughts. Affect behavior. Convince people they should vacate an area or that the stowaways on their flight are uninteresting and unimportant. But it's not always this easy."

Darius watched her, taking in the strain she was clearly under. "This is *easy*?"

"I'm not working *against* them," Thorn said. "They want to believe what I'm asking them to believe, so it's accepted without a second thought. If I'm Influencing someone to do something that goes against their judgment, their training, or their objectives, it doesn't work this well. Takes longer to catch on, and they're more likely to see through it."

Then Thorn moved. Darius glanced up to her face as she tilted her head back, but she still didn't open her eyes. He noticed dark rings sprouting up beneath them. She took a couple of slow breaths before she continued.

"Puppetting connects people to a hive mind," she said through a sigh. "We think they're linked to the actual essence of a Sin, which is why Forgotten Sins can't do it. Their consciousness turns off, and they do whatever the Sin wants them to do. People rarely break through."

Darius shook his head. "Does that mean the Sins can control entire *armies*?"

"Yes and no," Thorn said. "Some people are resistant to Puppetting—most of the Martyrs and anyone with Virtue exposure. Puppetting is also exhausting. The Sins can't maintain Puppets indefinitely, and the more Puppets they have, the easier it is for those Puppets to be cut off from the hive."

"How do you cut them off?"

"Pain, mostly. Because my power is linked to Wrath's, I can use my Influence to sever her connection to her Puppets, too. It's harder when she only has a few of them. Her control is a lot tighter when it's focused on one or two…"

Thorn's voice faded, and she brought her head forward

again. Now that Darius was paying closer attention, he noticed more than her hands were shaking. Her arms quivered, and her skin seemed dull. It was almost like he was looking at her in grayscale while the rest of the world stood out in color.

"This kind of Influence must be exhausting, too."

Thorn simply nodded. Slowly. Carefully.

"I'm fading," she acknowledged. "It's time to land."

Darius frowned and opened his mouth to ask what the hell she meant, but before he could speak, the pilot's voice came over the loudspeaker.

"Attention, everyone," she said. "I know we were all planning on arriving in Philadelphia in a few hours, but unfortunately, we're experiencing some minor issues with the aircraft. Nothing to worry about, but we are going to have to do an emergency landing in Chicago."

Darius turned to Thorn, hardly hearing as the pilot continued to explain how the passengers were to proceed upon arrival to make sure they got to their final destination. Thorn finally opened her eyes and looked at him. Her cheeks were hollow, her dry lips pressed together, and the whites of her eyes shone out, bright red and angry. Darius had never seen Thorn look so... *human*.

"You okay?"

"Yes," she said. "Go get Waters and Wolfe. I want to be the first people off this damn plane."

Forty minutes later, the aircraft touched down and slowly rolled to a stop outside one of the gates. John and Nicholas came down the center aisle, and Thorn got to her feet. She stumbled a little, and as Darius moved to assist, she just held up her hand and shook her head. Then, she led them forward. Slowly. With every step, she reached forward and grabbed onto the walls for balance, her fingers quaking.

Darius looked back at John and Nicholas. John seemed

just as concerned about Thorn as Darius felt. Nicholas's brows furrowed hard over his eyes, and he watched the back of her head with dark, suspicious curiosity.

"It's almost over," John murmured. Darius nodded.

But before they disembarked, two uniformed air marshals climbed into the aircraft. Thorn didn't stop walking. She strode right past them as they spoke with the flight attendant, and Darius and the others followed after her. As he passed, Darius overheard what they were whispering about.

The marshals were asking about two people—people who sounded remarkably like...

"Thorn, they're looking for us," Darius said as he rushed to her side.

"Yep," she said with a nod, but she didn't seem concerned. "Wrath knew which plane we were on. I'm sure she orchestrated an ambush in Philly, and when they heard the plane was landing early, they called to see if they could catch us here instead. But, since the Sins aren't *actually* here, we're just dealing with regular people trying to do their jobs. Thank god."

Darius looked her over, and he had to agree. There was no way Thorn could take on a Sin right now.

Thorn maintained a general bubble of Influence around them until they reached the baggage claim, well away from the marshals and any security personnel. As soon as she dropped it, relief visibly flooded her body. All the muscles along her throat, shoulders, and back relaxed, and she stumbled again. This time, she found a bench, and she lowered herself onto it.

"We need a car," Thorn said as she rubbed her forehead with the pads of her fingers. Her voice was harsh and dry. She cleared her throat, but it didn't help. "John, can you go handle that?"

Darius had never heard her call John by his first name. It seemed neither had he. He stared at her for a moment in quiet surprise before he agreed and disappeared around the corner. Nicholas watched after him before turning back to

Thorn and Darius with a dark, quiet look. He paid a little closer attention to Thorn this time, his eyes wandering from her face to her shoulders to her back—even to her left wrist and the mark and scars around it. Darius wondered if he was keeping a tab in his head of all the things he wanted to ask Darius as soon as he had the chance.

But Darius didn't have the time to worry about that. Right now, he was worried about something else.

He turned to Thorn. She had leaned forward, dipping her face into her hands. The muscles in her arms quivered enough for Darius to see it from where he was standing. He came to sit beside her. Nicholas wandered closer and stood by the end of the bench.

"Are you okay?"

He knew he'd already asked once, but he couldn't help it. Thorn moved her head just enough to look at Darius, then Nicholas. She sat up straight again and stretched her neck from side to side. From here, even her cheeks looked empty. "I'm tired, that's all."

"Why?" Nicholas asked. "Mind control?"

He looked down at her, and Thorn's eyes darkened. She didn't answer him, so he kept going.

"Healing? Are you like him?"

He thrust a thumb at Darius.

"No," Darius said.

Thorn cast him a dark look. "Jones…"

"Now's not the time to talk about this," Darius said, exasperated. The last thing he needed was for Thorn to punch Nicholas in the face again. Even with her Forgotten Sin strength, he thought she'd be weak enough for the new Virtue to take down. Darius got to his feet and looked around the airport. His anxiety had faded, and his sense of dread was gone, but it felt too easy. "How close are they?"

"It's hard to say," Thorn said. "They could be anywhere from one to four hours behind us now. That doesn't mean they won't come here. That doesn't mean they can't still catch up."

She and Darius shared a heavy look. Were they the only two who had seen Wrath at the gate? Were they the only ones who knew just how lucky they'd been to get out at all?

"Then we can't stay," Darius said.

"So, where do we go?" Nicholas asked.

Thorn closed her eyes and rubbed them with the fingers and thumb from one hand. "We're driving to the Underground—tonight. Today. Whatever the fuck time it is."

"Where is that?"

Darius opened his mouth to say—and he couldn't. Damn that Programming.

"Near New York," he said with a sigh. "Kind of." Nicholas's eyes widened, but he didn't seem upset. Maybe he was just too deep in now to get any more pissed off than he already was.

A few minutes later, John showed up with the keys to a rental sedan. They piled their gear into the back of the vehicle and jumped in. John offered to drive, which seemed to suit Thorn just fine. She was in no position to do it herself. Instead, she sat in the front seat. With her legs pulled up underneath her, and her arms wrapped tightly around her body, Thorn rested her forehead against the window. Sleep came on hard and fast. Sparkie curled up on her lap, and soon their breathing was rhythmic and synchronized.

Darius waited a half-hour before he unbuckled and leaned over Thorn's chair. He touched her arm, shook her shoulder a little, and prodded Sparkie a couple of times. She didn't budge.

John frowned. "What are you doing?"

"I'm about to break a bunch of rules," Darius said through a yawn. God, he hadn't realized how tired he was, but if he wanted to keep his promise to Nicholas, he'd have to do it now. "If you want, you can say you told me to shut up, and I ignored you."

John laughed. It was hollow. "Whatever, man. You're technically my superior officer. Do whatever you want..."

So Darius turned to Nicholas and took a deep breath.

Nicholas watched him with a dark, calculating, but curious expression. "All right," Darius started. "What do you know about the Seven Deadly Sins?"

CHAPTER NINE

"So," Nicholas said. He looked as exhausted as Darius felt—his hair frazzled, his freckled cheeks peppered with blonde stubble. Thorn shifted in her sleep and took a deep, shuddering breath. Nicholas glanced at her, his eyes narrow. "Is *she* a Sin?"

John cast Darius a dark look.

Darius had told Nicholas everything—about the Sins, the Virtues, the Martyrs—but he'd stopped just short of telling him about *this*... About Thorn Rose and Alan Blaine and the very long, tormented history they had with Wrath.

It felt wrong. This wasn't his story to tell.

For the last few hours, Nicholas had soaked in every word Darius said with thirsty curiosity. He had been eager to know everything. He lacked the skepticism Darius remembered having when he'd been thrown into this world, probably because the evidence in front of Nicholas was much more damning.

While he lacked skepticism, he didn't lack doubt. The doubt, though, came in a place Darius hadn't expected. Nicholas hardly batted an eye when Darius told him that not only was he himself a Virtue but Nicholas was, too. Upon hearing that Virtues had to die to destroy the Sins, Nicholas simply nodded, as though he wouldn't have expected anything less. Every so often, Nicholas would fixate on Thorn and the strange creature curled up on her lap. As soon as Darius paused, he asked that question:

Was Thorn a Sin?

Darius couldn't blame him. He'd told Nicholas what powers the Sins had at their disposal: accelerated healing, Influence, strength. Just as he'd seen Darius present Virtue abilities, he'd also seen Thorn display every single one of the Sins'. Of course he'd jump to the conclusion that she was one. How could he possibly think any differently? If Darius hadn't been able to sense, without a doubt, that Thorn was distinctly *unlike* the Sins, he probably would have thought she was, too.

He took a deep breath and exhaled it in a slow, thoughtful sigh. "No," Darius said at last. "Not anymore." He saw John glance at Thorn, but she was still breathing deep and heavy. Thank god. Darius knew she'd be furious if she heard what he was about to say, but he couldn't leave it alone. Not now.

Nicholas deserved to know.

So he shared as much of Thorn's story as he knew. He explained how she was possessed by Wrath and later escaped it. He told Nicholas about Alan Blaine and Cain Guttuso and how they founded the Martyrs and kept it up and running for more than one hundred and fifty years.

Now Nicholas was skeptical. His forehead stitched into a deep furrow, and his mouth tightened around his teeth. "So," he said slowly, like he was measuring every word before it slipped from his mouth. "She has that *thing*—" a gesture to Sparkie "—and those powers—" a gesture to Thorn "—because part of her soul is still corrupted by a Sin?"

"Yeah," Darius said. "Until we find Patience and destroy Wrath. When that happens, her energy will be purified, and she'll be human again."

"But she's got a part of Wrath still kicking around in there?"

Darius frowned. "I mean, I guess—"

"Then how do you know she's *really* one of the good guys?"

Darius blanched. John's hands tightened on the steering wheel, and he cast Darius a nervous look in the rearview mirror. "I—what? Of course she's one of the good guys. She wants the Sins dead more than anyone else here."

"Yeah," Nicholas said, and his tone darkened. "Because it serves *her*. She's doing the right things, but not for the right *reasons*."

"No." Darius shook his head and took a deep breath. "That's not the *only* reason—"

"You said it yourself," Nicholas interrupted. "She—and others like her—they're still *corrupted* by these Sins. That kind of thing has to come with consequences. Maybe their souls are poisoned."

"Listen," Darius said, a sharp, angry tone raising his voice. "It doesn't work that way. Everyone's got some good and evil in them—everyone. Even Virtues. It's not about whether or not we've got that kind of darkness. It's about fighting it and working to do good. Thorn works harder than anyone I know, and she *saved your damn life* today. She saved *all* of our lives."

Nicholas watched Darius for a quiet moment after that.

"So why didn't she want *you* to tell me about all of this?" he asked at last.

Darius sighed and rubbed his eyes. God, he was so tired.

"I don't know," he admitted at last. "But I had to. You deserve to know everything."

Nicholas frowned. "Would she *not* tell me everything?"

Darius didn't respond—because telling the truth, saying "I don't know" a second time, wouldn't help him now. Nicholas seemed to get the hint, though. From there on, he kept any further thoughts to himself, and he stared out the window in thoughtful, shrewd silence.

And that silence was deafening. It hung heavy in the car, absorbing the three of them in mutual discomfort for almost half an hour. John was the first one to cave in to its tension. He cleared his throat.

"Anyone need to stop?"

"Don't stop."

Thorn's voice caught them all off guard. Darius jumped. He saw Nicholas do the same. John swore and swerved into the other lane.

"Shit," he said. "I thought you were asleep."

Thorn didn't say anything as she straightened up and stretched her arms behind her back. Every sign of her battle—both physical and mental—had disappeared. Six hours of sleep rejuvenated her; the circles under her eyes had faded, and her pale skin looked more pink than gray. Her dark hair was still a mess, tousled and thrown from the bun in matted locks. She took the rest of it out of the elastic and ran her fingers through to smooth it, working out the knots with care and patience. Every so often, she pulled out a bobby pin and tossed it into the center console with a soft *plink!* Sparkie unwrapped himself from a cocoon of leathery wings and peered over the seat in Nicholas's direction. Nicholas ignored the lizard and focused solely on Thorn.

"We've got to get back to the Underground as soon as possible," she stated. Her voice had regained its stone-like resolution. "Wrath is close."

Nicholas cast Darius a heavy look. His eyebrows pinched hard over his eyes.

So they didn't stop. The only time they pulled the car over was to fill up the tank with gas, and they only had to do it once. Thorn handled everything, refusing to let the three men leave the car, even to use the restroom. Darius was grateful for the one time they'd already pulled over to relieve themselves when Thorn had been fast asleep and figured this was the only time it paid to be dehydrated. His mouth was parched, his eyes dry, and his throat stuck together as he tried to swallow down saliva. He was exhausted. How long had it been since he'd slept? He didn't remember, but he couldn't risk falling asleep now.

What if Nicholas did something—said something—that keyed Thorn into the conversation they'd had? Darius wanted to break the news to her himself. In private.

The last four hours passed in silence. After detangling her hair, pulling it back into a messy ponytail at the base of her neck, and putting on a fresh pair of fingerless gloves from her satchel, Thorn had taken over for John. They flew down the highways at speeds that made Darius's stomach flip every time they descended a hill or went around a blind corner, but Thorn was able to anticipate other drivers in a way Darius had never seen before. It was like she had a sixth sense that helped her maneuver her way right around death.

That seemed truer now than it ever had before. Darius thought back to the bomb with a shudder. That had been almost two weeks ago, but it felt like so much longer. Darius wondered if, and when, Thorn's luck would run out, and someone would manage to put her down for good...

And he wondered if that person would be Wrath.

Thorn didn't take them directly to the Underground. John spent several minutes on the phone with Mackenzie, planning to drop the rental car off at an agency in Newark, New Jersey. When they pulled up in the parking lot, Alan was there to greet them. He stood by the vehicle drop-off with his hands clasped quietly behind him. Darius was surprised. Alan rarely left the Underground.

It was three in the afternoon, and the July sun blared down on them with an unforgiving, humid heat. Alan did not dress differently for the summer than he did in winter. His black slacks were pressed and clean, his red, button-up shirt tucked precisely into his waistband. As they parked, he was rolling up his sleeves, squinting through the sun like he didn't see it often. When Darius and the others climbed out of the car, Alan's attention was first drawn to Thorn.

"It seems I owe you an apology," he said. It was direct

and humorless.

Thorn's face set into a stern frown. "You sure as hell do."

Darius glanced between the two. The bright light made his eyes ache. He rubbed them with his fingertips. "Well, *we* owe Thorn a lot more than an apology," he said as he gestured to himself, John, and Nicholas. "We'd be dead without her." Thorn watched him with a soft, quiet look—surprise?—before she gave a single nod Darius took to be a sign of gratitude.

"So I've heard," Alan said. He grabbed Thorn's shoulder in a firm, familiar grip before he turned to take them in, and he paused on Nicholas. Thorn disappeared to move their things out of the rental and into the back of the black Martyr SUV. John jumped up to help her. "This must be Mr. Wolfe," Alan said.

"It's Nicholas," the new Virtue clarified, and he extended his hand.

Darius wasn't sure how much Alan knew about Nicholas or what had happened in Spokane. Their contact had been limited, with Thorn's phone lost at the Davenport and Darius's battery dead. Eva would be back in the Underground by now, and she'd probably sent him a hundred frantic and worried texts. John was the only one with a functional cell, and he'd been texting back and forth—with Chris, with Mackenzie, and with Holly—since their plane had landed in Chicago. Who knew what information filtered back to Alan from those conversations? None of that mattered much now, anyway. Like the Sins, Alan wouldn't be able to feel the new Virtue's energy at all. He would know what Nicholas was immediately.

But as always, he was unreadable. He simply reached out and took Nicholas's palm in his. "It's a pleasure to meet you," Alan said. "Though I do wish it was under better circumstances."

Nicholas nodded. His keen, baby-blue eyes didn't leave Alan's face.

For a quiet, tense moment, Alan didn't look away, either. Darius's stomach twisted into a knot. Could Alan sense that Nicholas knew more than he was supposed to?

Thorn walked around the Martyr vehicle and came up beside her uncle. The tension broke as Alan finally looked away from Nicholas to consider her, and she said, "Waters is turning in the keys. Should take two, three minutes."

Alan nodded quietly. The knot in Darius's gut loosened. This was almost over. Soon, they'd be back in the Underground, and he could take Alan aside and explain to him what had happened. Then, he was going to sleep.

"*What the fuck?*"

Nicholas's voice cut through the parking lot like a gunshot. He grabbed the sides of his head and backed up several paces, all the while staring at Alan with wide, furious eyes. The color drained from his cheeks, leaving freckles behind on pale, white skin. Darius stared after him in shock, his foggy brain grappling for what could possibly be happening. It all clicked into place a moment too late. He opened his mouth to interject, but Nicholas was already speaking.

"You're doing it right now," Nicholas exclaimed. "Aren't you? You're trying to Program me!"

A heavy, hot, and fuming silence fell around them. Darius felt numb. The world stopped spinning, and here he was, trapped in the mess he'd made himself. Alan stared at Nicholas with the purest look of surprise Darius had ever seen on his normally-inscrutable face, his eyes wide and motionless, his lips parted just enough for Darius to see the glint of white teeth behind them.

Thorn, though... Thorn's mouth had all but disappeared into a fine line as she looked at Darius. He could almost see the flames of rage flickering inside her half-empty, black eyes.

The illusion shattered. Alan shook his head. "Mr. Wolfe, please let me—"

"Don't," Nicholas said, and he pointed a finger at Alan's

face. A flash of anger crossed Alan's expression. "I know what you are, and I know what you're trying to do."

Thorn's glare deepened. She didn't even look to Nicholas as he spoke. Her fury was focused on Darius. All he could do was stare back, mouth agape, as Nicholas continued.

"Stay the *fuck* out of my head."

Alan's anger grew, but alongside it, fear. Darius remembered what Thorn had said hours ago: "Wrath is close."

And now she knew where they were.

"We do not have time for this," Alan said. He turned to Thorn, and she tore her glare away from Darius. "We must leave. Now."

John was just coming back from the building. Thorn caught his eye and thrust her head toward the Martyr SUV. "Move, Waters!" She opened one of the back doors with such force it ricocheted back at her, and she caught it in one deft, angry hand. Darius saw the metal bow, just a little, under her fingers. "Everyone, get in the car."

Darius hurried past Alan and jumped into the back seat. John rushed in beside him. Alan strode around and opened the driver's side door. "We will discuss this later," he said. His voice was curt and calm—almost *too* calm, like he was holding himself back and forcing the rage down. Darius couldn't tell who he meant to address: himself or Nicholas. Alan's dark eyes passed between them, disappointed. Thorn jumped in shotgun. She rifled through the glove box and pulled out a small, black pistol.

Nicholas hesitated. He looked from the gun in Thorn's hands, to the dangerous look on Alan's face, and to Darius. Darius widened his eyes and nodded to the empty seat beside him, but Nicholas didn't move.

Alan made to shut the driver's side door, but he paused and watched Nicholas with a frown. "You're welcome to stay here," he said, "but Wrath *is* coming, and she will kill you."

Nicholas's nostrils flared, but a look of fear passed over

his face, and he climbed in beside Darius. The minute his door shut, they peeled out of the lot and headed southbound toward the Underground.

The drive back was awkward and uncomfortable. No one said a word. John was still rapidly texting Chris, none the wiser to the tense situation that had played out outside the rental car agency when he'd been inside. Nicholas sat on Darius's other side, his shoulders pulled back, his spine board-straight and rigid, as he glared at the back of Alan's head. When it was clear they were out of harm's way, Thorn returned the gun to its place in the dash. Then she'd pulled her cigarettes from her pocket, but she didn't light one. Instead, she rapped the box on her armrest with rapid, angry taps.

For fifty minutes, Darius daydreamed about his bed, about curling up around Eva and falling into a deep sleep that would last for twelve hours, maybe thirteen, but he knew the chances were slim that Thorn would let him get away without nailing him to the wall for disobeying her direct orders.

As soon as the car pulled up to the car wash outside the Martyr-owned gas station, he knew that was exactly what she planned to do. Alan slipped his card into the slot and pulled into the dark, dank enclosure. The doors shut, and the ramp below them opened. Thorn turned to consider Darius from over her headrest, and the look on her face said it all.

You're dead, Jones.

The entrance to the Underground was crowded. Chris and Mackenzie, waiting for John; Abraham, ready to take Nicholas in and talk to him about everything that had happened in the last twenty-four hours; Eva, tired and frazzled and so, so relieved as soon as she saw Darius's face in the window. Daniel Park—

Sara's husband.

His eyes were red and swollen, his black hair disheveled, and a day's worth of patchy stubble dotted his cheeks. As Alan pulled up to the entrance and turned off the ignition, he peered into the car.

John let out a pained sigh. "What's Dan doing here? Did no one tell him?"

Darius looked up to him. John's deep, blue eyes welled with unshed tears, and he sucked in a fast, hard breath through his nose. At one of their stops, when Thorn and John had traded spots so she could drive, she had given him the collection of things she'd taken from Sara's room. Her identification. The photograph of her and Daniel. The oversized headphones she always wore. He'd put them in his backpack, and now John clutched it with white, shaking fingers.

"I spoke with him," Alan said, and though his tone was even, Darius thought he heard a hint of cold compassion behind the words. "However, it is my experience that we never truly believe the ones we love are no longer with us until we see it for ourselves…"

Alan seemed to be spot on. Darius's heart sank into his stomach as Daniel stood on the balls of his feet and craned his neck to see into the car when they parked. The moment he saw that Sara was not with them, he broke down. Darius had seen a lot since joining the Martyrs, but there was something about watching a grown man sob that made his whole chest ache. Mackenzie knelt down and wrapped her arms around his shoulders, tears glistening in her vibrant, blue eyes, too. Darius's throat tightened up, and he looked away.

The hardest part of death was the people it left behind.

They opened the car. While the rest of the Martyrs embraced their loved ones, Mackenzie helped Daniel to his feet and led him back into the Underground. Darius watched them retreat and felt their energy move through the hallways with a lump in his throat.

This wasn't how it was supposed to go.

Darius heaved a sigh and stepped out of the car. As soon as his feet hit the asphalt, Eva wrapped her arms around his shoulders in a tight, desperate embrace.

"Thank god," she whispered against his ear. "Are you okay?"

"Yeah," Darius said. "I'm fine." His voice felt frayed. His throat was tight, his stomach empty, but he *was* fine—he couldn't compare what he was feeling to Daniel Park. It felt dishonest and cruel. None of this would have happened if Darius hadn't dragged them across the country.

Eva pulled back and grabbed his scruffy face in her hands. Her rich, chestnut eyes were heavy and tired, but her mouth was firmly set. "You did what you could," she said. "And you were *right*."

Then she glanced to Nicholas. Abraham was leading him through the double doors and into the Underground. He cast Darius a final look over his shoulder before disappearing around the corner. Eva turned back to him.

"He's a Virtue, right? Chris told me you found one."

Darius nodded. He *had* been right.

But so had Thorn.

"Jones."

Thorn. She wasn't done with him. Darius turned and found that he, Eva, and Thorn were the last people left in the garage. The Martyr second-in-command waited by the glass doors, her arms crossed dangerously around her chest as she watched Darius with narrow lips and even narrower eyes.

"I gotta go," Darius murmured to Eva. "I'll tell you everything later, okay? I promise."

How many times was that promise going to get him into trouble today?

Eva's brows fell, concerned. She stroked the stubble on his cheeks with her thumbs. "Okay," she whispered. Then she leaned in and gave him a long, tender kiss. "I'll be downstairs."

When Eva left, Darius turned to Thorn. She said nothing

as she led him through the upper level of the Underground. He walked after her quietly, painfully aware of the tired ache in his muscles as they wandered through the drab, beige hallways. They passed tactical, the conference rooms, the four offices taken by other Martyr directors. They went through the private lounge outside two doors, one labeled "Blaine" and the other "Rose." Thorn opened the latter and ushered Darius inside. Once he was in, she followed behind him and slammed the door shut so forcefully it made his fatigued ears ring.

God, he knew she was angry, but did she have to be so *loud?*

Darius had never been in Thorn's office before. It was much different than Alan's. Where Alan's was set up for research and reading, filled with bookshelves and memorabilia, Thorn's looked like the work of a madman. The walls were papered with candid photographs of the Sins, hundreds of newspaper articles, and large, intricate maps of different New York boroughs. These maps were strewn with thumbtacks and red string, marking what Darius could only assume were standard areas of operation for each of the seven. He also noticed photographs of her team: Eva, Elena, Jacob, Caleb, Alexis, and Peter. Each of these was placed in different areas around Manhattan. Thorn's own photograph was the only one set further south, down in Brooklyn beside an image of Autumn Hunt herself.

Was that Wrath's stomping ground?

"Sit the fuck down."

There were only four pieces of furniture: a wide, wooden desk, covered with more maps, more papers, more photographs; an office chair; a narrow coffee table; and a well-used, but comfortable, crimson couch where Thorn kept a pillow and a blanket, neatly folded on the arm. Darius wondered absently if she slept here and wished, again, he could be sleeping right now. He lowered himself onto the cushions and looked up at her.

She was fuming. Darius was getting good at recognizing

the subtleties of Thorn's emotions, but her rage was always so easy to see. It liked to play out in the tight muscles along her throat and the way her thin lips became even thinner. A few weeks ago, Darius may have been intimidated by this mood, but today, he was too damn tired. He just took a deep breath and rubbed his eyes again.

"Look, Thorn—"

"I can't believe you," she interrupted. She began pacing in front of him, like she just needed to release some of this pent-up energy to ensure she didn't lose control and break his nose the same way she'd broken Nicholas's. Her hands tightened into hard, white fists. "It was one order, Jones. *One fucking order.* And you broke it. Immediately! How long did you wait after I passed out to tell him?"

Darius continued to watch her quietly. There was no point in lying. "Twenty minutes. Maybe thirty."

She swore again.

"You realize Alan's Programming didn't work, don't you?" Her voice was rising. Anger seeped out of her and into the air around them. "That little *jackass* was able to hold it off. Now he's a god damned *liability.*"

Darius didn't say anything. What could he say? They both knew what he'd done, and he didn't feel bad about it. Not really. They could Program Nicholas later. They couldn't get a second shot of making a good first impression.

Though, to be honest, Darius wasn't sure they'd managed to pull *that* off. How could Nicholas possibly have a good impression after being punched in the face?

Darius's silence seemed to infuriate Thorn even more. She spun around and slammed her fist down on top of her desk. Papers fluttered. The wood groaned in protest.

After a few heavy, hard breaths, she turned to face him again, and Darius noticed her eyes were full of more than rage. There was something else there.

Pain.

That made his heart flutter a little uncomfortably.

"Why?" she asked at last. "Why do this?"

"It's how I got him to come with us," Darius said. "I promised I'd tell him everything."

Thorn's frown deepened, and she shook her head. "Then why hide it?"

Darius took a deep breath and released it in a sigh. "I thought you'd stop me. I figured there were things you didn't want him to know."

Thorn's eyes narrowed as her mouth curled into a snarl. "Like *what?*"

"C'mon, Thorn," Darius said, and he ran his hands over his face as he laid back against the couch. Every muscle in his body ached, longing to rest, but he pushed on. "You guys didn't tell me *so many* important details for months. You didn't tell me about my Virtue. You didn't tell me you two are Forgotten Sins... I don't want the Martyrs to run off lies and secrets, so I told him everything I know."

Thorn's mouth fell open, just barely, and she slammed it closed again. She stood directly in front of Darius now, with her arms propped defiantly on her hips. She considered him for a long time before she shook her head. "You don't trust us?"

"That's not fair—"

"Isn't it?" Thorn spat. "You didn't think Alan and I would keep the promise you made to Wolfe—the promise *we* made to *you.*"

Darius frowned, but he said nothing. Of course he hadn't.

"Damnit, Darius," Thorn dropped her face into one of her hands and rubbed at the tension behind her eyes. "You went *behind my back* to tell him something because *you didn't think I'd have the decency to tell him myself.* It's a god damned miracle he even decided to get in the car after Alan tried to Program him—"

"Maybe Alan shouldn't be Programming people without their consent," Darius interrupted. Thorn's nostrils flared.

"Without this Programming, you would be *dead!*" She

was yelling now. "We all would be! It's non-negotiable!"

"But you *have* to be more transparent about it," Darius shouted back, and he got to his feet. "I can get behind Programming. Fine. Whatever. But people have the right to know what's going on!"

A lot of feelings were bubbling to the surface—feelings Darius had thought he was over, but that clearly wasn't the case. He shook his head, trying to loosen that bitterness, but he couldn't help it.

It wasn't just about being a Virtue. Alan and Thorn hadn't willingly told him who they really were—*what* they really were. Darius had to find out after Thorn took a couple of bullets for him. He remembered watching as blood gurgled from a hole between her ribs. When his healing hadn't worked, and he realized Thorn's energy was as empty as a dry rain barrel in a drought, he'd found the *Peccostium* seared into the flesh on her wrist.

Thorn and Alan had known Darius was a Virtue from the moment they met him, but they hadn't wanted *him* to know *them*...

Thorn just watched him for a moment in tense, charged silence. Then she turned around and walked back toward her desk. He saw her shoulders rise and fall as she took a deep breath. When she spoke again, she was calmer.

"How do you think he feels about Alan and me now," she asked quietly. Forcefully so. She turned to face him. "Do you think *he* trusts us?"

The look on her face let Darius know she suspected the answer already.

"I don't know—"

"You do know."

There was a tense silence, and Darius and Thorn just stared at each other. She shook her head and spoke again.

"You saw the way he reacted. You *saw* the way he looked at us. That Virtue out there—" she pointed toward her door "—he *hates* us, and now we don't have the opportunity to prove to him that we'd have done right by him!"

151

"Give him some credit," Darius said. "He's been through hell. He'll come around."

"Will he?" Thorn said bitterly. "You're the only other Virtue in the Underground, and you just *proved* to him that even you don't trust us. Not really. Why the hell should he?"

Darius groaned, dropped his face into his hand, and rubbed his eyelids. This didn't seem to be a fight about Nicholas anymore.

"Yeah," Darius said. "Why *should* he trust you?" Thorn was taken aback. Her eyes widened, and her mouth fell open as Darius continued. "You don't just *get* trust, Thorn. It has to be earned. There are a lot of things I trust you with—the Martyrs, the Sins, my *life*... but making sure people know what's going on—what's *really* going on? For all I knew, you were under strict orders from Alan not to say anything about it, and I figured you'd follow them. Nicholas deserves to know everything. Give him a chance. Give *me* a chance."

Her expression darkened, and more of that pain shone through her half-empty eyes. "Darius, you didn't give *me* a chance," she said quietly.

Darius nodded. "You're right. I couldn't risk it."

Then he turned to go. He was done talking about this. He was hungry, he was sweaty, and he was so, *so* tired. So Darius left, with one final, polite nod in Thorn's direction, and her eyes drove into the back of his head until the door swung shut behind him.

CHAPTER TEN

Two days later, Darius laid awake in bed, too anxious to sleep, and he read the Bhagavad Gita.

This was his thirteenth time through the poems. Reading them had become a habit of comfort since Teresa Solomon had died. Everything else in her expansive collection had gone right to the R&D headquarters, but this book... this book was different. "For Darius," the note on the cover read—a note Darius had kept taped there for nothing more than the bittersweet sentimentality of it. For *him*. It had been a long time since he'd had anything exclusively his.

The book was full of Teresa's touch. She had highlighted sections that seemed to mean something to her, written notes in the margins in tight, beautiful print. Going through them was like getting to have a private conversation with the old woman again. Darius missed those conversations. He missed her.

He wondered what she would say about the situation he found himself in now and what she would have done about Nicholas Wolfe.

One thing was for sure: she probably wouldn't have messed things up this badly.

Alan hadn't been as angry as Thorn had been about

Darius's decision to tell Nicholas everything. In fact, he had praised Darius for his quick thinking and finding a way to convince the new Virtue to join them on a trip across the country. Very likely, it had saved the man's life.

All the same, though, now they were left with a big problem: how were they going to get Nicholas Programmed?

The question kept Darius up at night. He flipped through The Bhagavad Gita and heaved a sigh. He never related to Arjuna more. Oh, Krishna, the mind is restless...

Eva shifted beside him. She was sprawled out, her smooth legs tangled in the sheets. Her naked body teased him with soft curves and delicate features beneath the thin, white fabric. One of her rich, chestnut eyes opened into a narrow slit, and she looked up at him from the pillow.

"What're you doing up?"

The words came out through a yawn, and she propped herself up on one elbow.

"Nothing," Darius said. "I'm sorry. Is the light too bright?"

She didn't buy that. Eva's eyes darted between the red, leather-bound book in his hand to the look on his face. By now, she knew the tells—she knew this was a habit he had when he was unsettled. It wasn't the first time Darius had woken her up at the break of dawn this way.

She frowned at him, much more awake now. "What's wrong?"

Darius looked down at the book again, and he shook his head.

"It's just this whole problem with Nicholas refusing to let Alan Program him."

Darius tried to tell himself this was all still so new—that Nicholas was just in the process of taking in all of the information provided to him—but he knew it wasn't true. Nicholas wasn't resistant to Programming because the concept was foreign and scary to him. He was resistant because he didn't trust Alan, and he sure as hell didn't trust Thorn. He didn't want either of them poking around inside his head.

Darius couldn't blame him.

But they were running out of options. Jeremiah Montgomery was adamant the mess they'd had last year after Eva's disappearance wouldn't happen again. He assigned security details to monitor every single entrance into the Underground, from the doors to the subterranean garage to the stairs leading up to the convenience store above and every maintenance corridor in between. If Nicholas was paying attention—and Darius knew he was—he'd know the Martyrs were locking down and that *he* was the reason.

Eva was silent for a moment. "Is there anything I can do to help?"

Darius shook his head. "No, I don't think so. Unless you can Program him."

Eva gave him a small, sympathetic smile. "I thought *you* were going to give it a shot."

That was another point of anxiety entirely. After Nicholas had refused all attempts from Alan to talk to him about Programming, someone had suggested *Darius* try his hand at it. That someone had, of course, been Mackenzie. Virtues had many of the same powers as the Sins, so it stood to reason this was one of them.

But as much as Alan Programming the Martyrs made Darius uncomfortable, the idea of doing it himself was nauseating. He couldn't stop thinking about Jacob Locke and what Programming had done to him.

"Yeah, we're going to practice tomorrow," Darius said. He leaned over to put the book back on his nightstand and caught a look at the clock. Three a.m. "Today. Damn." Darius groaned and rubbed his hands over his face. "We don't even know if this is *possible.*"

Eva nodded and nestled in close to Darius's side. Her arm wrapped around his hips, and her fingers played gently on his far thigh. "Either way, it will be fine. You'll see," she murmured against his chest. "But you should get some sleep… and let *me* get some sleep." She playfully bit her lower lip.

Darius chuckled, turned off the side light, and sank back into bed. Eva kissed him and wound herself around his body. The warmth from her skin and the warmth from her soul enveloped him in a cocoon. It was almost *too* warm to be comfortable.

She quickly fell back asleep. When Darius eventually did, too, it was fitful, full of half-dreams about Jacob Locke and just how badly Programming could break the human brain.

"Okay, so how exactly does this work?"

Darius sat across from Mackenzie. The Irishwoman's heart-shaped face had a broad smile plastered across it, and her feet bounced excitedly against the plush, red carpet in Alan's office. She happily volunteered to be a guinea pig for their Programming test. Darius wished he shared even half of her enthusiasm. As it was, he was just worried he was going to turn her into a drooling mess on the floor.

"It's simple," Alan said. He leaned against his desk, his long arms crossed around his narrow chest. His Familiar, a black wolf named Rae, sat at his side, watching the room with intelligent blue eyes. "You input your thoughts into your target, as with normal Influencing, but instead of *ideas*, you plant rules, which the target is expected to follow."

"Rules," Darius said. He rubbed his hands together. "Okay. Like what?"

"The simplest are 'if this, then that' statements," said Skylar Fulton. She stood beside Alan, her hands jammed into the front pockets of her tight skinny jeans. Her graphic tee had some retro cartoon character Darius vaguely remembered from his childhood—before he'd lost his home and, with it, any connection to pop culture other people his age typically understood.

Today, she was here in place of Holly. The tech lead was swamped, doing whatever she could to scrub any photographs and videos from the disaster in Spokane from the internet. This was a monumental—and impossible—task. Once something was online, it was online forever, Holly had explained, but that didn't mean you couldn't make it *harder* to track down.

Luckily, only one piece of media had garnered attention. Unluckily, it was footage of Thorn effortlessly snapping a man's neck. She ducked under his arm as he fired bullets into the crowd and twisted his head in her hands like he was made of paper.

The video was being shared so widely on so many platforms that Holly's whole team was busy tracking it down, hacking into servers, and burying it. If Skylar hadn't been sent up here to help Darius learn to Program, she'd be down in the basement, stuck behind a screen, trying to stop Thorn's image from going more viral than it already was.

"If this, then that," Darius repeated to himself quietly. "So like, 'If you start to say something about the Underground, then shut up?'"

Alan chuckled. "My Program is a little more complex, but that is the idea. However, an 'if' statement is inherently single use in human Programming. To make it stick, you will want to use the term 'whenever' instead."

"*Whenever* 'this' then 'that?'" Darius clarified. A nervous bubble expanded in his throat, and he swallowed against it. "God, this is more complicated than I thought…"

Alan nodded, his mouth curled up into a kind smile. "Yes, it can be. Today we'll start with something simple. This is primarily a test of concept, just to see if it is possible for a Virtue to Program an individual, so we should start small."

"Make it easy," Skylar agreed. "Maybe 'whenever someone says your name, then you say, 'Hello world.'"

"Why 'Hello world?'" Darius asked.

Skylar smiled, coy and playful. "It's where all programmers have to start."

"So, I'll just be saying, 'hello world' every time someone says my name for the rest of my life?" Mackenzie asked.

Alan shook his head. "If Darius can implant a Program, he can also remove it. It will be a short inconvenience."

"Right," Mackenzie said, and she rubbed her hands together. "Well, if that's the case, let's make it *fun*. How about, 'Whenever someone says your name, then do a backflip!'"

Darius frowned. "Can you do a backflip?"

"Nope! But maybe with some brilliant Virtue magic, I could!"

"Yeah," Skylar said, shaking her head. "I'm gonna go ahead and say we *shouldn't* do anything that might make Mackenzie break her neck."

"Oh, boo. You're no fun."

"I like Miss Fulton's idea," Alan said. "It's simple yet obvious. We will know right away if you have succeeded. Are you ready to give it a try?"

Darius cleared his throat. "One last thing. How do I know I'm not gonna, like... mess her up?"

Alan's brows furrowed. "What do you mean?"

"I mean like Jacob Locke."

Alan's face shifted as though a veil had been lifted, and he suddenly understood. "Jacob Locke is an extraordinary case," he said with a somber sigh, and he ran a hand over his black goatee. "The level of Programming Jacob had to undergo to remove what Pride had done to him was something I had never tried before and have not tried since. It is not possible for you to permanently damage Miss McKay's brain with this kind of simple Programming."

"You're not going deep enough to *do* damage," Skylar said, shrugging. "I figure it's the equivalent of creating a program on the desktop. You're in a very superficial level of her brain. You're not trying to rewrite core subroutines in the operating system itself. Worst case scenario, your code breaks because it's being taken *too* literally, and it can cause some issues with the functionality. Since you're just in that surface level of consciousness, that code never causes any damage to the *hard drive*—or brain. Whatever. You just rewrite it until it does what you want it to do."

None of that made much sense to Darius, but he was comforted that both Alan and Skylar thought it was extremely unlikely that he would kill his test subject. He took a deep breath and shook out his hands. Mackenzie raised her eyebrows high into her neon-blue bangs.

"All right," Darius said. He cleared his throat again. "Let's get this over with."

Mackenzie dipped her fingers into Darius's palms, and he held them in a firm grip. He closed his eyes and thought back to the last time he'd used his Direct Influence. The *only* time. Had it been just four days ago? God, it felt like so much longer. Thorn joked with him then that maybe they'd teach him to do the Programming. He couldn't believe that's what they were actually doing.

Nothing was happening. Darius wasn't focused. He shook his head, squared his shoulders, and did what he'd done that evening. He opened his energy and felt the border between where his ended and Mackenzie's began. The line where they met was fuzzy, mingling together, and he gently pushed forward the thought.

Whenever I say your name, then you'll say, "Hello, world."

He felt a small surge of *something* move from his body and into Mackenzie's, but not the same kind of energy transfer he felt when he healed. It was more abstract. More ethereal. He opened his eyes and found Mackenzie staring at him. She'd inched forward in the chair, and her face was barely a foot away from his, her eyes bright and eager.

"Did it work?" she asked as she looked around the room.

"Mackenzie," Skylar stated. Mackenzie said nothing.

Alan frowned. "No. It appears it did not."

Darius's gut dipped, and he swore quietly under his breath. Mackenzie looked back at him, her fingers squeezing his a little tighter. "Okay, let's try again."

Darius sighed. "Mackenzie, I—"

But as her name slipped out of his mouth, she suddenly blurted out the words, "Hello world!"

The room went silent. Mackenzie's eyes widened, and

her mouth dropped. She squealed, pulled her hands out of Darius's grasp, and playfully punched him on the arm. "Damn, Jones! You did it!"

Skylar shook her head. "Something wasn't right, though. It didn't work for me. What was the exact rule you set?"

"Ah, that's it," Darius said, snapping his fingers. "I said, 'when *I* say your name.'"

Alan nodded, but his thin lips were set into a smile. "Yes, with Programming, your language matters quite a bit. Even a simple word change can make the whole thing nonfunctional—at least, not in a way that is beneficial to us."

"Do it again!" Mackenzie exclaimed. She tapped her feet on the ground and bounced in her chair. Darius laughed, and his smile stretched across his face. He couldn't believe it had worked! Proud of himself, he looked across at Mackenzie and said her name again.

But this time, she remained silent.

Darius's excitement deflated a bit, and he frowned. Mackenzie bit her lip and waited, but still, nothing happened.

"Were you fucking with us the first time?" Skylar asked.

The Irishwoman vehemently shook her head, almost offended. "No!"

"Hmmm…" Alan's brows furrowed as he walked away from his desk and around to Mackenzie's other side. Rae remained in position and looked between Darius and Mackenzie with those bright, alert eyes. Her black ears perked forward and followed Alan's movements. "I have a theory. Darius, if you would, please Program her again."

Darius grabbed Mackenzie's hands again. This time, he changed it up a little so he would *know* Mackenzie wasn't pulling a prank.

Whenever anyone says your name, then touch your nose.

He opened his eyes and said, "Mackenzie."

Both her hands pulled out of his, and her pointer fingers pressed to either side of her nose. She let out a great, loud laugh.

"Brilliant!"

As soon as she removed her fingers from her face, Alan said her name. This time, she did nothing.

"Did you Program her only to respond if *you* said her name again?" Alan asked.

Darius shook his head. "No. I made it 'anyone' this time."

Alan took a deep breath and shook his head. "This is what I feared," he said, and he looked down at Darius. "Your Programming disappears as soon as you no longer maintain physical contact."

That sucked the rest of Darius's excitement out right through his gut. Of course. It made sense. All of the Virtues' active powers—healing, Influencing, and destroying their Sin—had to be done with direct contact. Programming could only be maintained under the same circumstances.

Which made it useless to him.

"Damn it," Darius grumbled. "It was looking *so good*, too…"

If this had worked, it would have solved the biggest problem he had. Now, it looked like he would have to find some way to convince Nicholas he *needed* to let Alan Program him.

"Well," Mackenzie said with a shrug. "Look at the bright side—now you've got a pretty bang on party trick." Skylar was the only one who laughed. Darius just looked up at Alan and sighed.

Thorn fell onto the bed, her naked body glistening with a fine layer of sweat in the midday heat. Jay let out a deep, contented groan as he laid down, too. He rolled onto his side and admired her. One of his hands came and gently rested on her flat stomach, just below her navel, as his eyes traveled slowly up her body. They started at her toes and drank in every single detail—the strong muscles in her thighs, the way her throat sloped gracefully into her collarbone, the angles of her face…

Well… every detail except one. Even when they had sex, Jay avoided the thick, heavy scars dripping down Thorn's left forearm. In the last three years, he had never once asked about them. That was fine with Thorn. She'd just have to come up with another lie.

Only Alan and Cain knew the real story, and Thorn planned on keeping it that way.

Jay leaned forward and kissed the hollow of Thorn's throat. His hand wandered down from her stomach, running along the inside of her thigh. His closeness chilled her. The sensation of his cold energy against her bare skin made goosebumps rise along her arms.

Thorn allowed herself a smile. She knew this wasn't love, but fuck, it felt good to let herself go, especially when things were so frustrating at the Underground.

And damn, they were *frustrating*.

Her smile disappeared.

"What's on your mind?"

Jay's voice brought her out of her thoughts. She turned to look at him and found him staring at her with those blue eyes wide and concerned.

What was on her mind?

Programming Nicholas Wolfe and protecting the Underground. Figuring out why Wrath didn't seem to know about the assassination attempt that had blown her half to hell. Holding Darius Jones down and forcing him to understand that, damn it, she was *trying* to rewrite all the mistakes she'd made in the last nine months, but she couldn't fucking do it if he didn't give her a *chance*.

"Nothing," Thorn said.

"You sure?"

"Yes," Thorn insisted, and she sat up in bed. Jay laid back, frowning at the ceiling, as he propped his hands behind his head. Thorn watched him for a moment. She had the sense he wanted to say something but wasn't sure if he should.

Then his focus came back to her, and Thorn knew what was going to come out of his mouth before he opened it.

"I gotta know—what the *fuck* happened at The Cross the other night?"

A flicker of anger came to life in Thorn's chest. She rolled her eyes and got to her feet. "What about our 'no questions' policy?" she asked.

Jay's brows pinched together. He leapt up and followed as she walked around the bed, toward the spot on the floor where he'd thrown her clothes.

"I'm pretty sure that policy goes out the fucking window when you pull a knife on some guy in my bar."

"Jay," Thorn said. "Drop it." Her teeth gritted together, and whatever sense of peace she'd gotten from their tryst started to smolder. She leaned down to grab her boy shorts and leggings.

"No," he said as he crossed his arms. He looked ridiculous, standing there stark naked, glaring down at Thorn as she began to get dressed. "I *always* drop it. I dropped it last time, when I saw you climbing into the back of that car *covered in blood.*"

Thorn closed her eyes and pulled her shirt on over her head. "Jay—"

"And *this time,*" he pressed on. "You came into The Cross all bloodied up, then you tried to kill someone, and *then* a car exploded around the corner, and I didn't hear from you for two fucking weeks! I can't drop that!"

Fuck, this was the *exact* thing she came here to *avoid*—talk about *work,* talk about *the Sins,* talk about *her.*

"Well, you're going to have to," Thorn snarled. Her fingers curled into a fist, the muscles so tight she felt her hand quivering.

"Why can't you just—"

"*Fuck, just STOP.*"

Thorn wheeled around and slammed her fist into the wall. Her knuckles pushed through the sheetrock in a smooth, crackling pop. The room went silent. The sounds from the city outside filtered through an open window. Cars honking. People walking. The distant wailing of sirens.

But inside the studio, Jay and Thorn said nothing. A flash of bitter disappointment tugged at Thorn's anger, dragging it from the hollow in her chest until it sat in her stomach like a block of iron.

Fuck.

Thorn pulled her fist from the hole she'd made and took a deep breath before she turned back around to face him. His eyes were wide, his mouth open, as he stared at her.

Scared of her.

Thorn shook her head.

"I'm sorry," she said, and she meant it—*fuck*, did she mean it. "But I can't tell you what you want to know. I can *never* tell you. So we have two options here. Either you *drop it*, or we stop doing *this*." Thorn gestured around the room. It still spoke of sex—clothes strewn across the floor, sheets in disarray, Jay standing there, naked. Thorn pressed on. "And *I* don't want to quit doing this."

"Neither do I," Jay said, but it was quieter now. He seemed smaller than he had a few minutes ago. Thorn felt like she'd chopped him up and dried him out. She looked away and dropped back to the ground to put her shoes and socks on—anything to not have to see the harrowed look on his face.

"So, can we be done talking about this?"

"Yeah."

Thorn sighed. Thank god.

"Okay," she said. "Good."

She stood up again, breathing in the heavy, *angry* air between them. Thorn looked to Jay, and he looked down at himself, as though realizing for the first time he was nude. As he began to hunt for his clothes awkwardly, a sensation blipped to life at the edge of Thorn's awareness. A pull. Tight. Pure. Evil.

Wrath's Influence.

And it was *close*.

Her heart skipped a beat. She reached into her bag and pulled out a fresh pair of fingerless gloves.

"I've gotta go," Thorn muttered as she pulled them on and flung the satchel over her shoulder. "I'll catch you later?"

"Yeah," Jay said, but the look he threw her was tense and fleeting. "Sure."

Thorn's mouth tightened. She thought to say more, but what the fuck could she say to make *this* shitshow any better? So she simply nodded as she walked toward the door and left.

She could worry about Jay later. Now, she had more pressing matters.

The hot, humid air of New York's summer bombarded Thorn as she hurried down the street. The little pings of Wrath's Influence—quick, tiny flashes of cold energy—drew her somewhere to the northeast. Her rage flared with it. Usually, sex with Jay was a release, providing her time where the monster inside got to rest, but today had fucking backfired.

Thorn left his apartment feeling more pent up, more high-strung, than she had when she'd arrived, and she was running out of outlets. Since Witham had shown up at The Cross, Thorn hadn't been back. Sloth had clearly marked the place, and Thorn worried that meant the rest of the Sins knew about it, too. She had Holly monitoring it from that little camera across the street she thought Thorn didn't know about.

So far, so good. No Sins had made an appearance, but Thorn wouldn't take chances. She couldn't risk getting all the people there killed. They were the closest things she had to a community in this fucking city. It made her gut lurch to imagine Autumn Hunt walking through that door and cutting them all the pieces...

But even if she didn't have The Cross, she had Jay. She *thought* she had him. He was always eager when she called, and the man was good at what he did, but today, sex hadn't done the trick.

And Wrath's Influence kept *tempting* her.

Thorn's pace increased. The Sin was close. Three miles, Thorn estimated, based on the strength of the pull. In the heart of the Bronx. Wrath was *never* in the Bronx.

But Sloth was.

What were the chances that the two Sins were together? They weren't known to cooperate much, but Thorn couldn't ignore the possibility... and the chance to get information out of them about what the hell was going on here.

She pulled out her phone and navigated to her tactical map. Holly had developed this program to show Thorn and the rest of TAC which units were nearby—and to streamline calling for backup, which was the standard procedure when any potential Sin interaction was anticipated. Thorn glanced at the aerial view of the nearby neighborhoods. Chris and Jeremiah were on patrol in Harlem. Just across the bridge. They could be here in a matter of minutes. Thorn's thumb hovered over the alert button...

But Wrath's Influence kept *calling* at her... That call stoked Thorn's anger, her resentment, and god, she needed a fucking release.

So she put her phone back in her bag, pulled out an elastic band, and tied her hair into a low ponytail. As she opened the satchel, Sparkie darted out and took to the sky.

Three miles? She could sprint three miles.

Thorn ran tirelessly. Her muscles, resistant to the fatigue normal humans had to deal with, pushed her forward, and her lungs opened up and sucked in air with steady, practiced drive. She rushed past people on the sidewalks, hurried across streets, darted in-between pedestrians and honking traffic with deft agility.

All the while, Wrath's pulsing Influence moved, slowly pulling away. Thorn was quickly closing the gap. She rushed through the South Bronx neighborhoods, from Melrose through Morrisania. The summer heat, the warm, humid air coming in from the Atlantic, coated Thorn in sweat, but she kept running. Her heart beat hard, almost *excited*, at the chance to get her hands dirty.

The beacon stopped.

Wrath's call toward wherever she was blinked out. Thorn's pace slowed, just barely, as she kept on the same general heading.

Maybe it would come back.

It didn't.

After another mile, Thorn slowed to a stop along the side of the Bronx River in Starlight Park. She propped her hands on her hips, her breathing measured, as she looked around and waited… for nothing. Autumn Hunt's Influence was gone. Thorn had no more thread to follow.

"Fuck!"

She thrashed around and kicked a trashcan chained to a nearby post, sending it swinging around. Thorn's toes ached for a couple of seconds before the broken bones mended themselves. A woman at the nearby play structure quietly gathered her children up and drew them away, watching her with angry, nervous eyes.

Fuck. Wrath was gone.

Thorn dipped her hand into her satchel and found her cigarettes and lighter. She sat on a nearby park bench and lit one, staring through the trees in the general direction she'd last felt Wrath's Influence. She could always use her own, draw Wrath to *her*, but she knew Alan would feel it, too, and she was already going to have a hard time convincing him that she hadn't gone *looking* for trouble…

With a sigh, Thorn sucked a heavy lungful of smoke deep into her chest. Every single drag felt like the very first time she'd tried a cigarette, almost sixty years ago. Hot, painful, and satisfying. The habit helped calm the beast inside. Thorn had realized it shortly after Donovan's death, and she'd been smoking ever since. She wasn't addicted—she couldn't be—but now it was as much of a part of Thorn as her wrath was. The two went hand-in-hand, like an abusive couple who both brought out the worst in her.

She took another mouthful of smoke and held it in deep as she stared out into the distance, where Wrath's Influence had disappeared.

What the hell was that bitch up to in this part of town?

Thorn stood in her office, her brows knit together in a hard furrow as she considered the map of the Bronx hung upon her wall. She dipped her left hand into a tin of push-pins, pulled one out, and stuck it among a handful of others she'd already placed at various neighborhoods around the area. Crotona. Parkchester. Allerton. This one she jammed into "Van Nest," and she frowned. Sparkie perched on Thorn's shoulder, tilting his head.

Something had been bugging Thorn since they'd gotten back from the West Coast. Every night, before she fell asleep, she replayed the fight she and Wrath had in the alley outside of the Davenport Hotel. Every night, she saw the shocked, *furious* look on Autumn Hunt's face when she learned that Witham had tried to kill her. Every night, she heard those words:

"You're not going to die… but you'll wish you had."

Thorn had a lot of problems right now… a lot of problems she had no idea how to handle.

Jay, prying into her life and making it hard for her to justify why she hadn't disappeared on him yet.

Nicholas, refusing to be Programmed, putting the whole damned organization in danger.

And Darius… Fuck, that was the hardest one. Thorn's heart felt heavy, and her stomach twisted up in knots at the thought of *him*. She never should have listened to Alan. If she'd told Darius everything from the start, like she'd wanted to when they found him, he'd trust her.

She hated that he didn't.

Then there was Wrath. Thorn may not have been able

to do anything about any of the other big problems in her life, but she *could* do something about Wrath.

Starting with finding out why she was spending her time in the Bronx…

Thorn moved to grab another pushpin out of the box when a familiar movement in the waiting room outside her office caught her attention. She recognized the cold signature—cold to Thorn, but less so than all the other Martyrs who lived here. The energy moved toward her door, and Thorn didn't bother going to answer it. This visitor knew she was always welcome.

Thorn turned around as Chris let herself in without knocking. By the look of her, she'd recently gotten off shift. Her holster and pistol had been put back in her locker in the tactical room, but she was still wearing the beige cargo pants and black turtleneck of her uniform. To Thorn's surprise, she also carried a hot plate of food between her hands. When Thorn glanced at it with a frown, Chris raised her brows.

"You need to eat."

"I'm fine," Thorn said, and she turned back to the map on her wall. When she got to the bottom of this, she *would* be fine. Sparkie's wings ruffled irritably. Obviously so. Thorn took a deep breath as the animal scampered off, leaping from her shoulder to her desk. He retreated to the darkness of a half-open drawer, and Thorn released her breath in a sigh.

Chris watched the lizard, and she watched Thorn. Thorn felt her cool energy walk away—heard the sound of ceramic being placed upon wood—before Chris came back to her side. Thorn reached down to grab a fifth pin, but Chris's hand came out and took the tin from her fingers. She replaced it with a slice of bread.

"Sure," Chris said, but in a kind, placating way Thorn knew meant she didn't believe her. Chris walked back to the desk and placed the tin beside the plate. Then she turned to Thorn with a serious look. "I heard Alan and the others still aren't convinced the attack in Spokane is what Sloth meant when he talked to you. How are you handling that?"

Chris might not have been *in* the Martyr leadership, but she was close enough with the people in that room to know all the details of every meeting anyway. Including, it seemed, the tension surrounding this whole damned situation. A tiny spark lit up Thorn's empty, aching chest. She shook her head, and for the first time, she admitted something out loud.

"I think they're right."

Even saying the words put a bad taste in Thorn's mouth. She'd been convinced the attack in Spokane had been the Sins' big plot all along. When shit had hit the fan at the gala, she'd felt vindicated, but the more time passed, the more her conviction cracked.

"What?" Chris asked, her eyes wide. "What do you mean?"

"It just doesn't make sense," Thorn muttered. "If they knew about the trip, Hunt would have *known* there was a Virtue there, but she was shocked when she saw Wolfe."

Chris said nothing. She just nodded quietly, leaning to the side and resting her hip against the corner of Thorn's desk. Thorn came back around and put the slice of bread back on the plate.

"And it was too easy for us to escape," she went on. "If they'd planned it ahead of time, we never would have gotten out of that fucking city. It was too messy."

"If they didn't plan it, how did they find you?" Chris asked.

"Sentries, probably," Thorn said with a sigh. "Alan suspects the Sins have been setting Sentries in the nearest airports to New York, Programmed to spot me. Holly's team is looking for any links between the Sins and Newark Liberty International. Lina was right. She said it didn't make fucking sense at the beginning. I should have listened to her. I was just too damned stubborn."

And too focused on keeping Darius safe that she put

him, and others, into danger in the first place.

Chris took a deep breath. "What does that mean for the Recon teams?"

"John's fine," Thorn said shortly, and she closed her eyes and shook her head. When she spoke again, she kept her voice more level. "Mackenzie is going to start using airports south of here instead. They're further, and smaller, but there's almost no chance the Sins have people there."

"Ah. Well, good."

Yeah. Good. Good for John Waters, who had to find a new partner before going out on any more Recon missions because Thorn had gotten Sara Park killed.

A tense silence fell between the women then. They were accustomed to silence. Thorn and Chris spent much of their time together not speaking, but today, the silence felt different. Charged. Thorn looked Chris over, and she frowned.

"That's not what you came here to talk to me about," she asked, "is it?"

"No," Chris said through a sigh, and she crossed her arms in a way that reminded Thorn eerily of herself. She was sure she'd used this exact same posture on Chris during more than one training session over the last twelve years. "I read your report from today."

Thorn reached for the plate sitting on the desk. "Anything interesting?"

"Only that you went after Wrath without calling for backup."

"There wasn't time."

Chris raised an eyebrow. Again, Thorn felt like she was looking in a mirror, where the reflection showed light eyes, light hair, and a light spirit Thorn could never hope to achieve herself. Chris looked past Thorn's head, at the map mounted to the wall, and took a deep breath.

"You should've called," Chris said, and she focused back on Thorn. "Jeremiah and I weren't far away. We could have been there."

"It didn't even matter," Thorn said. She grabbed the

plate from the desk and made her way to the couch along the far wall. "I lost her somewhere in here." Thorn picked up the bread, took a bite, and gestured toward the pins. Then she sat down and put her food on the coffee table. Chris sat beside her.

"You still should have called," Chris said. "It's dangerous—"

"If you've been reading my reports," Thorn cut in irritably, but it was a tired irritation. Tired of *being* irritated. "You'd know Wrath doesn't want me dead. I'd have been *fine*."

"I did read that one," Chris said. She leaned back and turned to her side, pulling her legs up beneath herself as she looked Thorn over. "That doesn't mean you should go looking for a fight. Even if she doesn't want you dead, there are worse things she could do."

Chris's green eyes glinted in a concern that sent a guilty shiver down Thorn's spine. Chris had lost both of her parents to the war with the Sins, and Thorn stepped up to fill the void. She knew, deep down, Chris was terrified of losing her, too.

"I wasn't looking for a fight," Thorn said.

"Liar."

Chris cracked a half-hearted smile, and Thorn couldn't help but give a cold chuckle.

"I wasn't," Thorn insisted, but even she knew how fake it felt. Even when Thorn wasn't "looking" for one, fights always seemed to find her... and she didn't always mind. "I was looking for intel. There's something I *need* to know."

Chris frowned. "What?"

Thorn didn't answer right away. Her throat tightened, squashing any semblance of an appetite she had left, and she put the bread back on the plate beside the chicken and vegetables. Then she took a deep breath and shook her head.

"If Wrath's the *only one* who won't kill me," Thorn said at last.

Chris's frown deepened. "What do you mean?"

"Sloth tried to blow me to pieces," Thorn said. She remembered the bombing—or, rather, she remembered what she *could* of the bombing. The stink of propellant. The light and heat as fire overwhelmed her body. Vaguely, the hulking shape of Jeremiah lifting her from the ground. Opening her eyes in the hospital to find Alan hovering over her. His long face had seemed so gaunt and colorless.

"He didn't think I'd survive," Thorn went on, shaking her head. "And Wrath *didn't know about it*. The way I see it, there are only two options here."

"Either Sloth is a rogue Sin," Chris started slowly.

"Or Wrath has lost her control over all of them," Thorn finished. "Sloth might not be the only one who wants me dead. They *all* might. And if that's the case, if I have four Sins out to get me, I'm pretty much *fucked*."

Chris's face paled. Her eyes went distant. Though they were pointed at Thorn, they didn't really see her. Thorn could tell they'd focused somewhere beyond her, somewhere anchored outside reality. Her forehead tightened into a worried furrow.

"What are you going to do?" She asked it quietly, and her attention finally zeroed back in on Thorn's face.

Thorn shook her head. "I don't know," she said. "But if Wrath still wants to keep me around, maybe she'll kill the rest of them off for me and save my neck. What a fucked up situation *that* would be…"

She tried to smile, to break the tension, but she could tell Chris's mind was elsewhere. Thorn extended her hand and held it, palm up. Chris looked down at it, considered the white fingers sticking out from Thorn's gloves, and dipped her hand into them. Thorn squeezed firmly, confidently, but she didn't say anything.

She wasn't about to make promises she couldn't keep.

Suddenly, Thorn's phone trilled to life. She got to her feet and walked to her desk to grab it. Caleb Claytor, the Gray Unit member she had on Lust's case. Thorn frowned and answered.

"What's up?"

"Hey," Caleb said. His voice sounded a little unsure. "The new girl, Eva? Didn't she have a brother?"

Thorn's brows drew even closer together.

"Yes," she said. Saul Torres and two other people from Darius's orphanage hadn't been among the dead. The Martyrs had run under the assumption that he'd survived for a while, but their search for him had fallen into the background. With no guarantee that he'd made it out alive—or that he'd stayed in the city, even if he had—they had never focused on finding him. "Why?"

"Was his name Saul?"

Thorn closed her eyes and pinched the bridge of her nose. God fucking damn it. She sensed Chris stand up and walk a little closer. "What happened?"

"I just checked out a proof of tomorrow's paper with one of the editors I work with at the *Times*," Caleb said. "You need to see it. I'll send you a screenshot."

The device in Thorn's hand buzzed, and she pulled it back to open the text. She scanned the article, and her stomach dropped.

"Print me a copy," Thorn snapped into the phone. "I want it on my desk as soon as fucking possible."

"Yes, ma'am."

Then Thorn hung up and swore.

"What happened?" Chris asked.

"The Sins happened," Thorn snarled. "I think I know what they're planning."

CHAPTER ELEVEN

"Start at the beginning."

Darius sat in Jeremiah's office. Eva was in the chair to his left, holding his hand so tightly that his fingers ached. Jeremiah was situated behind his desk. His huge, hulking form made the furniture look small. Thorn stood at the back of the room. Darius couldn't truly sense her, but he felt her attention on the back of their heads all the same, focused and hot.

"Miss Torres?" Jeremiah said when Eva still hadn't spoken, and she looked up to him. His deep, brown eyes were serious but sympathetic. "I understand this might be difficult for you, but I need to know about your life before the Martyrs to rule out Sin involvement here."

Then he gestured a massive hand at the printout from the *Times* on his desk. Darius looked down at it, still just as shocked as he had been an hour ago at who was looking back up at him from the paper.

It was *Saul.*

He was younger than he'd been when Darius met him six years ago, but there was no mistaking it: the kid staring back up at him was Saul Torres. The caption below the image stated it was a yearbook photograph from when Saul

175

was just seventeen. His cheeks were clean-shaven, his eyes full, wide, and hopeful. Beside the photograph was a digital rendition of what Saul would look like today, almost twelve years later. It was eerily accurate. Add stubble and take away twenty or so pounds, and it looked just like him.

Darius's attention shifted up to the headline: _Have You Seen This Man?_ Beneath the photograph, a blurb, quick and concise, read, "Saul Torres, 30, was involved in a domestic incident, and his safety may be in jeopardy. The New York Police Department is offering a $1,000 reward for anyone who comes forward with information that leads to Torres's whereabouts."

Eva took a deep breath. "How could the Sins be involved?" There was a forced hopefulness to her tone, and she shook her head. "This doesn't seem _bad…_ "

"Terrance Moore—Gluttony—runs the police," Jeremiah said grimly. "I think it's too much of a coincidence that they would be looking for your brother without Sin involvement."

"What could they even do with him?" Darius asked. "He's not a Martyr."

"They may be trying to lure you out of the Underground," Thorn said. Her voice was low and serious, and both Eva and Darius turned toward her. "If Lina was right and the Sins' plan had nothing to do with the trip to Washington, maybe _this_ is what they were working on."

"How would they even know about him?" Darius asked.

"Both Pride and Envy saw him," Jeremiah said. "And in the report Thorn provided from the incident last winter, Eva admitted to Dane that she was looking for her brother when she was captured. They could very well have started planning this back then, and Dane's death slowed them down."

"There's been _no_ evidence of Saul at all," Darius said with a frown. Thorn looked down at him, and her eyebrows pinched together. "We have no idea if he's alive or even in the city."

"The Sins don't care where he is," she said, crossing her arms. "They know you'll look for him. If he's in the city, and they find him, they can use him as bait. If he's not, it doesn't matter if it gets you out there searching for him, too. In the end, they have one goal: they're after *you*."

Thorn's eyes flashed with white-hot, angry concern, and her fingers tightened around her bicep.

"Before we jump to conclusions," Jeremiah said, and Darius and Eva spun to face the desk again, "it's important for us to determine if this search for Saul Torres is legitimate."

"What if it is?" Eva asked.

"Then I'll be less worried that the Sins are involved here," Jeremiah said. He wore a look that made it all too obvious he didn't believe that was true. Darius was sure both he and Thorn knew the tells by now—they could almost sense when Sins were stirring things up—but the Tactical director rattled on his keyboard for a few strokes and opened a reporting program. "If there are no *real* reasons someone would be searching for him, it's likely the Sins are using this to spread their search as well as to let us know they are hunting him down."

She nodded. "What kind of thing are you looking for?"

"This story claims he's a 'person of interest,'" Jeremiah said, and he faced Eva again. "That could mean any number of things. Theft and petty crime. Connections to radical groups or individuals. Illicit drug use. Violence."

Eva's face drained of color. She looked down at her lap, and her fingers tightened around Darius's palm.

"Yeah… there are a few things it could be about," Eva said as she cleared her throat.

Jeremiah turned back to his computer. "Please, tell me everything."

"First," Eva began, "we're undocumented. Mom and dad tried to bring us into the country when Saul was seven, and I was just a couple of years old. Venezuela was a mess. It still is. They wanted a better life for us here."

She glanced down at her hands and took a deep breath before she continued. "Anyway, we were seeking asylum, so we thought we'd be safe, but they forced us into camps at the border. Saul and I were separated from our parents, stuck in this big, concrete room with other scared, dirty kids. We lived like that for months until they finally decided we didn't have a case and threw us back on the southern side of the border. We were reunited with Mom, but none of us ever saw Dad again. I'm pretty sure he died."

"That must have been very hard," Jeremiah said.

"Honestly, I don't remember most of it," Eva said. "Most of what I know, I learned from Saul."

Jeremiah nodded, watching her with dark, sympathetic patience. His brown fingers were laced in front of his face, and he pressed his full lips against them. "Do you know how you entered the country?"

"Well, we couldn't go back to Venezuela," Eva said, and she shifted a little in her chair. She pulled her hand out of Darius's grip and wrung it with the other one in her lap. "So Mom found some people willing to smuggle us across. One of them was this man, Luis Mendez."

Her voice tightened around the name, and Darius watched her. Jeremiah's keyboard rattled as he typed it into his notes.

"Who was Luis?" Jeremiah asked.

"Eventually," Eva said, "he was our stepdad. But first, he was just the guy who helped us get into the States and up to New York. He said it was safer for us to disappear up here, but I think he knew it was just going to be harder for us to get away from him. He and Mom would date for a while, then he'd hit her, and she'd leave, but she always came back. They got married when I was twelve, and Saul was sixteen. That's when—"

Her voice cracked. She cleared her throat again and looked down at her hands.

"When what?" Jeremiah pressed.

"He... started coming into my room at night, and..."

Eva's voice broke. The room went cold and quiet.

Darius's mouth fell open, and an angry bubble broiled in his stomach. Jeremiah seemed equally disconcerted. His professionalism faded for a moment, his eyes widened and jaw dropped. Eva looked up to the TAC director with a strong, resolute expression on her face, but Darius could see the cracks forming. Her lower lip quivered. A brush of tears built up behind her eyelashes.

Two firm, half-gloved hands came down on Eva's shoulders. Darius glanced up to Thorn. She'd been so quiet that he'd almost forgotten she was there. Her mouth was set, her brows furrowed, but she said nothing. Eva took a deep breath, used her ring fingers to wipe the tears from the corners of her eyes, and kept going.

"It went on for a year, I think," Eva said. Thorn removed her hands, but she stayed close. As Eva spoke, Thorn watched her with furious compassion. "I can't really remember. He was careful about it—only when Mom worked late, and Saul wasn't home. But Saul could tell something was wrong. One night, I begged him not to go to baseball practice. I cried so hard I threw up. He went anyway but then felt guilty. He came home early and caught Luis in my room."

"What did he do?" Darius asked. His voice felt foreign to him—strangled with an anger he was trying to hold in, to not burden Eva with it—but he had to know.

"He beat the shit out of him," she said. "Took his bat and hit him until he quit moving. Our neighbor heard Luis screaming and called the cops, so we ran. I don't know if he was alive. I don't really care, either."

Darius reached for her hand again, and she dipped her fingers into his palm.

"Did you ever see your mother again?" Jeremiah asked.

"No," Eva said. "After that, we made do by stealing what we needed. We never got caught—at least, never got arrested. A couple of times, employees would chase us out, but that's it. About eight years later, we met Darius." She squeezed his hand.

"And there were no other incidents after that?" Jeremiah asked.

"None," Eva said.

Jeremiah nodded and turned back to his computer. "All right. I'm sending this report to Intelligence," he said, glancing up at Thorn and giving her a nod of acknowledgment, "as well as Security. As weird as this is going to sound, it's a little comforting to know there are a few incidents this article could be about. Maybe it has nothing to do with the Sins after all. We should know soon." The Tactical director's stern face broke into a supportive smile as he picked up the printout and handed it to Eva over the desk. "And either way, we will do everything in our power to bring your brother home."

Darius and Eva thanked him as they got to their feet and made their way out. Thorn walked around them and approached Jeremiah's desk. She didn't meet Darius's eyes as she did so. Just as Thorn sat down, Darius closed the door to the office behind them.

He and Eva stood alone in the hallway for a few quiet moments. Eva took a deep breath and tried to smile. It made Darius's heart give a little flip in his chest, and he put an arm around her shoulders.

"Let's get something to eat, yeah?" he said.

She nodded.

A few minutes later, they were sitting at a table toward the edge of the courtyard. It was a little early for dinner, and the room was mostly empty. The high, concrete ceilings echoed with quiet footsteps and voices as Darius set a glass of water and plate of pasta down in front of Eva. She didn't acknowledge him. She'd placed the paper out over the table, and she stared down at Saul's face.

Darius sat down across from her and set his dinner to the side, too. He reached over the *Times* printout and held his hands out. Eva looked up at him, her eyes glistening, and laid her fingers into his palms.

"Are you okay?" Darius asked her.

It was a stupid question. He knew it. It felt hollow and flat, but he felt like he needed to say *something* to acknowledge the old wounds Eva had just torn open.

She sniffed and nodded, but a few new tears streamed down her face. She pulled her hands back and wiped them away with the pads of her fingers. "Yeah," she said. "But now we know someone is looking for Saul. Someone other than us. I've got to find him first. I *have* to."

Darius gave her a soft smile. He'd always known she and Saul had been through a lot, but he hadn't imagined *this*. All he wanted to do was reach out, wrap his arms around her, and tell her they'd find him—that everything would be okay.

He opened his mouth to say as much, but then a peculiar sensation neared the courtyard. That magnetic pull. Darius glanced over his shoulder to see Nicholas Wolfe coming out from the west wing of bedrooms. His blonde hair was styled back from his face, and his suit had been replaced by the same standard Martyr clothing Darius had been provided with when he'd first arrived. Drab. Gray. Uniform. It looked strange on Nicholas—a harsh conflict to the sharp attire he'd had when Darius had met him.

Nicholas hit the courtyard and paused. His bright eyes scanned the vast, empty area and landed on Darius. As soon as they made contact, Nicholas came right toward him.

While Darius had grown accustomed to feeling normal people around the Underground, having a Virtue here was strange, unfamiliar, and distracting. When he was in a more central part of the complex, he could almost always sense Nicholas's presence. At night, he could tell when Nicholas was laying in his quarters two hallways away or if he was in the break room.

That's where Nicholas spent most of his time, watching the news, browsing the Internet on the community computers, and refusing any request from Alan to talk.

"Hey."

Nicholas didn't ask if it was okay to sit with them. He

just pulled up a chair and straddled it backward, facing the table. As he lowered himself down, he held a hand out to Eva. She hesitated but shook it all the same.

"You must be Eva," Nicholas said. He didn't introduce himself, and he thrust a thumb in Darius's direction. "This guy told me a lot about you on the trip out here."

Eva nodded. "Good things, I hope." She raised her eyebrows at Darius, and he smiled.

"Glowing," Nicholas said. The corners of his mouth moved, like he was considering a smile but never quite made it.

"How are you adjusting?" Darius asked. Nicholas turned to look at him and furrowed his brow.

"Oh, great," he said. Sarcasm flooded the words and made them heavy. "Just great. I've been declared dead, so that's fun. I guess the Sins lit up the Davenport before they left, and over fifty people burned to death. They're saying I was one of them. Real cool reading the interview they did with my dad. Great to see he's still pretending we had a 'close' relationship. Oh, and there was also my obituary. Is this place behind that?"

He gestured widely around the room. Darius frowned.

"I don't think so," he said, and he passed Eva a look. All she could do was shrug. "Holly's just been removing the evidence of our activity in Spokane—"

"So they *do* manipulate the media," Nicholas said, and his eyes narrowed even further. "I thought they must because I can't find *anything* about what really happened out there. There was a video of that Rose woman killing Steve Munchin, the guard from the Davenport. Breaking his neck. She didn't have to do that, right?"

"What do you mean?" Darius asked.

"You told me this 'Influence' stuff could be taken out with pain, right? So she didn't have to kill Steve?"

Darius's mouth fell open. "It's not that cut and dry—"

"Huh…" Nicholas bit his lower lip before he shook his head. "Doesn't matter anymore, I guess, and the video seems to have disappeared. I can't find it anywhere…"

He watched Darius with dark, suspicious eyes.

"We do what we can to keep a low profile," Darius said, "but that's *it*. They wouldn't kill you in the media. Not without your permission."

"Uh-huh…" Nicholas sat up a little bit straighter. "Right. Well, there's plenty of *other* shit they're willing to do without permission."

Darius took a deep breath. Eva glared at the side of Nicholas's handsome face.

"I also noticed," Nicholas went on. He reached into the pocket of his sweatpants, drew out a cellphone, and placed it down on top of the paper on the table—right over Saul's face. Eva's eyes grew darker. Nicholas didn't see that. His attention was focused solely on Darius now. "My phone doesn't work, and the guest access on the Internet is restricted. I can't even get into my email—not that it matters, since I'm dead."

It definitely seemed to matter. Nicholas's mouth was set into a deep frown. Darius squared his shoulders and sat up straighter in his chair.

"I told you security measures were tight."

"Too tight," Nicholas said. "I have a *guard?*"

He pointed over his shoulder to a big, burly man with buzzed-short hair. Conrad Carter. He'd just sat down and was absently scrolling through his phone, but Darius knew it was a ruse. Conrad was part of the Tactical Unit, and he'd been assigned to watch Nicholas. Additional TAC members were also posted at every exit, just in case he tried to leave.

Like Eva had.

"When you told me about this place," Nicholas said hotly. "I didn't realize it was a *prison*."

"It's not a prison," Darius started, but Nicholas didn't let him finish.

"The locked doors and armed guards are standard protocol, huh?"

"The locks and guards are for *you*."

Eva said the words quietly, barely loud enough for Darius to hear them, but they were still crystal clear. Nicholas seemed taken aback. His eyebrows shot up as Eva kept talking.

"You're being a fucking moron."

He shook his head. "Excuse me?"

"I've been where you are," Eva said. "I didn't trust the Martyrs, so I left before I was Programmed, and you know what it got me? I got *stabbed*. I almost died. The Sins had me, and if Thorn hadn't shown up, they'd have found this place. Now they're probably looking for my brother—because I was *stupid*."

With the back of her hand, she swept Nicholas's phone off the table and pointed at Saul's face. His cell clattered to the concrete tile.

"Hey!" Nicholas dove down and grabbed it. The glass screen had shattered. Spiderweb cracks reached out from the corner. "What the fuck is your problem?"

"*You* are my problem," Eva hissed. "You're acting like a victim, but you're just a jerk. You're not Programmed, and the Sins know you're a Virtue. Wrath and Lust have seen your face. They'll have people looking for you, and they'll find you. I didn't understand what was at stake when I left. *You do*. You're going to get people killed, you *selfish pendejo*."

Then Eva got to her feet, grabbed the printout, and stormed out of the courtyard. Darius rose to follow her, but he paused and looked down at Nicholas first. Nicholas stared after Eva, dumbstruck and furious. White fingers held tight around his broken phone.

"As soon as you're Programmed, you're free to go," Darius said. "No more locks. No more guards. You can just leave. Alan would probably even pay to relocate you. He offered it to me, and he probably will to you, too, if you'd talk to him. But even if he *would* relocate you, I don't think you'd want to go."

Nicholas looked back up to him. His eyes were narrow, his nostrils flared, but there was something familiar in the way he watched Darius. That was the thing about being a Virtue. Even before he'd known what he was, before he'd accepted the responsibilities that came with it, Darius had *known* his place was here. With the Martyrs. Fighting this war.

He was banking on Nicholas feeling the same—even if he hated it.

———

The air was warm. Humid. The scent of chlorine filled his nose; the dead, echoing sound of an empty tile room, his ears. Darius sat cross-legged on the far wall, nothing but a stagnant pool between him and the doors to the locker rooms. He straightened his back, rested his hands, palm up, on his knees, and took a deep breath.

One... two... three... four...

He held the air in and focused on nothing but the sensation of his lungs being full. The stretch across his chest. His shoulder blades pulled, just slightly, apart. Then, he slowly breathed out.

One... two... three... four...

Months ago, Darius had stumbled upon this room. It had become his favorite place to meditate.

Since joining the Martyrs, Darius had picked up a handful of healthy habits to keep him sane. In the mornings, he ran a couple of miles on the treadmill. It wasn't as refreshing as running outside, but it was better than nothing. Twice a week, he and Chris did weight routines. Like Thorn, she was stronger than he was, but Darius was quickly catching up.

And every single night, Darius came here, and he meditated alone.

Thorn initially taught him meditation techniques to block out Direct Influence. Before he'd Initiated his Virtue, he'd made the mistake of letting Wrath in, and her Influence on him had almost cost him his life. Now, though, meditation was a comfort that stopped his head from spinning.

After the rough day he'd had, his brain was wound tight, worrying about the future—and his lack of one.

Usually, it didn't upset him. Darius had come to terms with dying to destroy Envy months ago. He wasn't happy about it, but he wasn't really sad, either. The necessity and value in the act were clear, and in some ways, empowering. While the thought of *dying* didn't upset him, he hated thinking about the things he'd miss out on and the people he'd leave behind.

Like Eva.

His heart gave a painful lurch.

Listening to her relive her childhood traumas, watching the wounds of Saul's loss reopen, had been hard for Darius. He felt so *useless*. All he wanted to do was hold her close and tell her that, no matter what, he'd always be there for her...

But he couldn't. Darius couldn't make those kinds of promises.

He was going to die, and Eva would be alone.

Damn it! His mind had wandered. Darius rolled his shoulders, stretched his neck from side to side, and started his breathing exercises again.

In for one... two... three... four...

Hold.

And out for one... two... three... four...

If they could find Saul, though, Eva would be okay. Maybe they'd find more than just Saul. The article hadn't mentioned Juniper or Lindsay, but they'd all disappeared together. If the Martyrs could find all of them, Eva could have a family again, and she wouldn't ever be—

"Damn it," Darius swore, and he ran his hands over his face.

"What are you doing?"

Darius jumped so hard at the sound of Thorn's voice he slammed his head on the concrete wall behind him. He groaned and peeked one eye open.

Thorn stood in the door to the women's locker room,

wearing a sleek, black swimsuit, her dark hair pulled back into a tight ponytail. She propped her arms on her hips as she watched Darius from across the pool. He just stared back, surprised.

He'd never been interrupted here before.

"Meditating," he said with a wince. His voice echoed across the tile room, making even quiet words loud and clear. "Or trying to."

Thorn frowned and walked toward him. He noticed a rubber swim cap in her left hand, and her forearm was bare. The thick scars looked searing white in the bright, fluorescent lights overhead. Thorn took him in for a moment; her half-empty eyes glanced at his bare feet, at the towel under his legs, and up to his face.

"Why *here*?"

Then she gestured around the pool room. Darius chuckled.

"Because it's always empty," he said, and he didn't just mean there were no *people* here. It was far enough away from the rest of the Underground he could only sense others' warm energy when they were in the locker rooms or the gym. This late at night, it was rarely a problem. For thirty beautiful minutes, he got to exist alone.

Except today.

"Ah," Thorn said. "I'll come back later." There was an awkwardness to her tone—the kind of awkwardness brought to life from unresolved conflict and unsaid words. She started to turn away, but Darius jumped to his feet.

"No, it's fine," he said, and he let out a short, uncomfortable laugh. "It wasn't working anyway. My brain's too... I don't know. Wired."

Thorn paused and watched him. He still wasn't used to the way she seemed to laser focus in whenever the two of them spoke. It felt a little more pointed today. Everything with Thorn had felt more pointed lately. Darius found himself wishing he could go back to their time at Teresa Solomon's estate. He knew Thorn had been miserable, but at least it had felt like they were in it together.

Now they were so far apart.

At last, Thorn took a slow breath and turned to look at the water. "Mine, too."

"Bad day?"

"Bad *month*."

Darius gave a conceding shrug. They were only halfway through July, and they'd kicked it off with Thorn getting blown up. Since then, they'd run into the Sins across the country, lost a Martyr, and were now facing the impossible task of dealing with a stubborn, powerful Virtue. The whole Underground was on edge.

"Yeah," Darius said. "It's been hard."

Thorn simply nodded, pulled her swim cap out, and began to stretch it over her head. Darius watched as she deftly tucked her long, black hair neatly away with practiced skill.

"How's Eva?" Thorn asked.

He sighed and rubbed his eyes. "She's okay. I think. She didn't want to talk about it much."

"I can't blame her," Thorn said. "She probably spent most of her life trying to forget it ever happened." Then she sighed and, almost without thinking, touched her fingers to the *Peccostium* beneath her wrist. Her eyes stared out at the far wall, but they were unfocused. Distant.

Darius glanced down at the mark of the Sins and the tangled web of scars around it. When he looked back up to Thorn, she caught his eye and let go of her arm.

"You okay?" he asked.

"Yes."

And that was it. Thorn didn't say anything else. Instead, she cleared her throat and made her way to the narrow edge of the pool. Darius watched her slip into the shallow end with the same lithe power she brought to everything she did. In the empty, echoing chamber, the light, quiet sloshing of water moving away from Thorn's body and lapping lazily at the edges sounded robust and melodic. She glanced up at Darius from across the room.

"You're welcome to stay," she said.

Darius shook his head. "Thanks, but I'll leave you to it. I should go to bed anyway."

She nodded, and as Darius began to make his way around the edge of the pool, she dipped her head into the water and pushed off the wall. When Darius got to the door, though, he turned and watched her. She was strong and elegant. Every other stroke, her left arm broke the surface, and the stark, black *Peccostium* peered out at him.

Then he quietly stepped into the locker room, exited into the gym, and walked out to the courtyard.

Nicholas was waiting for him.

Darius had known he was nearby. That Virtuous pull was the only thing Darius couldn't escape from at the back of the pool room. He was surprised, though, to see him sitting at a nearby table, watching the gym doors. As soon as Darius stepped through them, Nicholas got to his feet.

"Hey," he said, shoving his hands deep into his pockets. "Eva said you were meditating. I didn't want to interrupt..."

"Thanks," Darius said, but his brows furrowed curiously. "What's up?"

"I just wanted to let you know that I decided to do it. The Programming."

Darius's eyes widened. "Really? Can I ask why?"

"I won't be responsible for any more death," Nicholas said, and his mouth set into a firm line. "And because... I trust you. You were upfront with me. You're the only one who has been, so I want you there when they do it."

Darius nodded. "Absolutely. I'll talk with Alan tomorrow morning."

"Good," Nicholas said. Then he nodded and walked away. Darius waited until he disappeared into the west wing of rooms before he turned right back around, his heart racing excitedly in his chest.

He had to tell Thorn.

CHAPTER TWELVE

The next evening, Darius sat in the front seat while Alan drove them to Staten Island, where they had reservations at one of the restaurants the Martyrs favored for Programming. Nicholas was behind Alan, staring out the window. Every so often, he threw the Martyr leader a dubious look.

"Freehold is a long way from New York," Nicholas commented as he watched a road sign fly by. "It'll take us, what, an hour? Why build your hideout so far away from the city?"

Darius glanced at Alan. He wondered if Nicholas was doing this on purpose—stating the names of the towns closest to the Underground just to prove he still could. Alan maintained the same firm composure he usually had as he answered.

"For security. Establishing our base further from the Sins' hot spots makes it more difficult for them to track us. It also provides us with more opportunities to lose them in the rare cases they have found and followed our vehicles. That, along with Programming, has kept the Martyrs safe for over a hundred years."

"Over a hundred?" Nicholas nodded. His arms were crossed over his chest, and his baby blue eyes drove into the back of Alan's head. "That's pretty vague. When exactly did you build the Underground?"

"Construction was completed in the late 1950s," Alan went on. Again, his tone was level and his face impassive.

"How'd you pay for it?"

"One of the other founding members of the Martyrs, a Forgotten Sin named Judith Gladstone, had built up an impressive wealth."

"What, she used to be Greed?"

"Yes," Alan said. That was the first hint of annoyance. His lips twitched downward.

"What happened to her?" Nicholas asked.

"She was killed."

"By whom?"

Alan cast a dark look at Nicholas in the rearview mirror. "Who do you *think*, Mr. Wolfe?"

"For all I know, it could've been you," Nicholas said. He didn't look away from Alan—didn't even blink. Darius's breath caught in his throat. Maybe this had been a mistake. He should have asked John to drive them into town.

But Alan just gave a single, cold chuckle. "I assure you, Mr. Wolfe, digging into my past will provide you with plenty of reasons to dislike me, as you seem so determined to do. There is no need to fabricate a murder."

"Really?" Nicholas said, and he sat up a little straighter. "What kind of things are you hiding in your past, Mr. Blaine?"

The words "Mr. Blaine" came out almost mockingly. The muscles all along Darius's shoulders tightened.

The sooner they got this over with, the better.

"I was once Wrath," Alan said. It was short. Curt. "Use your imagination."

That carried a tone of finality, and Darius knew Alan was done with this conversation. Darius wasn't sure Nicholas was going to catch the hint—or if he did, if he'd follow it.

But to his great relief, Nicholas decided not to press the subject. Instead, he changed it.

"So, where's Rose?" he asked a couple of minutes later.

"She will meet us at the restaurant," Alan said.

"Do you always treat people to fancy dinners before you brainwash them?"

"Nicholas," Darius started, but Alan held his hand up.

"He has a right to ask questions," he said, and he passed Darius a slow, calm look before he focused on the road again and called back to Nicholas. "When I Program new members of my team, I typically do take them out to dinner. There are a handful of areas in town that are well lit and well monitored. It ensures we can safely perform the Programming and get out before the Sins show up."

"You mean before Wrath shows up," Nicholas said.

"Yes. I do."

"Because you and Wrath are still connected," Nicholas pressed.

"We are."

"Mmhmm."

Nicholas stopped talking after that. He cast Darius a look, and Darius sighed. Maybe he could convince Alan to skip the whole dinner thing and just program Nicholas on the road. Otherwise, the next couple of hours were going to be exhausting.

⎯⎯⎯⎯⎯⎯

They met outside a little, high-end bistro in Northern Staten Island, which had exploded in the last decade once the subway connecting it to mainland New York had been completed. Apartment buildings and businesses had popped up, filling this once-isolated suburb with renewed life and activity.

Alan had the car valeted, and as they walked up the sidewalk, Darius saw Thorn standing by the entrance, smoking a cigarette. The sun had already set behind tall buildings to the west, and while the sky directly above was still bright blue, Thorn and the rest of the street were cast in soft shadow. When she saw them, her cold, dark eyes looked Nicholas over, and they narrowed.

Thorn had been just as surprised—and relieved—as Darius had been when he'd run back to tell her Nicholas agreed to be Programmed. She'd also been suspicious. Maybe Nicholas was just going to use the opportunity for a chance to escape into the city, she had said.

Now that they were here, Darius saw just how easy it would be to do. The sidewalks were filled with people, their warmth pushing on him from all sides. If Nicholas slipped into the throng of hurried, busy New Yorkers, what could Darius do to stop him?

Probably not much, but he had no doubt Thorn could chase Nicholas down and tackle him into the pavement before he made it ten yards. Based on the way Nicholas was watching her, he thought that was true, too. His jaw was set, and his fists clenched at his sides.

"Good evening," Alan said to his niece. Thorn nodded. She didn't take her eyes off of Nicholas.

"Our table is ready," she said tersely.

They walked in the front of the bistro and followed a hostess through the busy interior to a gated back patio. Bright string lights hung over their heads, draping down low enough that Alan had to duck a couple of times to avoid them. Their table was in the far back, along a waist-high, wrought-iron fence. On the other side, a row of bushes separated them from a narrow, gentrified alleyway paved with bricks and lined with fancy pole lights. People walked past, talking and laughing in the warm, summer air. Darius let Nicholas into the table first and sat beside him, across from Alan and Thorn.

"So... what now?" Nicholas looked from Alan to Thorn to Darius. "You just... do your Sin magic?"

Thorn's eyebrows twitched.

"In time," Alan said with a short nod. He had his hands folded politely on the table in front of him. "I thought you may have more questions about the process. I want to make sure you are as comfortable with it as possible before we proceed."

"Oh, now you're worried about my comfort?" Nicholas said.

"What happened before was a mis—"

"Don't tell me it was a mistake," Nicholas interrupted. Alan quietly closed his mouth, but his eyebrows raised, and he watched as the Virtue went on. "The only reason you feel bad about it is because you got caught."

"I don't feel bad about it," Thorn said. Nicholas glared at her. Thorn's lips thinned out, and she glared back until Alan spoke.

"It was a *misunderstanding*," the Martyr leader said. "I wasn't aware that you already knew so much about us and our organization. If I had, I assure you, we would have had more of a conversation beforehand."

As Alan finished, Thorn's fiery attention shifted away from Nicholas for the first time and landed squarely on Darius. He felt heat rise to his cheeks, but he just gave her a small, sheepish shrug.

"You'll understand if I don't believe that," Nicholas said. He leaned back in his chair and crossed his arms.

Alan raised one brow high on his head. "My first priority is not convincing you of my motives, Mr. Wolfe. It is keeping the men and women who have entrusted their lives to me as safe as I can. Programming is part of that. I am sorry for how this situation has played out, but frankly, I don't care what you believe."

Nicholas's eyes widened, and he opened his mouth to interject, but Alan didn't let him. His voice grew louder—not loud enough to draw attention from neighboring tables but enough to stop Nicholas in his tracks.

"I don't care if you decide to leave the Martyrs and never set foot in the Underground again. I don't care if you never Initiate your Virtue. I don't care if you *die,* as long as you do not take any of my people down with you when you do."

Darius was dumbstruck. He'd never heard Alan talk like

that before. Nicholas scoffed and leaned across the table. His nostrils flared furiously.

"Is that supposed to make me want to go through with this?" he growled.

"You seem to be under the impression this is about *you*," Alan said. "But this has *never* been about you. It is about the people who could die because of you.

"Now." Alan cleared his throat and unfolded his napkin. He laid the white cloth across his lap. "Do you have any questions about the *process* for Programming, or would you like to disparage me further?"

For the first time since coming to the Underground, Nicholas seemed to have lost his voice. Darius hadn't realized he'd been breathing so shallow until he finally took in a gulp of air. He glanced across the table at Thorn to see her rage had softened a bit. A very subtle, little smirk curled up one half of her mouth as she opened her menu and looked down at the selection.

Darius couldn't decide if this was going well or if it was a total disaster.

Nicholas was silent for a few more seconds before he started asking real questions about Programming. While they ordered their food and Thorn got a scotch, he asked about the process and if Virtues were capable of it, as well. Darius and Alan told him about their failed experiment and explained the difference between Influence and the specialty of Programming. Then Nicholas wanted details on what had happened to Jacob Locke. Alan laid out the same tragic story Thorn had told Darius and reiterated how that kind of side effect had never been seen with the simple Programming they were here to perform today.

Then Nicholas wanted to know how permanent it was.

"Programming can be unwritten," Alan said. "Though, as Jacob Locke's situation indicates, it is very challenging. If you know the basic rules, you can use the same technique to 'erase' them, for lack of a better term. Programming also fades when the host who did the Programming is killed. It doesn't happen immediately, but eventually, it disappears."

"I wonder… can Virtues unwrite Programs the Sins have installed?" Nicholas thought aloud, and he glanced to Darius with a curious look. All Darius could do was shrug.

Alan nodded thoughtfully. "I suppose it *is* possible. Not only would you need to know the original rules, but you would need to get close enough to maintain physical contact while you removed them. Even Thorn and I struggle with rewriting or unwriting Programming that isn't our own."

"So, what do you do when you run into people who have been Programmed?" Nicholas asked.

"Knock them out," Thorn said shortly.

Nicholas frowned. "Oh, you don't just kill them? Sneak up behind them and snap their necks?"

Thorn raised her eyebrows and took a sip of her scotch. Before she placed the glass back on the table, her cell rang. Alan's and Darius's both blipped with alerts. As Thorn answered the call, Darius glanced down at his screen. His heart sank. It was from Holly:

"Sloth ITA. Sending Backup."

"Where is he?" Thorn said into the phone.

All at once, the atmosphere at the table shifted. Thorn pulled a set of wireless headphones out of her satchel and quickly put them on. Sparkie slipped out of the bag, crawled under the table, beneath the fence, and disappeared into the bushes just on the other side. Alan turned to Nicholas and said, "It looks like we won't get to finish our meal. Mr. Wolfe, if you are ready, we must set the Program *now*."

"What's going on?" Nicholas asked.

"Lead me to him," Thorn said, speaking to Holly as she got to her feet. She slipped her phone into her thigh pocket and tied her hair back. Then she quietly grabbed a handgun out of her satchel and tossed the bag to Darius. He barely managed to catch it. "Get out of here," she said as she hid the gun behind her waistband and the hem of her shirt. "*Now*."

"A Sin is in the area," Alan said to Nicholas. "Are you

ready for the Programming? You *must* lower your guard and let me in."

Nicholas's eyes went wide, and he nodded.

Thorn disappeared. A handful of patrons whispered and stared after her as she leapt over the wrought-iron fence and into the alleyway. Nicholas closed his eyes, and Alan watched him intently for a few moments. Darius got to his feet, flinging Thorn's bag around his shoulder. He craned his neck to see if he could spot her down the alley, but she had vanished into the bustling crowd of people.

"There," Alan said. Nicholas rubbed his temples, and Alan got to his feet. "Now, we should—"

An explosion rocked the street. People screamed. All around them, men and women got to their feet, abandoning their belongings as they rushed into the restaurant. Alan's face went stark white, and his eyes were round with terror. He leapt over the fence and called Thorn's name into the panic. His voice was rough. His calm demeanor, gone. He turned to Darius and Nicholas.

"Get to the car," he yelled over the screaming, the blaring car alarms, and the sound of hundreds of feet pounding against the asphalt.

Then he took off. His tall, black form cut like a knife through the crowd until he was overtaken by smoke and dust.

Nicholas and Darius exchanged a horrified look. The minute their eyes met, Darius knew they were *not* going back to the car. Together, they nodded and jumped over the fence, too.

Pedestrians rushed down the alley, pushing against them as they fought through the flow of frantic, screaming people. The air filled with sound and dust. Smoke clouded Darius's nostrils and stung his eyes. He was surrounded by oppressive heat—the massive energy force of hundreds of bodies, hot and humid around him.

That was his first indication that the flood of people was thinning. It got cooler. Then quieter. Shoulders stopped bumping him. Hands stopped shoving him to the side. Finally, Darius could see what was happening.

A building face had been blown to pieces. Debris littered the ground. Hunks of brick, beams of sharp steel, and bodies—

People groaned and cried or laid motionless. Little, warm lights of human life flickered out around him. As dust settled and smoke cleared, bright, red blood highlighted the mayhem. It streaked across the ground—pooled under dead and dying people. Men and women. Mothers, fathers, and children...

"Look for Thorn," he said to Nicholas, and he knelt by a teen girl crumbled on the sidewalk.

"My mom!" the girl cried. "Where's my mom?"

"It's okay," Darius said. He glanced over her shoulder and saw the cold, lifeless body of a woman ten feet away. His heart clenched. Then he gently lifted the girl's blouse to get a look at the injury. Her stomach was torn open—ripped from belly button to hip. Blood poured from the wound and soaked her clothing.

"It's not that bad," Darius lied, and he placed his hands over the gash. Nicholas stared as power surged into Darius's fingertips and flowed into the girl.

She gasped. "What are you doing to me?"

A tickle ran up the back of Darius's neck, and he swallowed hard. He shifted gears—felt the boundary between their consciousnesses and gave a little Influence, too.

"I'm a medic," he said. "You're hurt. Get some rest."

The girl's eyelids fluttered, and she drifted off. As Darius released her, Nicholas yelped above him.

"Darius, look!"

Darius glanced up—through the carnage, through more people moaning, crying, and bleeding out on the street—to see the horrifying shape of a man rushing toward them. Darius's gut twisted.

Half of the man's face was charred, and one bright, round eye had been blown from a black socket. His skin looked like melted wax, and his hair stuck to the misshapen remains of his scalp like a nest of blackened knots. As he moved, his left arm drooped down at his side, swinging loosely. When he saw Darius and Nicholas, he let out a strangled cry.

"Should we help him?" Nicholas said, but the words were strained. Darius's anxiety roared, and Alan's voice screamed over them.

"Get down!"

The man's one good eye went wide, and he abruptly changed direction. He sprinted through the chaos and disappeared as Alan barreled after him.

"Find Thorn!" he shouted over his shoulder before he was overtaken by smoke, too.

"Was that...?" Nicholas began to ask.

"I think so," Darius said, his heart pounding hard. He turned back to the wreckage. "Come on!"

Sirens sounded in the distance. As they moved, people groaned and begged for help. Darius knew he needed to find Thorn, but couldn't let them suffer. He stopped occasionally, trying to heal as many as possible, but there were simply too many, and he didn't have time. So he ignored those with minor wounds, helped others enough to where they would survive until first responders arrived, and used his Influence to give the dying a sense of peace and calm before the end. More human lives flickered out around him. Every one of them made Darius's chest feel heavy.

The closer they got to the epicenter of the explosion, the more devastating the damage became and the fewer survivors they found. Body parts and torn flesh lay around them. Darius felt a familiar wave of nausea, and he bit it down.

Nicholas didn't. Darius heard the other Virtue vomit behind him.

Then something chirped.

Darius looked down. Sparkie was clawing his way toward him through shards of brick and broken glass. The lizard was filthy, his smooth, blue scales coated in gray dust.

Darius scooped him up. The Familiar winced, but seeing him filled Darius with a surge of relief.

A scrape of metal. "Darius!" Someone screamed his name, muffled and desperate. He turned to see the blown-off hood of a car shifting on the sidewalk. They called him again. Darius opened Thorn's satchel and gently tilted Sparkie into it before making his way toward the sound. Nicholas followed after him.

Together, they moved the giant, dented piece of metal to find Thorn sprawled beneath it. The blood drained from Darius's face.

She looked awful. Her complexion was sickly pale, and heavy, dark circles filled in beneath her eyes. Her legs were in a horrible state—pants had been shredded, blown half-way up to her mid-thigh, and her calves were bloody, mangled masses of sinew and flesh. She tried to sit up and swore. Her arms shook beneath her.

"What the fuck are you doing here?" she snarled, but a hint of gratitude sneaked into her tone.

Darius knelt beside her. "Saving your life."

He hoisted her arm over his shoulder. Her skin was slick and clammy in the sweltering heat. Thorn let out a harsh, gasping cry as Darius's fingers closed around her wrist and the *Peccostium* hidden beneath her glove. He quickly adjusted his grip and moved to lift her, but the muscles in her legs were weak. Damn it, the healing had taken a lot out of him.

"Nicholas," he said, "help me!"

The other Virtue came to Thorn's right side. His face was white as death beneath his freckles as he grabbed her other arm and pulled it over his shoulders, too. They dragged her from the wreckage. She tried to put weight on her feet and stand, but her legs crumpled beneath her. She cried out. The sound was sharp and piercing.

"We've got you," Darius said.

"Where's Witham?" Thorn asked.

"He ran off," Darius said. "Alan went after him."

They made their way back the way they'd come. The

sirens were closer. Darius was shocked to find the alley empty—no lingerers, no helpers, nobody trying to film the disaster. Even in the midst of chaos, the streets of New York City were never this empty.

Nicholas noticed the same thing. He looked around. "Where is everybody?" he murmured.

"Alan's pushing them away," Thorn bit through a wince, and she jutted her chin forward.

The two Virtues looked up to see Alan rushing down the alley toward them. His face was white, his hands covered in blood, and when his eyes landed on Thorn, they widened.

"Did you get him?" Darius asked.

Alan shook his head. "No. We must leave." His voice was hoarse, and he lifted Thorn off of Darius and Nicholas as though she were as light as a child. She cried out again. The sound of her pain made Darius's stomach twist and his chest constrict. "Wrath will be coming," Alan went on. He hurried down the alley. "Go. Quickly, now. Quickly."

Then he led the way down the street—still abandoned—back to the valet. The attendant had left his post, but Alan dug through the podium with shaking fingers until he found the keys. Then, they were off. While Alan drove them southbound through the city, and Nicholas sat, pale and stiff, in the front seat beside him, Thorn laid in the far back and groaned.

"That little *fucker*," she hissed through clenched teeth. "I'm going to rip him to *fucking shreds*."

Darius turned around and looked her over. Her lips were turning blue, and she'd begun to shake as the shock set in. Darius unbuckled himself and crawled back to her. He didn't have much—no jacket or blanket—so he wrapped his arms around her shoulders and held her as close to his body as he could. Thorn's skin was staunched in sticky, cold sweat. Despite Darius's attempts, she shivered violently. One pale hand reached around, gripped overtop his, and held it tight. Her fingernails were blue, too. Darius's stomach flipped.

"Alan, hurry," Darius called out to the front of the car.

The SUV surged forward. Darius held Thorn closer. He felt disassociated from himself, like his muscles and brain weren't coordinating. While his body seemed to move in slow motion, his mind was on fire with questions and fears...

Because Gregory Witham had just tried to assassinate Thorn *again*.

Darius could hardly watch the screen.

He sat in the conference room with the Martyr leadership, Holly, and Nicholas. While Thorn had been rushed into surgery, Alan had called them together to figure out what the hell they were going to do next.

Holly played footage of the attack on a large, drop-down display at the far end of the room. It was gruesome, and Darius's stomach churned. Seeing it in real-time was somehow more shocking than the aftermath. There had been a handful of people so close to the blast site that they were blown to pieces immediately. Dozens more, caught further away, left to die slowly. Darius recognized a few faces— some he had healed and others he'd been too late to help.

As Holly rewound the tape, Darius shook his head and looked down at his feet. Nicholas was sitting beside him. The color still hadn't returned to his face, and he stared at the screen with a sickened, blanched expression.

"*Fuck...*" Mackenzie murmured as her eyebrows raised high into her vibrant, blue bangs. She hadn't taken a seat and was instead standing behind her chair, gripping its back with stiff, white fingers. Lina raised her hand over her mouth, gray eyes wide and tearful.

"Now," Holly said. She pushed her thick-rimmed glasses up the bridge of her nose as she started the video over again, at a slower speed. "You can see here... this is Sloth." She had a laser pointer in one hand, and she used it to indicate the bottom of the screen. Through the busy crowd of New York residents, a figure hunched in a nearby stoop. His face wasn't visible, but beneath the black beanie, long strings of oily, blonde hair fell down his shoulders. He looked nothing like the gnarled mess Darius had seen.

"In about three seconds, he moves to face the camera," Holly continued. The hunched figure turned. His thin, sallow face stared out at the crowd, in the general direction where Darius, Nicholas, Thorn, and Alan had been at dinner. Holly went on. "That's when my facial recognition system caught him. In about four minutes, Thorn shows up."

Holly sped up the video and slowed it down again as Thorn entered the frame from the far-right edge.

"As soon as he saw her—basically as soon as we can even see her in the shot—he hit the detonator." Holly paused the video again and zoomed in on the image. Sloth's eyes were wide, almost manic, and he had pulled something from the pocket of his ratty, stained sweatshirt. Holly circled it a couple of times. It was a small, metal rod with a button at the top and a wire coming out the bottom. "She was about thirty feet away from him, but the bomb was *here*."

Holly zoomed out of the frame one more time and indicated a trashcan about halfway between the Sin and Thorn.

"God, don't play that part again," Abraham said, looking a little green as he covered his long face with his hands. When Holly nodded solemnly, he cleared his throat. "Do you think this was an attack against Thorn, specifically?"

"I don't know," Holly said, and she glanced around, from Alan to Jeremiah. "I doubt it was premeditated. He had no way of knowing she would be in this area, and he seemed shocked to see her. But, I mean, the woman's been blown up by Sloth *twice*. Seems hard to say it's just bad luck."

"How long had he been there?" Lina asked.

"According to the security feed, just before dawn this morning," Holly replied. "Seemed like he was just hanging out, trying to keep his head low."

Jeremiah's brows fell low over his eyes, and his full lips

turned into a deep frown. He looked to Alan. "Are you ready to seriously consider that the Sins may finally be sick of keeping Thorn around?" he asked. Alan turned to consider Jeremiah with a dark—and maybe scared—glean in his eyes.

Nicholas frowned, and he leaned in over the table. "What does that mean, 'sick of keeping her around?'"

"It's Wrath," Darius said as he rubbed his eyes with his fingertips. He'd washed up as soon as they'd gotten back, but his hands still smelled like dust and burned plastic. "She's had standing orders not to kill Thorn for decades."

"What?" Nicholas seemed shocked. "Why?"

"All that crazy bitch cares about is revenge," Mackenzie said. The Irishwoman's eyes seemed duller as she crossed her arms, and her fingers tapped erratically on her bicep. She didn't make eye contact with anyone around the room; she just stared at the screen. At Sloth. "Wrath *hates* Thorn—and loves that she has a victim who will last as long as she will."

"So she won't let the other Sins kill her?" Nicholas asked.

"No," Abraham said, "and none of them have been stupid enough to try."

"That's not entirely true," Alan said. Abraham, Darius, and Nicholas looked up to him, and Alan continued. "There have been occasional instances of a Sin going rogue and attempting to kill Thorn despite Autumn Hunt's orders."

"Sloth?" Lina asked, her fingers anxiously toying with a silver pendant at her throat.

Alan shook his head. "Pride once. Gluttony most recently. Clearly, they were not successful. Wrath even killed Pride's host at the time to make her stance on the matter very clear."

"Well, she's trying to kill Sloth this time," Holly said. She turned toward the table and looked over to Alan. Even though she was standing and Alan was seated, she was so short that he was still almost as tall as she was. "Wrath has been in the Bronx a lot lately. That's Witham's usual neighborhood. If she's hunting him down, it gives more credit to the theory that he's trying to murder Thorn, and Wrath isn't happy about it."

"Good," Mackenzie said coldly. She looked away from the screen for the first time. Her mouth was set into a grim line as she turned to Alan. "With both Wrath *and* Thorn out for his head, he's bound to get caught. Son of a bitch doesn't know what's coming."

"We can hope," Alan said. He got to his feet and briefly wrapped a firm hand around one of Mackenzie's shoulders. She'd drawn them up, tense and rigid. At Alan's touch, she seemed to realize it. She relaxed, and he released her as he looked down the table at the rest of them again.

"Perhaps we simply have a rogue Sin situation here," Alan continued quietly. He was doing a much better job at maintaining his composure than Mackenzie was, but Darius could still see the tiny cracks in it that betrayed his worry. His wide eyes. Tight jaw. The slight pull in his voice when he spoke.

"We can't assume he's gone rogue," Jeremiah said, and all eyes in the room turned to him. He crossed his massive arms around his chest. "We can clear Hunt and figure she doesn't want Thorn dead, but we should move forward under the assumption the others are working together until proven otherwise. We can't get complacent."

"I agree," Alan said, and he steepled his fingers, pressing them against his lips. "If that is the case, we may be in for some luck. Wrath could very well kill them all. That would certainly make things easier on us for a few years."

"She'd do that?" Nicholas asked, shocked. "That weakens her side!"

"The Sins are more like allies than teammates," Lina said. "They work together, but they're all driven first and foremost by their own agendas. Sometimes, those agendas don't go hand in hand, and there's conflict."

"Thank god for that," Mackenzie grumbled, throwing herself into the empty chair beside Lina as she ran a hand through her hair. "Fingers crossed Hunt takes Sloth out."

"She might not have the opportunity to," Alan said. "He almost did it himself."

Lina shook her head. "What do you mean?"

"He was caught in the blast," Alan said. A shocked murmur rushed through the room as Holly began to speed through the video.

"I'll just fast forward through the bloody part," she murmured. "And... there."

She paused again. From here, there was no avoiding "the bloody part." Lina winced and looked down at her laced fingers again. Darius focused on the section of the frame Holly was highlighting with her laser pointer, and he tried to ignore the dead bodies littering the rest of the image.

"See this?" Holly said. "That's Sloth."

This was the figure Darius recognized. His body burned. His hair singed off. His face a blackened mess of melted flesh.

"Looks like the bomb and the detonator were wired," Holly said. "He couldn't get far enough away."

"I hope it fucking *hurt*," Mackenzie muttered. Her voice filled with a loathing Darius hadn't heard in her before. He glanced up as Lina reached over and patted the top of Mackenzie's leg with a firm, comfortable movement. Mackenzie's jaw clenched, and she took a deep breath.

"Why the hell would he wire the bomb?" Nicholas asked.

Holly shrugged. "I think he's learning," she said. "It's probably the same setup he used for the car bomb, but this time, he kept the detonator on hand. I bet he had no idea how big the blast would actually be."

"He's learning?" Nicholas asked incredulously. "Isn't he thousands of years old? How has he *not* figured out he shouldn't stand next to a bomb by now?"

"Sin memories are fragmented every time the host is lost," Alan said. "Sloth has lost its host more than any of the others—maybe more than the other six combined—

since we've been tracking it. Its memory has been damaged significantly."

"It makes him paranoid," Jeremiah said. He passed Nicholas a dark look from across the table. "And dangerous. This isn't the first time Sloth has caused this kind of damage." At that, Mackenzie glanced down at her lap and furiously picked at her cuticles.

"Well, we need to fucking stop him," Nicholas said, gesturing open-handed at the screen. "Where did he go after this?"

"I followed him south on Bay Street," Alan said, "but he managed to get away."

"Is there another video we can check?" Nicholas asked.

Holly shook her head. "No. The other three cameras I've tapped into in this area were damaged in the explosion. After he runs off-screen on this one, I lose him."

Nicholas frowned. "What about the internet?"

Holly raised a brow. "You wanna do my job?"

"Everyone has a camera on them," Nicholas went on, glaring at her. "Someone on the scene *had* to get a picture or video or *something* we can go off of."

"No one was *on* the scene," Darius said. He glanced up to Alan, and Nicholas followed his gaze. Then, Nicholas's expression darkened.

"Damnit," he said. He got to his feet and pointed at the still image of Gregory Witham's grotesque face. "If you hadn't *brainwashed* everyone, we'd have some kind of lead on this asshole!"

"There would also be photographic and video evidence of our people—"

"Why does it matter if there's '*photographic and video evidence of your people*?' This is about *saving lives*—"

"You are exactly right, and that is what I'm doing here, Mr. Wolfe," Alan snapped, cutting Nicholas off, and shattering the somber mood of the room. A tense silence fell, and Mackenzie turned to Darius. They shared a stunned look as Alan went on. His voice was quieter but no less firm.

"I used my Influence to get people to evacuate the area in order to keep both Martyrs and innocent civilians safe. We may have lost Sloth, but we have saved hundreds of others."

"*This time*," Nicholas exclaimed, and he began to pace behind the table. "What about the next time this fucker decides to blow up a street corner?"

"That is what we are trying to discuss here," Alan said, "and if you cannot keep your mouth shut, you can leave."

He and Nicholas stared at one another for a moment longer before Nicholas stormed from the room and slammed the door behind him.

The air was silent for a moment. Then Mackenzie, the sarcasm and joviality Darius was used to creeping back into her tone, said, "Anyone got any thoughts on which Virtue he is? I bet it's Chastity."

Abraham frowned. "Why Chastity?"

"Cause the only thing that can make a man that grumpy is massive sexual repression."

Darius smiled at her, and Jeremiah cleared his throat to stifle a laugh as Alan pinched the bridge of his nose. "We don't have time for this," he said. His forehead was knit into tense, angry lines. "Our next course of action should be determining the breadth of this threat. Is Thorn the target? Is Sloth working alone? These are questions we need answered. Miss Andrews." Alan turned to Holly, and she squared her shoulders. "I want an even closer eye on all of the Sins, and *find Gregory Witham.* Miss McKay." He turned toward her, as well. The lightness Mackenzie had allowed herself to have darkened again. "I know it has been a long time since you were in Sloth's company, but I want an updated report on his patterns of behavior. Anything you can remember."

Mackenzie nodded as Alan moved to give his next orders. When his back was turned, her jaw clenched together, and she swallowed hard.

"Jeremiah," Alan went on, "please establish more patrols in high-risk areas. Until we know more, Thorn must keep a lower profile in the city, perhaps not going into the city at all."

"We can't afford to keep her here," Jeremiah said. "With Wrath hunting for Witham, too, Thorn is one of our best chances at finding him."

Alan sighed and rubbed his eyes with the pads of his fingers. He looked older, more tired, than Darius was used to. "Then required check-ins and a curfew."

Abraham shook his head and ran a hand through his curly hair. "She's not going to like that…"

"I will talk with her," Alan conceded. "In the meantime, we all have work to do, or our new Virtue will be correct. More people are going to die if we do not find Sloth—*soon*."

Alan closed the meeting, and they all filtered out of the conference room. When Darius reached the waiting room outside the hospital, he found Nicholas Wolfe, standing against the wall with his arms crossed. Darius paused, and while the others moved toward the elevator, Alan turned the opposite direction and headed into the hospital without passing Nicholas a second glance. He disappeared through the double doors, and Nicholas watched him go until his dark back vanished through the windows. Then he turned to Darius.

"I want a job," he said.

Darius blinked, surprised. "Really? Well, you kind of already have one."

"This Virtue thing?" Nicholas asked. Darius nodded, and Nicholas quietly, slowly, did the same. "How do I turn it on?"

"I… god, I don't know. You just accept it."

"Haven't I done that already?" Nicholas asked.

"Clearly not. Trust me. You'd know." Darius thought back to Initiating his own Virtue and the hellish couple of days that followed. "Part of you must be resisting it still, for some reason. Do you have any idea why?"

"No," Nicholas said. He uncrossed his arms and took a deep breath. "But I have time to figure it out. Until then, what else can I do? I'm sick of sitting here. Now that I'm Programmed, I should be good to go, right?"

"Yeah," Darius said. "That's right. I'll see what I can do."

Nicholas nodded. "Good. Let me know."

He started to walk toward the elevators, and Darius rushed to catch up to him.

"You hungry?" he asked, and Nicholas glanced at him as he pressed the down button. "Seeing as we never got a chance to have dinner…"

A small smile curled up in the corner of Nicholas's mouth. Darius realized it was the first time he'd ever seen this expression on his face. It felt right on him.

"I *am* starving," Nicholas said.

So the two Virtues—the two Martyrs—headed down to the kitchen together.

CHAPTER THIRTEEN

"Damn, that Wolfe guy is *intense*."

John groaned and flopped down onto the couch beside Raquel. She and Darius were in the middle of a card game Darius didn't really understand, but Raquel had insisted on teaching him. She was winning with almost embarrassing ease, which seemed to frustrate her more than it did him. The local New York news was on in the background, and every chance they got, they ran the same story about Saul that had been in the *Times*. Darius couldn't help it—whenever Saul's face showed up on the screen, he was distracted, and Raquel had to fight to get his attention back. She tossed her cards onto the table with a sigh as John ran his hands down his face.

"Do you have any idea how many articles he found using that old Virtue's computer program?" John went on, leaning forward for emphasis. "*Five hundred and sixty-three.*"

"Well, at least he's eager," Darius said as he gathered up the cards and put them back into a neat stack.

When Nicholas had asked for a job, Darius put him in the only department he had any power over: R&D. Nicholas didn't have the training for anything else, and Mackenzie was in the unique position of needing to replace one of her

Recon members. Since Sara Park's death, John was without a partner. For the last seven days, he'd been training Nicholas for the position.

"Eager doesn't even begin to cover it," John said. "The man's an animal. He's spent at *least* ten hours a day in the R&D headquarters. I haven't found five hundred leads in my whole career."

"Are any of them viable?" Darius asked.

"I don't know." John sighed. He rested back against the couch and stared at the television screen, but his eyes weren't focused on it. "I haven't had the chance to go through them all. He's organizing them by location right now. Most are in New York, but he has pretty big piles for Pennsylvania, Vermont, and Georgia, too. I told him to focus on those three since Sara and I have been all over New York."

The timbre of John's voice faltered a bit, and his eyes darted down to his lap. Darius and Raquel shared a sad look. This was the first time Darius had heard John talk about Sara since her death. A surge of guilt welled up in his gut and made his stomach feel heavy and full.

"I'm so sorry, man," he said.

He wasn't sure what exactly he was sorry about—for not being able to heal Sara, for not paying attention to his instincts at the event, for dragging them across the country in the first place? It didn't matter. His friend was hurting, and Darius felt responsible.

But John didn't respond to that. Not really. "It's not your fault," he said as he shook his head and cleared his throat. Then he nodded toward the television. "How's Eva doing with *this* mess?"

Darius turned to look. Saul's face again. Same vague story. Saul Torres. Person of interest. Cash reward for information that led to his whereabouts.

"Frustrated," Darius said. "Scared, I think. With everything that's going on, Thorn changed her assignment. Finding Sloth is the number one priority, so Eva's being transferred to the Bronx. She's not happy about it. She wants to focus on looking for Saul."

"Of course she does," Raquel said. "I can't even imagine knowing my brother was being hunted by the Sins and not being able to do anything about it."

"Well," Darius said with a sigh, "she's trying to hold onto the hope that it's *not* the Sins. She wants to believe Luis Mendez tried to file charges or maybe Immigration is after him."

"Oh, it's the Sins."

A new voice entered the room and made the three of them turn. It was Skylar; Darius had felt her warmth walking across the courtyard toward them. She shook her head, her dangling, hoop earrings slapping against her neck as she flung a file on the table in front of him. Then she took a seat beside Raquel and grabbed the other woman's hand. Her brown eyes were cold and serious.

"That's all the information we've found about Saul Torres," Skylar said. Darius frowned and opened the folder. It was a single sheet. Somehow, he knew the *less* information they could dig up, the worse it was.

"There's nothing here," Darius said.

"Nada," Skylar said. "There's literally *no* record of him. All we could find was some old school information and that photograph." She gestured at the paper; the same old picture circulating the media was printed here, too. "It's like he didn't exist."

"What about the stepdad?" Darius asked.

"Luis Mendez is dead," Skylar said, "but not because of Saul. Eva's mother left him a couple of years ago and was living in a woman's shelter, but he tracked her down and killed her, then himself."

Darius groaned and pinched the bridge of his nose. He wondered if he should tell Eva. Part of her probably suspected this kind of thing had happened ages ago.

"Anyway," Skylar went on, clearing her throat. "The point is, Mendez never reported Saul for the assault or his and Eva's disappearance, so the police didn't look for them. Since they weren't documented, the State doesn't even know they exist. This is all we've got." She gestured to the one-sheet. "There's *nothing* incriminating in the system about Saul Torres."

"So... it's the Sins."

Darius had known for weeks, but confirming it made his throat tighten.

"Yep," Skylar said. "It's gotta be."

"But you don't think they have him already?" Darius asked. He felt the pitch to his voice rise a bit.

Skylar shook her head. "I don't. If they had him, we'd be seeing a lot more than this old picture." She gestured at the television again. "They'd use a recent one, probably one where he looks roughed up and hurt. They'd let us know exactly where he was being held. Trust me. If they had him, they'd make it ridiculously easy for us to find him and walk right into their trap."

Darius's chest felt heavy. He wondered how many Martyrs had been used this way.

"If they don't have him," John mused, "and they can't lay a trap for us, then what the hell are they doing showing his picture around town?" He looked up to Darius with a frown.

"Who said it's a trap for *us?*" Skylar said. "If they want to catch the big prize, first they have to dig up the bait."

She, Raquel, and John looked to Darius, and Darius's stomach twisted.

When Darius had found out Eva was being relocated to South Bronx, he'd tried to ease his concerns by talking to Thorn about it. All that conversation had done was make him *more* nervous.

In the last several decades, while Manhattan, Queens, and Staten Island had become more wealthy and prosperous (for those who already had the fortune of being wealthy and prosperous in the first place), the Bronx had never really changed. New York City generally ignored it, instead funneling money and resources to people who already had more of both than they knew what to do with.

The result was a dangerous, isolated, and traumatized borough that had to fend for itself just as much as the Williamsburg Bridge Market crowd had to do. Housing was crowded, scarce, and hazardous. Schools were underfunded and understaffed. The unsheltered population had burgeoned, moving further and further north every year, slowly pulling more neighborhoods under the blanket of "not worth saving," as far as Mayor Bently and the rest of the city government was concerned.

It didn't help that Sloth had moved in.

Most of the Sins stuck to Manhattan, but Sloth had hopped the Harlem River long ago and made his home on the Bronx streets. The neighborhoods were full of vices Sloth thrived on and promoted—drug use, alcoholism, gambling, and worse things Darius didn't even want to think about. Whatever hope the men and women trying to survive in that part of town had was narrow. What else could they do, swimming upstream against the tide of Sloth's Influence?

And Eva was set to start her new assignment first thing tomorrow morning.

"God, I don't want to go up to the *Bronx*," she moaned. She and Darius were laying on their bed as they looked over the map Thorn had made her. Thorn's handwriting was beautiful, neat script—a style that had fallen out of fashion decades ago and somehow made the map look dated. She'd used thick, red ink to lay out the areas Eva was meant to focus on. Suggested routes zig-zagged throughout the neighborhood. Scribbled stars highlighted the best corners for Eva to sit on, parks she could rest in, and other areas where the unsheltered were known to gather. The point was to cover as much ground as possible, getting close to the places and people Sloth was known to target.

"He's probably not even there," Eva went on. "His last known location was way the hell down in Staten Island, over thirty miles away."

She flopped around and laid on her back, staring at the ceiling. Her brows were knitted together, and there was a glisten of emotion wetting her eyes that hadn't faded since Darius had broken the news that the Sins were after Saul.

"The sighting before that was in Mott Haven," he said, and he looked down at the map in front of him. His attention wandered to the corner of Bruckner and Lincoln, where Sloth's first attack had almost killed Thorn. Like the other bombing location, she had marked it with a massive, red X. "That's barely a mile away from your new apartment."

"That was weeks ago," Eva said. "All I'm saying is, I doubt Sloth will be up there. He has to know we're looking for him. Why would he go back to where we know he hangs out?"

"It's what he's used to," Darius reasoned. "So we can't rule it *out*, either. We need to cover all our bases."

Eva turned and frowned in Darius's direction, heaving a sigh. "Darius, *Saul* is out there. The Sins are looking for him, and I'm sitting here doing nothing! I feel so *useless.*"

There it was. Darius had known most of Eva's frustration wasn't in where she was relocated but in *why*. He knew part of her—maybe even *most* of her—wanted to join in the search for Saul. But she couldn't. It wasn't her job.

"You're not useless," Darius said. It felt flat and hollow, and from the incredulous look Eva threw him, he knew it hadn't helped. "And you're not doing nothing. You gave Holly's team all the information you have about Saul and where he might be going. Let them take it from here. Thorn *needs* you on the lookout for Sloth."

"I should be looking for my brother," she said, dismissing his comment. She gave a guilty scoff and glanced back up at the ceiling. "If our places were swapped, he never would have *stopped* looking for me." Her voice broke over the last word. She rolled onto her side and stared at the distant wall in silence. Darius watched the back of her head for a moment before he sighed and looked over the map again.

The Bronx. Even just seeing the name printed out on the page made his stomach swirl with emotions he hadn't had to think about in a long time. Though it had easily been more than fifteen years since he'd been in the area, it was where he'd been born. It was where he'd been living when Teresa Solomon had sensed his Virtue on a rare visit to the city.

And it was where his mother had died.

Darius grew up in a shabby apartment in Melrose, and one afternoon, as he and his mother walked home from school, a drunk driver swerved onto the sidewalk. At the time, Darius hadn't understood why he had a sudden, terrifying urge to release her hand and dive to the side. Not until he looked back up and saw her pinned between a building and the front bumper of a battered sedan. She'd died instantly. The ER doctor told Darius and his father that she didn't feel anything. Ayda Jones hadn't suffered.

Darius had, though. The next two years were the darkest of his life. Depression. Anxiety. Wishing, constantly, that he hadn't let go. That he could have gone with his mother, wherever she had gone, rather than stay in the living hell his father created for them. Garret Jones hadn't handled his wife's death well. He fell back into the bottle, and within twelve months, they'd lost their home. Then they lived in St. Mary's Park.

That's where he'd met Juniper.

His heart gave a painful surge, and he looked over at Eva again. Maybe he understood her better than he realized. In many ways, Juniper had been to him what Saul was to her. For so long, they'd just had each other. Without Juniper, Darius probably would have starved in some back alley.

Darius folded the map up, placed it on his nightstand, and came to lay with Eva. Her arms were wrapped around her body, her shoulders set in frustration and sadness. He curled around her, wrapping her up in a tight embrace. He found one of her hands and held it firmly. She didn't look at him, but her fingers squeezed his.

"D'you think all three of them are out there together?" Darius asked quietly. "Saul, Juniper, and Lindsay?"

Eva turned to him with a thoughtful frown. She shifted and laid down on her back, nestled in the curve between his legs and shoulders. Her warmth was soothing and comfortable. "I think so," she said. Her voice was also low, like she was afraid to say these hopeful thoughts aloud. "Saul wouldn't leave them to struggle alone."

Darius didn't doubt that about Saul, but he also knew Juniper wouldn't struggle. Not really. She'd been living on the streets for years before she'd found Darius. She was the one who taught *him* how to survive.

She'd taught him a lot more than that. He and Juniper had been alone, just the two of them, for seven years. They'd shared a lot of firsts—and experienced a lot of heartbreaks.

"I hope they're safe," Darius said.

"Especially Lindsay," Eva agreed with a sigh.

Another painful lurch clenched Darius's chest. He couldn't imagine Lindsay had survived long without those antibiotics—the antibiotics he'd fought so hard for. It all seemed so meaningless now.

"I wonder what the Sins are doing, putting his name up all over the place," Eva went on after a quiet moment.

"Like Skylar said, they're probably trying to catch him so they can lay a trap for me," Darius said. "Hell, maybe they hope I'll go out and look for him myself."

Eva frowned. "They really think you'd be dumb enough to put yourself in danger like that?"

Darius gave a cold laugh. "I mean, I've done it once before…"

Eva shook her head with a chuckle and gently shoved his shoulder. Darius smirked. It had been a while since he'd seen a real smile on Eva's face, and he was glad he got one more before she went back into the city. The thought of her leaving made his heart a little sick, and he leaned down and caught her lips up in a tender, loving kiss. It silenced the laugh in her throat, and she kissed him back fervently.

This was how he wanted their last night together for the next few weeks to go. This is how he wanted her to think about him, and the Underground, while she was gone. And this was how he wanted to think about her, too.

———

Thorn stood down the street from her regular coffee shop, leaning against a cool, brick wall as a cigarette smoldered between her lips. The sun had risen an hour or so ago, and its light reflected hot white against the distant buildings. Faraway high-rises jutted into the blue sky, breaking up the horizon and taunting the Bronx with wealth and status this part of the city never got to enjoy. Thorn had been in town for a couple of hours already. She'd left the Underground as soon as she was cleared to go because she just needed to fucking *breathe*.

She exhaled a thick fog of cigarette smoke and took a deep inhale of the city's air. It was tainted with the smell of asphalt and rubber, of stinking garbage in the gutter, but it was refreshing, if only because it meant she was back here. In New York.

Where Sloth was hiding, somewhere.

The thought made Thorn's stomach broil, and her fingers tightened around the end of her cigarette.

Eight days. It had been eight days since she'd run into Witham outside of that restaurant in Staten Island. Eight days of healing, of *fighting* with Alan and Jeremiah about their stupid curfews and check-ins, of providing Mackenzie a safe space to relive her years with Sloth without reaching for a pipe again…

And itching to get back out here so she could find the son of a bitch herself and pummel him into a bloody lump on the sidewalk.

It had been a *long* time since one of the Sins had gotten this close to killing her. Sixty-seven years, almost exactly. Thorn gently touched her scalp, just behind her hairline at her right temple, and felt the ragged circle of scarred skin.

Gluttony had been even closer to taking her out. Scary close. Reed had been convinced Thorn wasn't going to pull through. The doctor even wanted to pull the plug on her...

But she'd made it, hadn't she? She always managed to. Somehow. Sometimes she thought her drive for vengeance was the fuel that kept her going. God, that's what she needed. *Another* way she and Wrath were alike.

Vengeance would have to wait, though. Just a little longer. A few more days. Maybe weeks. It didn't matter. Thorn had nothing but time. She could be patient. Finding Gregory Witham wouldn't happen through brute strength and untethered rage.

It would happen through people like Eva.

Thorn brought her cigarette up to her lips and slowly drew a mouthful of bitter air into her lungs as she looked down the street. Pedestrian traffic to Grind House Coffee was starting to pick up. Thorn was rarely here this late in the morning. She preferred to slip in when the doors first opened and avoid the crowds. Thorn *hated* crowds. Being surrounded by all that energy just reminded her how corrupted people were—and how she did nothing but add to it.

New York was cold, even on a hot summer day like this, because of the Sins—and Forgotten Sins like her.

Crowds had value, though. It was easy to disappear within them. Stay anonymous. Go unnoticed. That was why Thorn instructed Jacob Locke to drop Eva off here for her first day in the Bronx.

A green hatchback turned the corner and made its way down the street. Thorn pushed herself off the wall and tucked inside a nearby stoop. She pulled the hood of her kevlar bike jacket up and slouched down, sacrificing her posture for the sake of fitting in and disappearing. She'd told

Jacob to drop Eva off, but she hadn't told either of them she would be here waiting for her. Thorn didn't want Eva to think she didn't trust her. It was everyone *else* in this city Thorn didn't trust.

But neither Eva nor Jacob noticed her. Eva sat in the front seat and looked out the window with a tight jaw and hard eyes. She was one of the only Martyrs who didn't know how to drive. It was one of the many concerns Jeremiah and Abraham had raised when Thorn told them she wanted Eva on the Gray Unit. She would have to rely on others for transportation to and from the city, and once she *was* in New York, public transit would be her only option.

But Thorn saw it as another facet of why Eva would be so good at this—because she knew what it was like to survive in the city. She had the privilege of being *unprivileged*. For most of her life, Eva had lived here with nothing, and she could get access to places the Martyrs had never been able to successfully infiltrate.

Places Sloth liked to hide.

Jacob slowed the car, but he drove right past the drop-off point. Thorn felt his and Eva's energies continue down the street until they went by her and turned a corner.

"God damn it, Locke," she murmured under her breath. Thorn shook her head and took a final drag on her cigarette before she threw it to the ground and suffocated it with her heel. Sparkie, who was already watching from the air, glided silently above Jacob's vehicle as it turned down another side street and found a more secluded area. Thorn started walking that way, too.

Good old Jacob. Always making sure he found the safest spot he could before he let loose a Martyr into this dangerous city. His paranoia made him one of the most secure drivers they had, even if it made Thorn's life a little more complicated.

When she turned the corner, Eva had already hopped out of the car. Thorn watched as the green hatchback disappeared down another street, and she paused. Eva still hadn't noticed her.

And no one seemed to notice Eva. People walked by her without a second glance. Her hair was tied back; a gray hoodie pulled over her head obscured much of her face and made her look bland and unimportant. They didn't have to worry about Sentries who may recognize her anymore—with Pride obliterated and Envy without a host, all the old Programming they'd installed would have long since worn off by now—but Eva still preferred to keep herself as inconspicuous as possible.

She turned and started heading toward Thorn, and Thorn slipped quietly around the corner and into an alley. She pulled another cigarette out and lit it as Eva walked by. Thorn waited until she was a little further away before she turned down another street and situated herself parallel to Eva's path. Thorn followed her, a block of buildings between them, and Sparkie tracked Eva from the sky to ensure Thorn never lost her.

Whenever Eva was dropped off in, or picked up from, New York, she met her ride at some previously disclosed location several blocks from her actual apartment. The spots rotated and randomized to keep Eva from being traced or from familiar patterns being noticed by nosy observers. It was part of the plan: protect her by making her hard to predict, and she needed all the protection she could get. The Bronx was more dangerous, more unforgiving, than Harlem ever was.

It was even *more* dangerous now, with Wrath spending so much time here.

That was one of the reasons Thorn had insisted on being the one to get Eva established this morning. Usually, one of Holly's team came down to handle it, but Thorn wanted to check on all the security systems *personally*. She hadn't placed someone in the Bronx in decades, and the last Gray Unit man who'd been assigned here had died six months later. Stabbed in a mugging—no Sin involvement whatsoever. It had felt like such a waste…

God, Thorn could only imagine what Darius would say if Eva were killed on the job. Would he blame Thorn for not taking enough precautions? For assigning her a risky position in a dangerous part of town? She wanted to believe he would understand why it was so critical to have someone searching for Sloth with boots on the ground, but she wasn't sure anymore. She'd already believed he had understood why she'd lied to him, but that hadn't been true, had it?

A blip of something unfamiliar—the tinge of hurt feelings that Thorn didn't think *could* be hurt anymore—bubbled between her lungs. She sucked it down with more nicotine.

Thorn arrived at Eva's apartment first. She slipped around the corner and walked up to the door. The doorknob looked unassuming, but Thorn knew better. She wrapped her hand around it, felt for the smooth circle at the base of the metal, and pressed the pad of her first finger against it.

The mechanism in the lock clicked and opened. Thorn let herself into the apartment and closed it behind her. Then she turned on the light and looked around.

This little studio was anything but glamorous. Nothing in this neighborhood ever was. The apartment was barely larger than the largest dormitory room at the Underground. A bed in the corner was undressed, the mattress yellow and splotchy. The couch and coffee table were musky, the television mounted to the wall coated in a fine layer of gray dust. The attached kitchen had maybe three feet of counter space, and the tiny bathroom was barely large enough to fit the shower they'd squeezed into the corner, and it smelled like mildew.

But like the doorknob, it was more than it seemed.

The Martyrs owned a handful of apartments across the city, and each of them had been equipped with the same basic security features. The walls here were reinforced, the doors fortified, and the windows equipped with bullet-resistant, shatterproof glass. An alarm linked to the electrical system sent alerts directly to Holly's computer, Thorn's phone, and the nearest TAC units. Hidden buttons were spread throughout the room: on the inside windowsill beside the door, under the kitchen counter by the sink, and on the side of the medicine cabinet in the bathroom. They were subtle, painted to match the surrounding areas so visitors wouldn't easily spot them.

Though Thorn doubted Eva would entertain visitors.

A cold energy approached the door. Thorn opened it right as Eva knocked. Eva jumped, startled, but Thorn reached out and grabbed her by the shoulder.

"Hurry."

Thorn ushered Eva into the room as Sparkie perched on the top of the building, looking down at the street to ensure they weren't being watched. The last thing Thorn needed was to be spotted with someone on her team by the Sins or their Sentries. She closed the door and spun to see Eva taking in the apartment. Her expression was hard to read.

"Welcome home," Thorn said darkly.

Eva only shrugged. She pulled the hood off her head and dropped her bag onto the couch. "I've lived in worse."

Thorn didn't doubt it. The bar she and Darius squatted in hadn't been anything special—except for what he had turned it into.

"Let's get you set up," Thorn said.

They took a few minutes to get Eva's fingerprint programmed into the door. Then Thorn gave her a "tour" of the single, three-hundred and fifty square foot studio. She showed her where all the alarm buttons were located, reminding her how to use them and when she should. It was all familiar: the same basic training she'd gotten when Skylar had set her up in Harlem five months ago.

"Your clothing and belongings will be delivered later today," Thorn said as they walked back to the center of the room. "There are towels in the cupboard above the toilet. Sheets and blankets in the closet. A gun strapped under the sink in the bathroom." Eva nodded, but her face went a little pale. Thorn went on. "Your television has the same communications system you had in Harlem. Do you remember how to set it up?"

Eva glanced at the screen on the wall and gave a sheepish shrug. "No, not really."

Thorn nodded, grabbed the remote, and turned the television on. The local news blared to life. Thorn muted it and began the process of signing Eva in.

"You navigate it using the app on your phone," Thorn said, and Eva pulled her device out of her pocket. "Use your Martyrs access codes, then sync it to the television when I tell you to…"

Thorn typed in her private passcode, telling the system that an administrator was requesting access. The news disappeared, replaced by a blank screen.

"Okay," Thorn said. "Sync now."

Like the security system, the communication system was a closed link directly to the Underground. Thorn didn't understand fully how it all worked—something with blocks and chains?—but Holly set it up, so she trusted it. When the two devices finished syncing and Eva was all signed in, the screen changed again. A large, black rectangle, where the video feed would show, took up most of it. Eva's contacts list populated down the left-hand side. The name "Darius Jones" stood out at the top, followed by Thorn's and the rest of the Gray Unit. Thorn glanced at Darius's name briefly before she turned back to Eva.

"Hit the alarm," she said.

Eva walked the two steps it took to get from the center of the room to her front door and hit the button sitting on the side of the windowsill. The screen flashed, and suddenly the empty black rectangle blinked to life. Holly Andrews stared out at them. Her face looked particularly round in the webcam.

"Systems test?" Holly said. There was an almost bored, annoyed cadence to her voice.

"Does it look good to you?" Thorn asked.

"Is that Thorn?" Mackenzie's vibrant, loud voice broke through the speakers. "Tell her I say, 'Hi!'"

Holly rolled her eyes as Mackenzie forced herself into the camera's viewfinder. For a moment, her vibrant, blue hair and the top of her face took up half the screen. Over Holly's shoulder, Thorn could see Nicholas Wolfe standing against the blue backdrop they used for identification photos. His freckled face was set into a sneer.

"Sorry," Holly said, and she pushed the top of Mackenzie's head away. Thorn heard something clatter to the floor off-screen, and Mackenzie swore. "If you didn't notice, I'm a little busy. Everything looks good to go on my end. Did you let the nearest TAC team know you were running this test?"

"Yes," Thorn said. Chris was the only person she'd told about helping Eva today. "Thanks, Andrews."

Holly nodded as Mackenzie squeezed in beside Nicholas and waved excitedly at the camera. "You got it," Holly said. Then she hung up without saying goodbye, and the video feed went black. Thorn shut the system down, and the news came back on the screen. The announcer's mouth was moving noiselessly as Thorn turned back to Eva.

"There you go," she said.

"Thanks." Eva pressed her lips together and looked around the room again. Thorn watched as the other woman took in the space, lingering a little on the twin mattress, the threadbare carpet, and the door outside…

"You ready for this?" Thorn asked.

"Oh, yeah," Eva said, and she cleared her throat as she walked back to her bag. She dropped her phone into it and slung it over her shoulder. "It's the same old thing, just a new part of town."

Thorn frowned. "It's not the same," she said. "Stick to the areas we talked about, and keep an eye out for *more* than just Sloth. Be vigilant. Take care of yourself."

Please, god, don't get yourself killed.

Eva cast Thorn a quick, sardonic look. "I'll be fine."

Thorn raised her brows. "You better be. You're damned good at what you do. I don't want to replace you. I don't think I *could*."

Eva seemed caught off guard. She turned around again, but her eyes suddenly darted to the television screen behind Thorn's back. They went wide, and the color drained from her face.

Thorn looked over her shoulder, and her breath caught in her throat.

"Shit," she said as she quickly turned on the volume.

"—Torres was spotted in Crown Heights early this morning shoplifting food from a bodega," the newscaster was saying. "With him was a woman and child who have not yet been identified. They were leaving the scene with Torres as they moved north up Brooklyn Avenue."

Thorn and Eva watched in tense silence as the screen shifted and showed security footage from outside a quick stop convenience store. A tall, Latino man rushed out the door and onto the sidewalk. He grabbed a skinny, red-headed woman by the hand, lifted a toddler into his other arm, and the three of them darted off and out of sight.

But not before someone else got a picture of him. The newscaster was back, this time showing a full-face photo of Saul. He looked different from the school photograph. His face was covered in a trimmed, black beard. His cheeks were deep and hollow.

A scar extended from just above his left eye nearly to his ear.

"Oh my god," Eva whispered.

Thorn swore and started to gather up her things. Crown Heights was right next to one of Wrath's most frequented neighborhoods. Thorn flew toward the door, and Eva followed behind her.

"I'm coming," she said.

"No."

Thorn spun on her heels and faced Eva again. The other woman had a familiar look on her face—furious, scared, and determined. *This* was the other reason Abraham and Jeremiah worried about putting Eva on the Gray Unit. If Saul Torres showed up, could Eva focus on her work, or would she disappear again?

Thorn fought for her then—and she was going to fight for her now.

"You have a job to do here," Thorn said, her voice hard and firm, "and I *need* you to do it."

Eva's brows twitched as her mouth fell open. "But Saul—"

"I know you want to find him," Thorn cut in, and, god, did she know. When the Sins had kidnapped her son, Thorn hunted for him for months. Three *agonizing* months. She hadn't slept. Hadn't eaten. Hardly even breathed.

But Saul wasn't Donovan, and the Sins hadn't captured him. Not yet. Thorn went on, "But your *job* comes first. Is that going to be a problem?"

Eva's mouth was still wide open, and the corners of her eyes filled with quiet, angry tears. When she spoke, the words were hoarse and heavy. "He's my *brother.*"

One of the things Thorn respected most about Eva was her loyalty to Saul and her single-track mind when it came to finding him. That kind of quality was admirable—and relatable.

It also made Thorn's life harder.

She'd known the moment that paper with Saul's picture had come in that this could become a problem. Thorn wasn't stupid. At the end of the day, she knew Saul mattered more to Eva than her work with the Martyrs.

And there was nothing Thorn could do to change that.

"Let *me* handle this," Thorn said. "*You* help me find Sloth. I need to know I can rely on you. Can I rely on you?"

Eva just stared at Thorn for a few long, tense seconds. A flicker of rage nestled in that empty pit in Thorn's chest— the pit left behind when Wrath had ripped her to shreds. It worked like a fireplace, giving oxygen and fuel to the flames of her fury.

Damnit, she didn't have the time for this.

But then Eva squared her shoulders and sighed.

"Yes."

Thorn paused and watched her. So far, Eva had been excellent at her job. She'd given Thorn no reason not to trust her—so, fuck, she'd have to trust her.

"Good."

Thorn rushed from the studio. The street was searingly bright, and the sun blared down on Thorn with oppressive heat. Sparkie had already taken to the air and was halfway across town, headed southward toward Crown Heights. Thorn sprinted to her motorcycle.

Hopefully, Saul Torres had gotten as far away from Brooklyn as he could, or Wrath would be close on his tail.

CHAPTER FOURTEEN

Once the news broke that Saul was officially in the city, the Sins doubled down on their attempts to weed him out—and with him, Darius.

Saul's face started popping up *everywhere*, and the stories were getting more antagonistic. Instead of just a "person of interest," now they claimed Saul was "potentially danger-ous," but what he was being investigated for, no one would say. The updated image was printed on every newspaper still in circulation and posted on every website local to New York. The fresh scar across his face added to the paranoia. He looked much less innocent than he had in the old high school photo. Between Alexis Claytor, the Gray Unit agent working in dispatch, and Holly, who had hacked into the police tip hotline, the Martyrs tracked every reported sight-ing of Saul around the city.

Within a week, there were so many that the tech team couldn't possibly keep up with sorting through all of them, even with their advanced face detection software, so that job fell to Darius and the rest of the Research and Discovery Department.

Much like they had when Eva had disappeared last year, R&D was reassigned. Instead of hunting for Virtues, they were going through hours upon hours of video footage for any sign of Saul, Juniper, or Lindsay, and they weren't having much luck.

"Yeah…" Nicholas said with a sigh to Darius's right. They had brought a few extra computers into the conference room, and Darius and Nicholas, along with John and a few other R&D members, were quietly scrolling through video footage from various areas of town with multiple reported sightings. Nicholas shook his head. "This can't be him unless he ate two *thousand* donuts in the last week."

Darius glanced over his shoulder. Nicholas's screen was paused on a grainy shot of an overweight man coming out of a post office. Holly's facial recognition software wasn't foolproof, and most of what they were doing was ruling out false positives the program called up. It was slow, tedious work, so they tried to make it fun.

"Or this guy," John said on Nicholas's other side. "Look at this hair. It goes down to his ass."

Nicholas and John laughed, but Darius turned back to his screen and took a deep breath. He didn't think there was a lot to laugh about.

For a fleeting moment, Darius had been *relieved* to learn Saul was alive and well and that Juniper and Lindsay were with him. Seeing their faces again brought back a spark of hope he hadn't felt since he first realized they weren't among the dead over nine months ago. That hope was quickly squashed. Their survival was just the beginning. Saul, Juniper, and Lindsey were out there, totally unaware that the Sins and their army of Programmed Sentries were searching for them. Eva was trapped at her tiny apartment, unable to do anything but watch the news to see if anyone else spotted her brother. The Martyrs were stretched so thin it felt like they weren't making any progress at all. Holly and her team were busy maintaining all their standard security procedures on top of hunting for Sloth and *now* searching for Saul and the others.

It was hard for Darius to feel optimistic. How the hell

could they expect to find *anyone* this way?

Many of the researchers seemed equally disheartened. Parker had lost her usual luster, instead frowning at the screen and scratching her head beneath a mop of tight ringlets. Daniel Park looked haggard and wasted. In the month since Sara had died, he hadn't missed a day of work, but sometimes it was like he wasn't here at all. His black eyes had dark circles underneath them, and he occasionally threw John or Nicholas reproachful looks over his shoulder.

"Can you two just shut the fuck up?" Daniel finally asked. The muscles along his jaw flexed. Nicholas and John glanced at him. John seemed abashed; a pink tint rose to his cheeks, and he quietly turned back to his computer. Nicholas, however, frowned.

"It's just a joke, man," he said. "Calm down."

The energy of the room shifted. The dull, monotonous cadence of clicks and typing disappeared, almost like someone had slammed their thumb on a mute button. In its place, the static tension of silence fell. Daniel turned fully around in his chair. He gritted his teeth. Moved to stand—

Darius cleared his throat and spun to face the room.

"Hey," he said loudly, trying to carry the same kind of authority Alan commanded that could still the room with a single word. He held a hand up toward Daniel, but his eyes landed on Nicholas. He raised his brows and gave his head a single, gentle shake. "C'mon, guys. We've got a job to do. Let's focus on that."

Nicholas took Darius in for a moment. John, who had glanced at the scene from over his shoulder, quietly turned back and started working again. Neither Daniel nor Nicholas moved right away, like both were determined not to be the guy who backed down first, but after an awkward minute, Daniel rolled his eyes and turned back to his screen, too.

When Nicholas finally relented, Darius rubbed his eyes with his thumb and fingertips. He pulled his hand back to see Parker watching him. She gave him a supportive smile, which he returned before getting back to work.

After that, things were quiet… for a while.

"I don't know why we're looking in Midtown," Nicholas said with a sigh a couple of minutes later. "Or anywhere in Western Manhattan, really. I figure he's more likely to be on the Lower East Side."

The tension roared back. Darius felt eyes move onto him from around the room.

"He *was* on the Lower East Side," Darius said shortly. He moved another low-resolution video file to the "irrelevant" folder. His cursor moved slowly on the screen. Slowly enough to be irritating. With so many people working on the server, it delayed, and Darius was struck with the urge to smack the side of his machine. He felt Nicholas shift in his chair to watch him.

"That's right," he said. It was quiet. Almost contrite, but not quite. "That's where you were all living before coming here, wasn't it?"

Darius just nodded.

"I've never really been to that part of Manhattan," Nicholas continued. "Seemed too… I dunno, grungy for me."

"You've been to New York before?" John asked. There was a relief to his voice, and that relief moved through the rest of the room in a soft wave.

"Oh yeah," Nicholas said—dismissively, almost as though it was a stupid question. "I was born on Long Island, and I went to Columbia University."

Darius paused and glanced over his shoulder again. Nicholas was a perfect example of why the Martyrs couldn't restrict their Virtue search to the areas around New York exclusively. Though Teresa had learned that Virtues tended to be born close to the Sins they were meant to destroy, they didn't always stick around.

"How'd you end up all the way out in Washington State?" John asked. He'd stopped working so he could listen to Nicholas, too, and he spun his chair around to face him.

"It's a long story," Nicholas said, but the smile on his

face told Darius he was excited to tell it. "I got my MBA and started helping my mom out with her little restaurant in Islip. We grew it into a pretty big business. Until Mom got cancer. Her treatments were too expensive, so we had to sell, and she died a couple of months later."

John winced. "Yikes, man. I'm sorry."

Nicholas gave a half-shrug. "It is what it is. Mom worked hard and fought harder. I learned a lot from her. Like not to trust my dad. He abandoned my mom, my kid sister, and me when I was ten and moved across the country. We saw him maybe once or twice a year. When he heard Mom died, he offered me a job at his consulting agency, and being the dumb thirty-year-old that I was, I took him up on it.

"Well," Nicholas went on, leaning back in his chair and stretching his arms behind his head. He'd gone ahead and gotten new clothing ordered, and his fitted, button-up shirt made him look somehow both younger and more dignified. "That turned out to be a *huge* mistake. He just wanted me in the company to take advantage of my credentials to charge clients more money. As soon as I figured out what was going on, I told him to fuck off, and I bailed."

"What did you do then?" John asked.

"I worked my ass off!"

Nicholas recounted his life from thirty to forty-five. He'd started at the bottom of an event center, working his way up from an intern to a coordination manager. That job had provided him opportunities to move, and he moved a *lot*. In the last fifteen years, Nicholas had worked in seven states with five different companies. Every one had been a move up in his career until he got into organizing charitable events. He'd raised *billions* of dollars.

"Three years ago, I got transferred to Spokane—you know the rest from there."

His voice darkened a bit, and his eyes glossed over as he stared, aimlessly, at the screen in front of him.

"Had to be hard to say goodbye to all of that," John said. He seemed both impressed and sympathetic.

But Nicholas's mood shifted back toward nonchalance, and he shrugged. "Yes and no. I was getting bored. It was time for a change."

"Just like that?"

"Just like that."

"What about your friends and family?" John asked.

"I didn't really have any," Nicholas said. "My dad and I don't talk, and I haven't seen my sister in years. I had connections. Associates. The closest thing I had to a friend was my assistant. I hope they took care of her after that last event..." His voice drifted off for a bit, but he quickly shook his head. "Doesn't matter, though. It all seems pretty pointless now. I'm just going to die anyway."

A lump caught in Darius's windpipe. John cast him a wide-eyed look. A few other Martyrs who had been listening in did the same.

People didn't talk much about the fate of the Virtues—especially not around Darius.

He cleared his throat and turned back to his computer, frustrated that he'd let himself get sucked away from his work. All the same, he couldn't let that last comment sit. It didn't feel right.

"At least your death will mean something," he said. "Most people don't get that."

Daniel Park looked down at his feet, his eyes glassy and sad, as Nicholas turned to consider Darius. Darius didn't turn around. He just watched Nicholas's reflection in his screen. The other Virtue's face was impassive and hard to read. For a few quiet moments, the room watched the two of them.

"That's true," Nicholas finally said. "It's probably more meaningful than anything I've done in my whole career."

He wasn't joking. Darius looked back again and found Nicholas's face set into an earnest and honest determination. The lump in his throat started to dissolve.

Then something dinged on Darius's screen, and he turned to look at it: a batch of videos collected from more tips to the NYPD hotline. Darius sighed as he opened the file.

"Another two hundred and fifty videos," he called out to the room. People around him groaned, and Nicholas shook his head.

"This bullshit is going to take forever," he said. "There has to be a better way."

"If you can find it," John said as he opened the new folder up and started grabbing the files for the neighborhoods he was assigned to search, "the beer's on me."

Nicholas cast him a look over his shoulder with a sly smile.

"Game on."

In the days that followed, Nicholas went into overdrive to find an alternative solution to hunt for Saul without wasting hours going through useless leads. He started by annoying the security team until Holly finally got so fed up with him calling all the time that she assigned Skylar to help him. Then, the two of them worked on ways to better sort and prioritize the videos coming in.

First, they started by cross-sorting the footage of people who looked similar to Saul with people who looked similar to Juniper. If they were still homeless, Nicholas reasoned, chances were they would be spotted together. After that, he read Eva's report about Saul's life and habits. The idea was to sort out the most likely areas of town he'd be frequenting.

Thanks to Nicholas, just two weeks after the first sighting of Saul, they found him again.

"I'm a man of my word," John said as he cracked open a bottle of lager and handed it over to Nicholas. Darius stood beside them, his heart beating hard in his throat.

More security camera footage of Saul, Juniper, and Lindsey looked up from the screen. This time, they were in Astoria.

"This is old footage," Nicholas said, and he tipped the bottle to his lips and took a sip. He sucked in through his teeth and furrowed his brow as he looked back down at the computer. "About eight days old? Still, it's better than nothing."

It was a tiny snippet—no more than thirty seconds—showing Saul, Juniper, and Lindsay quickly leaving a fast-food place just off of 21st Avenue. They were clearly taking precautions to avoid being recognized now. All three of them covered as much of their faces and heads as possible, with hoodies and scarves and oversized sunglasses. They looked ridiculous in the early August heat, but Darius had to admit, it certainly made it hard for Holly's system to catch them.

And, hopefully, harder for the Sins' Sentries.

"So they're moving North," Darius said with a frown, and he crossed one arm over his chest while his other hand ran over his lips thoughtfully. "I wonder where they're headed."

"Wherever it is, they're not moving fast," Nicholas said. "They've seen the news. They know someone's after Saul. Clearly, he doesn't want to get caught, either."

"Maybe they're trying to leave the city?" John asked.

Nicholas shook his head. "It would've been faster to go south through the Staten Island train or even to Atlantic Terminal. Hell, they should just high tail it right to Grand Central if they want to get out. Maybe they're trying to lay low until this all blows over."

Darius took in a deep breath and shook his head. "It won't blow over. Not with the Sins."

"Then we just gotta find him before they do," Nicholas said. "And now, we stand a fighting chance."

That was true, but somehow it didn't help the sense of uneasiness that had settled in Darius's stomach. It felt like something was wrong—like there was tension somewhere nearby, and he was soaking it in.

Darius turned toward the door just as it opened, and Lina poked her head in. She looked him right in the eye.

"There's been another bombing," she said, her face pale. "You're needed in the hospital."

A weight dropped into the pit of Darius's stomach. "Someone's hurt?" he asked, and Lina nodded. The weight sank deeper. "Is it Thorn?"

"No. It's Alexis."

The dread lifted a little—but just a little—as Darius nodded and rushed from the room. Nicholas followed promptly on his heels.

———

Gregory Witham was standing on a wood plank dock, staring down the sidewalk. He looked better than he had the last time Darius had seen him. His face wasn't black and charred, and his eye was placed back in its socket. If it wasn't for his hair, which had been singed so short it was practically buzzed, it wouldn't look like he'd been caught in one of his explosions at all.

The Sin was skittish. Anxious. His eyes darted toward a cyclist that passed by, then to a woman pushing a stroller, like he expected them to lash out. His head twitched to the left, and he shoved both hands deep into the pockets of his ratty, old hoodie.

For several seconds, he stared at a man fifty feet down the walkway.

Darius recognized him. Anton Claytor—Greed. In many ways, Greed seemed like a *light* version of who Derek Dane had been. Like the late Pride, he had the same affinity for expensive, tailored suits. His platinum blonde hair was slicked back and stylish. He had a haughty air of superiority.

But he was much less confident. Where Dane had carried himself with a poise that demanded attention, Greed was meeker. His facade of bravery was fraying as his icy eyes took in Gregory Witham. His right hand played absently with the buttons of his suit jacket as he opened his mouth to speak.

And his voice was lost. His lips moved to form words Darius couldn't make out above the hiss of the wind coming off the Hudson River. He leaned forward, straining to hear, but it was no use.

Whatever Greed had said, though, elicited a reaction in Sloth. Witham's twitching became a little more erratic, and he exclaimed something back. Anton Claytor just shook his head and raised his hands as though to say, "This isn't up to me."

Then he took a step toward Witham, and Witham drew something out from his pocket.

The trashcan beside Greed exploded. Darius had been expecting it, but he still startled as Anton Claytor screamed. A dogwalker nearby, along with her tethered pack of animals, were blown back, and a piece of sharp metal flew at Darius—

The scene suddenly jolted upward—a furious flurry of green leaves and blue sky. Alexis Claytor swore violently, and her face appeared overhead. One of the lenses from her sunglasses had been blown out, and dark red droplets of blood dribbled from under the brim of her ball cap as she leaned down.

Then the footage shut off, and Darius was left looking at a blank screen.

Eight of them were gathered together in the conference room. The whole of the Martyr Leadership—Alan and Thorn, Jeremiah and Abraham, Lina and Mackenzie, and Darius. The room sat for a moment, silent following a chorus of gasps and curse words as the projector went black. Lina's fingers covered her lips, and Mackenzie had jumped so much she'd come right out of her chair and was now pacing, agitated, by the table.

Alexis Claytor was also there. She sat on the far end of the room, one arm around her chest while her other hand gingerly touched the side of her forehead. Less than twenty minutes ago, she'd come into the Underground with deep lacerations across her face and shoulder where sharp, metal shards from the trashcan had ripped through her. After Darius healed her up and the hospital staff provided her with a clean change of clothes, Thorn had thundered into the Underground. She flew through the door to the hospital room with her jaw set tight and her eyes dark and narrow.

Then she'd demanded that Darius and Alexis join her in the conference room. Nicholas had tried to follow, but Thorn refused to let him.

Now he was waiting just outside the door. Darius felt his energy and the pull of his Virtue stomping back and forth down the hallway.

"What the hell is going on here?" Mackenzie asked with a frown. She stopped pacing, clicked her tongue piercing against her teeth, and furrowed her brow as she grabbed the laptop and rewound the footage to the beginning, where Sloth and Greed met at the edge of the water. "Is this one of those piers in Hudson River Park? That's not Greed's normal hangout, is it?"

"No," Thorn confirmed. "Cortez was at an event he was hosting at the United Nations building and overheard him make plans to meet with someone at Pier 66, in Claytor's territory." Thorn nodded her head in Alexis's direction.

"Cortez," Darius murmured, and he glanced to Thorn. "Is that Elena?"

Thorn nodded. "She works with Greed's preferred caterer."

"Why didn't Cortez follow him?" Jeremiah asked as he cast Alexis a dark, almost suspicious look. The blonde woman's cheeks went a violent shade of pink, and she opened her mouth to argue, but Thorn silenced her by holding up a hand.

"She couldn't get away without risking her job and her position within the city," Thorn shot back, and Jeremiah turned to her. "Are you questioning the way I run my team, Montgomery?"

There was a pointed criticism in Jeremiah's eyes. Darius knew what this was all about. Anton Claytor was Alexis's father. At least, he had been before the possession. Both Alexis and her younger brother, Caleb, were Gray Unit members, but they were explicitly removed from situations involving Greed. While Caleb worked as a freelance photographer, keeping tabs on Lust, Alexis was a night shift dispatcher following Gluttony's movements. Elena Cortez was the operative assigned to Greed.

Jeremiah watched Thorn, and Thorn glared back, almost daring him to challenge her. The air around her felt dangerously charged. After a tense moment, Jeremiah seemed to accept her answer and turned back to Alexis. He gestured to the screen. "Did you hear what they said?"

"No," Alexis said. "They were too far away."

Jeremiah nodded before taking the laptop over from Mackenzie and dragging the footage forward a bit. "Look at this," he said. He paused on a shot of both Sins, just before the bomb went off. Greed stood right beside the trashcan that would soon explode, and Sloth had just drawn his hand out of his pocket. Jeremiah got to his feet and pointed at the item in Sloth's fingers. "No wires. He's progressed to remote detonation. Didn't want to get blown up again…"

"What do you think, McKay?" Thorn asked. She turned toward Mackenzie, and Darius was surprised to see her expression wasn't as hard as usual. There was a concerned note there. Mackenzie shrugged and took a deep breath.

"Well, clearly he planned this," she said. There was a steely note in her voice. "Sloth doesn't come out of his hole without a good reason. This was intentional."

"Do you think he wanted to kill Greed?" Alan asked.

"Nope," Mackenzie said. "If he just wanted him dead, he'd send a Puppet. Sloth doesn't do his own dirty work. He makes others do it for him."

Mackenzie's mouth settled into a rigid line, and the room went quiet. Thorn stepped up, drawing attention to herself as she said, "So, he wanted to talk."

"Why the bomb, then?" Abraham asked.

Lina's eyes widened. "Oh, god! As a failsafe? To make sure he had a way to escape if the talk didn't go well?"

"What the hell would he want to talk to Greed about

that could be dangerous enough to merit *this* kind of escape plan?" Jeremiah asked, crossing his arms as he looked down at Lina.

"He needs a partner," Alan said quietly. The whole room turned to face him. "All of the Sins have maintained normalcy—all of them *except* for Gregory Witham and Autumn Hunt. While Lust, Greed, and Gluttony have been going about business as normal, Sloth has all but disappeared from his typical territories, and Wrath has been extraordinarily active in parts of town where Witham is usually found. We can surmise she is trying to stop him from, or simply punish him for, trying to kill Thorn." He gestured to his niece with a curt nod.

"So," Mackenzie said with a frown. "Greed says, 'fuck off,' and Sloth blows him to hell, along with a pier full of people…"

"It must be more than that," Lina said. "He didn't hit the detonator until Greed started to move toward him. I think he felt threatened."

"Maybe Greed did more than refuse to help him," Abraham said, exhaling a long, weary sigh as he ran a hand through his curly hair.

"Yeah," Thorn growled. The corners of her mouth turned up in a snarl. "He made it clear he was on Wrath's side."

Alan nodded. "It seems likely. Not many Sins are willing to work against her."

"And if they're *not*," Thorn said, and she threw Alan a hot look. "It means I'm *not* a target, and I can resume duty as normal."

"We will discuss that as we get more information," Alan said. He turned to Alexis and shifted the subject. Thorn bristled behind him, but she said nothing. "Miss Claytor, how many people were injured in the attack today?"

"I don't know," Alexis said. "That dog walker, for sure. There were a few other people down the sidewalk and more by me at the park. I don't know if anyone died. I got out of there as quickly as I could."

"I see." Alan turned to Abraham. His face remained mostly impassive, but a tug at the corner of his mouth told Darius he was troubled. "Mr. Locke, please find out how severe the damage from this attack has been. Jeremiah, talk to Miss Andrews. Finding Sloth is an absolute priority. If he is willing to attack not just Thorn—not just the *Martyrs*—but the other Sins as well, things will get much, much worse. We *must* track him down."

"What about Greed?" Alexis asked. Her voice was strong and clear, but there was a hint of panic curling up the edges. Darius turned to look at her. Her mouth was set, her jaw tight, but her chilling eyes watched Alan with an unashamed resolution. Darius's chest clenched. He couldn't imagine how hard it was for her, fighting the Sins when her father was one of them. "Are we going to look for him, too?"

Mackenzie and Lina exchanged a tense look. Abraham glanced down at his feet, and Jeremiah's eyes went unfocused as he looked out at a point just beyond Alexis's shoulders. Only Alan and Thorn watched her with the familiar cold and unreadable expression the two of them often shared. At long last, Alan shook his head.

"No. We are not."

"He could be hurt," Alexis insisted.

"He *is* hurt," Thorn said. She gestured to the video footage again. "He was too close to get away without serious damage."

Alexis's face paled.

"Miss Claytor," Alan said quietly. Compassionately. "He is not the man you once knew. Not anymore. He is a Sin."

"So were you," Alexis said hotly. A glint of anger crossed Alan's eyes. "He has a chance—"

"The chance is extraordinarily slim," Alan said. "The longer the host has been under a Sin's control, the more challenging for them to escape—"

"Thorn was Wrath for twenty years!" Alexis exclaimed,

and she got to her feet. "He's only been Greed for twelve."

"Miss Claytor." The name was spoken with a hard, dangerous note of finality, and Alexis's lips slammed shut. They were so tight they turned white on her face. Alan went on. "I regret that your father is Greed. Truly, I do. I, more than anyone, know the pain of having a Sin take someone from your family and turn them into a monster." The room went silent. Thorn slowly turned to look at her uncle, but her face was stoic and impenetrable. Alan pressed on. "If there comes a time when Anton is able to escape Greed, then we will welcome him with open arms, but we cannot forget what we are here to do. If Anton Claytor was killed today, we must consider it a victory. Not only will Greed's Influence begin to diminish, but your father will finally get to rest."

That solution didn't satisfy Alexis. She mumbled an ungrateful "Yes, sir" before she spun on her heels and stormed out. The door slammed shut behind her, and her warm energy stalked down the hallway. Darius turned back to the room, and Alan pinched the bridge of his nose.

"We must find Sloth," he reiterated. "Whatever it takes."

The rest of the meeting passed quickly, though not without more tension. Alan instructed Jeremiah to keep the Tactical Unit teams to the same increased patrols they had been working since the last attack. He spoke with Mackenzie and Lina about reallocating more than half of their team to start helping Holly track down Gregory Witham instead of searching for Saul. And new orders were made:

If Sloth was spotted, no one was to engage him. With remote bombs, there was no way to guarantee any team's safety.

Then they adjourned, and the room slowly emptied.

Nicholas stood outside the door as everyone dispersed. Alan, Lina, and Mackenzie headed back to their offices to move around the resources they needed for the changes to come. Jeremiah and Abraham disappeared down the hallway toward the elevators. Nicholas rounded immediately on

Darius as Thorn started toward the garage.

"What's happening?" he asked.

"Sloth attacked another Sin," Darius said.

"Were more people hurt?"

"Yes," Darius said with a sigh. "We don't have an exact number."

"He needs to be stopped," Nicholas said.

"We're trying—"

"Not hard enough, clearly."

"*Excuse me?*" Thorn's voice cut through the foyer like a knife through flesh. Nicholas and Darius turned to look at her as she paused in the doorway and slowly spun to face them. Her eyes were narrow, her lips thin, as she shut the door and walked back into the room. "We're *not trying hard enough?*"

She took a couple of steps toward Nicholas, and he squared his shoulders. His face was set into a deep, determined frown.

"He's still out there, isn't he?"

"It's not that simple—"

"It can't be this complicated, either," Nicholas growled. "You knew where he was today. Why the hell didn't you send all your units out to find him?"

Thorn paused, and her mouth opened a sliver in disbelief. "You want me to send my people into an *unknown situation* where our target has been using *explosives?* How many people are you willing to kill in this fight? How many innocent lives are you okay sacrificing to take down a single Sin?"

"He'll kill even *more* people if he's allowed to run around New York without being stopped!" Nicholas yelled. "Isn't that what this damned place is all about? Protecting people? Or is it just about protecting *your* people? And yourselves."

Thorn's nostrils flared. She flew across the room, grabbed Nicholas by the collar, and slammed his back into the wall. Darius gasped and rushed forward, but Thorn put her other hand out and held him back. Her fingers were firm against his chest, her nails digging in even through his shirt as she leaned in close to Nicholas and hissed:

"Not that it's any of your business, but since you seem so *determined* to make me the bad guy, I'll tell you anyway."

"Oh *yeah*, you definitely don't seem like a bad guy right now," Nicholas started, but Thorn cut him off.

"Do you know what I'm doing? I'm on my way out to hunt for Sloth *by myself* because if anyone in this god damned place can survive a run-in with him, it's *me*. Am I willing to sacrifice my team to get rid of one problem Sin? No. But don't you *dare* assume I'm happy to sit here while civilians die."

She let go of his shirt, then, but she didn't back off. Her nose was still inches away from his, her rage seeping out of her body and into the room around her. "You talk a lot about how selfish we are, but what the *fuck* have you done? Sit behind a computer and make fun of people on video feeds while my team is out there risking their lives? You've bitched and moaned and told everyone else what *they* should be doing while you sit here and do *nothing*."

Then she turned on her heels and made to walk away, but Nicholas, his fists balled tight, his forehead knitted into a series of furious lines, called out again.

"The only reason I'm not doing anything is because you won't fucking let me," he yelled, and Thorn turned back. "I'm not afraid to go out there and fight. I was on board with this shit weeks ago, but you're too scared of your precious Virtues getting hurt to let us do any real work!"

The air around Nicholas began to change. Darius stared as the magnetic pull around him became electric and crackled with energy. Nicholas kept shouting.

"I'm not fucking afraid to die for this," he said. "And I'm done waiting for *your* permission to help. I'll find him. I'll take the fucker out—"

Suddenly, that crackling magnetism shattered and pulsed, taking Darius's breath away in an electric wave. He stumbled back, but Thorn didn't seem to notice. She was focused on Nicholas.

And Nicholas was screaming. His baby blue eyes went wide as he looked around the room—at Darius, at the far wall, at Thorn—and then down at his hands.

"What's happening?" he shouted. "I—I'm on fire!"

Darius rushed over to him and put his hand on Nicholas's shoulder, but Nicholas cried out in pain and pulled away. Thorn's mood shifted. She came forward and grabbed onto Nicholas. He didn't seem bothered by her touch. She pulled him toward the hospital ward, but he fought against her.

"It's hot—*that's hot*," Nicholas said, gesturing toward the double doors. "Jesus, why is it *so hot*?"

"Welcome to being a Virtue," Thorn said. Her voice was stern and cold, and she threw Darius a dark, knowing look over Nicholas's shoulder. Then Nicholas stopped struggling. His eyes went even wider, and his mouth fell open.

"Oh god," he murmured. Sweat had broken out across his forehead and torso. His shirt was already sticking to his skin. "It's me. I'm the one."

"What do you mean?" Darius asked. He tried to get closer, but Nicholas recoiled as he neared. Somehow, he seemed oblivious to Thorn's hands on him, guiding him toward the hospital doors.

"I was right," Nicholas said, and, through the heat and the pain and the unfamiliar *newness* of this situation, his mouth broke into a manic smile. "I'm the one that's gonna kill that bastard. I'm *Diligence*."

CHAPTER FIFTEEN

Alan's office felt suffocating.

Thorn sat across from her uncle. Or rather, she *tried* to sit, but she was wound up with so much rage and frustration that her back was pin-straight and rigid, and the muscles in her legs tightened explosively, aching to spring up and go... *somewhere*. Anywhere.

But she took a deep breath as Alan looked down at the map she'd brought in, a pair of reading glasses perched at the end of his long, prominent nose. Several bright red Xs were scrawled in various neighborhoods around the city.

"This is the seventh bombing precipitated by Sin activity in the last two weeks," he reflected out loud. His deep voice was quiet, dulled by his thoughts, as a frown formed behind his black goatee.

"I know the fucking number," Thorn snapped, and Alan looked up to her. His dark eyes were cool and collected, and one eyebrow slowly raised on his forehead. She went on. "I was there. My point is that the other Sins are clearly *not* trying to kill me, so my restrictions should be lifted." Alan's brows raised even higher. Thorn held up a hand and counted off on her fingers. "No more curfews. No more check-ins. No more talking with Holly to make sure I didn't sneak out in the middle of the night."

She sent a pointed look his way, but Alan deflected it as naturally as he deflected all of his other smothering behavior—by simply not acknowledging it at all. He was shameless. Thorn was about the only person Alan had let himself get truly attached to in the sixty years since Teresa Solomon had left the Underground. She couldn't say she blamed him, but it could be infuriating.

Especially when he treated her like a delinquent teenager.

Alan sat up straighter in his chair, sighed, and whipped the glasses off his face.

"It might be premature to—"

"It's not, and you damn well know it," Thorn cut in. Her legs seized, ready to run and roar and rage, but she closed her eyes and shook her head to beat the feeling down. "Damn it, Alan, there have been *seven* attacks—"

"I know the number."

"—and I can't do a damn thing to stop them if I'm *stuck here.*"

"You don't know that you would be able to prevent them if you *were* there," Alan said, and he folded the map up and set it to the side. "In fact, you *have* been on the scene for three of these incidents, including the one just hours ago, and it changed nothing of the outcome. Besides, you seem to be conveniently missing one very critical point."

He watched her with a stern, concerned expression that almost made her feel sympathetic.

Almost.

"What's that?" she asked bitterly.

"Sloth *does* want you dead, and *he* is the one with the explosives."

Sloth. Just the mention of him made Thorn so furious she couldn't sit still anymore. She burst up from her chair and propped her hands on her hips. Alan watched her, as did Rae. The wolf sat at her spot on the side of Alan's desk, and now that Thorn was pacing, her keen, blue eyes stared at her. Thorn ignored her. She ignored Alan. She tried to ground herself, to soothe the white-hot fire burning in the cavern of her chest. The walls of Alan's office felt like they were closing in around her. The dark, maroon carpet. The mahogany shelves. The books and artifacts and Sin paraphernalia—it all slowly constricted her.

No matter how hard she tried, Thorn couldn't escape. Her mind was alight with the sights and sounds of this evening's attack. The cinder-block smell of broken buildings. Terrified, screaming people. Bright white eyes in bruised and dirty faces—and the gut-wrenching sensation of watching the life fade from those eyes. Feeling cold energy blink out forever.

Thorn sensed herself slipping. Her vision went gray and dead in cold, senseless rage.

"Are you all right?"

She rushed back to reality, stopped pacing, and snapped her head to look at Alan. He hadn't moved. He was still a figure of perfect, fucking *statuesque* calm. He had clasped his hands, fingers laced, on top of his desk, and while his face was mostly impassive, Thorn saw the worry line crinkling a little bit between his eyebrows. She looked away again, her fingers so hard on her hip bones that they were almost painful. She took a deep breath—

"Thorn?"

"No!" She exploded, throwing her hands up in the air and spinning toward Alan. "No, I'm not fucking *all right*. That mother fucker has detonated *seven* more bombs, and *every fucking time*, I get there too late to do a damn thing about it! People are dead! Buildings are ruined! My people have seen carnage I can't even begin to explain to them, and Gregory Witham keeps getting away! And that's not even the worst fucking part!"

Thorn's voice caught in her throat, an angry lump between her lungs trapping the air there. Alan steeped in the pause for a moment before he asked, "What is the worst part?"

She didn't answer him. Thorn turned away from her uncle, away from his level-headedness, away from his *superiority*, and clenched her teeth. She couldn't feel him move, but she felt the mood of the room shift and heard the quiet sounds of his shoes on the carpet as he walked around his desk.

Thorn didn't turn back to him as she said, "I want that fucker *dead.*" Now she was quiet, the words almost a whisper. "I want to rip him to pieces. I want to wrap my hands around his fucking throat and *squeeze* until I feel the vertebrae snap in my palms."

A rage of hatred and shame swelled in Thorn's gut, but Alan said nothing. She knew he wouldn't. He was the only person she felt comfortable admitting these kinds of thoughts to.

Because, whether he showed it or not, Alan understood what it was like to have Wrath tainting his soul, feeding his fury, and making every situation more violent, more aggressive than it had to be.

"But I *can't,*" Thorn went on, "because Nicholas Wolfe is fucking *Diligence.*"

The rest of the Underground was reveling in Nicholas's acceptance of his Virtue, ecstatic that they had a fully Initiated Diligence, but Thorn was not. She wanted to be—*god,* did she want to be—but that selfish bubble just wouldn't burst.

Thorn may be able to *kill* Gregory Witham, but only Wolfe could eradicate the Sin and remove it from the planet... *forever.*

"Have you spoken with Abraham?" Alan asked.

Thorn barked a harsh, humorless laugh. "The poor man's already terrified of me. No need to make it worse."

Alan came up beside her, and Thorn could sense him looking down at the side of her face. Rae padded up to the other hip, and she gently touched Thorn's thigh with the tip of her nose. It was cool even through the fabric of Thorn's leggings. She turned to Alan at last.

"He is a trained counselor," he offered in a way that was painfully *not* helpful. "And he has a standing appointment to meet with you every week."

"I haven't gone before, and I'm not going to start now," Thorn snapped.

"Thorn," Alan said, and he let out a sigh. One hand came out to grab firmly onto her shoulder. Her muscles relaxed a bit beneath it. "I am concerned for you. I have not seen you this tightly wound since—"

"Since when, Alan?" Thorn growled, twisting out of his grip furiously. "Since Cain left the Underground? Since Donovan died? Or since last fucking *week*, because I've got news for you—I am *always* tightly wound."

Alan frowned. "You need to control your—"

"What the *fuck* do you think I'm trying to do?" Thorn exclaimed. She threw her hands up again. "That's why I need to be back out there, *without any god damned restrictions*. I cannot *breathe* here. Please, *let me go.*"

The room went quiet. Thorn and Alan stared at one another in mounting apprehension. She gritted her teeth. The muscles along her throat were so tight it made the bones in her neck grind together. Alan's face was a canvas of worry he rarely showed, so Thorn knew his concern was deeper than he wanted to admit.

Concerned she would do something stupid and get herself killed.

But at last, he took a deep breath and said, "All right. No more restrictions—"

Thorn didn't even wait for the word to leave his mouth before she turned around and opened the door. "Thank you," she murmured, and the words came out with such a heavy relief that, for a moment, Thorn felt overwhelmed. Alan followed her into the lounge. Sparkie squeezed himself out of the gap beneath Thorn's office door and vaulted onto her shoulder. His tiny body was a ball of anxious energy. He shuddered as she breathed.

"Where are you going?" Alan asked.

"Into the city," Thorn said shortly. She didn't want to talk about this anymore, so she didn't wait for him to respond as she headed into the hallway, brusquely passed Jeremiah as he left for the day, and rushed to the parking garage. Her bike was parked by the door, and Thorn threw a leg over it.

It was late, but maybe Wrath would be hunting for Sloth. Maybe Witham would send Puppets after her. Maybe Jay was still awake, and she could pick a fight then fuck him to release some of this rage.

Whatever it was, Thorn didn't care.

She was back.

———

The sun was barely rising over New York, dawn breaking in red hot reflections in the bright, glass facades of distant skyscrapers as Thorn walked into Grind House Coffee early the next day. She paused outside the door, sucked her morning cigarette down to its final dregs, and flicked the butt onto the sidewalk. Then she drove her heel into it harder than she had to, like it was a cockroach that needed squashing.

Being back in New York hadn't quelled her anger as much as Thorn had hoped it would. Instead of a sedated beast, it growled low from the cage between her ribs in a rhythmic beat.

Last night had been a bust. No Sins. No Jay. No *release*.

But it was still better than being stuck in the Underground.

"Good morning, sunshine," the barista said with a smile. He looked older than Thorn remembered; his brown hair was thinning at his forehead, and he'd grown it out a bit to try to hide that fact. His round face felt a little thinner than she was used to, and the lines beneath his eyes a little deeper.

It was almost time for her to find a new coffee shop. If Thorn noticed he was aging, it was only a matter of time before he realized she was *not*. The thought sent a dull pang of loss through her chest. She'd miss this place.

"Good morning," Thorn said.

The barista grabbed a to-go cup off the stack and started preparing her standard order: a tall black coffee—no cream, no sugar. He glanced at the clock above the door. "You're here early, even for you."

Thorn scoffed. She hadn't slept much last night—or any night, really, for the last few months. But last night had been particularly bad. Tossing and turning in one of the Martyr-owned apartments in Harlem, tormented by Sloth, obsessing over finding him and wondering what the fuck she would even do when she did.

Would she have to kill him, right then and there, to *guarantee* the bombings would come to an end? Or would she try to apprehend him, to hold him in one place, until fucking *Nicholas Wolfe* could get down there and save the day? She'd have to at least try, wouldn't she?

Just the thought of that left a bitter taste in Thorn's mouth.

"I've been busy," she said.

"Oh yeah? With what?"

Rage bubbled. Irrationally, she knew, but it bubbled all the same. It wasn't his fault. Even without knowing the man's name, Thorn knew this barista well enough to know he was a talker. He thrived on drama and gossip, using it to connect to his customers and get bigger tips. Sometimes, the drama helped. He'd cued her into strange incidents linked to the Sins on more than one occasion.

But lately, it was exhausting. She didn't want to talk—especially not when he was just one more person she had to lie to—one more person she had to pretend to be this *other woman* around.

She bit the rage back, though. Dug her nails into her palm to keep herself grounded as she shook her head. Alan was right. She had to stay in control. Keep a cool head. Thorn had a role to play. *Teagan Love* didn't lose her shit and punch through walls. "Just a big story," Thorn said. "I'm under a lot of pressure, and I have an intense deadline."

It wasn't a lie. Thorn had gotten good at that—at giving a glimpse of the truth without revealing anything substantial. Just enough to draw people in, to make them think they knew her.

The barista nodded as he passed her cup over the counter. "Well, I wish I could say we were busy here," he said with a sigh. "Business has been down the last couple of weeks."

Of course it was. The Sins were still working hard to keep Sloth's bombings out of the media. "Mass grid overcharges," they were being called. It suited them to keep the public unaware. If civilians realized a madman was running around New York, blowing things up, fewer people would be out on the streets. Where the Martyrs relied on a complicated network of security cameras and computer algorithms to keep an eye on what was happening in the city, the Sins relied upon Programming. Wrath was always working, Programming as many people as she could to spot Sloth and report his whereabouts. Thorn could feel it—tiny, fleeting beacons of Influence across the city. Undoubtedly, the other Sins were doing the same.

If the Sentries they Programmed got spooked and stayed home, it would be harder to track Sloth down.

But rumors were starting to circulate. It didn't matter if Lust could stop the truth from leaking into the news or that Wrath prevented onlookers from recording video: people could *sense* that this was bigger than deficient infrastructure.

In many ways, rumors were more dangerous than facts. Thorn could feel it in the people around her when she walked through the city. There was a quiet air of fear.

That air was seeping out of her barista that morning. His voice was casual, but the worry crept across his face—in the fine lines under his eyes, the creases in his forehead, and the way the corners of his lips were turned, just slightly, downward. Thorn took a deep breath.

She didn't have time for this *friend* thing. She didn't have the mental bandwidth to deal with tracking down Sloth and taking care of the emotional wellbeing of another human being.

"I'm sorry. That sucks." She meant it. She *was* sorry. It *did* suck. All of it was out of his hands, like so much of what happened in this fucking city. But what else could she say? She grabbed her coffee and raised it, about to say her good-byes and get the hell out of there, when he kept talking.

"I heard there's been attacks around the city."

He was looking her right in the face. Thorn paused mid-step as she backed away from the counter.

"I figured the heat was causing problems with the city's power," she lied with a shrug.

She moved to turn around, but the barista spoke again. Her rage bubbled more, popping just under the surface. Thorn's stomach twisted up, and she clenched her teeth together.

"One of my sister's coworkers went missing after an explosion in Midtown," he was saying. "The news said a power box blew up under the street, but my sister said it seemed like it was an above-ground thing."

"Really?" Thorn took another step back.

"Yeah," he said. "I don't think I buy it."

"Yeah, I don't know."

"Think it's a terrorist?"

"I have no idea."

"You gotta wonder, 'cause—"

Thorn's rage boiled past the tipping point. She was half-way between the door and the counter when the man just *kept fucking talking*, and she lost it. She shook her head and said, "Jesus, SHUT UP."

He stared at her—mouth open, eyes wide, with an expression of pain on his face so clear she may as well have slapped it onto him—but she couldn't stop. The words poured out in a tsunami of anger:

"I have no fucking idea what's going on, okay? And I

don't have the fucking *time* to make you feel better about it, so just *shut up*."

Then she turned and stormed out of the building. Her heart gave an uncomfortable flip at the way he stared after her, but she kept going. She strode down the street, around the corner, and finally, Thorn exploded. She roared, her fingers tightening around her to-go cup until she crumpled it in her fist and poured scalding coffee down her hand. It soaked into her black, fingerless glove and held the burning liquid tight against her skin. She threw the cup to the ground.

"God damn it!"

This was exactly why she didn't spend much time in the Underground when she was in a mood like this. She couldn't let the Martyrs—the people who trusted her with their *lives*—see her this way. She had to be better for them. She had to be the best that she could be.

And she certainly wasn't living up to that standard now.

Thorn removed her soaked gloves and opened her satchel, digging through her items until she found a clean pair. Sparkie vaulted into the dawn sky above her and flew in furious circles high over her head. As she pulled the gloves on, she looked down at the *Peccostium* on her wrist.

Fucking *Wrath*, still finding ways to screw her over almost one hundred years after Thorn had ripped it out of her body.

She finished putting the gloves on, grabbed out her pack of smokes, and stood up straight again. She lit a cigarette and sucked the nicotine deep into her lungs.

Tomorrow, she would come back and apologize. She'd make up some bullshit story about her boss being a dick and how she let the pressure get to her. Maybe she'd even buy him some gift certificate and a card. But that would come later because now, she had to get back to work.

Time to start another long, sweltering day of hunting for Gregory Witham on the busy, crowded, and ignorant streets of New York City.

Twelve hours later, Thorn had nothing to show for a day of stalking through Manhattan except an empty pack of cigarettes.

The Sins were quiet. Thorn had insisted on near-constant updates from her team about everything that was happening with them. Itching for a fight, maybe? Chris would certainly think so, but Thorn didn't care. And it hadn't mattered, anyway. The most exciting development was that Anton Claytor had raised his smug, little face again. Elena Cortez was working a fancy luncheon, and she'd called to let Thorn know he walked through the door an hour ago like nothing had happened.

That news had just sour her mood even further. Thorn had *really* been hoping he hadn't survived the bomb. One less active Sin meant a lot less Influence to contend with and fewer Sentries to avoid.

Beyond that was radio silence. Lust and Gluttony were maintaining business as usual, and Wrath was nowhere to be found. Not by Holly's cameras. Not by Thorn's senses. She could be anywhere, doing anything.

Wherever and whatever it was, Autumn Hunt wasn't using her Influence.

Thorn headed back toward Mott Haven, frustrated, empty-handed, and full of pent-up energy she needed to release. Sparkie flew far above her, so high that even on a bright day like this, no one on the ground would see him as anything other than the dark silhouette of a peregrine falcon gliding through the air. He fed off her irritation, dipping and diving and snapping at starlings that made the mistake of flying too close.

With a heart full of fire, Thorn decided to try her luck at The Cross. She'd been hounding Holly for any new developments there, but the bar was just as dreary and uneventful as usual. Aside from the occasional drunken brawl, there had been no violence or suspicious activity. Knowing now that the rest of the Sins weren't after her, Thorn wondered if the only one who knew about her regular hang out was Sloth…

And if so, maybe showing up there would lure him out.

She missed the bar. There was an emptiness in her chest, like she'd lost a good friend, and she was aching to get it back. What she wouldn't give to kill a couple of hours surrounded by the familiar coldness of The Cross's regular patrons, drowning her miseries in scotch she couldn't feel. It didn't matter that she couldn't get drunk. Alcohol, like nicotine and caffeine, wasn't about addiction. It was about dousing the fire.

And, god, she could use a drink right about now.

Just as she hit the Willis Bridge, her phone rang. She pulled it out to see Holly's face on the screen. She frowned, and she answered.

"Yeah?"

"Check your email."

There was an urgency in Holly's voice Thorn rarely heard. She slipped her headphones on so she could talk privately while she navigated to her protected, Martyr service email account.

"What's going on?" she asked.

"We picked up a tip that was sent in to the police. It's a video. Watch it."

Thorn started the clip and immediately spotted what had Holly so worried: footage of Saul Torres. Thorn's chest constricted. He'd been spotted near the Mitchel Houses, just half a mile away from The Cross.

Right in the heart of Eva's new territory.

"When did you get this?" Thorn asked.

"Three minutes ago. Maybe four."

"And it was anonymous? This wasn't on the public news?"

"I said it was from the police hotline," Holly snapped. "No, it wasn't public."

Thorn nodded. That meant Eva didn't know—or at

least, she *shouldn't* know. Good. The last thing Thorn needed was for her to run off and get herself into trouble trying to reach Saul before the Sins did.

Because the Sins *would* be coming. Gluttony was the police commissioner; he would undoubtedly share the information with the others. Wrath's Influence suddenly pinged to life. A tiny, flickering light that disappeared as soon as it came in. North—further north than the Cross. Sparkie arced one last time before rushing off, straight toward Autumn Hunt. Thorn pulled her hair back and said, "All right. I'm on my way—"

"Wait!" Holly cut her off. Her tone was more frantic now. "Look at the foreground at the end of the video—look at the man sitting on the corner. Is that who I think it is?"

Thorn stopped walking and squinted down at her phone. People pushed past her impatiently as she tried to get a good look at the guy Holly was talking about. She paused the clip on a still shot of Saul. It was just him. Juniper and Lindsay weren't anywhere in sight. Thorn allowed herself a petty moment of satisfaction in knowing Wolfe's new system wouldn't have worked in this case—not if Torres was traveling alone.

With her thumb, Thorn dragged the video forward frame by frame, watching as Saul walked back and forth outside the housing authority building. Then, as the camera came down, the lens caught sight of a homeless man huddled on the street corner just before the footage went black. He was filthy, covered head to toe in ratty, old clothes. His back was to her, and Thorn couldn't make out his face. What the fuck was Holly so—

And then he shifted, just enough, to where Thorn could see the *Peccostium* peek out above the collar of his sweatshirt. Her heart skipped a beat.

"*Fuck,*" Thorn breathed.

She didn't wait for Holly to answer. She just barked orders as she began to hurry down the sidewalk.

"Send backup. Whoever's closest. Call Eva. Tell her to

get to her apartment and *stay there*. Get me eyes on the scene. Record whatever you can. I'm on my way."

"Roger that," Holly said. Then she added, with a tiny hint of concern, "Be careful."

Thorn remembered what it felt like to be caught in Sloth's explosions. Flesh being blown from her body. Fire licking her chest and throat. The agonizing sensation of bone and muscle knitting themselves back together.

"I will be," Thorn said.

Then she hung up and ran. The hot, rank air from the Harlem River flew past Thorn's face as she sped across the Willis Street bridge. Her headphones bounced around her throat, and she ripped them from her ears and shoved them into her satchel. She darted through people, ignoring angry calls and empty threats as she pushed her way past them and sprinted furiously toward Mott Haven.

Wrath's Influence continued to blink sporadically as she moved. She was across the river. Past The Cross. Fuck. She was so close.

Thorn pushed harder. The bridge ended. Thorn leapt down the stairs three at a time, bounding from one to the next with footfalls so light they hardly made a sound on the concrete. People jumped or were pushed out of her way as she ran down Bruckner. Through screaming pedestrians. Through honking traffic. Through whatever path she could find that offered the least resistance and didn't slow her down.

Thorn ran to Lincoln and headed north. Past the scorched, black spot on the side of the road where Sloth tried to blow her up. Under the overpass. Through one last busy intersection. She didn't wait for the light to turn green—she just barreled around speeding cars. Drivers laid on their horns and swore at her, but she ignored them.

Finally, she reached the corner where Sloth had been sitting.

He wasn't there anymore.

She rushed to the tall, brick building where Saul Torres

had been spotted.

He was gone.

But Wrath was closing in. Her Influence felt closer now. Through the trees. Behind the building—

A figure in a dark, pullover hoodie came around the corner of the housing authority. He lifted his head, and Thorn saw the distinct, purple scar cutting his face from just above his left eye all the way to his ear.

Saul Torres.

Thorn darted across the lawn. She vaulted over one wrought iron fence. Then another. He saw her coming. As soon as he spotted her, his brown eyes went wide. Thorn's heart leapt into her throat as he turned to run away, back the way he'd come. Back toward where Wrath was closing in.

She couldn't let him go.

Thorn reached out with her Influence. She felt his energy—his consciousness—and she told him to stop.

He did.

Then Wrath's Influence flared to life. Excited. Earnest. Like the Sin was *happy* to find that her favorite plaything was nearby. That cold, vicious force grew, hungrily gorging, until it had doubled, tripled, quadrupled in size.

Fuck. Wrath was collecting Puppets.

Thorn couldn't focus on that. She rushed up to Saul and grabbed him by the bicep. He turned to her. Dazed. Shocked. He looked down at his own feet, as though wondering why they'd suddenly stopped working, before he looked at her and said, "Who the fuck—"

"We don't have time," Thorn snapped. "We need to get you out of here. Follow me."

"Follow you?" Saul ripped his shoulder out of her hands and took a step back. "Who the fuck *are* you?"

"Look," Thorn insisted, "I know Eva. I know your sister. And I know who is looking for you. I can keep you *safe,* but we need to *move.*"

Saul's whole expression opened up. His brown eyes

went wide, his mouth dropped, and he barely choked out the words, "Eva's *alive*?"

"Yes." Thorn reached out and grabbed his shoulder again. This time, he didn't fight back. Thorn's anxiety was mounting. Wrath was close—so close Thorn could almost feel the charge of her Influence buzzing in the cavern where her soul once was. "But if you want to see her, we need to *go.*"

She thought she'd have to fight him more, but Saul just nodded and tucked in close behind her as she pulled him around the building.

Now Thorn could sense more than Autumn Hunt's Influence coming at them like a frigid hurricane. She could sense her energy through the twenty-story, brick face of the housing authority.

"Come on," Thorn said. "This way." She broke into a run across the parking lot. Saul followed on her heels. "Where are the others?"

"Who?" Saul sped up to be beside her.

She cast a glance at him from over her shoulder. "Juniper and Lindsay. Where are they?"

Saul's face blanched, and for a moment, he seemed shocked. And scared. "Not here," was all he said.

That was good enough for Thorn.

"Okay." She focused on running again. "We can get them later."

"Where are we going?" Saul asked. His breathing was heavy and haggard.

She didn't answer. She didn't *have* an answer. She just had to get them out of here, hopefully before—

"Fuck!"

Saul's energy stumbled and fell behind her. Thorn turned to see him sprawled on the asphalt, his foot ankle-deep in a pothole the city hadn't bothered to fucking fix. She hurried to his side and helped him up. When he tried to put weight on his foot, he collapsed.

"Shit," he growled. "I twisted my ankle."

Thorn's heart dropped. Fuck. Time for a new plan.

"Come here." Thorn pulled Saul's arm over her shoulder, wrapped hers around his waist, and all but lifted him from the ground. They rushed toward the far end of the parking lot. Saul stared at the side of her face, awestruck, but Thorn ignored him as she stopped by the side of a car and put him down. Then she focused on the lot.

And the people in it.

Thorn pushed her Influence out. There was no point in trying to hide now. Wrath already knew she was here, and she knew Thorn was associated with the cold energy that belonged to Saul Torres. Even if Thorn tried to hide him and lure the Sin away, Hunt would be able to feel him. To track him down. Capture him.

And Thorn had no doubt she intended to capture him.

Like she had captured Donovan. Like she had tortured and killed him in order to wound Thorn, Wrath meant to torture and kill Saul to wound Darius.

Thorn wouldn't give her the satisfaction.

Instead, she would do what she could to turn this place into a better battleground. If she couldn't outrun the bitch, she'd have to turn and fight, and she wouldn't do it pressed up against a wall.

With one hand firmly around Saul's shoulder to stop him from trying to get up and leave, she pushed her Influence out, into the lot, and drove all the people from it. Fewer distractions. Fewer casualties. Fewer civilians Wrath could take over and add to her horde of Puppets.

As Wrath's army neared, the lot emptied. People left their cars and dashed away, their cold energies fleeing the area until Thorn couldn't feel them anymore. All but one. Thorn frowned and focused on it.

Her whole body went cold. "Oh, *fuck*!"

Saul turned to her, confused. "What?"

Thorn ignored him. She felt numb, distant, as Sparkie dove from the sky. He followed where Thorn sensed cold energy, quietly landed on the pavement near where Saul had fallen, and peeked around a car tire…

To see Gregory Witham hiding behind it, his blue eyes anxiously darting from where Thorn and Saul were hiding to where the energy of Wrath's Puppets bled through the housing building. He held a metal-plated device in his shaking hands.

Thorn's heart raced. She felt it in her fingertips, rushing through her ears in a disorienting flood. Sloth's face was white and terrified as he inched his way backward, abandoning his explosive beneath the car. For a moment, Thorn was frozen.

What the fuck was she supposed to do *now*?

She didn't have the time to figure it out. Wrath's Influence moved through the building, and suddenly, there they were.

Puppets rushed around the brick facade of the housing authority and made their way straight toward Thorn and Saul. They ran out from the front door and hurried into the parking lot. People with dead eyes—plastic, expressionless faces—as they blindly followed the strings Wrath pulled as she sent them barreling across the blacktop. Between parked cars. Around big, leafy trees.

Sloth inched further backward. He belly-crawled away until he was underneath another vehicle. Sparkie glanced between his retreating feet and the bomb he'd left behind…

Thorn swore and turned to Saul.

"Wait here," she growled. "When I tell you to run, *run*."

Saul shook his head. "Run where?"

"Away from here," Thorn said as she got to her feet, and turned toward Wrath's army. With a deep breath, she grabbed the gun from her satchel, deposited the bag at Saul's feet, and squared her shoulders.

There were twenty Puppets. Coordinated. Hive-minded. Sprinting in one mad dash through the old, beat-up cars like an organism. Then there was Wrath. She walked around the building slowly, with a wide, toothy smile plastered across her tawny face. Her long, brown hair was loose and wild around her shoulders as she strode out and into the open.

As soon as Wrath's feet hit the asphalt, Thorn charged.

She arced toward the edge of the lot, away from the bomb Sloth had planted, as she rushed the mass of Puppets. The tight muscles in her thighs pushed forward as fast as they could, putting as much distance between herself and Saul as possible before the Puppets could spread out to surround them.

Fifty feet back, they made to break around Thorn. She didn't let them.

She reached out with her Influence, feeling Wrath's grip around their minds. Vice-like, but brittle. With a sharp, mental twist, she stabbed her Influence in like a knife and snapped the connection with the first Puppet. He collapsed onto the ground, his bulky body landing with a hard thump.

She did the same for a second and a third—all the way through the first fourteen. Thorn dug in with her mind and flipped the switch. People dropped around her, unconscious, as Influence broke. She selected them strategically—working to thin the numbers and keep them dispersed so they would be easy to take on one-on-one when the time came.

It came quickly. As she disposed of Puppets, the ones that remained were harder to free. Wrath's Influence became more focused. More powerful. When there were just six left, Thorn's attempts to cut them off were slow and clumsy, like trying to slice through steel cable with wire cutters. It would take too long to break the link now.

She had to do it the old-fashioned way. Put a Puppet into enough pain, and the connection between them and the Sin shattered.

Thorn was good at inflicting pain.

A woman tried to barrel past her to where Saul was standing—and where Sloth's bomb lay hidden. Thorn's heart pounded as she jumped into the Puppet's path. She clawed at Thorn and swung her purse like a weapon, but Thorn deftly slipped under her arms and thrust her elbow up and into the Puppet's throat. She dropped, gasping for air, and went unconscious.

Freed from Wrath. Safe from Sloth.

For now.

Thorn kept moving. Rushing forward. Adding more feet to the space between herself and Saul. Herself and the bomb. Sparkie was still on Sloth's tail, keeping his eye on the detonator in the Sin's hand. So far, he was still army-crawling in the opposite direction, almost to the edge of the lot...

Thorn kept pushing forward. A Puppetted man moved to pass her. Thorn intercepted him, grabbed him by the shoulders, and kneed him in the groin.

He squealed and passed out.

Then Wrath roared, and she charged.

Her rage flared. It teased the edges of Thorn's anger, coaxing it forward and egging it on. Thorn fought to stay in control of herself as the Puppets changed focus.

They rounded on her. The four remaining Puppets suddenly dashed not past Thorn but *toward* her. Fingers grabbed at her arms and throat—pulled at the fabric around her wrists and wrapped themselves up in her ponytail. Thorn twisted around. She swept a foot in a circle around her and knocked two of the Puppets' feet out from under them. They jumped back up with robotic finesse. Thorn grabbed a woman by the arm, hoisted her over her shoulders, and flung her ten feet down the parking lot—right into Wrath as she came down upon them.

The Sin screamed and threw the Puppet to the side, where her unconscious body bounced along the asphalt. Thorn thrust the butt of her gun into a man's face and felt his Influence break as quickly as his nose. Blood gushed down his face, and he crumbled.

Then Wrath leapt on her back.

Autumn Hunt wrapped her legs around Thorn's middle, and while one arm held tight around her throat, the other clawed viciously at the gun in Thorn's hand. Thorn held it straight up, into the air, as Wrath snarled and dug her nails into the flesh around Thorn's fingers. Thorn's skin broke. She felt the blood drip down, slick, making the gun slippery in her hands.

The last two Puppets came in to help. They punched at Thorn, grabbed her hair and her clothes, trying to pull her to the ground. Wrath's arm tightened around Thorn's throat.

This wasn't good. Thorn had no advantage now.

She threw herself backward.

Thorn slammed down on top of Hunt. Her body crushed against Wrath's chest and forced the air from her lungs, but the fall knocked the gun from Thorn's hand. It clattered somewhere behind them as Wrath took deep, thirsty gasps in an attempt to breathe again. The Puppets hesitated, as though they were out of breath, too.

Without a weapon, Thorn changed tactics.

She spun around on the ground—rolled over until she was straddling Wrath's body on the hot, black asphalt. Autumn Hunt's gray eyes went wild with anger as Thorn threw the first punch into her face.

She felt Hunt's skull crack against the blacktop.

Thorn didn't stop punching. She struck Wrath over and over again, pummeling her face with her bare fists. Soon Hunt was almost unrecognizable. Her flesh was purple and blue, her lips cracked and bleeding.

The Sin roared in pain and caught Thorn's fist. She yanked, wrestled, writhed under Thorn's body until she'd lifted her up and got her legs up underneath her. Then she pivoted and flung Thorn back, further down the parking lot. Further away from Saul Torres. He was more than one hundred feet away from her now—and now, the Sin and her Puppets stood between them. Thorn landed hard on her back as Wrath, mangled and raw, got up and started to race toward Saul—

"Run!" Thorn screamed to him.

But he couldn't run, and Thorn knew it. As Saul turned

to limp away, Wrath gained ground. Thorn knew she couldn't catch up.

So she put her other plan—her *stupid*, desperate plan—into action.

Sparkie leapt on Gregory Witham.

Sloth screamed as the lizard jumped onto his face. Clawed at his eyes. Scurried to his right hand and the detonator he held there—

And Sparkie pushed the button.

The car exploded.

Thorn ducked down and took cover as debris flew by. She felt Wrath's energy sail over her head and crumple on the ground behind her. She felt Saul limping away…

And she felt Witham running.

Thorn jumped up. Sloth had gotten to his feet, not bothering to hide now, and taken off toward the east. He darted between cars, desperate to escape, and Saul Torres was running north, with an awkward, unbalanced gait, away from the fire and smoke.

For a brief second, Thorn paused.

Who should she follow?

Wrath made the decision for her. By some unholy miracle, her last two Puppets were still intact, and they were chasing after Saul. Gaining on him. Thorn swore and started after them.

She sensed Wrath's aura as soon as she took the first step. Hunt tackled her from behind and drove her back into the blacktop. She wrapped one hand up in Thorn's hair while the other clawed for her left wrist. Her fingers found the *Peccostium* and dug into it. Thorn cried out as acrid, paralyzing pain shot from the mark and followed the tangled web of scars up her arm. It settled into her spine, radiated through her extremities, pulverizing her muscles until they felt weak and jelly-like. Sparkie fell from the sky with a shriek. Thorn felt him drop onto the asphalt.

"Fucking *Witham*!" Wrath's voice was hot and caustic against Thorn's ear. The Sin shifted, raising herself up, and looked across the lot. Sloth's energy was fuzzy as he got away. "I'll get you next!" Wrath screamed after him.

But then she shifted, kneeling on top of Thorn's lower back, pulling her hair with a rough, joyous exuberance as she forced Thorn's head up.

To where the Puppets were chasing Saul.

"But for now... I've got something *better*. Jones will come for him," Hunt whispered. Her voice sent a furious chill down Thorn's spine. "Then I'll peel him like an orange and *squeeze him dry*."

Thorn's stomach dropped. She fought, weakly, *pathetically*, against Wrath's grip, but it was no use. The asphalt scalded against her skin—the stink of burned rubber and propellant clouded her senses, made her eyes thick and watery. Saul stumbled down 138th street. The Puppets were right on his heels—

A gunshot blasted. Wrath swore. Her grip on Thorn's left wrist loosened. Hot, syrupy liquid poured into the divot between Thorn's shoulder blades.

Another gunshot.

That one hit the ground. Chips of hot, black rock flaked off and dug into Thorn's face.

Wrath's Puppets collapsed. Her fingers released Thorn's wrist, and she darted away and hid behind a car. Saul disappeared around the corner as Thorn scrambled to get to her feet. Eva came at them from the housing authority building. Her pistol was held straight and even in her hands.

Thorn rushed to her, snatched the weapon, and pointed it right at the car Wrath was hiding behind. Thorn walked in a wide arc around the vehicle, and every time she got a glimpse of the Sin, she shot, and she shot until the clip was empty.

But Autumn Hunt was still alive.

The weapon clicked uselessly in Thorn's hands. Wrath got to her feet and started to back away, out of the lot, and across the street. Eva's shot had been right to the collarbone. Blood poured down the wound, coating Hunt's throat and chest in a slick of dark red streaks. Her face was starting to heal. The minced flesh was stitching together, and her swollen eyes were opening up again.

And Wrath looked right at Eva. Her pupils were pin-tight as she took in everything about her—from her face to the dirty sneakers she had on her feet. She pointed a finger and screamed over the sound of the burning car and distant sirens.

"You'll *fucking pay*, you little *bitch*."

Then she turned and ran.

Thorn watched her go, and though she *ached* to follow, her body still felt faint from Wrath's assault on her *Peccostium*, and she knew she'd never catch up. Instead, she swore and rounded on Eva.

"*What the fuck are you doing here?*"

Eva gawked at her. Her lips parted, her dark eyes wide.

"What am I—? I just *saved* you!" she choked out.

"And let Wrath see you!" Thorn roared. All the practiced restraint she'd been struggling with for the last few weeks shattered. The rage overflowed. Like a volcano, she felt the eruption rock through her—into her hands, her legs, her core—and she spun around and punched a nearby car. She punched it again. And again. Until the metal was warped and her knuckles were cut and bleeding.

Sloth had escaped! Wrath had survived! Eva had *ruined* her job in the city—had let *Autumn Hunt* see her face!

God fucking damn it!

Sparkie clambered up onto Thorn's shoulder and made a small, meek sound. Her anger quietly crawled back into its cage, but it still reached out with long, dangerous claws. Eva was staring at her—her mouth dropped open, her eyes wide. Shocked. Silent. Terrified.

Fucking *great*.

Now wasn't the time, though. Thorn had to get them out of there. Smoke was still furling high into the sky above them. A blaring signal. Sirens roared in the distance—but not that far in the distance.

"Come on," she snarled. "We've got to get back to the Underground."

"What about Saul?" Eva asked. The words were strong and clear, but her voice shook with emotion.

"Saul is *gone*!" Thorn screamed. She turned and pointed across the parking lot to where Saul had disappeared around the corner. "And we have to—"

But she paused because laying in the lot, beside another vehicle, was a peculiar, rectangular device.

Thorn's fury ebbed a little further as curiosity sank in. She furrowed her brow and hurried toward the object. Sparkie crawled from one shoulder to the other as Thorn leaned over and picked it up from the ground. Her heart stopped.

It was an undetonated bomb.

CHAPTER SIXTEEN

A small, rectangular item sat in the center of the table. Darius stared at it, feeling simultaneously disconnected from his body and yet crowded into it. The gray, concrete walls were covered with racks and shelves, stocked with so many rifles, handguns, and boxes of munitions Darius couldn't begin to imagine what kind of small army they could supply. The lack of softness in the room stole the buffering of sound, creating an uncomfortable loudness. Every foot shuffling, every throat clearing, every soft *plink!* of Mackenzie's tongue ring against her teeth felt magnified.

And in that not-quite-silent silence, the seven men and women of the Martyr leadership looked down at a bomb.

Thirty minutes ago, Thorn had come back to the Underground, filthy, furious, and empty-handed. *Almost* empty-handed. She hadn't rescued Saul. She hadn't captured Sloth.

But she had found *this*.

It seemed harmless. Just a metal box, fixed together with crude duct tape, sprouting cut wires like spider legs. Five minutes ago, Jeremiah had called them all into the tactical munitions locker to talk about it, but so far, no one said a thing. While Thorn and Alan stood by the door and Lina and Abraham were at the far side of the room, Darius was beside Mackenzie on the adjacent wall. The Irishwoman was quiet, but her fingers tapped wildly on her bare bicep.

At last, she threw her hands into the air and blurted out, "I'm just gonna say it—anyone else concerned that we have *all the Martyr leadership gathered in one room around a fucking bomb*?"

"It's not active," Jeremiah said, and he cast her an almost comical look. "You think I'd bring a live bomb in here?"

"If it's not a threat, why did you call us into the *god damned weapons vault*?" Mackenzie fired back. "This room has two-foot-thick walls and a *reinforced door*!"

Alan held up his hand to quiet Mackenzie, and she leaned back, her arms wrapped around herself like armor. He turned to Thorn. "Where did you say you found this?"

Thorn looked up at him. While Jeremiah was defusing the bomb, she had taken a quick shower to wash the blood and grime off. She was clean, dampness clinging to her throat and back, but the stink of burned rubber still floated off her and permeated the room.

"It was in the parking lot," Thorn said. She crossed her arms over her red tank top and looked back at the device. "About one hundred feet from where the other one went off."

"He placed multiple bombs?" Lina asked.

"It appears so," Jeremiah said with a nod. "Or he carries a spare."

"Well, *fuck that*," Mackenzie breathed. She shook her head and stepped a little closer to the table. "One bomb at a time is bad enough."

"Why would he even want more than one?" Abraham asked.

Jeremiah took a deep breath and shrugged. "There are a lot of reasons," he said, and his frown deepened as he thought about it. "To do more damage, for one. It would also make things more confusing if bombs were going off in multiple areas. Plus, it gives him a greater chance of killing his target."

"I don't think he had a target," Thorn said. "He didn't detonate the bomb. *I* did."

"*You?*" Jeremiah asked, shocked. His heavy eyebrows pinched together.

Before he had the chance to say anything further, Thorn propped her hands on her hips. "Yes," she said. "Wrath was going to get Torres, and I had to do *something*. For fuck's sake, Montgomery, that's not even the point. He wasn't trying to kill me or anyone else. Sloth was just trying to get the hell out of there."

"Just because he didn't detonate it doesn't mean that wasn't his plan," Jeremiah said hotly. "You and Wrath are both hunting him down. He would have to be out of his mind not to take this opportunity."

"Of course he's out of his damned mind," Thorn said. Her voice was dark. "But he wasn't even watching the fight to know when to blow the bomb in the first place."

"He also had no way of knowing they would be there," Abraham added, drawing his shoulders up in an anxious shrug. "Did he?"

Jeremiah nodded thoughtfully. "Then maybe the bomb was simply meant to be a diversion."

"Pretty fucking extreme diversion," Mackenzie grumbled.

"But it *is* effective," Jeremiah said. "I carry grenades when I'm on duty for this exact reason. When shit blows up, people get confused, and we can get away."

"It is possible this explosive was a way to guarantee that he could escape if he needed to," Alan said.

"Maybe they *all* have been," Jeremiah said. He was the only person in the room taller than Alan, and he looked down, just slightly, at him. "We've been assuming Witham is leading an attack, but maybe he's on the *defensive*."

"Like he was with Greed." Lina pressed the fingers of her right hand against her lips. "I'll talk to Holly about it. I know we have footage from at least half of the bombings. Maybe we can see who really instigated them."

Alan nodded. "That is an excellent idea. Please do so, Miss Brooks." Then Alan turned to Jeremiah and gestured toward the device on the table. "Is there any way this bomb can be useful to us?"

"We can reverse engineer his detonator," Jeremiah said. "The receiver is still intact."

"Translate that for those of us who don't speak bomb," Mackenzie said.

"The detonator sends a signal that is received by the bomb. If we can recreate it, we can find a way to jam the signal," Jeremiah said with a look in Mackenzie's direction. She provided a quick nod of gratitude, and he went on. "I'm afraid I know a lot more about how to cut the wires on a bomb like this than I do about how to stop the signal from reaching it."

"Would Holly know?" Abraham asked.

Alan frowned and stroked his goatee. "Perhaps. Her experience is more in software and computer engineering than in electrical or mechanical."

"She's basically a genius," Mackenzie said. "If anyone down here can figure it out, it's her."

"Jeremiah," Alan said, "ask Miss Andrews if she can help with this. Disabling Sloth's explosives would be more valuable to us than I can possibly describe."

"Yes, sir."

"Now, unless there is more we need to discuss," Alan started, but Thorn stepped up and cleared her throat before he had the chance to dismiss them.

"There is," she said, and she threw Darius a quick look. Her half-empty eyes were tinted with a regret that barely touched the rest of her expression. She turned back to her uncle. "Eva Torres is no longer safe in the Gray Unit."

The room quieted again. Darius's stomach twisted up in knots as Mackenzie swore and said, "One of them spotted her, huh?"

"Wrath," Thorn said. There was a hot edge to the words—an anger waiting, just beneath the surface—but her face remained neutral, if tense. "She showed up on the scene, and Autumn Hunt saw her."

"Clearly enough to be able to Program her face?" Alan asked.

"Yes," Thorn said. The muscles in her throat tightened. "Absolutely."

"Didn't Holly send her strict orders to return to her apartment and stay there?" Jeremiah observed with a frown.

Thorn nodded, but she was unapologetic as she said, "If she hadn't ignored those direct orders, the Sins would have Saul Torres right now. They would have *me*. She fucked over her job, but she damn well saved our lives out there today."

Then Thorn looked to Darius again, and he felt a surge of gratitude grow in his chest. This was one of the things he knew he could rely on Thorn for: she saw the value in her team, and she fought fiercely for them, even when she was fighting alone.

"Has she been informed?" Alan asked.

"No," Thorn said. "We were picked up just a couple of blocks away from the incident. I felt this conversation should be had in private. I'm going to speak with her when we're done here."

And, by the way Thorn's lips pressed together when she said the words, Darius assumed she hadn't been in a calm enough place to have that conversation without screaming.

"I'll handle it," Darius said.

Thorn shook her head. "No. Let me be the bad guy—"

"It's fine," Darius said, and he gave Thorn a weary smile. She got to be the bad guy often enough. He could take this bullet for her. God knew she'd taken some for him. "Really."

Thorn watched him for a quiet moment, but at last, she just nodded.

"All right," Alan said, taking a deep breath and looking around the room. "Jeremiah, Miss Brooks, you have your tasks. See to them." Jeremiah and Lina nodded and quietly exited the room. Alan addressed Mackenzie and Abraham.

"Miss McKay, let your team know Saul Torres has been spotted alone. They will have to adjust their search pattern based on this new information. Mr. Locke, once Darius has spoken with Miss Torres, I am going to insist she meet with you. This will undoubtedly be a challenging time for her. Please make room in your schedule this week." Abraham nodded, and he and Mackenzie left, too.

When the room was empty, Alan slowly turned to Darius and let out a slow, deep sigh.

"Good luck with Eva," he said quietly. Now that it was just the three of them, he let his formal, authoritative tone fade into a more familiar one, and his shoulders slumped in a small, sympathetic gesture. "I can only imagine how hard today has been for her."

Darius didn't even know. They hadn't had the chance to talk before Alan had called them all together. The last time he'd seen Eva, she'd been storming toward the elevators.

"Yeah," Darius said. "I have a feeling she already suspects she won't be able to go back."

Thorn crossed her arms and raised her brows. "She should. She knows the rules, and the most important one is not to blow your cover around a Sin."

"And now that she has," Alan said, "she isn't safe in New York City. Not until Autumn Hunt is killed."

Darius's heart sank. The Martyrs hadn't been able to kill Wrath's current host for over ninety years. He knew better than to get his hopes up that it would happen any time soon.

As the three of them walked into the hallway, Alan went to the left, toward his office. Darius moved to go the other direction, but Thorn called him back.

"Darius, wait."

Then she reached out and gently grabbed him by the shoulder. Darius turned to find an uncommon yet familiar expression across her face. Where had he seen that look before?

"Did you tell Eva?" Thorn asked. Her tone was quiet and earnest. "Did you tell her where to find Saul today?"

Suddenly, Darius recognized what it was. She'd worn the same look a month ago when he'd told her he hadn't trusted her to tell Nicholas the truth. *All* of the truth.

It was pain.

Darius was taken aback.

"No," he said. "No, of course not."

Thorn just watched him. Her thin, dark brows pinched in. Her black eyes narrowed. Her lips pressed together. Just barely. All of it was *just barely*. But Darius saw it, and he knew what it meant.

"What, you don't believe me?" he asked.

She didn't answer right away. She breathed through another pause before she said, "Could you blame me if I didn't?"

The words came out softly. Thorn's mouth hardly moved. Darius's chest constricted, and he frowned.

"No," he said, and he took a deep breath, shoving his hands into the front pockets of his jeans. "But I swear, I didn't tell her. I assumed she figured it out when Holly sent her the orders."

Thorn shook her head. "She knew about him before Holly ever called. I checked her phone's GPS records on the drive back. Eva was on her way to the Mitchel Houses well before she had orders to return to her apartment. The only other people who knew Saul was there were me and the Recon units looking for him."

The units Darius was working with. Another pointed look. Her piercing eyes dug into his, searching for some truth there—some truth she could trust in. "If you didn't tell her, who did?"

Oh, god. Darius's stomach flipped, and he rubbed his eyes with his fingers and thumb.

"Nicholas," he said with a sigh. He groaned and ran his hand down his face. "I bet it was Nicholas."

"Why would he do that?" Thorn asked, but the look on her face let Darius know she already suspected the reasons why. They were the same reasons Darius suspected, too.

"I think we both know," was all Darius said.

Thorn nodded. Slowly. Still a little bit hurt.

Darius hated that she was hurt, but at this point, he had no idea how to fix it.

"Fuck," Thorn said, after a few tense moments of silence threatened to make the air between them more awkward, more painful, than it already was. She uttered a sardonic laugh. "Maybe I should thank him. His lack of faith in me saved my life today. He'll *love* to know that."

Darius frowned. "Wrath wouldn't kill you," he said.

Thorn's face darkened a bit. "There are worse things," she said, and the air caught in Darius's lungs. Thorn cleared her throat and briefly looked away from his face. "Eva showed a lot of guts today. Without her, Saul and I would have been fucked. Make sure she knows that."

"I will," Darius said, "and I wanted to thank you for standing up for her."

Thorn's brows drew together, and she shook her head. "She was in a shitty position," she said. It was biting but not as harsh as Darius would expect. "We asked her to pick between her job and her brother. I should have known which one she'd choose."

"You would have chosen the same thing," Darius said.

Thorn's expression softened.

"Look," Darius said with a sigh. "All I meant is, I know today was probably hard. A lot went wrong. But not you. You *always* do right by your people, and I just wanted to let you know I see that, and I appreciate it."

Then something about Thorn changed. A flash of regret. She crossed her arms, glanced down at her feet, and took in a deep, heavy breath.

"That's not always true," she said, and she cleared her throat. When she looked back up to Darius, something was different. There was a peculiar openness he hadn't seen in her in a long time—not since they had lived together at Teresa Solomon's house.

"I've been having a really hard time the last couple of

months," Thorn went on. The admission caught Darius off guard. He leaned toward her as she continued. "I am so fucking *angry*. People are dying. The city's a mess. It's just— it's been hard to maintain control, and today…" She scoffed, and shame washed over her face. It settled into the pull at the corners of her lips—at the glistening rage in her black eyes. "Eva saw a side of me I don't like—a side I try to keep out of the Underground and away from the Martyrs."

Darius frowned. "The side that destroyed Teresa's sunroom and broke Nicholas's nose?"

"That's the one."

For a moment, Darius just watched Thorn. She didn't shy away from his focus. If anything, it made her expression a little more serious, more critical, and more penitent.

So Darius took a slow breath, and he said, "Good."

Thorn's brows furrowed together. "What?"

He shrugged. "We all lose our cool."

"Darius, this isn't a matter of just 'losing my cool,'" Thorn snapped. Her defenses were rising with a furious wall, and she glared at him. "I pulverized a car into scrap metal with my *bare fists*."

Darius couldn't help it. He chuckled. At first, it seemed to make Thorn angrier, but while her eyebrows knit closer together, the rest of her face began to relax with his laughter.

"What's so funny?" she asked, but the fire behind her voice was a little dampened.

"It's just, you know… I think a lot of people wish they could unload like that," Darius said, and Thorn seemed taken aback. "It's got to be cathartic. Sure, it might not be the *healthiest* outlet, but it's an outlet, and you needed it. Don't beat yourself up over it."

Thorn relaxed even further. Darius decided to keep pushing.

"And," he said slowly, "I think you should let the Martyrs see that side of you every once in a while."

"Ah, yes," Thorn said sarcastically, but her tone was

lighter. More playful. "Nothing builds confidence in your leadership ability like reminding people that you are capable of incredible, terrible violence."

"Well, sure," Darius said. "But what I mean is, you shouldn't feel like you have to hide yourself. It's got to be really lonely." Thorn's face fell, and Darius pressed on. "Let us see you—*all* of you. The good, the bad, and the terrible. I bet people aren't as worried about it as you think they are, and maybe you won't feel so out of control if you aren't always stuck behind this wall."

Thorn simply nodded, and something in that nod made Darius's chest constrict. It was short, quick, and unconvinced. Darius had never stopped to consider all the ways being a Forgotten Sin had impacted Thorn's life. How many people had already taught her to hide herself away? How many were afraid of her because of what she *used* to be?

It wasn't her fault she was possessed by Wrath.

"Anyway," Darius said with a sigh. He hated to walk away when he felt like he'd *finally* broken through with Thorn, but he had another difficult conversation to have. "I've got to go find Eva and tell her the bad news. You good?"

"I'm fine," Thorn said. Her vulnerability evaporated as though it had never existed in the first place.

"Great," Darius said. "I'll catch you later."

"Good luck, Jones," Thorn said. Before he turned away, though, she reached out and gently grabbed his arm in a secure, grateful grip. Her fingers felt cool against his skin in a way no one else's did anymore, and they sent a chill across his shoulders. "Thank you."

"Any time," Darius said with a smile. Then they went their separate ways: Thorn, back toward her office, and Darius, down the hallway to the elevator.

Eva was in their bedroom. He stood outside the door for a few quiet seconds, feeling the warmth of her aura pace back and forth across the room with quick, irritable energy.

This wasn't how he had pictured her return to the

Underground. He'd imagined something a little more celebratory… more intimate…

But he hadn't expected her to return under such complicated circumstances, either.

Darius paused, steeled himself, and opened the door.

As soon as he walked into the room, Eva stopped and turned to him. Her hair had fallen out of its clip and draped in fuzzy waves around her face. Her eyes were puffy and red. Angry tears streamed down her cheeks, leaving hot trails against her brown skin. She didn't even wait for Darius to close the door before she started talking. She was so worked up that she practically yelled.

"Am I fired?" she asked. Her voice was loud and shaky. She propped her hands on her hips and squared her shoulders. "Are they kicking me off the Gray Unit?"

Darius just sighed and raised his hands. "I'm sorry, Eva, but Wrath saw you."

She nodded. Slowly, at first, then more fervently as she slammed her teeth together and fought back another onslaught of tears. "Great," she snapped. "Just great! Damnit, I was *so close!*"

"I know," Darius started to say, and he took a step toward her, but Eva shook her head and cut him off.

"I *saved* her out there," Eva went on. She started pacing again. Darius lowered his hands to his sides and waited. Eva kept talking. Ranting. "If I hadn't shown up, Wrath would have *destroyed* her! When Nicholas told me where Saul was, he warned me this would happen. He knew Thorn would be pissed."

Darius shook his head. "Thorn's not pissed—"

"Not pissed?" Eva cut in, and she threw him a hot, affronted look. "She *beat the shit out of a car.* She punched it until she was *bleeding!*"

"It's not about you—"

"Then why am I the one being fired?"

"You're not being fired," Darius said. He felt himself swelling, getting caught up in Eva's fire, and he took a deep breath as he shook his head. "Eva, you were *seen* by Autumn Hunt. She can Program people to recognize your face now. You're not safe in the city."

"It's *bullshit!*"

"I know it is," Darius said. "I know you were in a shitty situation, but if you go out there now, there's a really good chance the Sins will find you and kill you—or worse, capture you."

"But if I stay in *here*," Eva said, "then I can't find Saul!"

"You're not the only one looking for him," Darius said. "We have a whole team of people tracking him down. We're not giving up."

Her mouth pursed together. Her nostrils flared. A new wave of tears started to stream, silently, from her rich, brown eyes. "It's not *fair*," she said. The words came out in hot, throaty sobs. "He's *my brother*. I should be out there looking for him!"

"I know. I get that," Darius said. "But is it worth finding Saul if you get yourself killed while you're doing it?"

Eva was taken aback. She blinked at him a couple of times, and she started to cry. "I *saved* him today! If I hadn't shown up, *he'd be dead!*"

Darius shook his head, his chest tight, his mind tired. "I know that. *Thorn* knows that. She made sure we knew they'd have been screwed if you weren't there, but you could have gotten yourself killed. And now you're talking about wanting to go back out there? Eva, that's suicide!"

She crossed her arms and glared at Darius from the far side of the room. "So, what? You want me to just stay in the Underground and *wait*, like a good little girl?"

"I want you *alive*," Darius said. His tone softened, and he took a step toward her, but she didn't reciprocate. Her arms remained locked around herself, her eyes dark and narrow. "I don't want to sit here, worried sick that Wrath is going to get you. Let us handle finding Saul. There are other ways you can help."

"Other ways?" Eva said quietly, and she breathed a bitter

scoff. "I don't *want* to do anything else."

Before Darius had the chance to respond, she turned away from him, opened the dresser drawer, and pulled out an armful of clothes.

"I'm going to go take a shower," she said, and she stormed past Darius, slamming the door on her way out. He stared at the knob and heaved a final, heavy sigh.

That had gone about as well as he'd expected. Now, he just needed to give her some time to let it settle.

Eva needed a lot of time.

Ten days later, Darius was having coffee in the courtyard with John and Chris. Eva was still devastated she had lost her position in the Gray Unit, and largely, she spent all of her spare time in their room.

Even when Darius was with her, she was distant. Their nights had become cold and quiet. Darius decided to give her space to process everything that had happened. It was a lot. He could only imagine the emotions she was sorting through.

And his imagination was all he had to go on. Eva didn't talk about it. Not with him. Not with anyone.

"How's she doing?" Chris asked. She pulled a long wisp of yellow hair behind her ear and watched Darius over the rim of her coffee cup. Right now, she and the rest of the Tactical Unit teams were working longer shifts than ever. Since Chris had partnered with Jeremiah, her work had become more irregular than the others. She never complained, but there were light, tired rings underneath her eyes that betrayed her exhaustion.

Darius sighed and shrugged. "I mean, as far as she says, she's fine, but I know she's not."

"Never believe a woman when she says she's 'fine,'" John said. Chris cast him a skeptical but good-natured look, and he gave a sheepish laugh. "What I mean is, a lot of women are raised to just 'be fine,' even when they're not."

"Nice save," Chris said, and she patted him on the top of the thigh.

John laughed again. "I'm serious! I grew up with *four* older sisters, and every one of them had a hard time with it. They didn't want to cause problems by standing up for themselves."

"Oh, Eva has no problem standing up for herself," Darius said. He remembered a few instances on the Williamsburg Street Market when sleazy men would try to get handsy with her. Eva hadn't needed Saul—or anyone else, for that matter—to step in and rescue her. She'd just start screaming in Spanish and throwing items until they got nervous and ran away. Eva wasn't afraid of causing problems.

Knowing what he knew now, Darius wondered if it stemmed from her childhood trauma. A man had touched her without her consent for a year. When she grew up, she made sure it never happened again.

"What kind of punishment did Alan dole out for her?" John asked.

"None," Darius said, shaking his head, and John's eyes widened. "He and Thorn had a private meeting with her, and Alan wanted to assign her a couple of weeks on maintenance, but Thorn convinced him that Eva losing her position in the Gray Unit was punishment enough."

For which Darius was grateful. He couldn't imagine how much more frustrated Eva would be if she'd not only lost her job but was delegated to working with Stevie's crew cleaning bathrooms.

"Damn," John said, raising his brows, and he elbowed Chris lightly in the arm. "Conrad's gonna be *so* mad. Didn't he get maintenance duty a couple of months ago because he punched Rossi?"

While John chuckled to himself, Chris focused back on Darius. "Does Eva know what her new assignment is yet?"

Darius shook his head. "No. Jeremiah doesn't want her on TAC unless she can show she's not a flight risk." Chris nodded, and Darius continued. "I talked with Mackenzie and Lina about having her help us scan through video footage for Saul, but they're worried she'd leave the Underground without telling anyone if she happens to find him first."

"I mean," John said, and he gave a half-grimace and shrugged. "I think that's a pretty legitimate concern."

"I do, too," Darius said. "But that means we're running out of places for her to go."

"We'll find something," Chris said. "There are a lot of little jobs that go into keeping the Underground running smoothly."

"Yeah," Darius said with a sigh, and he looked down into his coffee cup. "I'm just worried she's going to hate it."

She probably would. Darius had a feeling that no matter what job she was assigned, Eva was going to be miserable until they found Saul. That was just more motivation to track him down and bring him—and Juniper and Lindsay—to the Underground.

"Wow," John said, and his shift in tone caught Darius's attention. He looked up from his mug. "He really *is* an animal."

Darius and Chris turned to see what John was talking about, but Darius knew, from the sensation of the Virtue crossing the courtyard, who it involved. Nicholas Wolfe was coming out from the west wing of living quarters, a laptop in his hands. He quickly dropped the computer off before he darted into the kitchen and poured himself a bowl of cereal. Then he returned to his table, and he got to work.

"Isn't he off shift?" Darius asked, and he grabbed his phone to look at the time.

John did the same. "Shit. Yes. But I'm not. I've gotta get back to work. Maybe I could grab my computer and work down here, too…" He thought about it for a moment before he wrinkled his nose, shook his head, and dismissed the idea with a wave. "Nah, I'd get too distracted. You're off tonight, right?"

He said those last words to Chris directly, and she nodded. He flashed her a handsome grin and said, "Awesome!
I'll make dinner, get some candles, and then maybe we can
enjoy some *enthusiastically consensual* time together."

His grin widened, and Chris rolled her eyes.

"Oh my god. Go to work!"

He laughed and leaned over to kiss her. Then he said
goodbye to Darius and made his way across the courtyard.
Chris watched him go with a smile on her face, but the further he got, the smaller her smile became. When the elevator
doors closed behind him, she cleared her throat and turned
to Darius.

"Is it nice having Eva back in the Underground, at
least?" she asked.

"Yeah," Darius said, and his brows twitched a little bit
down in concern. "Even though it's been kind of tense, at
least I know she's safe. What about you? This is the longest
John has been back in the Underground in a long time, isn't
it?"

Chris nodded and took a sip of her coffee. When she
answered, she took her time, and she spoke slowly. "He was
usually gone for two weeks, then home for two. Now, he
hasn't left the Underground for almost two months."

She didn't seem as excited about it as Darius would have
thought she'd be. He frowned.

"Is that a problem?"

"No," Chris said, and it sounded genuine. "But I think
he's feeling a little trapped. He misses traveling. He misses
Sara. He misses *me*. With these double shifts, it's been hard
to get time together. Well, harder than usual." She passed
Darius a smile, but it didn't quite reach her green eyes.

"It'll normalize," Darius said.

"Oh, yeah," Chris said, and she gave a dismissive, little
head shake. "It always does. It's just part of the job, you
know?"

Darius nodded. He was figuring that out.

"And speaking of the job," Chris said. Darius sensed she

was trying to change the subject, so he just leaned forward and listened. "Do you know what Nicholas has been up to lately?"

She gestured her head in the other Virtue's direction. Darius glanced up to him again. Nicholas was now pouring over his laptop, spooning cereal into his mouth with a bizarre accuracy considering he wasn't watching what he was doing.

"Looking for Saul, like he's been assigned to do?" Darius asked.

Chris shook her head. "Nope. On his off time, he's going through all the footage we have of Gregory Witham."

Darius raised his eyebrows. "Really?"

He shouldn't have been surprised. From the minute Nicholas had recovered from his burnout period, he'd been working harder than ever. Darius rarely saw the other Virtue without a computer in hand. At meals. In the R&D headquarters. He even carried it back to his bedroom when he finally retired for the night. Darius should have known it would have something to do with Sloth.

"Yeah," Chris said. "I talked with Skylar. He's been asking her to send him any video files she and her team get of him. Particularly the bombings. He's really interested in the attacks."

"I wonder why," Darius mused out loud.

Chris shrugged. "I don't know, but Skylar is impressed with him. I guess the work they did together was some of the most intense hours she's ever worked in her life. She had to take a full three days off just to sleep and recover."

Darius whistled. "Damn."

"Yeah. Anyway." Chris glanced at the watch on her wrist. "I have to head out. Jeremiah and I have a meeting with the next group of units before they go on shift."

"What about?" Darius asked as Chris stood up.

"Honestly?" she said, and she gave a little, ironic laugh. "About *sleeping*. People are exhausted, so we need them to start taking their time off to rest."

"Looks like *you* need to hear that advice," Darius said.

Chris laughed. "Tell me about it. Take care, Darius."

Then she walked across the courtyard and disappeared up the elevators. When she'd gone, Darius got to his feet, strode over to Nicholas, and pulled up a chair.

"What're you working on?"

Nicholas didn't even glance up as he responded to Darius. The light from his screen cast his smile lines in deep, contrasted shadows, making his baby blue eyes look even brighter. Darius could see that subtle bags were developing beneath them, and the whites were a little bloodshot.

"Looking for patterns," he said. His computer showed footage from the most recent bombing. There had been two more in the week and a half since the incident by the Mitchel Houses. The latest one had been in Harlem. Nicholas had the sound muted, but that didn't stop Darius from wincing as a newspaper stand blew to pieces, and with it, another six human lives. His heart ached.

"Have you found any?"

"I've found a lot," Nicholas said, pausing the video at last as he looked to Darius. "First, he *is* only setting bombs off once he's been spotted. We have footage of six of the twelve attacks. In every single one of those, he didn't set off the explosive until Wrath saw him. Of the other five, Thorn was *at* two of them. The first doesn't count, obviously, since that one was a direct assassination attempt, but the other one? When we went to dinner? He only hit the trigger when she'd seen him."

"What do you think that means?" Darius asked.

"He's on the run," Nicholas said. "Makes sense with his bombing pattern, too. In that, there *isn't* a pattern. He seems to be erratically jumping from one neighborhood to the next."

"Trying to hide?" Darius offered.

"Most likely," Nicholas agreed. "I read everything Lina has collected about Sloth, and this isn't the first time he's had a violent streak like this. She thinks he was an infamous serial killer in London two hundred years ago. The guy was never found, and some people speculate he was impossible to catch because he was homeless or something. Did the same shit in LA in the 1980s. Thorn tracked him down, helped him frame someone else for the attacks, and brought him back to New York to join the rest of the Sins."

Darius shook his head. "What do you mean Thorn *helped* him?"

"My bad," Nicholas said, his tone biting. "I mean *Wrath* helped him. Back when Thorn was possessed."

Darius's heart skipped an uncomfortable beat. Though he knew Thorn had once been Wrath, sometimes he forgot that meant she would have had a history with the rest of the Sins, too. He cleared his throat and got back on track. "Why hasn't Sloth just left the city?" he asked. "If he's trying so hard to hide from both us *and* the other Sins?"

"How could he?" Nicholas crossed his arms, but there was an almost manic excitement to the way he was talking about this. That excitement bled into his eyes and made him look wild. "From what I understand, most of the major transits out of New York have some kind of Sin involvement. Skylar thinks they have Programmed a bunch of Sentries to recognize him if he tries to rent a car, hop on a plane, or take a train *anywhere*."

Darius nodded quietly. Of course the Sins would have people making sure Sloth didn't leave the city. That was the running theory on how they'd discovered the Martyrs had flown to Spokane, too.

"So, what," Darius said, and he watched Nicholas beneath furrowed brows. "You're trying to track him down?"

Nicholas shrugged as he focused back on the computer. "Track him down. Learn how he works. Find anything I can use against this son of a bitch that will help me take him out."

Darius's mouth twitched.

"Help *us* take him out," he said, and Nicholas glanced at him. "We're here to help you."

"Yeah," Nicholas dismissed with a wave of his hand. "That's what I meant."

Something on his laptop pinged. Darius saw an alert from Skylar pop up on the bottom, left corner of the screen. Nicholas opened it, and a new video came up. Darius's stomach dropped.

"Was there another bombing?"

"Maybe," Nicholas said. "Maybe not. I asked her to send me all clips of Gregory Witham—not just the attacks. She set up an automatic delivery program. As soon as Holly's system gets a match for his face, I get an email. Almost all of them are false positives."

Darius nodded, impressed. When Nicholas set his mind to getting something done, he didn't screw around.

"Well, I'll leave you to it," Darius said, and he heaved himself up off the chair, but something stopped him. Nicholas was staring at the computer screen. His bright eyes widened, and his mouth slowly curled up into an almost fanatical smile. Darius paused there, frowning, and looked back at the screen. Suddenly, though, Nicholas jumped to his feet and whooped.

"I've got him!"

"What?" Darius crouched over the computer. He wasn't sure what he was looking at. The clip was short—the only sign of Sloth came from his face, briefly visible, in the second-story window of an old, gritty apartment building. Then, he disappeared.

But there was no denying it. The man in that window was Gregory Witham.

"This footage was taken *this morning*," Nicholas exclaimed. He grabbed Darius by the shoulders and shook him. "Less than an hour ago! He's in that building *right now*."

And Nicholas pointed at the screen. Darius's heart started to race.

They'd found Sloth.

Now... what the hell were they going to do about it?

CHAPTER SEVENTEEN

Six of them gathered in the munitions locker, once again looking down at the bomb Thorn had picked up in Mott Haven. Alan and Thorn stood on one side, Darius and Nicholas on the other, and Holly and Jeremiah were situated near the door. They were almost comical side by side. Jeremiah stood at around six and a half feet, and Holly, at barely five. If the situation weren't so serious, Darius might have laughed.

But instead, he wrapped one arm around his chest, propped the other up, and pressed his fingers against his lips as he listened.

"This is a signal disruptor," Holly said. She gestured to a large, metal rack beside her. It was almost three feet tall, two feet wide, and just as deep. Most of the slots were empty, but the top two sections had sleek, black devices clicked into place. One was unassuming—nothing but wires, lights, and a power button, but the other had a large screen and a handful of knobs. Holly plugged the cord into an outlet and clicked on a switch. The devices whirred to life. "It'll stop the detonator and receiver from speaking to each other, so Sloth's bombs won't go off."

"How the hell is this supposed to work?" Nicholas

asked, incredulous, as he gestured toward it with an open palm. "What am I going to do? Walk in with this strapped to my back? With an *extension cord?*"

"No," Holly said. She threw him a skeptical look and shook her head. "We have three of these units. The plan is to put them in a couple of SUVs and park them in a perimeter around our target area. They should cover a full city block, give or take a few meters."

"This is impressive for less than two weeks of work, Miss Andrews," Alan said.

Holly threw him a smile, albeit a somber one. "Part of being a genius is knowing what you don't know," she told him. "I have connections with a bunch of people in different fields, and I worked with the same guy who helped set up our vehicles' short-range police interference devices. He told me this was a surprisingly simple job. I guess the signal used in this bomb is old—from the 2030s? It's less complicated to scramble than the things you see today."

Alan nodded. "All the better for us, I suppose."

"How are we going to set it up?" Jeremiah asked, and he leaned over to look at the signal disruptor more closely. "The units will be put into the vehicle just like this?"

Holly shrugged. "More or less. They'll need to have a power generator and an antenna on top of the car, but otherwise, it's the same setup."

"And you're positive it's going to work?" Thorn asked. Sparkie, perched on her shoulder, tilted his head in Holly's direction.

"I will be soon," she said. "We're going to test it."

She reached into the pocket of her oversized hoodie and pulled out a detonator. Darius and Nicholas both took a step back, and Holly smiled. "We removed the explosive elements, so it won't blow up, but I did wire up an electrolytic cap in there that will pop if the bomb gets the detonation signal… Let's see what happens, huh?"

She pressed her thumb onto the detonator. Nothing. Darius and Nicholas exchanged a look.

"How do we know the *detonator* works?" Nicholas asked.

Holly raised her eyebrows, flipped the signal disruptor off, and pushed the button again.

A loud *pop!* shot through the room. Even though Darius was expecting it, he still jumped. So did Nicholas. Alan, Thorn, and Jeremiah were unmoved. A fine line of smoke rose from the bomb, and the dense, tacky smell of burned chemicals filtered through the air, coating Darius's tongue. He swallowed against his dry mouth to try to get rid of it, but it didn't do any good.

Thorn nodded. "Good enough for me. What do you need from us to finish setup?"

"Nothing," Holly said, shaking her head. "My team is already putting the other two in a couple of SUVs. Just gotta get this guy in place, too. We're also putting in additional blockers on cell and police radio frequencies to slow down first responder times, just in case."

"Excellent," Alan said. "I want everything ready to go within the hour."

Holly nodded, unplugged the signal disruptor, and wheeled it out of the room. As soon as the door shut behind her, Alan turned to the rest of them.

"Now," he said, "what is *our* plan?"

Thorn stepped up to the table, unraveled a roll of paper she'd had tucked beneath her arm, and slapped it down, using the bomb to hold one edge while Sparkie pinned the other. Darius looked at a large, aerial printout of a brick building while Thorn leaned over it with a bright, red marker. Alan and Jeremiah stood on either side of her and watched as she drew four giant Xs next to different points around the building's perimeter.

"These are the only entrances, and this one—" another X "—is where the fire escape comes down. Witham was spotted in a second-story window on the east-facing wall, but he could be anywhere in the apartment complex."

"I want one TAC team on each exit to prevent Witham from escaping," Jeremiah said. He looked over to Alan, who nodded silently. "If he tries to leave, we'll get him."

"Then Wolfe and I will make our way through the building," Thorn said.

"*Just us?*" Nicholas asked, appalled.

"Neither you nor Thorn have an aura," Alan said with a tone of grim resolution. "Anyone else will be sensed by Sloth almost immediately. It will announce your presence and ruin any chance you have of catching him off guard."

"And catching him off guard is our best bet at taking this son of a bitch down," Thorn said. "I want *everyone* in full body armor, which means no one can step foot out of the cars or inside the building until I give the signal. If Sloth gets spooked, he's going to run. When I'm in the building, I'll be able to sense him. If he moves, I can alert the teams to get ready for an escape attempt."

"Or I can," Nicholas said, and he raised his eyebrows. "I can feel him, too."

"Yes, or our sweet, *innocent* Virtue who has never been in a combat situation can alert them," Thorn said. Nicholas crossed his arms and sneered at her.

"This is not the time for petty bickering," Alan said, his voice stern and testy. Thorn didn't seem abashed. She continued to watch Nicholas with a loaded expression. Nicholas glared back with just as much palpable distaste. Alan ignored them and went on. "What about tenants?"

"There are none," Jeremiah said. "This building was condemned in 2047 when it was busted as a major transit for trafficking methamphetamine and heroin. It's been abandoned ever since. From what I can tell, the only people we may have to worry about are the occasional squatters."

"If there are people in the building, we must assume Sloth will put them to use in some way," Alan said, and his brows pinched together over his dark, half-empty eyes. "We should proceed as though anyone inside has been Programmed."

"To do what?" Darius asked.

"Probably to let him know someone is coming," Thorn

said, and she propped her hands on her hips.

"So, what do we do about them?" Nicholas asked.

"We avoid them as best as we can," Thorn said.

"Why don't you just *knock them out?*" Nicholas commented with a cynical sneer, and Thorn slowly turned toward him. She was not amused.

"I will, if I'm close enough," she said.

"You can't just *Influence* them to pretend we're not there?"

"I could," Thorn said, and she turned back to the table, "If you want Wrath to come down on us—and she *will* come down on us. The plan is to avoid using Influence at all. The last thing we need is *more* Sins showing up to the party."

"Mackenzie and Lina are working on ensuring that does not happen," Alan said. "Since Holly's entire team will be busy managing the signal disruptors, R&D is going to take over surveillance on Lust, Greed, and Gluttony. If any of them make a move in our direction, we will be alerted immediately."

"They're not tracking Wrath?" Darius asked.

"They cannot *find* Wrath," Alan said darkly. Darius's stomach dropped.

"So we're just relying on our senses and Thorn's brutality to stop any Programmed tweakers from calling Sloth and cluing him in on the attack?" Nicholas asked with furrowed brows. "Sounds *great.*"

"I will be assisting as I can," Alan said. "I want you to take Rae into the building with you." He turned to Thorn, and she simply nodded. Alan went on. "I will also be situated on a rooftop to the east." He indicated a place vaguely off the frame of the printout. "I can help disable any Sentries whom I might be able to spot from the windows. Additionally, if Sloth is still on this side of the building, I should be able to get a lock on him."

"With what?" Darius asked.

Alan turned to consider him. "My rifle, Mr. Jones," he said. "We cannot afford to fail. If we do not succeed in obliterating Sloth from the planet, at the very least, we must succeed in destroying its host. These bombings end today, one way or another."

Thorn glanced up to her uncle. Her nostrils flared dangerously, and her half-empty, black eyes were alight with furious, cold fire.

"How long until your units are ready?" Alan asked Jeremiah.

"They're ready now, sir," Jeremiah said. "Chris prepared them."

"Excellent. I believe we all know the plan—"

"Wait," Darius said, and everyone in the room focused on him. "Where am I going to be?"

Thorn's eyes narrowed. "What the hell do you mean? You're going to be here—out of danger *and* out of the way."

Darius shook his head. "We're dealing with a Sin who's been blowing people up," he said. "Even after we stop the bombs, we know he's willing to go to pretty extreme lengths to get away. People are going to get hurt. I can help."

"So can Wolfe," Thorn snapped back.

"Not if everything goes according to plan," Darius said, and a thick silence filled the room. Nicholas turned and watched Darius with a solemn look, and Sparkie shuffled uncomfortably before leaping off the map and onto Thorn's shoulder, where he promptly hid behind her hair. Darius focused on her. "If everything goes the way we hope it will, Nicholas will be dead."

The silence grew. It felt suffocating. Thorn glanced at Nicholas before turning back to Darius. She took him in, slowly and thoughtfully, and as she did, her expression shifted. Her forehead tightened, her mouth relaxed, and her eyes flickered. Away from anger, annoyance, and resolution.

Back, a little bit, toward pain.

"He has a good point," Jeremiah said. His words jarred the room, broke Thorn's train of thought, and dragged her back to them. The hardness returned.

"Then we need a safe place for him to hide out," she

said. "And I mean *safe*. If anything happens to him, I'll—"

"He'll be safe," Jeremiah said, and he frowned down at Thorn. "The surveillance vehicle is one of our fully-reinforced SUVs, and it will be parked around the corner, away from the main fight. Fulton will be in there, monitoring the live footage from each of our people's body cams and directing units, if needed. If something goes wrong, she'll be the first to know, and they can get the hell out of there."

"Perfect," Thorn said, but she didn't sound pleased about it. "I want a guard posted, too. I'm not taking any chances."

"Yes, ma'am," Jeremiah said. "I'll get someone on it."

"Someone *good*." Then Thorn turned back to Darius. Her eyes were heavy, her jaw set. "Let's go take that bastard down."

"Finally," Nicholas said, and for a brief moment, that manic look rose to his eyes again.

They filed out of the tactical room to the parking lot. Just as they reached the foyer, though, Darius paused.

A familiar, warm energy rushed toward him.

He turned just in time to catch Eva as she threw herself into his arms. The rest of the group filtered into the garage. Thorn held the door open as Alan, Jeremiah, and Nicholas moved through. She caught Darius's eye over Eva's head. Before she turned to leave, she just gave him a quiet, understanding nod. Then she disappeared, leaving them alone.

Eva gripped him tightly. Her fingers dug into his shoulders, and her arms were so firm around him he couldn't take a full breath. But that was fine. He didn't care. He closed his eyes and nestled his face into her soft, brown hair.

"Be careful, *mi amorcito*," she whispered. "And come back. Okay?"

"I promise," Darius said.

They stood there for a few more quiet, precious moments—aching, scary moments—before Eva finally stepped back. She grabbed his face in her hands and kissed him passionately, like she was afraid it was the last time she'd have the chance to do it.

"Good luck," she said. This time, she forced a smile. "We're all rooting for you."

"Thanks," he said, and he tried to smile back.

Then they said goodbye, and Darius made his way into the garage. The Tactical Unit vehicles were already gone. Darius climbed into the back of a black SUV and strapped himself in. Driving was Conrad Carter, and beside him, Skylar Fulton.

Thorn was gone. Nicholas was gone. Alan and Jeremiah and the others, gone. Everyone went out ahead of them to scope out the scene. To do what they could to be ready to take down Gregory Witham once and for all.

As they pulled out of the parking lot, Darius stared through the back window. Eva watched from the other side of the glass doors, her eyes glued to his, until the SUV twisted up the ramp and out of sight.

———

Thorn sat in the back of the Martyr SUV as it rumbled through the streets of New York City, northbound toward Unionport. She pulled at the kevlar vest around her chest. Tugged on the straps. Cinched it so tight to her body it felt like a second skin. Nicholas sat beside her, and he swore as he struggled with his.

Even in the light of their serious situation, Thorn felt a spark of juvenile satisfaction. Anything that put that smug Virtue in his place—that showed him he wasn't God's gift to the Martyrs—was worth finding a little joy in.

But she didn't let that joy sit for long.

"Turn around," she said gruffly as she grabbed Nicholas by the shoulders and jerked him toward her. She quickly adjusted the straps, pulled them into place, and attached the arm and throat guards. He glared at her—his forehead furrowed into a sea of angry ridges, his bright eyes narrow and ungrateful.

"Put that on," Thorn said. She slammed a helmet into his hands and turned back to finish getting her armor together. Alan's wolf sat in the center seat, staring back at them with alert, critical eyes. Thorn saw the familiar look on the animal's face—the same look Alan had when he was fed up with her shitty attitude.

She knew Rae was here to help—and she *would* help—but part of Thorn felt like Alan wanted his Familiar along for the ride so he could keep an eye on her. To make sure she didn't punch Nicholas Wolfe in the face again.

Thorn tightened the ponytail at the base of her skull as Sparkie crawled onto her shoulder and glowered at Nicholas.

"We'll be stationed near the back entrance," Jeremiah called to them. Beside him, Chris stared out the window. Her armor was already on—her face all but hidden behind a black-tinted visor. "We'll wait for your signal. Hopefully, this is over fast, and we don't even need to get out of the car."

"That's the goal," Thorn said. She pulled her helmet over her head and adjusted the mouthpiece attached to the com unit inside. She pressed the button to turn it on. "Rose here. Mic test. Everyone, sound off."

Voices pinged in the speakers. Alan, from his post on a building down the street. Jeremiah and Chris. The rest of the Tactical Unit, one by one. Thorn elbowed Nicholas, and he jumped and said his name, too. She heard his voice both to her right and inside her ears.

"Good," Thorn said. "Get into position and standby." Then she turned off her mic and indicated for Nicholas to do the same.

It was almost time.

They were in Unionport now. Even in a shitty, little neighborhood like this, coated in a fine layer of graffiti and garbage, New York City was always full of people. Thorn was acutely aware of them all. Their cold energies filtered in and out of her senses as Jeremiah slowed the SUV to a stop toward the back of the foreclosed apartment building. Every human being here was a potential threat to Thorn and her people. She closed her eyes and paused for a moment to take them in…

She recognized a precious few of them. She could feel her team near the exit on the far side of the building. To her right, another set of Martyrs. To her left, two—one at the entrance and another at the fire escape. Then she took a little extra care to feel for the familiar essences of Conrad Carter and Skylar Fulton because then she would know exactly where Darius was…

Just around the corner. Behind Thorn. Far enough back that she could barely sense them, but Gregory Witham could not.

Good. That thought allowed a little relief to creep into her shoulders. The last thing she needed was the Sin to learn *two* Virtues were out of the Underground. She had enough on her plate just trying to keep the one alive…

Alive long enough for him to destroy Sloth—and himself with it.

Thorn shook her head—damnit, she couldn't get distracted right now—and she focused on her Tactical team. Their cold signatures were situated a little further back from the building. They'd arrived in staggered time slots to make sure Sloth didn't feel a sudden surge of fifteen people surround his position all at once.

Thorn wasn't even sure he would think twice about it, though. There were dozens of energies Thorn did *not* recognize, flittering around and within the complex. They moved in a bizarre, uncoordinated manner Thorn had started to associate with homelessness and drug addiction. Even as those energies moved, more came and went off the streets, passing close enough to her people that, for a few moments, they would blend into an almost-indistinguishable blur before separating again.

And then, there was one—*just one*—energy Thorn knew which did *not* belong to a Martyr.

"Sloth's here," she said, and she opened her eyes. She focused on Nicholas beside her. He had his helmet in place, his armor secured. While his eyes were wide, his jaw was set and determined.

Thorn had to admit, she respected that about him. He had drive.

"Do you feel him?" she asked, and she gestured her head toward the building out the back of the car. "He's moved up—on the fifth floor. Lock onto that energy. Memorize it. That's where we're headed."

Nicholas looked out the window, up the brick building face outside, and provided a grim nod. His face was a little paler now. Thorn grabbed him hard by the shoulder. It seemed to jolt him back, and he looked at her again.

"Are you ready?"

"As ready as I can be," he said.

Thorn nodded. "Whatever you do, stick close to me."

She opened the back of the SUV and jumped out.

Sparkie took to the air. He wouldn't be much use in closed spaces indoors, so he flew high in the sky to watch from above. Thorn didn't waste time on the street. In her black, full-body armor, she'd stand out like a burning building. She silently slipped into the back door and held it open for Nicholas and Rae to follow. As soon as they were all inside, Jeremiah and Chris drove down the street. Thorn closed the door, drew her pistol, and turned to Nicholas.

Then she nodded as she slowly started into the hallway.

The building was almost quiet. Mostly quiet. But not completely. The floorboards creaked beneath Thorn's feet as she walked around piles of trash, discarded needles, and empty plastic baggies. Voices occasionally broke through cracks in moldy, uneven doors. Every so often, a Martyr would sound off in Thorn's helmet. Alan confirming that Sloth was not visible from his position. Chris, that she and Jeremiah were officially in place and ready to go. Thorn felt Sloth high above them. Slow. Lazy. Completely unaware.

Suddenly, something moved, and Thorn paused. A

human energy was coming out from one of the old apartments. Thorn started to back up. Nicholas was already doing the same. They tucked into an empty room—Rae at their heels—just as the door opened and that energy stepped out. Thorn held her breath as it began to walk down the hallway... Then it headed past the room and out the back door.

Thorn heaved a sigh, turned to Nicholas, and gestured into the hallway again.

It was slow-moving. The stairwell nearest the back exit was so badly blocked by discarded furniture and stinking, rotting trash that the three of them couldn't climb it. They had to walk across the ground floor, silently darting into empty rooms or around corners to avoid people as they came and went.

Thorn had been right about the kind of person this place would attract. Their energies moved like addicts, and the place reeked of drug use. Rooms smelled heavily of chemical fire and burnt plastic. The sickly sweet scent of ammonia intermingled with the unmistakable odor of human waste. They turned the corner to the stairwell on the far end of the building, and Thorn heard Nicholas start to retch behind her.

Her heart leaping into her throat, she quickly spun around and slammed her hand over his mouth and nose. The action caught him off guard. He started to fall backward, and they both stumbled into a wall. Someone in a nearby room stopped moving. Thorn swore under her breath, but she didn't release Nicholas's face as she pulled him around the corner and up the stairs. They paused halfway up the second flight and listened.

A door opened. Heavy footfalls thudded down the hallway. A man grumbled, talking to himself, as he came toward them. He paused around the corner at the bottom of the stairs. Thorn froze. She felt Nicholas's breath, hot and moist against her ungloved fingers. A stark, cold energy sat right beneath them. If it started climbing the stairs...

Thorn looked to Rae and gestured downward. The wolf silently moved into position, ready to strike.

But the man waited a little longer. Thorn could hear heavy breathing, a rough, wet cough, and then he moved away, back to the room.

As soon as the door clicked closed, Nicholas tore out of Thorn's hands.

"Jesus, a little warning next time," he whispered.

"I'm sorry," Thorn snapped back. "If I had known you had such a weak stomach, I would have told you to hold your fucking breath."

Nicholas roughly got to his feet and rushed up the stairs. Thorn chased after him, trying to get ahead and lead the way. He threw an arm out to hold her back.

"I don't *need* you to protect me," he hissed.

"Damnit, Wolfe—"

Suddenly, Thorn felt someone moving twenty feet down the hall, and a door flew open.

Thorn swore and tried to hide back in the stairwell, but it was too late. The woman's gaze met hers. She was high as fuck. Her eyes were wide and blank, and they moved rapidly from side to side as she tried to make sense of what she was seeing. Her arms twitched, and she stumbled. The poor thing looked like a child in the oversized clothes she wore. A dirty sweatshirt hung off her like clothing on the rack to dry.

Then she reached into her pocket, and she drew out two items.

One was a phone.

The other, a detonator.

Thorn's stomach clenched. She raised her gun. Shot. The bullet hit the woman in the shoulder. She floundered back and dropped her cell phone, but her thumb tightened around the button.

She exploded.

Her body tore to pieces as a bomb went off beneath her sweatshirt. Thorn and Nicholas were thrown back into the stairwell. Nicholas crumpled on the set of steps going up, but Thorn was thrown back down, halfway to the first floor. She crunched and rolled until her body slammed into the far wall.

Suddenly, the building was a flurry of activity.

Energies darted all around them. Above. Below. On either side. Thorn jumped to her feet. Her ears rang. Dust settled around her. Sloth was moving now—frantically running around three floors above them. Through the hallways. From room to room. He did *not* start coming down. Thorn unmuted her mic and barked orders into her headset.

"Backup!" she screamed. "The bombs are live. We've been compromised. Send in the backup. Now!"

More energies moved in. More people. *Her* people. Thorn felt them swarm the building. Voices flooded her ears as the Tactical Unit communicated back and forth with one another. Alan came in, too. His voice was a drone of calm in the chaos. He alerted the Martyrs without Sin or Virtue senses which rooms he could see people in from his vantage point.

Thorn tuned him out. She tuned all of them out. Instead, she focused on her job—getting Diligence to Sloth. She reached the second story. Nicholas swore and got to his feet.

"*What the fuck,*" he exclaimed. "I thought the bombs weren't supposed to go off!"

Thorn's teeth gnashed together. So had she.

"We don't have time to worry about that right now. Come on." She grabbed Nicholas by the arm and started pulling him back upward. Gunfire echoed in the stairwell. Dull shots bounced around the concrete cavern. Rae was ahead of them. Thorn couldn't hear her, but she could feel people running away as she chased them down.

His bombs might have worked, but Witham hadn't Programmed his people to pull the trigger when they were face to face with a *wolf*.

But as Thorn moved up and hit the third-floor landing,

people stopped running. All around her, the energies Thorn didn't recognize *stopped*. And when they moved again, it wasn't in the unpredictable, manic way panicked human beings would typically move.

They moved as a *unit*.

Her lungs constricted.

"He's Puppetting them," Thorn shouted into her headset. "I repeat—everyone is a Puppet. Shoot on sight. Alan, get him—"

Another bomb rocked the building. Three energies blinked out. Thorn's heart sank into the empty pit of her soul.

Two of them were Martyrs.

Their names were called in her headset. "Man down," Jeremiah said. "Get them out of here. Bring them to Jones."

It was too late.

"Fuck!"

Thorn kept running upward. Rae ripped through the third floor. Another bomb rocked that level, and Alan swore in her ear. On the fourth floor. There were two Puppets here, moving to the stairwell, getting ready to intercept—

Thorn raised her gun and shot the first man to come around the corner. She hit him in the shoulder. He spun around, flipped backward over the railing, and landed with a crunch on the steps between her and Nicholas. To Thorn's horror, though, he got back to his feet. His eyes were wild and crazy. Thorn's stomach dropped as she realized what was happening.

They were drugged. They were so fucking high they didn't feel pain. Thorn couldn't knock them out of Sloth's Influence. The man reached into his jacket. Thorn saw a bomb strapped to his chest—

She shot him right between the eyes. Blood sprayed out in the stairwell. Coating the filthy walls. The yellow window. The clear visor of Nicholas's helmet. His face blanched.

"You killed him!" he said.

Thorn didn't have the time to argue. "They're drugged,"

she said, as much to Nicholas as the voices in her headset. "Aim to kill!"

The second energy was coming around the stairs now. A woman rounded the corner, and Thorn shot her in the throat. She fell backward, unconscious.

But not dead.

Nicholas pushed past Thorn. He dropped his weapon and put his hands against the woman's neck. Vibrant red ribbons pumped through his fingers. She was bleeding out fast—so fast that Thorn feared healing her would drain too much of Nicholas's power. She tore him away.

"What the fuck are you doing?" she screamed.

"Saving this woman's life!" Nicholas yelled back.

"You need to save your energy for Sloth. This isn't our job—"

"Killing innocent people isn't our job, either!"

Thorn grabbed Nicholas by the vest and slammed him into the wall. "Damnit, Wolfe, there are casualties in war!"

The woman's energy flickered out. Thorn's lips pressed tight together. Nicholas glared at her with a fervent hatred.

Then another bomb rocked the bottom floor. One death—the bomber. Three injured Martyrs. Thorn heard Chris yelling orders to get the casualties back to Darius. She roughly released Nicholas and started back up the stairwell. There was only one person there now.

Gregory fucking Witham.

The fire in Thorn's chest roared. She and Nicholas rushed up the stairs. Another bomb went off below. The building rattled. Thorn was knocked to the side and steadied herself on the doorframe.

"It's getting unstable down here." Jeremiah's voice crackled in her ear. "We need to pull back. This whole thing could come down on top of us."

"Get out," Thorn said, but she said it quietly. "Pull his Puppets onto the street. Away from the building. We're here."

They were there—and Gregory Witham had no idea.

Thorn looked to Nicholas.

"This ends *now*."

She felt Witham moving frantically. The Sin walked in big circles, checking rooms. At one point, Thorn heard a glass window shatter, and Witham ran from the apartment. Across the fifth floor. Alan sighed into Thorn's headset.

"I just missed my shot," he said. "Witham isn't in any east-facing rooms now."

"Help on the ground floor," Thorn said. "Take out as many of Sloth's people as you can. Keep the Martyrs *safe*." Thorn felt them leaving the building—felt the Puppets follow after them. A bomb exploded. A car alarm wailed. A life blinked out—not a Martyr. Thank *god* it wasn't a Martyr.

Thorn and Nicholas rushed through the top floor. Down the hallway. Around the corner. To the room where Gregory Witham was spinning...

And they slammed through the door.

Thorn pulled back and kicked it off its hinges. It clattered into the room. Sloth cried out. He was standing at the back wall, a pistol clutched in his shaking hands. He turned and immediately fired. A bullet zoomed past Thorn's shoulder, and one hit her square in the chest. It thudded painfully against her armor, threw her off balance—

Nicholas shot back. He missed, but the distraction—the *pure shock* on Sloth's face as he took in everything Nicholas was and was *not*—gave Thorn the chance to tackle the Sin to the ground.

They grappled. Both Thorn and Sloth's guns clattered to the floor. Gregory Witham made up for his lack of brute muscle with desperate wildness. He was wiry and unpredictable. Thorn rolled around with him, fighting to catch his arms and yank them around his head or to grab him by the back of the neck where she knew the *Peccostium* was waiting, but he was quick, and her armor made her clunky and uncoordinated. Witham managed to slam the heel of his palm into Thorn's chin.

She swore and twisted, just enough to jam her elbow into

his Adam's apple. He spluttered for breath as she reached out and grabbed his throat.

Thorn wrapped her fingers around it—dug her nails into the *Peccostium* just beneath his hairline. He cried out in pain, and then he stopped… because Thorn's hands tightened so hard around his windpipe that he couldn't force the air out.

For an agonizing moment, Thorn felt her control slipping. The anger inside swelled, overtaking her. Her vision blurred around the edges, and her senses dulled so much that she hardly had the sense to notice something new approaching. A new energy from beneath them, moving up the stairs. She didn't even hear Nicholas calling her name. She was too focused on the prize between her palms. God, how long had she been waiting for *this* moment?

It would take *so little* for her to crush his vertebrae. Break his neck. Cut him open, from jugular to jugular, and let the blood pour out—

"Thorn!"

Nicholas Wolfe's voice finally broke through. The room came into focus again. Thorn's breath caught in her throat, and she loosened her grip. Sloth sucked air deep into his lungs with hungry, haggard gasps, and he screamed.

"Get the fuck off of me, you crazy bitch!"

Spit bubbled on his lips. It clung to the dry, flaky patches and dripped down his chin. He tried to move, but the motions were weak. His crazy eyes darted between Thorn and Nicholas. He twitched. Writhed. Twitched again.

Nicholas just stared down at him, a look of contempt contorting his otherwise handsome face. Thorn turned to him—but something suddenly caught her attention.

That energy. Moving up.

Oh, god, Sloth had a Puppet on the way! How the *fuck* had she let herself get too distracted to notice?

"Send backup! One of them got away. It's on its way here," she cried into the headset. She felt Jeremiah break off from the fight and move into the building. He wouldn't be fast enough. He wouldn't catch up. She turned to Nicholas.

"Do it. Now."

Nicholas snapped back to reality. He hurried beside them and reached his hands out toward Sloth.

Gregory Witham's breathing grew harsh again. "Do— Do what? Do it? Oh, god! *Fuck*! *You're Diligence*!"

And as Nicholas went to touch him, Witham's panic exploded. He screamed, and his voice didn't sound human anymore.

"*What the fuck are you doing to me? What did you do? I'm trapped! I'm fucking trapped in this body! Why the fuck can't I get out? LET ME OUT!*"

Thorn's brows furrowed, and her heart beat hard against her ribcage. Sloth continued to scream—to cry out about being trapped and unable to escape—but Nicholas's hands were pressed firmly against the Sin's fingers, and *nothing happened.*

"*What the fuck are you waiting for?*" Thorn screamed. "Do it! Do it *now*!"

"I'm trying!" Nicholas's eyes were wide, and his teeth gritted together.

"Try fucking harder! We don't have time!"

"I know—"

The door slammed open. A Puppet barreled into the room. He already had a detonator in his hand—

Thorn desperately dug her nails deeper into Sloth's *Peccostium*—as hard as she fucking could—and he screamed. His link to the Puppet faltered. The man hesitated. But it wasn't enough. Thorn knew it wouldn't be enough.

His thumb came over the button.

Thorn leapt to her feet. She grabbed the Puppet by the collar of his shirt, and with a roar, she threw him toward the window. The glass broke behind his back, and he was out, over the street—

The bomb exploded. It blew the wall into the apartment. The blast scalded Thorn's face and hands, sent her flying backward in a cloud of debris. She was thrown against the far wall, and it collapsed, burying her under broken brick and drywall. The building quaked. Sloth's energy moved away, desperately fighting out from beneath the wreckage. Down the stairs. It collided with Jeremiah's. Thorn felt Jeremiah go flying over the railing in the stairwell, where he collapsed, motionless, on the level below.

Then Sloth was gone. Out of the building. Onto the streets. His energy faded away into nothing.

Wrath's Influence pinged in the distance.

God *fucking* damn it!

"Wrath is coming," Alan said into his headset. Thorn heard the distinct clicking of his rifle being disassembled and put back into its case. "All units, retreat."

"Thorn, Wolfe, and Jeremiah are still in the building," Chris's voice crackled in Thorn's ear. "It's coming down!"

The rage in Thorn's chest caught fire. It sent power through her body. Adrenaline through her veins. She tore her way out of the debris. The bottom half of her face felt raw and wet, and her exposed fingers were charred and searing. Her arms, her legs—everything hurt. But she didn't have time to focus on just how badly damaged she was. She had to get the fuck out of here before the building went down and took her, Nicholas, and Jeremiah with it.

"I'll get them," Thorn roared into her mic. "Leave one car. Everyone else, *get out.*"

Then she hurried around the room. Nicholas was pinned under a pile of bricks. She dug him out. Her raw fingers screamed at her, but she kept digging until she had uncovered his head. His visor was cracked; his face, scraped and bleeding. Nicholas just stared at her with a blank, confused expression.

"Can you stand?" she asked him.

"I-I don't know."

Thorn pulled one of Nicholas's arms over her shoulders, dragged him from the rubble, and rushed toward the stairwell. Sparkie zipped into the gaping hole in the wall and landed on her back. He kept an eye on the walls, on the ceiling, on the crumbling building around them for any sign of a collapse as Thorn flew down the steps. She found Jeremiah on the landing to the fourth floor. He had pulled himself to standing, but his left leg was twisted out of shape.

"We need to go," she said.

"I can't walk," Jeremiah said through a wince.

Thorn adjusted Nicholas, and Jeremiah wrapped his arm around her shoulders, too. Then, she hauled them away. Their combined weight strained her aching body. She could feel that her ribs were broken, and the muscles in her arms had been lacerated by shrapnel, but she pushed on.

Down the stairs. Through the decimated skeleton of the broken building. Parts of it started to crumble around them. Thorn had to stop on the second landing and avoid a beam as it fell from overhead. She heard deep, heavy crashes from above. She pushed faster. Past bricks. Past bodies. She hauled Jeremiah and Nicholas over massive piles of rubble as she made her way into the street.

Darius's SUV was waiting for them.

He opened the door and helped Thorn heave Nicholas and Jeremiah into the back. Thorn hopped in, closing them inside as Carter pulled the car into drive and took off. Darius healed Nicholas first, then Jeremiah. His tan complexion lost its luster, and even his shining, green eyes seemed dull and tired.

In the distance, the apartment building rumbled. Thorn looked out the back window to see the whole south face of the structure come down. Gray dust furled around it like a cloud of toxic smoke.

When Jeremiah's leg was mended and Nicholas's cuts and bruises cured, Darius took a deep, heavy breath, and he looked up to Thorn. His hands were shaking, his lips dry, but his jaw was set and grim. Thorn shook her head, punched her wounded, weeping hand into her thigh, and swore.

They had failed.

CHAPTER EIGHTEEN

As soon as Conrad parked, Thorn threw open the back of the surveillance vehicle and stormed out. She didn't make a sound, her jaw slammed shut, but her eyes were wide and wild. She tore the doors to the foyer open so furiously they ricocheted back, groaning, and she barely caught them. Jeremiah got out of the car, stared after her, and shook his head.

"This is going to be a rough one," he murmured through a sigh. Before Darius had the chance to ask what he meant, the TAC director followed Thorn into the Underground, Nicholas on his heels. Darius watched them quietly and ran his hands down his face.

"You okay?" Skylar asked.

Darius glanced over his shoulder to see her and Conrad staring at him from the front of the SUV. He waved dismissively. "Yeah. I'm fine. Just a little tired."

That was an understatement. Darius was *exhausted*. His muscles felt weak, and his mind was lost in a haze. As Conrad and Skylar set about removing the equipment from their vehicle, Darius took a deep breath, got out, and walked into the Underground.

Thanks to Darius's hard work on the field, Dr. Harris's

hospital ward was empty, but people were gathered around the waiting room anyway. Seven soot-stained, blood-streaked, traumatized people who had managed to make it through the bombings and get back to the Underground in one piece. Elijah and his wife, Colette, walked among them, providing the surviving Tactical Unit team with hot tea and nerve-soothing medications. As Darius passed through the room, a few people caught his eye and gave him grateful nods. Chris spotted him. Before he disappeared down the hallway, she jumped up, came over, and put a hand on his shoulder.

"Thank you," she murmured, and he grabbed her fingers and smiled back. The fatigued muscles on his face felt strained.

But his day still wasn't done. There was a lot they had to figure out.

Like why everything had gone so *wrong*.

Thorn had the same question. As soon as Darius walked into the conference room, she slammed the door shut behind him.

"What the hell happened out there?"

She tore her armor off and threw the pieces onto the table. Sparkie perched on her shoulder. His wings flared in a massive, red arch behind her head. The leathery webbing quivered as he kneaded his tiny claws into the black fabric on her shoulder.

"That was a fucking *disaster*." Thorn's voice was so tight it shook. The muscles along her throat were tense to the point that Darius could see the outline of each ligament and tendon through her pale, gritty skin. The wounds she'd sustained in the final explosion had almost totally healed on the drive. There was a fine, pink boundary between the fresher flesh on the bottom of her face and the undamaged skin above.

"How the fuck were the bombs able to go off?" Thorn snarled. She was pacing back and forth along the wall. Her nostrils flared. Her lips tight and thin. Thorn's frazzled hair was falling out of its ponytail and frayed like static around her head as her wild, black eyes moved across the room—from Holly and Jeremiah, Lina and Mackenzie, to Darius and Nicholas. Finally, they landed on Alan at the head of the table. He watched her back with a practiced reserve. Rae sat beside him, stoic as a statue.

Alan stepped toward Thorn and tried to put a hand on her shoulder. "Thorn, please—"

She tore away from him. "And *you*," she hissed. "Why the *fuck* did you leave *Darius* behind? I said I needed *one car*. *His* had to be the one?"

"That was my call," Darius said. He tried not to let any weariness seep into his voice, but it was hard. He took a deep breath. "Jeremiah and Nicholas were injured. I wanted to—"

"I don't give a damn what you wanted," Thorn screamed. Sparkie screeched from her shoulder. The sound was deafening. "It was irresponsible to leave a fucking Virtue behind with Sloth on the run and Wrath on the way!"

"Thorn." Alan stepped closer to her again. Rae got to her feet and followed. Thorn retreated, out of arm's reach. "Thorn, you need to—"

"Don't you dare tell me to calm down!" Thorn raged. Spit was flying from her dry lips. Her eyes were wide. Her voice raspy and guttural. The air around her seemed charged, like her fury was so palpable it was saturating the room. She spun away from Alan and slammed her fist into the wall behind her so forcefully Darius heard the disorienting *crack!* of bones breaking against the concrete. Thorn roared again and turned back to the room. Her injured knuckles dripped with blood.

"We lost *two people* today because our damned disruptors didn't work," she went on. "Sloth strapped bombs onto *innocent people* and let them *blow themselves to fucking pieces*. Over twenty people died—*over twenty*. And we didn't even fucking *get him*. Gregory Witham escaped because this damned, arrogant Virtue—"

"Excuse me?"

Nicholas stood up, and his eyebrows pinched hard over steely, blue eyes. Now that he was healed, Nicholas was full of fire and energy. His hands clenched at his sides. Thorn turned to face him. Her shoulders raised. Her fingers dug so deep into her palms that Darius was sure her nails would break the skin.

"*I'm* the reason that son of a bitch escaped?" Nicholas said.

"You didn't destroy him! You were right there—we were *right fucking there!*"

"Oh, I'm sorry," Nicholas said, raising his hands in furious disbelief. "I've never fucking done this before—"

"You know how!" Thorn screamed. "We *all* know how! You have to be prepared to sacrifice yourself for the greater good, but you're too fucking arrogant to see past yourself!"

"Or maybe," Nicholas yelled back, "having someone scream 'try fucking harder' in your ear doesn't make this decision—"

"Decision?" Thorn barked with a harsh, critical laugh. She took a step toward Nicholas. His eyes widened, and he took a half-step back. "The decision should have been made before you ever got into that room!"

"Whoa, Thorn," Mackenzie said. She jumped up to help as Alan rushed upon Thorn again. He tried to grab her by the shoulder, but she twisted away and shoved him backward. Mackenzie ducked under his arm and approached Thorn, holding her hands out like she was coming upon a wild animal. Her bright eyes were wide, cautious, but compassionate. "This isn't the time—"

"This is the perfect time," Thorn screamed. "Teresa Solomon spent *her entire life* learning how to destroy the Sins so that *assholes like this*—" she jabbed a finger right into Nicholas's chest so forcefully that she almost knocked him backward "—wouldn't have to! That woman gave up her life for you! For all of us! And *you* selfish little—"

"That is *enough.*"

Alan pushed past Mackenzie and grabbed for Thorn. She tried to bat him away, but Alan managed to catch her by the arms. The edges of his fingers tightened just below the *Peccostium* on her wrist, and she froze. For a few quiet moments, they shared a look—Thorn, contemptuous and furious, and Alan, piercing and steady.

"If you cannot get a grip on yourself," he said, "you need to *leave.*"

The tone was off, and Darius frowned. It was almost a threat, but he caught a subtle note—a hint of caution.

Thorn didn't respond. Her lips curled up in disgust as she tore her arms out of Alan's hands, spun on her heels, and stomped out the door. She slammed it behind her so hard that the wood along the frame cracked.

The room went quiet. Silence hung around them like a fog. Darius looked around. Most of the Martyr leadership shared the same expression—a blend of awkward tension and familiar relief.

This wasn't the first time Thorn had an outburst in this room with these people.

Not *all* of these people, though. Nicholas was aghast. He just stared at the door, his mouth gaping, his eyes dark and heavy. He tenderly touched the spot on his chest where Thorn had jabbed him with her finger. Darius had no doubt it would bruise.

Alan allowed himself those few moments to recover. He took a deep breath, rolled his shoulders, and turned back to the room. If he saw Nicholas's expression, he did a damn good job not showing it. Instead, he looked right at Holly.

"Miss Andrews," he said. His tone was even again— back to the curt, professional attitude Darius was used to. "Why did our signal disruptors fail?"

"They didn't," Holly began, but she didn't get to finish the thought. Nicholas raised his hand and stepped forward.

"Hold the fuck up," he said, and he looked around at all of them. His eyebrows furrowed, his jaw clenched, and he gestured a wide arm at the door sitting in its cracked frame.

"That's *it?* She gets to come in here and freak the fuck out, and we're just going to act like it didn't happen?"

"We have more important business to attend to," Alan said, but Nicholas cut him off, too.

"The *fuck* you do! The second-in-command of your organization is *insane*. How can you stand by and let that woman have any power here? She's out of control."

"Mr. Wolfe, that is enough," Alan said, and his calm demeanor disappeared. He raised himself to full height and rounded on the new Virtue. The sharp lines of Alan's face were somehow sharper, his eyes darker. Suddenly, Rae was at his heels. She bared sharp, white fangs and gave a deep, heavy growl. Her hackles raised and made her look even more massive. More formidable. The pin-tight pupils inside her shining blue irises focused on Nicholas's face.

Nicholas's confidence wavered. His eyes widened, and he took a step back. Alan went on, and this time, his tone was *not* even. The fires of his Wrath singed at its edges, tinting it with a fury Darius hadn't seen up close before.

"Just because *you* cannot see the reasons Thorn is in the position she's in does *not mean* she does not deserve every ounce of power she has here. It is *my* job to manage and contain her. Not yours. Your job—your *only job*—is to learn how to destroy Sloth… A job at which you have *failed miserably.*"

Those last words sank in, slowly hovering in the room, and Darius's breath caught in his throat. He cast a glance at Mackenzie, and she stared back, jaw dropped, with her eyebrows raised so high on her head they disappeared behind her electric blue bangs.

"I *suggest*," Alan continued, his piercing glare driving deep into Nicholas's shocked eyes, "you stop blaming everyone else for their shortcomings and focus instead on how *your failure* allowed two Martyrs and nineteen civilians to die in vain today. Now get out."

Without looking away from Nicholas's face, Alan opened the door to the conference room. Nicholas's facade of confidence quickly built back up, and he furiously strode out the door and disappeared down the hallway. Darius was half-convinced he'd leave the Underground, but to his relief, he felt the Virtue move around the corner and toward the elevators. Alan turned back to the room. This time, his resolve did not return so quickly. His nostrils were flared, his mouth a hot line, and his fists clenched when he looked to Darius.

"We need to find out what went wrong," he said again. Rae slowly mellowed out. Her fur flattened against her body. Her pupils widened and relaxed. Alan took a deep breath and shook his head. "We *must* understand why Sloth was not destroyed. There must be something we missed…"

"If there is," Darius said, "I'll find it."

He had to.

Derek Dane's voice echoed in a dark, resonant laugh. It bounced around inside Darius's skull, somehow distant and near, as his broad hand wrapped around Teresa's throat. The Sin lifted her from the dark, foggy ground. His *Peccostium* glared out from just beneath his wrist, almost like an eye—like a serpent's slitted pupil—carnal and hungry.

"I've been waiting for this for a *long time*," Pride said.

And Teresa smiled. She wrapped her hands around Dane's arm. The *Peccostium* disappeared behind her palm. She was too weak to put enough pressure on it to hurt him.

But she didn't need to. She had something else. Something stronger.

"Me too," Teresa said. A bright, shining light erupted from her palms, into Pride's flesh.

And Dane screamed.

Loud and guttural, it tore from his throat like a gale—poured out of his mouth on a river of heavy smoke and hot ash. It pierced the sky, the darkness, the sides of Darius's head…

He startled awake.

Darius snapped up. The Bhagavad Gita lay open on the table in front of him, a full cup of cold coffee beside it. Darius blinked a couple of times to get his bearings and looked around the courtyard. It was quiet. Empty. The overhead lights had been dimmed—something they were programmed to do past nine p.m. to give this sunless cavern some sense of a circadian rhythm. Jesus, how long had he been asleep?

He looked at the time. It was almost midnight. Darius groaned and rubbed his eyes. These last few days had really worn on him, but he couldn't *believe* he'd passed out in the courtyard.

Ever since their failed attack on Sloth, Darius had done nothing but eat, sleep, and try to find out why Nicholas hadn't been able to destroy the Sin. It was the final piece of the puzzle—the final mystery that needed solving about why everything had gone *so* south. Holly's signal disruptors hadn't worked because the bombs Sloth was using now didn't match the frequency of the one they'd found earlier. He'd adapted. It was simple, if not devastating.

But they hadn't found any explanation as to why *Nicholas* hadn't worked. All of Darius's time was spent digging through research to figure it out. His eyes ached from reading. His back was sore from hunching over books and reports and computer screens. His brain was tired—*so tired*—but he kept pushing forward. He had to.

Teresa had unlocked the secret. She'd *died* to prove her theory.

And before she'd gone, she'd given Darius *this*... He looked down at The Bhagavad Gita again and touched it with light, gentle fingers.

The answer was in here. Whatever Teresa had uncovered, whatever final key she had found, was somewhere between these pages.

He leaned back in the chair and lifted the book again. Carefully, Darius thumbed through it, but his tired brain didn't have the energy to focus on the words printed there anymore. He'd read them so much that he felt like he could recite them, line by line. He understood the concepts, the theories, the morals of the story. He felt confident in his interpretations...

But something *had* to be missing.

Darius put it down, closed his eyes, and ran his hands over his face. His palms caught on the stubble he'd been too busy to shave. He sighed and took a deep, full breath.

Derek Dane's death had revitalized the Martyrs. It had changed the whole energy of this dark, lonely place. When Teresa Solomon had reduced Pride to a pile of ash on the ground at her feet, it had proven the Martyrs were still a force to be reckoned with—that they wouldn't just fight to the end, but they could, and *would*, fight until the Sins were destroyed. It had given them a confidence they hadn't seen in decades.

But now, that confidence was hanging by a delicate thread, and Darius had heard the rumors. The whispers. The deep, primal fears...

What if Teresa's destruction of Pride had been a *mistake*?

What if the secret hadn't been uncovered after all, and now the Martyrs were trapped fighting against one *fewer* Sin, but the remaining six were driven, angry, and thirsty for revenge?

Darius couldn't stand it. He could let them down. He'd worked hard to build up a sense of camaraderie inside these walls, and he'd be damned if he let this setback tear it down.

The Underground—the *Martyrs*—were too important to him.

For a moment, Darius let himself sink into this place. The familiarity of the Underground and the energies of the people sleeping there helped center him. During the day, this entire structure moved, bustling with an invisible activity Darius had the privilege of experiencing with his Virtue senses. At night, though, when people finally laid down to rest, the chaos settled. From the center of the courtyard,

Darius could feel almost every single Martyr. He spent a few minutes checking in with them. Mackenzie, lukewarm and still in a way she never was when she was awake. Skylar and Raquel, their energies curled comfortably and lovingly around one another, so close they blurred into one. John, sitting up, still awake while he waited for Chris to get home from her night shift in the city.

They were all calm. Peaceful. Motionless.

Mostly motionless.

Every so often, he felt movement. In their bed on the western block, Eva tossed and turned in her sleep. The search for her brother had been paused to put more people on Gregory Witham's trail, and she'd finally been given a new assignment: with the Cleaning Crew. She was devastated and restless. Darius couldn't blame her, and his heart ached.

Then there was Nicholas. His strong, Virtuous pull flickered with activity. Undoubtedly, he was in his bedroom, pouring over even *more* videos of Gregory Witham after their failed attempt to kill him. Shortly after he'd been kicked out of the conference room, Nicholas asked Skylar for all the body cam footage from their mission. Instead of helping Darius uncover the missing piece to destroying Sloth, he was obsessively going over the botched operation.

And finally, one more element moved—one more person. He felt her above him, leaving the R&D headquarters and walking down the hallway to the elevator. Darius turned toward it as her warmth moved down. The light blinked on, the doors opened, and Lina Brooks stepped into the courtyard.

She looked just as tired as Darius felt. Rings had sprung up beneath her eyes, and her neat, braided hair was fuzzy around the edges. She yawned as she headed toward the eastern block of rooms. Darius yawned, too. God, he *was* tired. As she was about to pass him, he called out to her.

"Late night, huh?"

She leapt and let out a little shriek of surprise. "God,

Darius," she said, smiling as she pressed a hand to her heart. "I didn't see you there!"

He gave a sheepish chuckle. "I didn't mean to scare you," he said. "I didn't expect anyone else to be up this late."

Lina laughed, too. The sound echoed through the concrete chamber. "I got caught up in some reading. What are *you* doing up?"

"Trying to figure out what the hell is going on with Nicholas," Darius said through a sigh as he pinched the bridge of his nose.

"With his Virtue?"

"Yeah."

Lina paused for a moment before she came and sat across from him. Darius looked down at the table with a frown. "He's not being helpful with it, either," he said. "Every time I try to talk with him, he brushes me off. He's just obsessed with Sloth."

Lina shook her head. "That won't do us a lot of good if he doesn't know how to destroy it."

"Tell me about it." Darius groaned and rubbed his tired eyes with his fingertips. "We were *so close*. I thought we had everything figured out."

"When it comes to the Sins, I don't think it's *possible* to have everything figured out," Lina said with a small smile, but there was a glint of excitement behind her eyes. "We're always learning new things. Did you read the report Thorn wrote about the latest mission?"

Darius's chest clenched. He hadn't. He hadn't even *seen* Thorn since she'd stormed out of the conference room four days ago. He'd asked Mackenzie if she'd heard from her, and all she'd said was that Thorn was keeping herself busy in the city. Darius thought about calling or texting to see if she was okay, but he wasn't sure she'd want to hear from him.

After all, it wasn't that long ago he'd suggested that she stop hiding her anger. He could just imagine the shame in her voice as she said, "I fucking told you, Jones."

Darius shook his head, coming back into the courtyard, where Lina was watching him. "I didn't even know she wrote a report," he said at last.

"She submitted it this evening," Lina said. "A little late, but late's better than never. You should read it. It's fascinating."

"Does she have any idea why Nicholas couldn't destroy Sloth?"

"Only the idea she's already shared with us," Lina said. "She thinks he's not ready to sacrifice his life yet. But that's not what I'm talking about. She posed an amazing theory— that the Sins *can't escape* their hosts if the Virtue that can kill them is nearby."

That caught Darius's attention. His eyebrows shot up, and he leaned across the table. "Really? What makes her think that?"

"Her report outlines it in more detail," Lina said, "but I guess she had him disabled, and when he realized that Nicholas was Diligence, he started panicking about how he was trapped in his body. I watched the footage from Thorn's body cam to see it for myself, and I think she's right."

Darius's eyes widened, and he felt a little excited bubble swell between his lungs. "He was probably trying to abandon ship," he said quietly. It made sense. Sins could abandon their hosts whenever it suited them, but they rarely did since it messed with their memory. When face to face with the Virtue that could destroy it, though, the better option would always be to leave the host and find someone new to possess. A fragmented memory was better than annihilation. The implications of this theory, the idea that the Sins could *not* escape their host if the opposite Virtue was nearby, were incredible.

Darius's heart sank as he realized what *else* it meant.

"Then Envy knows I'm Kindness," Darius said, and he looked at Lina. "When Chris killed her, she would have tried to escape and wouldn't have been able to get away."

Lina nodded. "I know. Wrath even said the Sins are

afraid of you, right? That protection will only last until Envy repossesses—unless, of course, it lost its memory of that in the trauma."

"Let's hope," Darius said. "But we can't rely on that. Has this ever been documented before?"

"Not that I've seen," Lina said. "Alan had never heard of it, either. He was going to reach out to Cain and see if he knew anything, and he asked me to see what I can find. So far there's nothing. I was so engrossed in my reading that I didn't realize it was so late until all the words started blurring together!"

"Hah!" Darius laughed and sat back in the chair again. "Well, I'm glad *you're* having fun. I just feel like I'm banging my head against a wall."

"Where are you stuck?" Lina asked, and though she was tired, her excitement brought a little more energy to her face. "I love this kind of thing."

"Well," Darius said, and he tapped the front cover of The Bhagavad Gita on the table between them. Lina picked it up. She started flipping through pages as Darius went on. "This is a book Teresa wanted me to have. I've read it probably a hundred times now. Most of her notes have to do with *accepting* your Virtue. Her theory was that Arjuna was an Uninitiated Virtue—probably Diligence—and Krishna was Patience. Teresa thought Krishna was trying to teach Arjuna how to finally initiate his Virtue, so most of her notes talk about that.

"But," Darius continued with a sigh, and he stifled a yawn. "There are a few newer notes there that talk about *destroying* the Sin. Especially the one on *that* scrap of paper."

Lina had just pulled the note Darius used as a bookmark from between the pages. She read it to herself, but Darius knew exactly what it said. Those words were chiseled onto his brain like a commandment:

'To end the cycle of possession and rebirth, we must come together and pass in the light—as One.'

"As far as I can tell," Darius said, "It's all about the self-sacrifice. The whole book is about self-sacrifice."

For a moment, Lina nodded thoughtfully. Her thin eyebrows pinched together. "I didn't see this in Dr. Solomon's research," she said after a moment. It had the cadence of a question, and she glanced up to Darius. He shook his head.

"No. I kept it. As a memento, I guess."

Just saying that made his chest give a painful twinge. Lina smiled at him from across the table and nodded.

"Of course," she said. "Do you mind if I borrow this? I need to sleep, but I promise I'll read it and get it back to you as soon as I can."

"Help yourself," Darius said. A new perspective could only help him at this point. "Thank you so much, Lina."

"Oh," she said, and she dismissively waved him away as she got to her feet. "It's my pleasure. Really. I meant it when I said I *love* this stuff. I'll get right on this first thing tomorrow. In the meantime, take a break, okay? We'll figure this out."

Then she said goodnight, tucked The Bhagavad Gita under her arm and headed back to the eastern set of rooms. Darius watched her go until her aura quietly settled into place in her quarters. It felt weird going back to his without the book in his hands—strange to see his bedside table empty. He laid beside Eva and wrapped himself around her. Her warmth pierced into his soul, comforting him from the inside out. She relaxed in his embrace. For the first time all night, Eva's restlessness disappeared.

But even in sleep, Darius struggled to "take a break." His mind replayed everything he knew—or thought he knew—about how to destroy the Sins. As his eyes closed and his mind settled, he found himself back in the same dream, where Teresa Solomon destroyed Pride with hands that glowed like the sun.

CHAPTER NINETEEN

The next day, Eva started training for her new place in the Cleaning Crew, and Darius found himself in the rec room trying to take a break.

But he wasn't familiar with this. When he'd been living in Alphabet City, surviving off his skills in the Williamsburg Bridge Street Market, there wasn't such a thing as downtime. Any moment he wasn't busy bartering for goods, he was at home, sorting items, washing clothing, preparing food, reading to children, breaking up fights, and, finally, falling asleep, just to start over and do it all again the next morning.

What did people usually do when they had nothing else *to* do?

Darius decided to try reading. He had a book in his hands—a collection of Arthurian legends they had pulled from Teresa's house last January—and his eyes moved meaninglessly along the same opening line, over and over again, seeing it without reading it.

Because a couple of TAC members, also on a break, were watching the news at the other end of the room.

"There have been no sightings of Saul Torres since he was spotted in Mott Haven on August twenty-first, just over two weeks ago," the newscaster was saying. Darius glanced up at the screen. "Authorities have now started calling Torres a 'suspect,' instead of a person of interest, believing he may be tied to the explosion outside the Mitchel Houses. While the motive for the bombing is still unclear, Torres was last seen outside the housing authority just minutes before the bomb went off. Commissioner Moore recently announced the reward for information leading to Torres's arrest has increased from ten-thousand dollars to fifty thousand."

"Holy shit," Darius grumbled, and he ran a hand over his face.

"Police are also warning the public," the newscaster went on, "not to approach Torres. He may be armed, and he certainly is dangerous. If you see him, call the police tip hotline. You can also send photos and videos to the NYPD's tip email address scrolling at the bottom of your screen—"

Darius swore, his fingers tightening around the book. The pages groaned in his hands. For a moment, he found himself wondering if this was how Thorn felt all the time. Always *this* close to throwing something across the room.

The TAC agents glanced up to him. Darius took a deep breath and set the book down.

The Sins weren't the only people who hadn't seen any sign of Saul since the bombing at the Mitchel Houses. Neither had the Martyrs. Even Nicholas and Skylar's new system hadn't been able to spot him in the busy throngs of New York City.

And now, the Sins were weaponizing him. Alan had called Darius in to talk about this new development a couple of days ago. Saul was being blamed for the attacks, making him a higher target for civilians who just wanted everything to go back to normal. Alan thought it was a two-pronged approach. Putting the spotlight on Saul would mobilize the Martyrs, too—make them *more* proactive in trying to stop Sloth and get Saul out of danger. It could also make Saul nervous enough to make a mistake. Get himself caught.

And if the Sins caught him, Alan was sure they'd use him as bait to lure Darius out of the Underground.

But they hadn't caught him. Not yet. Maybe not ever. So the Martyrs weren't focusing on Saul. All their energy was going toward Sloth. Every single day, an air of tension clouded the Martyrs as they waited for news of *another* bombing their people had been too late to stop.

It made Darius sick.

He got to his feet and made his way out to the courtyard. This place was empty, too. More and more, lately, the Underground felt empty. The Gray Units were on long-term placement in the city. Tactical Units were working double shifts. Research and Discovery teams were upstairs, helping Holly's team sort through hours and hours of video footage.

Only a handful of people were left down here, on the second level, including Nicholas Wolfe.

He sat at the counter in the kitchen, like he did every afternoon, hunched over his laptop and writing in his notebook. Darius approached him. He didn't bother announcing himself, and Nicholas didn't bother looking up to acknowledge him. He was too intently focused on his screen. As Darius came to his side, he saw what it was. Bodycam footage. But not just anyone's footage…

It was Thorn's.

The screen showed Nicholas's face, up close, as he and Thorn argued in the stairwell. Then Nicholas took off, and Thorn followed after him. They reached the second level. A door opened, and a woman slipped out. Darius had to look away as she took out her detonator.

"Jesus, why are you watching this?" he asked.

"I'm learning," Nicholas said.

"Learning what?"

Nicholas didn't answer as he rewound the video. He started playing it over from the moment when he first tore out of Thorn's hands. Behind his visor, Nicholas had glared at her with a hot, heavy rage. Darius couldn't imagine how the hell rewatching this footage could help him uncover how to destroy Sloth. Unless that wasn't what he was trying to do at all.

Darius's stomach dropped, and he took in a small, shocked gasp.

"Are you building a case against *Thorn*?"

"What?" Nicholas said, spinning toward Darius at last. On the screen behind his head, the woman exploded again. Darius focused on Nicholas's face.

"Why are you watching Thorn's body cam?" Darius pressed. "What could you possibly get out of it unless you're trying to prove how unstable you think she is?"

"For one," Nicholas said as he crossed his arms. "She *is* unstable, whether the rest of you want to see it or not. And you're right. This footage would do a damn good job of showing that off. Just watch." He looked over his shoulder and gestured to the screen. Darius glanced up to it, too, just in time to see Thorn shoot a woman in the throat. "I was going to save her, but Thorn pulled me off. And when we got to Sloth? She went *dark*. You want to believe these people aren't as close to Wrath as they once were, but you're wrong. She wants to do the right thing, but one push too far, that bitch will snap, and she'll take you down with her."

"No," Darius said. "She won't. Thorn has lived as a Forgotten Sin for almost a century. She's never snapped—"

"Do you know that for sure?" Nicholas asked. His eyes narrowed, and his lips pressed together. "You've been here, what? A year? She's been here for almost *ninety*. I've looked at the files about her in the database, and details from tons of them have been redacted—including her real name. You don't really know *her*, so how can you *possibly* know she hasn't snapped?"

Darius didn't have an answer for that, because Nicholas was right. There was a lot of Thorn's history Darius didn't know. It was more than possible she had lost control in a way that resulted in horrifying violence.

But Darius found he didn't care. He didn't want to dig

into who Thorn had been, what Thorn might have done. All he cared about was the woman he knew now.

"She's got an empty pit in her chest instead of a soul," Darius said at last, and his voice deepened. "She's capable of a lot more than either of us can imagine, including a lot of *good*. You would see that if you'd just stop making her out as the enemy."

Nicholas's expression hadn't faltered. He focused a little harder on Darius, his eyes narrow, his mouth set, and his brows heavy. He was about to argue, but they both suddenly stopped and turned toward the elevator. Lina's energy was descending, and as the doors opened, she looked around the courtyard. Her eyes landed on them.

"Oh, good!" She rushed over to the pair of Virtues, holding The Bhagavad Gita in her hands. Darius could see hundreds of new sticky notes poking out at its edges. "I'm glad you're both here!" Lina exclaimed, but then she paused. Her excitement wavered a bit as she looked between Nicholas and Darius. "...Am I interrupting something?"

Nicholas turned to look at Darius, like a challenge, and Darius shook his head.

"It's nothing," he said. Then he gestured to the book in her hands. The familiar, comforting little book. "Did you find something?"

Lina's smile lit up the room. For a beautiful, painful moment, she reminded Darius of Teresa. "*Yes!*" she said. "I think I've got it! I know how you have to destroy the Sins!"

Nicholas finally unwrapped his arms from around his torso, and his expression moved from anger to what Darius was more accustomed to: intense, almost devoted ambition. And he realized Nicholas was willing to die to destroy the Sin. That wasn't the problem. There had to be something more, something deeper.

Lina, Darius, and Nicholas sat down around one of the tables in the courtyard. Nicholas started flipping through the pages of The Bhagavad Gita while Lina talked.

"This version of The Gita is really interesting," Lina was

saying. Compared to the night before, she looked well-rested and vibrant. Her braid was tight and smooth, and her gray eyes glistened with excitement. "I had to read this text a couple of times while I was getting my undergraduate and doctorate degrees, but this translation is different. Instead of talking about himself in the individual, the 'I' of a higher being, he talks in regards to 'we.' For example, in this section, he says, 'We are the goodness of the virtuous.' That definitely lends credit to this being a story of one Virtue talking to another."

"So this whole conversation really happened?" Nicholas asked.

Lina shook her head. "No," she said. "At least, not like this. For all the things this book says about the nature of Virtues, it's also full of opinions about good and evil that are clearly coming from more of an establishment point of view. Ultimately, this text is like The Bible. It's got some great stuff in there, but you need to dig through a lot of human folly to find it. Most religious books and stories were ultimately designed to keep a budding society bound by standard rules and moralities, and The Bhagavad Gita is no different.

"But," Lina went on, "like The Bible, parts of this story are likely drawn from real experiences and people, real Sins and Virtues, who were Influencing the culture of the time. Back then, Virtues and Sins would have been seen as holy or unholy creatures, depending on who you're looking at. Greeks revered Sins as gods, while Vyasa regarded them as demons. Some of the most ancient cultures, like the Egyptians, *only* talk about the Sins. The Virtues don't seem to exist at all, probably because—"

"Lina," Darius said, and he raised his hand to quiet her. When she was excited about something, she could go off about it for hours. Right now, Darius didn't have that kind of time. Or patience. "What does The Gita say about destroying the Sins?"

"Right," Lina said, and she cleared her throat. "Like I

said, I definitely see this being a conversation between two Virtues, but where Dr. Solomon originally thought it was an Initiated Virtue talking to an Uninitiated Virtue, I think it's more likely a Virtue who *has* destroyed its Sin talking to one who hasn't."

"That's impossible," Nicholas said. "Virtues have to die to destroy the Sin."

"Yes, I realize that," Lina said with a polite nod, but her cheeks turned pink. "Remember how I said it's like The Bible? It's mostly a work of fiction. It's more likely that these lessons were passed down in Virtuous orders, and over the centuries, this story developed as a way to *teach* the lessons."

"What makes you think it's a lesson about destroying the Sins instead of Initiating a Virtue?" Darius asked.

"It's mostly in the way Krishna describes himself. He seems to have reached this new level of existence, which *could* be a metaphor for accepting his Virtue. However," Lina said, and she paused a little for dramatic effect, "if we take into account Dr. Solomon's belief that the Virtue and the Sin are two halves of the same whole and therefore must come together to be mutually destroyed, a lot of Krishna's dialogue has a whole new meaning. Take this, for example."

She reached her hand out for the book, and Nicholas dropped it into her fingers. She flipped through to a particular bookmark and read a couple of passages from the pages. "*We are the ritual and the sacrifice; We are true medicine and the mantra. We are the offering and the fire which consumes it, and those to whom it is offered. We give and withhold the rain. We are immortality, and We are death; We are what is and what is not.*"

Then she looked up to Nicholas and Darius with an enthusiastic, expectant look. When neither of them said anything, she raised her hands. "Doesn't that sound like what Dr. Solomon meant?"

"I'm sorry, but I'm not following," Darius said.

Lina took to flipping through the book again. "The idea is that Krishna is everything, a unified being above the rest of humanity. Here's another passage that shows how this combination, or 'unity,' may be the clue to destroying the Sins: '*The wise unify their consciousness and abandon the fruits of action, which binds a person to continual rebirth. Thus they attain a state beyond all evil.*' You see? The 'rebirth' can mean both the Virtues' literal rebirth and the Sins' repossession. And Krishna has achieved this state—being *beyond* all evil, beyond the Sin—by bringing them together as one."

"Okay," Nicholas said, closing his eyes, and he rubbed his temples with his fingertips. "Okay, fine. Let's say that *is* what this book is about—some fairytale about a dead Virtue talking to a living one. Why the *hell* do we need to know that to know how to destroy the Sins?"

"For *context*," Lina said, with a slight affront to her voice. "If that's what this book is about—destroying the Sins instead of accepting the Virtue—then the answer as to *how* to destroy them is actually pretty obvious. Wouldn't you agree, Darius?"

Then she looked right at him, and for a moment, Darius didn't think it was. He frowned and watched Lina back, trying to think about what he knew of The Bhagavad Gita—what would be different if it applied to *destroying* the Sins instead...

Suddenly, it clicked. His eyes widened, and his mouth fell open.

"Oh my god. It's more than just the sacrifice."

"Precisely," Lina said.

"What?" Nicholas asked, and he grabbed for the book again, but Lina held it closer to her chest. "What do you mean it's more than just the sacrifice?"

"Of course," Darius said. "I can't believe I didn't see that before." And he couldn't. He'd been so consumed with thinking it had to be *bigger* than this—that it had to be more complicated. But, in its simplicity, it *was* complicated.

"What the *fuck* is going on?" Nicholas said with a frustrated groan.

"The sacrifice is only a part of the equation," Lina said. "It's not enough to be willing to give up your life. You have to do it *selflessly.*"

Then she paused and let the gravity of that sink in, but Darius could tell the effect was lost. Nicholas didn't get it. Up until thirty seconds ago, neither had he.

"Isn't that the whole point of a sacrifice?" Nicholas finally asked. "Killing yourself to get rid of the Sin is *inherently* selfless."

"Not according to The Gita—"

"How the hell not?" Nicholas cut in. He crossed his arms and furrowed his brows. "What the fuck do I have to gain by giving up my life to destroy Sloth? I'll be a dead-man."

"Well, there are a lot of things," Lina said, and though the blush on her cheeks deepened, and she didn't make eye contact with Nicholas, she didn't back down. She held out The Bhagavad Gita again and flipped open to a page. Then, she read out loud:

"*You should never engage in action for the sake of reward. Perform work in this world as a man established within himself—without selfish attachments, and alike in success and defeat. For this is perfect evenness of mind.*" She flipped to another page and read again: "*He must work not for his own sake, but for the welfare of all.*" And another: "*Those whose consciousness is unified abandon all attachment to the results of action, but those who are selfishly attached to the results of their work are bound.*"

But Nicholas shook his head again. "That's just the same bullshit over and over. It doesn't explain how being willing to die for this battle isn't inherently selfless."

"It's about the intent," Darius said, and he looked at Lina. "Did you mark that verse, too?"

"Of course I did," Lina said, and she flipped to yet another page and read yet another passage. A damning passage.

"*Self-important, obstinate, swept away by pride, they ostentatiously perform sacrifices without regard for their purpose. Egotistical, violent, arrogant, lustful, angry, envious - they abuse our presence within their own bodies.*"

Then she stopped and looked back up to Nicholas. His face had paled, his jaw set, and the muscles along his neck went tight and hard.

"So you think I'm *self-important*?"

"No," Lina said, and she glanced back down at the pages in front of her. "But I think your reasons for wanting to destroy Sloth are." Then she took a deep breath, and instead of focusing back on Nicholas, she turned to Darius. "It doesn't matter how pure and good a Virtue is. If your motives for destroying the Sin are clouded with ego or vengeance or anger, you're going to fail. That's why this was lost for so long—because it's not a trick or a tool or a technique. It's a *mindset,* and that's hard to teach."

For a few long seconds, none of them spoke. The echoing, vast silence of the courtyard closed in around them. Darius stared down at the book.

It was so simple, but still so—

"This is impossible," Nicholas scoffed, and he threw his hands up in the air. "Nobody—*nobody*—can go into something like this completely selflessly."

"Teresa could," Darius said as he leaned back in his chair and rubbed his eyes.

"The Gita has practices you can do to help you get to the right frame of mind," Lina offered, but from the tone of her voice, Darius could tell that even she wasn't sold on them. "I think, ultimately, it's just going to take a lot of practice."

"Practice doing *what*?" Nicholas asked.

Darius had an idea.

"In changing the way you think," he said, and he cast Nicholas a hard look. Nicholas shot one back.

Something told Darius that Nicholas wasn't one for having his mind changed.

The gentle, rhythmic sound of water lapping against

concrete filled Darius's ears. His mind. His spirit. His thoughts filtered in and out of his head like they were on slow-moving waves. His breathing was measured, his heart quiet and even, as he sat cross-legged on the ground, palms upon his knees, and he relaxed.

The stillness was disrupted by Nicholas clearing his throat. It broke Darius from his reprieve, allowing a flash of annoyance to intrude on the quiet of his mind. He fought to get back there.

"So..." Nicholas's voice echoed through the pool room. It bounced from distant, concrete walls and tiled floors, back at Darius somehow louder than it had been when it first left Nicholas's mouth. "How do I know if it's working?"

For the last few days, Darius had been focusing on opening up his mind, both for his benefit and for Nicholas's. While Nicholas had wandered off to think about what Lina had uncovered—and obsess more over the video footage he'd received from Skylar—Darius and Lina researched exercises in mindfulness. He was looking for something, *anything,* that could help Virtues achieve the right state to destroy the Sins, and he wanted to make sure Nicholas tried it all.

At every possible opportunity, Darius was tearing the other Virtue away from his laptop and forcing him to participate in whatever technique he was working on that day. It ranged from yoga to writing prompts, breathing exercises to meditation.

Nicholas went along with it, though not without complaining.

"If you're wondering if it's working," Darius said through a sigh, "then it's not. Just focus on your breathing." He tried to recenter himself, but it was hard. He was frustrated—with Nicholas, with Sloth, with *everything.* And now, he was spending hours on what felt like a futile effort to convince a stubborn Virtue to work on being *more* virtuous.

"Breathing. Got it."

Then Nicholas went quiet again, but he sure as hell didn't focus on his breathing. He shuffled where he sat. Quiet, but not restful. Darius just shook his head and took a deep breath in.

One... two... three... four...

Then Nicholas's phone went off. Darius's concentration shattered again. He clenched his fists as Nicholas dug into his pocket. Darius had insisted, as he always did, Nicholas leave his phone behind. Nicholas—as *he* always did—ignored him. He looked down at the screen, and Darius chanced a glance over. Skylar's name shone up at the top of the message. It was *always* Skylar. Before Darius had the chance to read it, Nicholas jumped to his feet.

"Whelp, this has been fun," he said with a tone that distinctly implied it was *not* fun. "Same time tomorrow?"

"Every evening," Darius said, and he shook his head. "Man, you gotta take this seriously."

"I *am* taking it seriously," Nicholas said. His tone was more on-message this time. He looked down at Darius, conviction in his eyes. "I'll figure this out. Don't worry."

"That's the problem, though," Darius said, and he got to his feet, too. Nicholas didn't stop walking, and Darius followed him into the men's locker room. The whole time, he kept talking. "I *do* worry. You've had this lone-wolf attitude since you got here, acting like you can do it all by yourself, but we've already seen that you can't. We're here to help you. *Let us* help you."

Nicholas had just walked into the gym, where he finally stopped and turned around. At first, Nicholas just took Darius in. Slowly. Intently. Then, he opened his mouth to say something, but the doors to the gym swung open.

Thorn walked in.

A tense, quiet moment passed between the three of them. Thorn stood in the doorframe. It was the first time Darius had seen her in the Underground since she'd lost control in the conference room. If he hadn't been there in person, he never would have pictured it. She was poised, though cold, and stone-faced as she watched Nicholas with those hard, dark eyes. Sparkie peered his little head out of the top of her gym bag and looked between Darius and Nicholas with quiet interest.

Then Thorn turned to Darius. "Jones," she said as she stepped the rest of the way into the room. She didn't acknowledge Nicholas.

"You know," Nicholas said, but while he was speaking *to* Darius, he wasn't looking at him. He was watching as Thorn made her way across the padded gym floor. "I think it's pretty fucking funny that I'm being asked to be more selfless when this whole god damned organization is run by a couple of Forgotten Sins who only care about what benefits them. They're willing to let us Virtues die so they can be human again."

Thorn paused with her hand outstretched to the women's locker room door. She turned and cast Nicholas a hot, venomous look over her shoulder—a look he returned with just as much fire, just as much poison. She seemed to be trying to decide what she wanted to say. At last, she came back to face him.

"You are *so* much more like the Sins than I think you realize," Thorn said—and while her words were quiet, there was a sharp point on them that sent a chill down Darius's spine. Nicholas's nostrils flared, and his mouth dropped open.

"*What?*"

"You think it's so cut and dry—about good and evil—but it's not," Thorn went on. "I've been around the Sins. I've *been* a Sin. I know how they act, how they *think*. You're blinded by such a single-focused view on what's right, on what needs to be done, you can't see past your own agenda, and anyone who doesn't fit with your worldview is the enemy. You know who else thinks like that?"

Thorn didn't say it out loud. Her lips slammed together, and her eyebrows fell heavy over her dark eyes. Nicholas just gaped at her with furious indignation. He threw a look to Darius, who gave a conceding half-nod.

"She's ri—"

"I don't need to take this," Nicholas spat, and he spun on his heels and stalked out of the room.

Then Thorn and Darius were left there alone. Somehow, the tension only grew.

"I'm sorry about him," Darius began, but Thorn raised her hand.

"It's not your fault," she said, but she didn't look back at him. She was still staring out the windows of the gym doors, where Nicholas could be seen walking across the courtyard. Her expression was hard to read. Her brows were down, her lips tight, but there was a strangled sort of reserve on her face. At last, she turned to him. "Though I do wonder how different things would be if you'd trusted us to talk to him in the first place."

Darius shook his head and stumbled for words. "I— god, it wouldn't have mattered. He's—"

"Stubborn?" Thorn said hotly. The corners of her lips began to curl, but she caught herself. She closed her eyes and took a deep breath. Her hand gripped the strings of her gym bag so tightly that her fingers were white. Sparkie ducked his head back down and out of sight. "Angry? *Proud?* He can't destroy the Sin because he's got too much of an ego standing in the way. I wonder if he wouldn't have so much of an ego if he weren't trying to prove how much better he is than we are."

"He would have, Thorn. That's just who he is," Darius said, and he took a deep breath. "But you are right about one thing. I should have trusted you, and I'm sorry."

For a moment, Thorn only looked at him. Her expression softened, brows raising a bit in surprise and relief as the edges of her hard surface slowly chipped away. She rubbed her eyes with the fingers and thumb of one hand and sighed. "It doesn't matter. Nothing we did would have made a fucking difference. I'm sorry. I shouldn't take this out on you. I'm just… god, I'm just so tired."

Darius knew she wasn't talking about a physical tired, but a deep, spiritual, emotional exhaustion.

"Me too," he said with a sigh. He crossed his arms and looked down at his feet. "This summer has been rough… Saul, Eva… And I'm scared Nicholas doesn't have what it takes to destroy Sloth. Sometimes I wish I was Diligence so we could end this once and for all."

He looked back up to Thorn. She was staring at him again. The anger and fatigue faded, and her eyes pooled with a remorseful, ardent pain. Darius's stomach flipped.

"Thank god you're not," she said. "We need you."

The intensity of the way Thorn was looking at him filled Darius with an awkward guilt, so he tried to break the heaviness with a laugh. "Yeah, you'd be lost without those theme nights you never show up for."

Thorn shook her head. "That's not what I meant, and you know it."

Darius didn't know what to say to that, so he said nothing. Thorn watched him in silence for a moment before she turned back toward the locker room. Sparkie peeked out of her gym bag again, tilting his head at Darius curiously as Thorn's fingers wrapped around the doorknob, but she paused before she opened it. Then, she threw an obliging look over her shoulder. The corner of her mouth raised in one of her familiar, half-smiles.

"When you host a scotch and coffee night, I'll be the first in line," she said.

And she slipped through the door. He smiled after her, but that smile faded as soon as she was gone. In the wake of all that had happened the last few weeks, Darius found himself wishing he could go back and change the way he handled Spokane. If he'd known Nicholas would be so difficult either way, it would have been nice to be on Thorn's side from the start.

Darius took a deep breath and released it through his nose in a long, quiet sigh. He stepped out of the gym to find the courtyard dark again. The lights were just beginning to dim as night set in. Darius was on his way toward his and Eva's room when suddenly his phone beeped in his pocket. Darius's heart caught in his throat.

It wasn't a text or a call alert. It was the warning system Holly had installed when she needed immediate attention. Only the Martyr leadership got this notification.

He fumbled with his device and looked down at the screen. It only said three words:

"We found Saul."

Before Darius had finished reading the message, Thorn came ripping out of the gym. She was already on her phone, talking heatedly as Darius chased after her.

"What happened?" Thorn barked into the receiver. She didn't go to the elevators—instead, she opened the door beside them and began to sprint up the stairs. Darius tried to stay close behind her, but she was faster than he was, and he could barely keep up.

"If it was sent into the police hotline, the Sins already know," Thorn went on. She wasn't even losing breath. "Was he alone?"

Then she hit the first-floor landing, opened the door, and paused. Her pale face went even whiter as she finally caught Darius's eye.

"Fuck," she whispered—to him, this time. "The girls are with him."

The air squeezed from Darius's lungs, and for a brief, haunting moment, he felt like he was going to suffocate.

Thorn snapped him out of it by turning on her heel and rushing through the foyer to the garage. "Send the coordinates straight to my car and have the nearest TAC unit head over," she said right before she hung up the phone. She ran to one of the black coupes, and Darius ran after her.

"What's going on? Where are you going?"

"They're in Staten Island," Thorn said. She opened the back of the coupe and did a quick look through the gear. Darius could see body armor, smoke grenades, a helmet, and a large, black weapons case. "If I leave now, I have a shot at getting there before the Sins do."

She opened the driver's door. Darius started to walk around the car.

"I'm coming with you."

"To hell you are," Thorn growled, and she reached out to stop him. He turned, and she shook her head. "I can't do my job if I'm worried about you. You're *staying here*." Then, though her face was set and stern, her eyes softened a little. She placed a hand on the crook of his neck. Her fingers were chilly to the touch but firm and reassuring.

"Darius," she said more quietly. "I'll do whatever it takes to bring them home."

And, even though Darius knew she could make no real promises, he nodded. He didn't think he'd be able to speak. His throat had tightened up, and his voice had nowhere to go. Thorn squeezed his shoulder once more before she jumped into the driver's seat and took off, spiraling up and out of the lot. Darius watched until her taillights disappeared around the corner.

Then he stood in the garage alone, in silence.

CHAPTER TWENTY

Thorn sprinted through a sea of indistinct, white moving vans. Dim lights at the edges of the parking lot created pockets of deep shadows as the Martyrs made their way toward a tall, wrought-iron gate. Sparkie spiraled above, circling a long storage complex pushed up against the shore of the Raritan Bay. Behind her, Conrad Carter and Liz Wright rushed to keep up, the sounds of their breathing hard in the silence of the night.

A silence that broke with sirens.

"They're getting close," Thorn roared. "Go, go!"

The whole neighborhood reeked of sewage and rot. Thorn remembered a time, decades ago, when this area had been a state park—a forest with walking trails, rich wildlife, and fresh air. The city mowed it down to make room for more fucking people, and now industrial warehouses and factories poured waste into the water.

Thorn made it to the gate just as a wave of frigid energy poured around the lot. She looked down at the lock, pulled out her pistol, and fired into the mechanism. It shattered and the door creaked open. Thorn pushed Carter and Wright through—

A bullet crashed into the concrete pillar by her shoulder.

She swore and ducked inside.

"Carter, help me with this!"

Together, Thorn and her Tactical team pulled a heavy dumpster from the side of the wall and barricaded it in front of the gate. Another bullet flew by, piercing a red, metal door in the storage locker behind them. Thorn cursed again.

"I've got six units en route," Jeremiah's voice drilled in her ear. "Do you have eyes on the target?"

"I *am* the target," Thorn snarled as she ushered Carter and Wright around the corner. Cold, human life drew nearer as the Sins pushed their people closer to the structure. Thorn took a moment to feel around, and at the very edge of her awareness, she sensed a different energy. One she knew. Thorn's stomach dropped.

"Torres is here," she said. "In the back of the complex."

"And the girls?"

"I'm assuming," she said as she came up next to the nearest building, caught Carter's attention, and gestured to the roof. She laced her fingers, which he stepped into, and she hoisted him up. "He's not alone."

Jeremiah swore into the headset as Thorn heaved Wright to the rooftop, too. A cold front of energy came closer to the gate, and Thorn heard Carter open fire above her. A rattling of shots echoed into the night. Once Wright was in position, Thorn stepped back, adjusted the rifle strap against her chest, and sprinted up the wall. She barely caught the edge of the roof with her fingertips.

"Can you get to them?" Jeremiah pressed as Thorn pulled herself up, crouched low, and came to Carter's side. She looked over a retaining wall and down into the parking lot below. Twenty people—twenty Puppets—moved in a mechanical line toward the gate. Beyond them, somewhere in the trove of vans, she felt four distinct energies on her cerebral map. The Sins. All but Sloth. She shook her head then ducked down as a volley of weapons fire slammed into the concrete in front of her.

"Not if you want us to defend the god damned gate,"

Thorn said. Sparkie was still circling, and what he saw made Thorn's stomach drop. The whole place was surrounded by tall, concrete walls topped with spikes and caging. The sides of the storage complex rode up against massive, industrial shipyards, and behind them, the back wall pushed to a rocky shoreline covered in tiny docks and little boats.

"Why do you need to defend the gate?" Jeremiah asked.

"If we don't, we won't have a way out of this death trap."

Gunfire roared again, echoing through the industrial yard in rapid, deafening bursts. Bullets slammed into the building just feet below where Thorn was positioned. The metal siding was already shredded. Now the gunfire decimated the naked concrete beneath it. Thorn pulled her head down until the firing stopped, then she signaled to the two TAC members laying on their stomachs to her right. They nodded, and the three of them rose up and shot back. A row of armored police officers in full SWAT gear pulled behind moving trucks and out of sight.

"Shit," Thorn said as she and her team ducked back down. "Montgomery, where the fuck *are* you?" A new wave of weapon fire assailed the building. She felt the vibrations of the shots as they rattled the concrete. The Puppets pushed forward. She popped up and shot again. More ducking. More avoiding. One man took a bullet right to the thigh. He cried out and collapsed.

"Three minutes out," Jeremiah said. "Keep holding."

More gunfire. The incessant sound was sharp, distracting. Thorn heard a pause. Felt the armored Puppets moving again. Came up. Fired. Another man down.

"Three minutes?" Carter grumbled beside her as he adjusted the rifle against his armored shoulder. "*Fuck.*"

"We don't have much of a choice," Thorn muttered. She glanced at Wright over Carter's shoulder, and the other woman watched her with a look of grim determination. "Keep the gate clear. On my mark. One. Two. Three—"

It was chaos. The air reeked of gunpowder and cement dust, and the noise was so overbearing that Thorn struggled to hear anything outside of rifles firing and the Tactical Unit voices right in her earpiece. The Sins' Puppets hid between moving trucks as they pushed toward the gate. Thorn waited out another round of gunfire before she came up and shot back. She managed to hit one of the officers in the throat. His life blinked out.

"God damn it," Thorn muttered. She ducked. Bullets riddled the side of the building again.

Thorn was hot. Even late at night, the summer was muggy and claustrophobic. Sweat dripped down her face, following the lines of her nose and wetting her lips. The firing paused, and Thorn and her team came up to shoot again.

More gunfire. Every time they put their heads down, the Puppets moved closer. Thorn could feel their energies gathering together—preparing for another attack. The Sins kept their distance, standing just far enough away to be harder to see—and harder to hit—as they led the Puppets to fight their way through. Letting innocent people *die* as they pushed closer to the gate.

And closer to Saul Torres.

Thorn could barely feel him and the girls. Three hazy, distant energies huddled together. The entire time she'd been driving, she hoped they'd find some reason to leave…

The Puppets pushed closer still. Thorn could no longer see them over the top of the perimeter wall. They braced up against it and tucked around the massive, concrete pillars on either side of the gate. A cold movement caught Thorn's attention. One of the men turned the corner and started fucking with the wrought-iron monstrosity, trying to force his way through. Thorn zeroed in on him and shot him in the chest plate. He was forced back, toppled over—unconscious.

Another storm of shots came their way, and Thorn pressed herself against the metal roof again. Wright swore.

"We can't hold them off forever," she said, checking her ammunition. They hadn't had time to prepare for a lengthy standoff, but Thorn wasn't worried about it.

"We won't have to," she said.

While Thorn and the TAC team lay flat on their bellies, Sparkie looked into the darkness. It was hard to make out much beyond vague shapes and the bright, flashing lights of gunfire in the night, but he could see the Tactical Unit vehicles, and they were closing in.

"Middle of the lot," Thorn screamed into her headset. "The Sins are in the middle of the lot!"

"Roger that," Chris's voice came through. "Units one, two, and three, take the eastern edge. Four, five, and six, western. Let's flank 'em."

"About damn time," Carter grumbled. Thorn indicated to him and Wright. Then they came up and fired into the Puppets pushing against the fence. As soon as Thorn's head lifted above the wall, a second line of Puppets, standing just behind the first, shot back. One of the bullets slammed into the armor on her shoulder. The force was enough to crack her collarbone. A painful surge jolted down her arm and across her chest. She swore and ducked down again.

The Tactical Unit changed the scene. Thorn felt it almost immediately. As the Martyrs got into place and twelve new energies surrounded the parking lot, the Sins shifted. Thorn felt them. Lust, Greed, Gluttony, and Wrath—fucking *Wrath*—moved forward as a new barrage rained on them from either side.

But the pressure made them more persistent—*more* chaotic. Now the assault came almost nonstop. Thorn's senses were flooded with constant feedback. The loud, screaming sound of automatic rifles firing, over and over again. Dust from the concrete being blown to bits on the wall below her floated up, obscuring her vision and caking inside her nostrils. She coughed and rolled over. It sent a fresh surge of pain from her injured shoulder.

Thorn felt the Sins push their way to the front of the line as their Puppets fired in a never-ending wave. She commanded her team to stay where they were and edged a little further to the side—a little further away from where Carter

349

and Wright were laying—where the Sins could feel their energy and the Puppets were focusing their attack.

She looked over the edge of the roof.

Autumn Hunt led the pack. Her face was contorted: nostrils flared, lips curled, eyes tight and wild. She was up against the gate beside Carlos Ruiz and the hulking, gratuitous form of Terrance Moore, and the three of them together pushed against the wrought iron bars and tried to force the gate open. It started to budge—

Thorn put her rifle into position and pulled the trigger.

Her aim was off—the kickback pushed against her injured shoulder and made it hard for her to shoot straight. Bullets cracked against the concrete pillars, metal bars, bodies. Moore fell back. A handful of Puppets went unconscious and collapsed where they stood, their energies low and stagnant. One blinked out of existence. Hunt's white-hot, rabid attention shifted. Searched the roofline. Spotted Thorn.

The Sin shouted something Thorn couldn't hear over the new assault of weapons fire focused on the building directly beneath her.

She ducked down again and screamed, "They're at the gate!"

Jeremiah started barking orders. Thorn could feel the Martyrs closing in. Some of the Puppets broke off and turned toward her people. Greed and Lust followed after them. The reprieve gave Thorn another chance to rise up and shoot—

Wrath beat her to it.

As soon as Thorn crested the roof, she was hit. A bullet slammed into her shoulder again and pierced the damaged spot in her armor. It ripped through her flesh. Shattered her bone. She swore and rolled down the roof as Sparkie cried out and fell from the sky. Thorn's rifle slipped from her grip and slid over the edge to the ground below. Blood dripped onto the metal sheet beneath her back.

Then Wrath was through. The gates were open. The

Puppets divided—half of them turned around to face off against the oncoming Martyrs, and the other half followed Hunt into the storage complex.

"Hunt's through," Thorn called into her headset.

"Phase two," Jeremiah's voice boomed. "Get me some smoke and flares in here!"

The Martyrs shifted. Thorn felt them move and switch weapons. She got to her feet as Carter and Wright rose, too. The two of them started shooting down into the flood of people pushing through the gate. A torrent of projectiles flew by. Thorn sprinted down the building as flash grenades and smoke bombs landed fifty, one hundred, two hundred yards deep into the storage complex. The aisles between the buildings were suddenly flooded with bright light and thick smoke. Someone screamed behind her, and Thorn was vaguely aware of Liz Wright's energy falling off the roof and crumpling, motionless, to the ground below.

But she didn't turn to check. She couldn't afford to.

Now that they'd broken through, no one bothered to shoot at Thorn anymore. She rushed toward Autumn Hunt—felt the energy of the Sin as she hurried to get around the corner, where she would have a straight shot down the complex, right to Saul Torres.

His energy was stagnant. Fuzzy. Sitting right at the limit of where Thorn could feel him. A wave of desperation—and not a small amount of rage—pushed Thorn forward faster. She pulled the handgun from its holster at her back as she ran.

When she reached the edge of the building, Wrath was just turning the corner. Thorn could barely see her outline through the heavy smoke, but she could fucking *feel* her, and that was close enough. Thorn pointed her gun at the signature and emptied the clip. The Sin's cold aura stumbled forward and stopped.

Thorn leapt to the ground and rolled to her feet. Her visibility was awful, but she could still feel her way around. The Puppets floundered by her. They moved slowly, uncoordinated, as they worked to get through the smoke. Wrath was up. She roared and spun toward Thorn, but in the dark and smoke, she couldn't see. Thorn reloaded her weapon. She was slower than usual, with her right arm stiff and awkward. Just as she slammed the fresh clip into place, a flash grenade went off a few dozen yards behind her and lit up the aisle. Hunt's wild eyes landed on Thorn, and she attacked.

Thorn leveled the weapon at Wrath's face, but she wasn't quick enough on the trigger. Hunt swiped one arm out to the side and forced Thorn's gun hand out of the way, sending the shot into the side of the storage unit. Then she jammed the heel of her palm into Thorn's chin and sent her sprawling back. Thorn twisted on the ground and looked up. Wrath was nothing but a dark shadow in the smoke. Thorn shot anyway, and by some miracle, the bullet crashed into the Sin's leg, and she went down swearing. Her Puppets dropped, too.

Then Thorn got up and pointed the weapon right at Autumn Hunt's face. Another flash grenade rocked the ground. Bright light illuminated them. Wrath stared up at Thorn with a loathing and a venom so potent it poisoned the link they shared, filling Thorn's mind with even more rage and hatred. Part of her wanted to do away with the gun entirely and grab a knife instead. To kill Wrath slowly, the way Wrath *liked* to kill.

Thorn's finger tightened on the trigger.

A thunderous explosion shook the whole block. Thorn's mouth fell open, and her eyes went wide as she stared into the distance—above the smoke and chaos and noise—toward the back of the storage complex. Massive flames furled up into a dark, starless sky. They made the smoke glow with eerie, orange light.

Before Thorn knew what was happening, Wrath reached up, grabbed her by the arm, and pulled her to the ground. They wrestled over the gun, but even with a bad leg, Hunt still had two good arms. She ripped the weapon out of

Thorn's grip and threw it away. Then she jammed her hand underneath the lip of Thorn's helmet and tightened her fingers around her throat.

For a brief moment, Thorn couldn't breathe. Cool energy converged around them as the Martyrs closed in. Wrath came in close and screamed at her, her face twisted with fury and terror. Spit speckled Thorn's visor.

"This doesn't matter," she snarled. "I'll still get your precious little Jones boy. *I'll fucking get him.*"

Then she slammed Thorn back to the ground and took off, running through the smoke toward the single exit before it was overrun entirely. Her damaged leg made her awkward, but not slow, as she rushed away from Thorn and the Martyrs. Away from the continued barrage of smoke bombs and flash grenades. Away from Saul Torres—

Thorn's heart skipped a beat.

Saul's energy was gone.

Forgetting about Wrath and the rest of the Sins, about the Puppets unconscious at her feet and the Martyrs wounded in the parking lot, Thorn jumped up. She ignored the pain in her shoulder as she sprinted down the aisle, past row upon row of concrete storage units and flashing red doors. She could hardly see where she was going through the smoke. The unconscious bodies of Wrath's Puppets worked as bread crumbs. She followed their cold energies until she hit the last building.

Then she stopped.

A section of units was completely engulfed in flames. The heat from the fire came at her in sweltering, unbearable waves. Thorn shielded her eyes from the bright, intense light. It reflected off the smoke and surrounded her in a hard, flickering glow. She wanted to push forward further, but she didn't need to. All Thorn felt was the fierce, hot flames in front of her. Nothing else. No cool, human essence. No life.

If Saul, Juniper, and Lindsey were still in that building when it burned, they were dead.

The Sins had retreated. The smoke faded. Thorn walked through the charred wreckage of one of the burned storage units slowly. Carefully. The Tactical Unit had managed to douse the flames with fire extinguishing devices they kept in their cars for just such emergencies, but while the fire was out, the structure was still smoldering and dangerous. Her people stood guard outside, securing the area and tending to their wounded while they waited for the Cleaning Crew to get here. Thorn couldn't wait, though. The look on Darius's face when she'd left the Underground—that painful, desperate, and helpless look—was all Thorn could see now.

She had been determined to bring Saul home tonight. She was hoping, now, that she wouldn't. Thorn wanted to believe he'd somehow managed to escape—climb the concrete wall, brave the barbed wire. Having nothing at all sure as hell beat bringing back a body in a bag.

The ground beneath her singed the bottom of her boots as Thorn made her way through the wreckage. If she lingered too long in one location, her feet stuck to the hot concrete. It was impossible to make out what exactly she was looking at. Several different storage units had been caught in the blast. Five had severe damage, and another two were peripheral casualties. The actual unit which had exploded was all but decimated. Nothing stood there now beyond three broken walls and a charred, black floor. The ones beside it, though, had burned down. Saul Torres and the girls had been in one of them.

That was the one Thorn was walking now. Looking for… something. She wasn't totally sure what. Bodies? A lack thereof?

The locker hadn't been empty when it went up in flames, and from what Thorn could gather, it had been used as a living space. The blackened remains of furniture and clothing were strewn around the room. Boxes of nonperishable food. Plates. A basin that had once been filled with water but now held nothing more than thick, muddy ash. Debris littered the ground around her feet. Thorn leaned down to lift a blanket. It was small—the perfect size for a child. A twinge ached through her chest as she shook her head and took a deep breath. It hurt. The hot smoke and ash went into her lungs and burned all the way down.

"Thorn," Chris called in from the gaping hole that was once a door. "We have lurkers."

Thorn stood up and walked back into the open. The rubber of her boots was tacky and malleable. Chris stood there, still dressed in full armor, with her rifle held at the ready in her hands.

"They're by the front," she said. "Conrad is trying to convince them he's law enforcement, but…"

"I got it," Thorn said, and she raised her hand to show she understood. The movement sent pain through her injured shoulder. She was lucky the bullet had passed all the way through instead of getting lodged in her scapula. It healed so much faster that way. "I'll take care of them."

Then Thorn focused. She could feel a handful of unfamiliar energies pressing up against the gate. Innocent, ignorant civilians. She quietly pushed out her Influence with a calm, simple command.

Go away. Nothing to see here.

Moments later, she felt them shuffle off.

"No concern about Wrath coming back?" Jeremiah asked. He was approaching from the other side of the unit. Like Chris, he was still equipped in his tactical gear. Thorn had disposed of hers as soon as the fire was out. It was so much hotter inside that unit covered in body armor.

"No," Thorn said. "She's hurt. She knows we could take her down."

"Then I wish she would," Jeremiah lamented. "How nice would it be for us to get her out of the picture?"

A furious, self-loathing flame lit up in Thorn's chest. She almost fucking had. She shook her head and cleared her throat.

"What's the status of our people?"

"We lost Rossi," Jeremiah said, and Thorn's stomach clenched furiously, "and Wright and Emerson are en route back to the Underground for serious injuries, but they should both survive. We have several other minor injuries in the team, but nothing anyone wanted to go home for."

Thorn nodded. All in all, it could've been fucking worse. "Property damage?" she asked.

"It's extensive," Chris said. "Most of the trucks in the front lot have been destroyed. The building you were holding out on is pretty bad, too. There's also *this*—" Chris gestured to the units in front of them. Streams of smoke were still floating up into the dark sky in thick, dancing whorls. "We're lucky that this area doesn't have any security cameras, so Holly doesn't have to do a lot of cleaning up there."

"What evidence of ours do we need to clear out?" Thorn asked.

"The only things that can be potentially tied to us are the vehicles," Jeremiah said. "Three of our reinforced SUVs were totaled in the firefight. Marcus and his team are bringing tow trucks in to carry them off the scene."

Marcus. Damn it, Thorn hadn't thought to talk to Marcus. She'd been so busy trying to determine if Saul, Juniper, and Lindsey had been caught in the fire she hadn't called ahead to tell him *not* to bring Eva Torres with him.

She wanted to believe he wouldn't be that stupid, but Thorn knew how tactless Marcus Boseman could be.

"I need to know what the fuck happened here," Thorn said. Her voice was harsh. She tried to reel it back, to hide how furious she really was, but a little bit managed to sneak out. It always did. "I need *everything* we can find on who owned that other unit and what was inside of it." She pointed at the unit two doors down, where the explosion had originated.

"I have Nichols on it," Jeremiah said. "He's breaking into the leasing office."

"Go check on him," Thorn said. "I want answers, and I

want them *now*."

"Yes, ma'am," Jeremiah said, brows furrowed heavily over his deep-set, serious eyes as he took off. Thorn felt him walking toward the front. Slower than she liked—slower than *she* would have gone.

For a few moments, Chris and Thorn stood there in silence. Thorn turned back to the storage unit and took a deep, slow breath. Chris edged in closer to her. Her energy helped Thorn feel a little cool relief in this sweltering environment.

"So," Chris started quietly, her tone becoming more intimate. "Do you think Saul was in there?"

Thorn cast a dark, heavy look over her shoulder. She didn't want to say the words out loud, but the fact remained... she had no idea how Saul could have possibly gotten himself, Juniper, and Lindsey out in time.

"I think," Thorn said, "we don't need to worry about the Sins hunting for him anymore."

Chris didn't say anything. That was one of Thorn's favorite things about Chris. She didn't feel the need to fill the space between them with empty words and platitudes. No "just look on the bright side" or "it could be worse." Simple silence and the space to process. Thorn reached out and placed a hand on Chris's shoulder in gratitude.

"Marcus is here," she said. The Cleaning Crew had just arrived on scene. Their energies came to life as they entered the structure. Thorn felt them walking down the aisle to the left of the storage units. "I'm going to go—"

But then she paused because she recognized something else. Her chest swelled, and her jaw clenched shut.

Eva Torres.

Thorn swore and rushed around the corner to head Marcus and his men off. There were six of them, dressed in thick, fire-retardant suits and heavy-duty hardhats. As soon as he saw Thorn, Marcus stopped, and his team followed his lead. Eva was standing at the back of the crowd. Her rich, brown complexion was pale and terrified, her dark eyes

357

wide, but her mouth was set and determined.

"What the fuck is wrong with you?" Thorn screamed at Marcus as she stormed toward him. He glanced to Martin Velasquez, his assistant supervisor, and nodded for him to get started. The other five members of the Cleaning Crew began to walk past Thorn, but Thorn reached out and grabbed Eva by the shoulder. "You understand what we're *doing* here, don't you?"

"We're covering up—"

"I can't believe you're this fucking stupid," Thorn snarled. Marcus's thick, gray eyebrows furrowed, and behind his neatly trimmed beard, his lips pursed. Thorn went on. She couldn't help it. The monster inside her was thrashing against her ribs—furiously hunting for an outlet at the injustices of the night. "Why the fuck did you bring *her*?"

"She needs on-the-job training," Marcus said. He was short for a man, just about eye level with Thorn, and he crossed his arms around his thick chest as he glared at her.

"She can wait for a *different fucking job*—"

"I asked to come," Eva cut in. Thorn turned to her. While she looked scared, her voice was strong and clear. She didn't shy away from Thorn. She just squared her shoulders and held herself high. Marcus quietly slipped away, and Thorn sighed.

"You understand what we're looking for here?" She asked it quietly, and she grabbed Eva by the shoulder again. The other woman tensed. "There is no life. No energy. If Saul is in that unit—"

"I know," Eva said. Her teeth pressed tight together, and she took a breath. Held it. Thorn watched her for a moment longer before she nodded.

Then they started back around the edge of the building, toward the heat and the smoke and the movement. But before they even turned the corner, Thorn could tell something was different. The Martyrs had gathered together, and their energies felt rushed and chaotic. She frowned as they came around to the scene.

Thorn's chest constricted tight around her lungs. Eva stopped dead beside her.

Marcus was opening a collapsible gurney. He glanced up to Thorn as two of his people carried a black body bag out from the unit. It was bulky, awkward, and roughly the shape of an adult man…

Then Eva was running. Chris reached out to stop her, but Eva pushed her arms away and rushed up to the gurney. As she went for the bag, Marcus grabbed her hand and held her fingers tightly inside his. He closed his eyes and shook his head.

"You don't want to do that," he said quietly. Then he looked at her, and Thorn saw the dull, familiar pain that so often came with this job reflected in his irises. "Do yourself a favor. Don't remember him this way."

Eva's resolve broke. All at once, the emotion she'd been holding back came flooding out of her on a wave of tears. Her legs collapsed beneath her, and she fell to her knees. Thorn hurried to her side and wrapped her arm around Eva's shaking shoulders. She looked up to Marcus with a dark, furious glare. All he could do was shrug.

"Yo, *jefe*," Velasquez called from inside the smoking structure. "Get another couple of gurneys. We got two more in here."

Eva choked out a sob. Chris came up to her other side, and together, she and Thorn gently lifted Eva to her feet. As they stood up, Jeremiah started making his way toward them. The look on his face made Thorn pause.

"What did you find?" she asked him.

Jeremiah shook his head and said, "The unit that blew up was leased to a man named 'G. Witham.'"

Thorn's stomach boiled; she felt the rage swell out into her muscles. They went tight, rigid, and angry. "That can't be a fucking coincidence," she said.

"I doubt it."

Her rage was just growing. Threatening to explode. To go up in flames like the decimated units in front of them.

She took a deep breath and forced her jaws open to say, "Get your people cleaned up and cleared out. We found what we were looking for."

Jeremiah nodded, dark and somber. He turned and started barking orders into his helmet. The Tactical Unit around them moved like a machine as they helped the Cleaning Crew collect their gear and head back toward the lot at the front of the complex.

Eva didn't move. She just cried into her hands as Thorn watched them wheel three gurneys away. Three bodies. One of them was so, so small. It made Thorn's heart ache.

"C'mon," she said. Her voice was low, but firm. Kind, but final. This wasn't the first time Thorn had to drag a crying Martyr away from the dead body of a loved one. She remembered the day Chris's mother had come into the Underground after an altercation with Pride. Dead on arrival. Chris had only been seventeen, and Thorn had never seen her so broken. Not before. Not since. "Let's get you home."

Something in Eva shifted then. The onset of shock. As Thorn led her away from the burned-out building, from the death and the pain, Eva went quiet. Her eyes were wide and empty, staring out into a distance Thorn couldn't see. She helped her into the car, buckled her in, and climbed into the driver's chair. The whole trip back to the Underground, Eva just watched the black dead of night flash by her window.

CHAPTER TWENTY-ONE

"I've finished the autopsy on the remains that were found inside the storage unit on Staten Island," Elijah Harris said. "I'm afraid I don't have a lot of good news."

A heavy, gray apprehension filled the small room. The doctor leaned forward and clasped his hands on top of his desk as he watched them both with steely, compassionate eyes. In the sixteen hours since Eva had returned to the Underground, Darius hadn't slept. He hadn't eaten. He'd just waited, painfully. Slowly. For this.

"The only comfort I can offer you is that they seem to have died before the flames reached their unit," Elijah said. "Likely suffocation from the smoke. It would've been relatively painless."

"How can you know that?" Darius asked.

"The way they were laying," Elijah went on. He spoke with practiced calm and poise, but the creases in his forehead betrayed his sadness and the fact that he felt this sadness often. "They were curled up together, almost like they were asleep. They probably lost consciousness trying to get out."

"And you know it's them?" Eva's voice cracked a little. "You know it's Saul?"

Elijah took a deep breath. "The remains were too badly damaged for us to make a positive identification visually," he said. "And, since Saul, Juniper, and Lindsay did not have any dental records in the system, we can't use that, either. That means I can't, in good conscience, say I'm one-hundred percent positive. However, we *are* looking at a male and female in their late twenties to early thirties and an adolescent around four years old. Knowing that, knowing that there is video evidence of the three of them entering the unit, and knowing that Thorn felt Saul's energy at the site, I am confident in saying that we have found Saul, Juniper, and Lindsay."

Eva swallowed a hard sob next to Darius. Silent tears streamed from her red, puffy eyes and trailed down her face. Darius just nodded. He felt numb. Distant. For a moment, it was almost as though he had traveled back in time, and instead of a twenty-eight-year-old man, he was a ten-year-old boy again. Instead of Eva sitting beside him, it was his father. He was overcome with the same disconnection, the same aching sense of loss deep in his chest.

"If you would like a more conclusive answer," Elijah went on, speaking solely to Eva now. Her gaze, which had been wide and distant, came back in and focused on him. "We can do a DNA analysis. It will take several weeks to get the results back, but…"

"No," Eva said, her voice tight. She cleared her throat and shook her head. When she spoke again, she was stronger. "No. That's not necessary."

Elijah nodded. His mouth curled into a frown, and he considered Eva for a moment longer before he glanced at Darius and brought him back into the conversation.

"We'll be preparing the bodies to send to Cain for cremation and burial," Elijah said. Then, he took a moment of silence before he continued. "I am so sorry. There is nothing I, or anyone else, can say to make this easier. I sure as hell wish there were. But, as your doctor, I want to make it clear that grief can be just as dangerous as any medical condition. If you need anything, please see me or talk to Abraham. We may be able to help."

Then he got to his feet and moved toward the door. Darius and Eva rose to follow him. She moved like a Puppet—mechanical, on autopilot. She even had the same blank, disconnected look on her face. Until they reached the door. Just as they stepped into the hospital ward, Eva's eyes lit up a little, and she quickly turned.

"Oh! Dr. Harris?" she asked. "Can I get some of Saul's ashes? Can Cain do that?"

The doctor provided a sad smile that didn't reach his eyes. "Of course he can. I'll make sure he gets the message. *Personally.*"

"Thank you."

Elijah nodded and disappeared into his office. Eva and Darius walked through the hospital ward toward the lobby. It felt surreal. Raquel was doing paperwork behind the nurses' station. Pretending to do paperwork. Her eyes weren't moving on the page, her hand hovering just above it. As they passed by, she glanced up and caught Darius's eye. All she did was give him a small, sympathetic smile.

The walk down to their room went like that. They passed by familiar faces, and all anyone could do was nod at them with quiet, somber understanding. Of course, they'd all heard the news by now. The Underground was small, and almost one-third of the Tactical Unit had been on the scene. A dozen people. A dozen opportunities for stories to be shared, rumors to be started, and truths to be told.

Only one person said anything to them. Mackenzie McKay was getting on the elevator in the courtyard when they were getting off. As soon as she saw them—and the looks in their eyes—her pixie-like face scrunched up. She wrapped her arms around them both and pulled them in for a hug.

"Fuck, I'm so sorry," she whispered.

And that was it. They muttered half-hearted thank-yous that sounded as empty as they felt. Minutes later, they were laying in their room, staring at the ceiling. Finally, in the dark and quiet, Eva broke down. She sobbed long and hard, with deep, guttural cries that poured into Darius's heart and made it break all over again. He curled up around her, silent tears streaming down his face and into her hair as he held her close against him.

Darius wished he could help her more—do *something* to take away the pain—but there were hurts even Virtues couldn't fix.

Grief was one of them.

The Martyr Memorial Garden was as beautiful as ever.

The last time Darius had been here was nine months ago. The trees had been barren then, their leaves long dead underneath the winter snow. Icicles had dangled from empty branches, glistening like crystal as they sent waves of bright light and dancing rainbows across white, snowy hills.

Now, it was lush and green and warm.

The large, full trees overhead sent a patchwork of shadows onto the footpath below as Cain Guttuso led Darius and Eva through the garden. Birds chirped and fluttered in distant branches. The gravel crunched under Darius's feet, and a warm breeze whipped through his hair. It was colored with a hint of the oncoming autumn—just a little cooler, a little crisper, than the breezes from a week ago. Darius took a deep breath, sucked in the fresh, earthy air, and let out a sigh. Cain's feline Familiar, Crescendo, trilled by Darius's feet and looked up at him with eager, lamp-like eyes.

"Not much further now," Cain said gleefully. He walked ahead of them, and if Darius wasn't mistaken, Cain had taken a little extra care to put himself together for their visit. His salt and pepper hair was sleek and styled, and his clothing looked recently pressed. He gestured ahead with one hand, and in the other, he delicately held a wine glass. The red liquid swirled around it as he looked back over at them with a grin.

Cain had been in exceptional spirits from the moment Abraham pulled the car into his driveway. The old Forgotten Sin all but ignored everyone else as they got out of the vehicle and instead had snatched Darius's palm up in an almost desperate handshake. When Abraham and Lina went off to visit Stella's grave, Cain had *insisted* on showing Darius and Eva through the garden himself.

Darius had just smiled and thanked him. There wasn't much else he *could* do. It wasn't Cain's fault Envy had possessed and later abandoned him, leaving him cursed with immortality and half a soul. He was empty, aching, and alone, like all other Forgotten Sins. Like Alan and Thorn.

Only two things could quiet that emptiness—Envy being destroyed, and Darius himself. Just being around Kindness masked the empty cavern in the pit of Cain's chest, if only for a moment. Darius made sure to remember that. Cain had lived with his emptiness for hundreds of years, so feeling it fade must have been a relief. What was it that Alan had said? It was *intoxicating.*

"I'm afraid I haven't had the chance to finish their name plaques," Cain said as he continued to walk deeper into the garden. He tried to make his tone a little more somber, but the emotion didn't translate, and the smile didn't fade from his face. He glanced over his shoulder and looked at Darius. "It's delicate work, after all. I have, however, put up temporary metal plates with sketches of the designs to show you what they will look like when I'm done. They're quite beautiful. I think you'll like them."

Darius's lips tightened. He'd almost forgotten how focused Cain was on his own work in the midst of all this death. They continued through the garden. Subtle grave markers showed up every few feet, making it impossible to forget this was a cemetery. Hundreds of them. Hundreds of lives lost. After six centuries, Darius figured Cain's art was his only constant. People died. Faded. Crumbled away into piles of ash. But art? Art lasted forever.

This garden was a testament to that. Darius looked around, at the carefully manicured flower beds and bushes, at the immaculately crafted memorial stones and statues. Not a leaf was out of place, not a weed left poking out between the seams in the stones. The granite was clean and polished. It was flawlessly beautiful and intimately loved.

By a man who had nothing else *to* love.

A surge of pity swelled through Darius's chest.

"I'm excited to see them," he said, and even though it was a lie—Darius was anything *but* excited to be back here, burying more friends and more family—he passed Cain a smile. The older man's eyes lit up, and his grin stretched from ear to ear. That made the lie worth it.

Then they kept walking. Cain all but ignored Eva, which seemed fine for her. She just followed after Darius quietly. Her gaze was distant and unfocused, and her brows pinched together in thought as they rounded the last corner and came upon the open clearing by the gazebo. Seeing it made Darius's breath catch in his throat. It was even more beautiful in the last days of summer than it had been in the middle of winter. The ashen-stained wood blended into the gray bark of the maple trees encircling it. Their young branches were still short, not quite high enough to reach the black-shingle roof, but they stood strong and proud. There had been thirteen of them before. One for Thad and the twelve children Envy and Pride had slaughtered. Now, three more had been added to the circle. The new trees were smaller and still supported by posts in the ground.

Darius's throat suddenly felt dry and tight. He tried to swallow through it.

"As you can see," Cain said as he gestured toward the gazebo, "I have planted three new maples with the remains of your loved ones. I also have this." He reached into the front pocket of his tight slacks and pulled out a small, glass bottle full of powdery, gray ashes. Darius felt the color drain from his face as Cain turned toward Eva and held it out.

"These are for you, my dear."

Eva's hand was steady as she grabbed the bottle from Cain's fingers. Her eyes filled with tears, but they didn't fall. She blinked them away, nodded, and cleared her throat. "Thank you."

"If you would like," Cain went on, indicating the ashes, "I can turn them into a piece of jewelry. Something you can keep on hand. A pendant, perhaps. Or a ring?" And for the first time since meeting him, Darius saw Cain give undivided attention to someone who *wasn't* him. The Forgotten Sin focused solely on Eva, and though it was half-formed and unpracticed, his face showed compassion. Crescendo rubbed himself against Eva's shins.

She seemed just as taken aback as Darius. At first, she just stared at Cain, her lips barely parted in surprise, before she shook her head. "Oh, no. It's fine. I have plans for them already."

Cain smiled, and all at once, the compassion and attention disappeared. "Of course," he said, promptly turning back to Darius. "Now, come! See what I've done inside…"

He led them along the small footpath, past the new trees, and up the stairs. Inside, the gazebo was just as elegant as Darius remembered. A circular bench sat in the center, sanded smooth and stained to match the rest of the structure. The open walls let in plenty of light, and beneath these openings, thirteen circular plaques hung to the wood. Darius looked down at one. "Sophie," it read. His heart clenched painfully in his chest.

"You can see here," Cain said. He cleared his throat and drew Darius's attention. Darius came back toward him but looked outside. Eva hadn't come with them. She was standing beside the new maple trees. Darius watched as she gently reached out and touched one of their branches. Tears glistened behind her eyelashes again. Cain cleared his throat one more time, and Darius turned. "I was not anticipating adding more people to this display," Cain continued when he was sure Darius was listening. "At the time I planned it, I didn't realize we were missing some of your friends. All the same, it didn't feel right to put these three in a separate location, so I sacrificed design for decorum, added the new trees to line the path, and set the plaques just inside the door. It loses some of its symmetry, which I did love, but I think it is still quite beautiful."

Darius had stopped listening a while back—because as far as he was concerned, the design could be damned. Instead, he was looking down at the metal disks nailed into the beams beside the entrance. It was surreal. Sobering. Seeing them written out made everything so much more *real*...

Saul was dead. Juniper and Lindsey were *dead*.

Darius's throat tightened up again, and he swallowed hard against it.

"Thanks so much for this," he said to Cain after a few quiet moments, and then he glanced up to Eva. She had fallen back into the same far-away look. Thoughtful and sad. Darius turned to the old Forgotten Sin again and tried to smile. It felt weak and placating. "It looks great, Cain. Thank you. Eva and I would like a little privacy now. We'll come back up to the house in a few minutes, all right?"

He made a conscious decision not to *ask* Cain to leave, and Cain seemed to get the hint. For a brief moment, a crestfallen expression flashed over his face. His smile faded. His eyes darkened. He pursed his lips together in a smirk and gave an almost theatrical bow. The wine glass tipped with him, and his merlot nearly spilled out.

"Of course," he said. "You are here to grieve. Please, take all the time you need."

Then he quickly and quietly excused himself and walked back down the path, the big, brown and black tabby following after him. Neither of them looked back as they disappeared into the foliage.

When Darius was sure they were gone, he walked back down the steps and came up beside Eva.

"Are you okay?"

Eva didn't look up to acknowledge him. Her eyes were

still distant, her brow furrowed, just slightly. Just enough to let Darius know she was thinking and that those thoughts were important. She took a deep breath and held it in for a few moments before she slowly exhaled and said, "I can't believe he's gone."

"Neither can I."

A sigh of silence fell between them. Nothing but the sounds of gently rustling leaves and buzzing insects. Darius reached out and put his arm around Eva, but she didn't seem to feel him. Her shoulders didn't loosen the way they usually did. Her tension didn't fade. Darius gave her a comforting squeeze.

Nothing.

"So," he said, "what are you planning?"

"Hmm?" Eva glanced up to him at last, and her eyes widened a bit.

"With his ashes?" Darius said. He gestured to the bottle in her hands. "You told Cain you had a plan."

"Oh." A note of relief flooded her voice, and she shook her head. A tiny, sad smile teased at the corners of her mouth. "Well, it's kind of silly... Maybe stupid."

Darius hugged Eva closer to his side. "I'm sure it's not stupid," he said. "Tell me."

"It's just..." Eva started, and she looked back down at the young maple standing in front of her. She reached out again—grabbed a leaf between her fingers and stroked it softly. "The Martyrs weren't important to Saul. They weren't home. The only place that ever felt like home to us was the orphanage."

She went quiet. A wave of tears pooled at the corners of her eyes, and she wiped them away with the pads of her ring fingers. Darius just watched her, held her, and waited as she recomposed herself. It hurt to see her this way. After a few seconds, she cleared her throat and continued. "We talked about it a lot, how the orphanage was the best thing that had ever happened to us... It gave us something to work for. Something *worth* working for. I want to bring part of him back there. I think that's where he would want to be."

Then she looked back down at the ashes in her hand. Darius's chest tightened up, and he kissed the top of Eva's head. Her soft hair caught in the stubble on his chin.

"That's not stupid," he said quietly. "I think it's a great idea. We'll do it together."

Eva's shoulders tensed underneath Darius's arm. He frowned and pulled away only to find her staring at the gravel path beneath her feet. More tears swelled, and this time, she let a few of them fall down her cheeks. Darius reached out to brush them away.

"Eva, what's wrong?"

"I'm sorry, Darius," she whispered, and she shook her head.

"Why?" There was something different in her voice—something that gave Darius a heavy feeling in the pit of his stomach. He gently grabbed her by the shoulders and turned her to face him, but she avoided his gaze. Instead, she looked off to the side as she hastily wiped her tears away on the backs of her hands. "You can talk to me," Darius said. "I'm here for you. No matter what."

"That's just it," she said. "You can't be. I... I'm leaving the Martyrs."

It felt as though his lungs had burst—like the air had been sucked right out of them, and Darius was left just staring. At Eva. Through Eva. She looked to him, reached up to grab one of his hands, and pulled it from her shoulder. The other fell beside it, and Eva took that one, too. Then she held them together and pressed his knuckles to her lips.

"I'm sorry," she whispered against his skin. "But the Martyrs have never really been *my* home either. Not the way it is for you. Now that Saul's gone, I can't stay here anymore... I don't belong here."

Darius nodded. His throat had tightened up, and he cleared it to speak. "Where are you going to go?" he asked.

"I don't know," Eva said. "But I'll figure it out. I always have. The Martyrs have given me a new start—a real identity, real papers. I can get a job, build a life, have a future... but that future isn't here. I'm so sorry."

Darius shook his head. He felt tears filling his own eyes now, and he blinked to clear them. It didn't do much. "Don't be sorry," he said, and though it hurt—though the idea of losing Eva and Saul in the same *week* was almost more than he could stand—he smiled. "You need to do what's right for *you*, and I support you in that. *No matter what.*"

Eva smiled back at him, and he reached up to brush her hair behind her ear. He traced the side of her warm, soft cheek with the pad of his thumb, and she closed her eyes.

"I wish you could come with me," she whispered.

"I know," Darius said, and he pulled her in for a tight hug. "Me too."

But they both knew he couldn't. Eva may have had a future outside of the Martyrs, but Darius didn't. Darius didn't have a future at all.

"I don't think you understand," Eva said, her voice beginning to shake. Her shoulders drew high and tight as her hands balled into fierce fists at her sides. "I wasn't asking for *permission.*"

Darius stared at the back of Eva's head, his eyes wide and lips parted, while she looked down at Alan from where she stood in front of his desk. Thorn leaned against the wall to Darius's left, and she crossed her arms as she watched Alan. He sighed and shook his head.

"I appreciate how difficult the last few days have been for you, Miss Torres," Alan reasoned, clasping his hands together, but when he opened his mouth to go on, Eva cut him off.

"I'm spreading Saul's ashes at the orphanage," she said, repeating it for the third time since she and Darius had come in here to talk about her plan. Alan's eyes darkened, and his jaw clenched shut. Eva didn't seem to care. She kept going. "You can either let me and Darius do it tomorrow, or you can drop me off at that train station in Newark, and I'll just take the first ride back here."

"There are risks," Alan insisted.

"I don't care," Eva said.

A few tense, quiet seconds passed. Eva glowered down at Alan, and Alan watched back with a static expression, but his nostrils flared enough for Darius to know he wasn't pleased. His wolf Familiar sat back on her haunches to the right of his desk, and her black tail flicked irritably. Thorn and Darius exchanged a look. Thorn's lips were set hard and serious, but there was an appreciative, maybe even impressed glint in the way her eyes moved to Eva.

"Holly *has* been monitoring the area since we pulled them out of there," Thorn said at last, and both Alan and Eva turned toward her. She didn't uncross her arms, but she shrugged her shoulders up and held them there for a beat. "She hasn't reported any strange activity."

Alan shook his head. "We know the Sins instilled a system of Programming in those neighborhoods after Darius was brought to the Underground."

"Envy instilled that system, and it's been nine months since her host was killed," Thorn argued. "All that Programming has dissolved by now."

Another silence. Alan considered Thorn, his brows pinched even harder together, and he took a slow, deep breath.

"You think this is a *good* idea?" he challenged.

"It's not about whether it's a good idea or not," Thorn said, pushing off the wall and propping her hands on her hips. "Eva said herself she's doing it no matter what we say here, and I'd rather her go to the orphanage with a guard than come back into the city alone. Wouldn't you?"

Alan's eyes moved from Thorn to Eva before glancing over Darius and landing back on Thorn again. His jaw was stern, and his throat moved as he swallowed against it. At last, he shook his head.

"This must be done with extraordinary caution," he began.

"Of course," Thorn said, nodding.

"I want additional patrols in the area."

"I'll talk to Jeremiah," she concurred, "and I'll call Jacob to drive them into the city. He knows how to avoid getting caught."

Alan nodded. "And the security detail?"

"I will meet them there personally," Thorn said, and she looked at Eva. The two women quietly took each other in. Darius watched as Eva's face softened, and she gave Thorn a grateful nod. Thorn returned it, and the corner of her mouth hinted at a smile. Alan leaned back in his chair and crossed his arms. The movement drew all their attention back to him.

"Very well," he said. "Do you have all your affairs in order, Miss Torres?"

"I'm meeting with Holly right now to get it all set up," she said.

"Good," Alan said. "You and Mr. Jones are free to go." Darius stood up, and they made to leave. As Thorn moved to follow them, Alan called her back, his tone testy. "Thorn, I have more I would like to discuss with you."

She paused, but before she went back, she glanced at Darius again. He chanced a smile, mouthed the words "thank you," and Thorn's hard face relaxed. Then she turned to her uncle as Darius and Eva walked into the lobby outside his office.

Once there, the stillness trapped them.

"So," Darius muttered. "We're all good, I guess."

"Yeah."

Another tense pause. More silence. Without speaking, they walked to the elevator. When they made it to the foyer, Darius reached for the door to the stairwell.

"What are you doing?" Eva asked.

"I was going to walk you down to Holly's," he said.

Eva's brown cheeks flushed. "Actually," she said, "Holly asked me not to bring you. If you don't know my new name or where I'm going, the Sins can't get it out of you, just in case they—"

The next words caught in her throat on a knot of emotion, and she looked at the ground. Darius's stomach dropped.

"Oh," he said. "Yeah. That's a good idea. I guess I'll wait for you in the courtyard."

"That sounds good. I'll... see you in a bit."

She brushed past him, opened the door, and disappeared into the stairwell. Darius stood, rooted to the spot, until her warmth was small and distant.

The courtyard pattered with dull, lazy energy, but Darius ignored it. People wandered in and out of the kitchens across the way to grab an early lunch. They came in from upstairs and from their bedrooms, walking past and around him. Their footsteps echoed in the high ceilings, caught up in the concrete walls and supports. Voices carried through on murmurs and laughs. Darius tuned them out. His eyes were looking down at his phone—looking, but not seeing—as he scrolled through news articles from *The Times*.

News articles that had finally stopped featuring Saul Torres.

The Martyrs were returning to a more "standard" routine, focusing all their efforts on tracking down Sloth before he set off another bomb, but Darius still floated in the space between grief and normalcy. The rest of his team seemed to understand. Lina and Mackenzie told him to take a break from work for a while, but he wasn't sure he could. What else would he do when Eva was gone?

God. Eva was going to be *gone*.

It wasn't just that he was losing a lover. Darius was losing a *friend*. Someone who had been through more hell with him than anyone else in the Underground could imagine.

A surge of emotion welled up in Darius's throat. He swallowed, shook his head, and wiped a tear from the corner of his eye. The last few days had been a blur of packing and planning for Eva's new life—far away from New York City. Far away from *him*. He looked up at the courtyard, across to the kitchen, where many Martyrs were sitting down to eat now. Their warmth called out to him, their auras a familiar reminder that he was in the right place and doing the right thing.

But it would feel a lot different when Eva's energy wasn't part of the crowd anymore.

Something shifted and drew Darius's attention from his thoughts. A different kind of energy. That magnetic pull. Nicholas had been in the basement all morning. Hell, Nicholas had been in the basement all *week*. For days now, Darius could feel him beneath his feet, that drawing sensation tugging at him almost constantly. Now it moved toward the stairs. Darius watched the door beside the elevator until it opened, and Nicholas emerged. Skylar Fulton was with him. They chatted briefly outside the door, continuing a conversation they'd clearly been deeply invested in. Nicholas's eyebrows were furrowed, but his blue eyes were wide and excited.

After a few seconds, Skylar disappeared back down the stairs, but Nicholas turned to the courtyard, and he looked right at Darius. Without pause, he headed across the room and pulled up a chair by Darius's side.

"So, Eva's getting a little seed money to start her new life, huh?" Nicholas asked as he straddled the chair and leaned toward Darius. "She's downstairs with Holly getting her accounts in order."

"I know where she is," Darius said.

Nicholas raised a brow but didn't comment on Darius's short attitude. "It's pretty nice of the Martyrs to help her out. Have you thought about going with her?"

Darius shook his head. "I can't. My place is here. I have

a job to do."

"I think you should go," Nicholas said. "The Martyrs aren't all that you think they are. I'm pretty sure they killed your friends."

It was as though a bucket of ice water had been poured over Darius's head. A deep, heavy chill went down his spine and made his whole body go rigid. He frowned, but Nicholas watched him with a pointed expectancy—like he'd been waiting days to drop this bit of news.

Darius shook his head. "What the hell are you talking about?"

"Look," Nicholas went on as he leaned even further over the table. His voice went quiet, his tone deepened, and he said, "I've been thinking about the night your friend was killed. A *lot*. And it just doesn't make any fucking sense. I mean, what a crazy coincidence that they just happened to pick a unit next to one that Witham was hiding his bomb shit in? And an even *crazier* coincidence that it just *happened* to blow up with the Martyrs there? I don't buy it."

An energy shifted, and Nicholas cast a cautious glance over his shoulder. John Waters stood up from his table and wandered back toward the elevators. Nicholas waited until he was gone before continuing. "I read all the reports. Wrath's Puppets got past Thorn and were on the way to the unit when the explosion went off. I think the Martyrs weren't just throwing flash-bangs and smoke bombs. I bet they blew the whole son of a bitch up to make sure the Sins couldn't get your buddy. An 'if we can't have him, nobody can,' situation."

Then Nicholas stopped talking, and he stared at Darius with that same eager look in his eye. Almost manic. Like he had done Darius a favor.

And for a moment, all Darius could do was stare back. A lot of thoughts flooded his head. A lot of feelings. He closed his eyes, pinched the bridge of his nose, and took a deep breath.

"You know what happened the night Saul died?" Darius

finally asked.

He opened his eyes and looked up at Nicholas. The other Virtue just shook his head.

"Thorn woke me up," Darius said. "At one in the morning. They'd just gotten back, and she was filthy and beat up, but she woke me up, brought me to her office, and spent the next two hours telling me what happened. Everything that happened."

"She was trying to cover her—"

Darius held up his hand and kept talking through whatever Nicholas had been trying to say.

"And the next day, Alan came to me and told me he was sorry. He asked if there was anything he could do to help. Lina and Mackenzie, too. Elijah. Abraham... Everyone else here—*every person* in this place—told me the same thing. That they were sorry, and they were here for me."

A warm flame lit inside Darius's chest, a comfort in saying out loud how many people he had in his life that cared about him. In the middle of losing Eva and all that he had left of his old life, he'd let himself lose sight of what he'd gained here.

And Nicholas was trying to taint that.

So Darius furrowed his brows as he took Nicholas in. Nicholas just watched him. His eagerness was gone. His jaw clenched tight.

"But not you," Darius said. "This is the first time you've said two words to me since Saul, Juniper, and Lindsey died, and you're here to accuse these people—the people who have been here for me—of *murder*?"

Nicholas's cheeks flushed red. Darius pressed on.

"You know how that looks to me? You know who looks like the bad guy right now? I can tell you, it sure as hell isn't the Martyrs."

"Look, man, I'm just trying to help you see what's happening here," Nicholas said. "I don't want you to be blind-sided—"

"Nicholas," Darius said, and he shook his head. Despite

everything that had happened in the last seven days—despite the numbness and heartache—he was surprised at how strong he felt now. Powerful and assured. "I'm not the one who's blind. You are *so trapped* by your own hatred and distrust that you just... you can't see past it. You've built yourself this cage, and until you learn how to take it down, all you're ever going to see is people you have to fight. I hope you get out someday, man. I really do. It's limiting you."

Darius got to his feet and started to walk away, but before he left, another thought occurred to him. He turned back to Nicholas.

"You know," he said slowly. Nicholas was still watching him. Darius was surprised to see he didn't look angry. Instead, he seemed sobered. "If you think the Martyrs are so misguided that they'd kill three innocent people, I think you need to leave. We've got a war to fight here. I'm not going to fight you, too."

Then, he turned around again and walked back to his room, the room he and Eva would share for one last night, and he didn't come out again until the next morning.

CHAPTER TWENTY-TWO

The city flashed by Darius's window. Buildings. People. Billboards and bus-side advertisements for attorneys, plastic surgery, and pharmaceutical drugs. The world around him felt warm. The mid-September air was hot against his face; the human energy, hotter. Eva sat beside him. Her fingers interlaced with his, and she held tightly onto his hand.

"We're doing Manhattan first," Jacob said. He spoke quickly, almost nervously, in the same manner he had the last time Darius had seen him, but now, there was a hint of annoyance, too. He cast a look at Nicholas from over his shoulder. His brows were furrowed heavily over his deep, brown eyes. "It's faster than stopping on the way back down from the Bronx."

"No problem," Nicholas said. "I'm just here for the ride." Darius turned and looked at him. Nicholas made a point *not* to look back.

Eva wasn't the only one leaving the Underground today.

Darius wasn't sure when exactly Nicholas had decided his time with the Martyrs was over or when he'd talked to Alan about his decision to leave. All Darius knew was, when he and Eva walked into the garage that afternoon, Nicholas was already there waiting for them. Packed, funded, and ready to go.

Maybe Darius should have felt guilty about it, but he didn't. His time on this planet was short. He didn't want to waste any more of it trying to change the heart of one man. He had more important things to worry about, like finding the rest of the Virtues and tracking down Envy's new host. Nicholas would have to figure things out on his own.

Maybe he'd get lucky, or maybe one day, Darius would find another, younger Diligence.

One with a better attitude.

Jacob Locke didn't share Darius's indifference to Nicholas tagging along for the ride. When he realized his job now included *three* separate stops—one to spread Saul's ashes in Lower Manhattan, one to drop Nicholas off in the East Bronx, and finally, one to take Eva to a train station in Newark, New Jersey—Jacob almost lost it. He had gotten fidgety as Alan explained the change in plans. When Jacob asked Darius for the address to his old orphanage and punched it into his phone, Darius thought he was going to break the device.

And it had only gotten worse. The nearer they got to Lower Manhattan, the more obsessive and hyper-alert Jacob became. Darius had warned Eva about his Programming-induced brain trauma and the behavior that came with it, but he hadn't reminded Nicholas. The other Virtue was watching the side of his face with cautious, narrow eyes.

"You okay, man?" he asked.

"Can't be too careful," Jacob said. The words came out quickly, like he was talking twice the normal speed. He didn't bother looking at Nicholas. He was too busy taking in the streets. The cars, the civilians, and the spaces between them. "People are dying out here."

Nicholas frowned, and Darius watched Jacob's eyes in the rearview mirror. There was more than caution there. Darius also saw anger.

"What do you mean?" Nicholas asked.

"The bombs," Jacob said. "Abraham told me. Sloth's

been setting them off. Hundreds of people are dead. *Hundreds.*" He shook his head, and his fingers tightened on the steering wheel. "It's gotta stop. It's making the city unsafe for the Martyrs, and I *don't like it.*"

"Ah," Nicholas said, and he turned back toward the window. There was a strange, confident glint behind his eye. "Well, I'm working on that. I'll get him."

Now Jacob looked at Nicholas. Darius couldn't tell if it was with skepticism or contempt.

Minutes later, they reached the old projects near Alphabet City. Darius was struck with an odd sense of bittersweet homecoming that just anchored more to the sadness he felt at Eva's leaving. He recognized these buildings, and though the individual faces weren't familiar, he recognized the *people.* The way they walked down the street. The cautious and distrustful way they watched Jacob's nice car roll through their part of town. Darius caught a glimpse of a young child playing in the gutter, slapping his bare feet in the filthy water as his mother gently worked knots from his hair with her nails. She glanced up and caught his eye through the window. Darius tried to pass her a smile.

He'd spent hours gently pulling his fingers through long, tangled locks on the heads of dozens of children. Those children had been dead for almost a year now.

A lump caught up in Darius's throat, and he cleared it away with a deep cough. Eva's grip tightened around his palm as they turned the corner.

Seeing the old bar again was harder on Darius than he'd thought it would be. Jacob pulled up along the sidewalk in almost the *exact* same place that Darius had come running out of the building with Eva's bloody body in his arms, screaming for help. He looked up. The studio where they had quarantined the sick kids overlooked the street. The window was still broken from when Envy had grabbed Darius by the throat and thrown him out of it. He could see sharp shards of glass sticking out around the edge of the frame.

He took a deep breath to steel himself and looked back down at the door to see Thorn sitting on the front stoop. A cigarette smoked between her fingers, and she watched them park with a cold, stoic expression.

"Hurry up," Jacob barked as he glanced at his watch. His knee bounced impatiently. "I'm driving around the neighborhood. Can't stay in one place. I'll be back to get you in twenty minutes."

Darius opened the door and stepped out of the car. Eva came with him. To Darius's surprise, so did Nicholas. He got out of the front seat and walked around the back of the vehicle as Jacob pulled away from the curb. When Darius threw him a questioning look, he just shrugged and said, "I wanted to pay my respects to Saul... Plus, I don't want to spend twenty minutes in the car with *that* guy..."

Darius was surprised. Nicholas seemed genuine. Behind his nonchalance was steady compassion, and he tried to give Darius a smile. Darius just nodded. "Thanks, man," he said. Then he turned to Eva. She was looking up at the old bar, her face tempered with conviction. "Are you ready?"

She nodded.

The two of them laced fingers and started up the stairs. Darius's heart felt heavy, and it grew heavier still as they neared the door. Thorn remained at the top of the stoop. She put her cigarette out, smothering it beneath her heel, but the air still smelled of smoke. When Darius and Eva reached her, she held her hand out and passed a solemn look between them. "The place is safe. No traps or wires," she said. Her voice carried a note of hard caution. "But it's not pretty. You're going to be facing some dark memories in there. Can you handle that?"

Eva nodded. "We're good," she said, and she sounded like she meant every word. Thorn nodded.

"I'll be out here," she said. Before she headed back down the steps, she gave Darius one last look. Then she disappeared, and he and Eva walked into the bar.

As soon as they passed through the door, a cold chill

washed over him. Darius knew seeing the orphanage again would be challenging, but he hadn't been prepared for *this*. Though the bodies were gone and the blood dried, heavy, dark stains soaked into the wood and colored it a deep, ruddy brown. The streaks told a story—of bodies being dragged, of children running, scared, down the hallway and up the stairs. Darius was overwhelmed for a moment. Vivid memories—images he now only saw in his deepest of sleeps—bombarded his senses. He could practically smell the sickly-sweet, iron scent of death in his nostrils again. The hairs at the base of his neck stood up in a familiar, telling way.

Whatever happy memories Darius had of this place were tainted. He could never think of the orphanage without re-membering the brutal, senseless way it all came crashing down on top of him.

"You're sure you want to spread Saul's ashes here?" Da-rius asked.

His sense of unease grew more intense.

Eva nodded. Her face was pale, almost sickly so, and her eyes wide, but she reached into her pocket and took out the glass tube of Saul's ashes. Darius's goosebumps spread from his neck, across his shoulders, and down his arms. As Eva went to open the vial, he let out a gasp.

Fuck, he'd been so *stupid*.

"What?" Eva asked.

"We're not safe."

Darius hardly heard Eva ask what he meant. The feeling of dread intensified. He felt out around them. Energies were converging on their location. The Virtuous pull from Nich-olas grew nearer. Toward the door. Darius rushed to the entrance of the bar—

But it flew open before he got there, and Thorn came barreling in. Nicholas followed on her heels. She slammed the door shut behind them as the first gunshot went off. It blasted part of the doorframe to splinters. Thorn swore and ducked down.

"What's happening?" Darius asked.

"The Sins," Thorn growled. She pulled her phone from her pocket, hit a button, and held it to her ear. "It has to be. *Fuck!* Locke! Pick up!" She hung up, hit an emergency button on her screen, and jammed the device into her pocket. "Son of a *bitch*. Come on. Stay down." She ushered them all to get low and move away from the doors and windows. Darius could feel the people outside coming closer. Fifteen of them. Their warmth pushed in like a wall, but then it stopped and surrounded the building.

"Puppets?" he asked.

Thorn shook her head. "I don't think so."

"They're cops," Nicholas said. He had sneaked to a window and peeked over the edge of the sill. The auras outside were hedging closer. Darius could feel them moving in a line toward the door. Nicholas stared back at Thorn in furious disbelief. "Why the hell would the cops be shooting at us? We haven't done anything!"

"That's never mattered," Thorn said bitterly. She reached into her satchel and drew out a weapon. Sparkie slipped out of the bag and disappeared into the back of the bar. Darius felt a handful of energies moving that way, toward the rear door. His panic increased as Thorn went on. "But I doubt they're here by coincidence. Someone in the area must be Programmed to let Gluttony know as soon as you show back up." She looked right at Darius. "Did you see anyone when you came in?"

Darius's heart dropped as he remembered the woman combing her son's hair on the street. The look on his face must have told Thorn everything she needed to know. She swore under her breath.

"What the fuck is your plan?" Nicholas asked. The other energies were at the back door now. Getting closer. Almost inside the building. "Kill a bunch of innocent people?"

Thorn glared at him. "It's too risky," she said. "We're outnumbered, I'm the only one with a weapon, and backup won't get here in time. I only have one option, but it won't be pretty. Center yourselves."

Darius frowned as Thorn closed her eyes. Then she reached out with her Influence in a broad stroke. It emanated out from her like a wave. Darius felt it tingling at the edge of his consciousness, pushing at his temples. Nicholas seemed to, as well. Eva felt it most of all. She faltered on her feet for a moment and almost fell over. Darius grabbed her by the shoulders to steady her.

Then all of the police around the building froze. Their energies were low and unmoving. Nicholas looked out the window again.

"What did you do?"

"I stopped them," Thorn said as she got to her feet, but she didn't put her weapon away. A flash of real, tangible fear filled her eyes. "But I can't hold them forever. They're fighting me, and now we have a different problem."

Thorn cast Darius a dark look, and he knew immediately what she was worried about.

Wrath.

"How close is she?" he asked.

"Too close," Thorn muttered. "Is there another way out of here?"

Darius thought about it. The cops were already at the back door, held off by nothing more than Thorn's fragile Influence. Even if they *did* get past the police, Alphabet City and the adjoining neighborhoods were full of people who could easily be Programmed. He just stared at Thorn for half a second, his eyes wide and unhelpful, as he watched her fear grow.

Then Eva said, "We can try the tunnels."

Thorn frowned. "What are the—"

"Prohibition tunnels," Darius breathed, and he hurried from the living area into the old kitchen. "They're from the drug prohibition. Or, we thought so, at least. We don't know where they lead—"

"I don't care," Thorn snapped. Panic hinted at the edge of her voice now. It was so subtle, Darius was sure no one else caught it. "We need to go. *Now.*"

The carnage from the massacre was less intense in the kitchen. All that remained were dark brown lines from where Thad's blood had fallen into the grout between the tiles. Darius ignored that. He rushed past the old table where he and Juniper had folded laundry, the counter where he and Saul had laid out the goods they'd acquired during the day, and the tarnished sink where he'd bathed little Lindsey. His heart ached at the memories, but he didn't have the time to mourn them right now. He moved to the back corner of the room. A massive, wooden trap door lay in the ground, coated in dust.

Darius squatted down to lift it, and as soon as it opened, his stomach turned.

A wretched smell poured from the cellar and saturated the room with hot, putrid air. Darius heard Nicholas gag behind him while Eva coughed and covered her nose with her shirt. Darius instinctively shut the door again and choked in the back of his throat.

Thorn took a deep breath, put her gun back into her satchel, and reached down for the door. She threw it all the way open and wrinkled her nose. The rot was so intense it made Darius's eyes sting. He followed Eva's lead and pulled his shirt up over his face, too.

"Where is it?" Thorn said. Her voice sounded strangled, like her throat was closing up to stop the rank stench from getting into her lungs.

"Behind the shelf," Darius said through a cough. Thorn nodded and jumped down into the cellar. Darius followed after her. He carefully climbed down the narrow steps and saw what was creating such an awful smell.

All the food they'd collected down here had gone bad. Boxes of produce were now sopping wet and puke green. Sticky slime melted down the sides and coated the dirt floor beneath his feet. Loaves of bread were so covered in mold that they looked like fuzzy, green rocks. Even the dried meats had begun to putrefy. Flies buzzed around, batting into Darius's face as he fought down the urge to throw up and followed Thorn to the back of the long, narrow room. Eva and Nicholas came down behind them. Darius heard Nicholas vomit as Eva closed the door.

Now the only light they had to go by came through a frosted window at the edge of the ceiling. Thorn navigated them through the dark, reeking room with finesse. At the far end stood the bookshelf. It was covered with nonperishable goods—cans of peas and corn, fruits steeped in syrup, and pickled things in green jars. It had been pulled away from the hole in the wall already.

"Someone's been here," Darius said as he came up beside Thorn. Cooler, staler air filtered slowly into the cellar, and it was a welcome reprieve from the stink. Darius stepped through the crumbling wall and into the tunnel beyond it. "We always kept this shut."

"There's no way in hell anyone came through recently," Nicholas said with a gag as he quickly pushed past Thorn and climbed into the tunnel, too. Darius grabbed his shoulder to keep him from going too deep in. "No one's been down here in months."

"We don't have the time to worry about it now," Thorn snarled. She pulled Eva through, turned back to the shelf, and grabbed it with the tips of her fingers. With a grunt, she shifted it closed behind them. It must have been heavy, but somehow Thorn managed to cinch it so closely against the wall it obstructed the light coming through the cellar window. They were cast in total darkness. Darius heard people fumbling around in their pockets, and both Thorn and Nicholas turned on the lights from their cell phones. It illuminated them all in bright, white light, casting dark shadows across their faces and the stone walls around them. Thorn looked down at her screen. The harsh glow put her sharp features into even more contrast.

"No signal," she said, then she looked up and down the long tunnel. The flashlight on her phone only lit about ten feet ahead of them, beyond which was just darkness. "Let's keep moving. We'll find the surface eventually."

She pushed past them, and Darius came in behind her. "Be careful," he said. "Thad tried to map these tunnels out but had to stop because of cave-ins."

"Getting caught in a cave-in is better than getting caught by the Sins," Thorn muttered. Then she kept walking.

For several yards, the tunnel moved in one straight line. The stagnant air was quiet and still. Their breathing echoed back at them, and their footsteps were loud and disorienting. Even more disorienting was the sense of energy around them—*above them*. Darius could feel people overhead as they hurried through the underground path. It made him feel somehow open and exposed, even though he *knew* they couldn't feel them back...

Unless they were Sins.

"Hey," Eva suddenly said. "What's this?"

Thorn turned around, and she and Nicholas both focused their light on the wall by Eva's hand. Darius leaned in closer for a better look. It was a brown streak that almost looked like a handprint...

"It's blood," Thorn said, and she cast Darius a look. "Old blood. I think I know who came through the tunnels."

Eva let out a small, emotional gasp. Darius heard the sadness in her voice more than he could see it on her face. "It was *Saul*..."

"This must be how they escaped," Thorn said as she turned back down the tunnel. Now, though, she moved with a different kind of purpose. She swept her phone from side to side, walking more slowly, taking in more detail. "And we *know* they found a way out... Maybe we can—ah, here's more."

She stopped and showed another bloody handprint on the wall. Darius heard Eva stifle a sniff behind him.

"He must have gotten hurt," Thorn said.

"The scar on his face," Eva said. "He didn't have that before."

Thorn nodded, but she didn't say anything as she

continued down the tunnel. After that, they were all on the lookout for more blood, and as they started paying attention, it was easier to find. It had dribbled onto the ground, and when Saul had touched the walls, he left streaks behind. They reached the first fork in their path, and Thorn made the others stay in one spot as she explored both routes, looking for more markers of Saul's journey through the caverns. When she found one, she called them down to join her. It felt strange to follow a dead man's messages, and stranger to know Saul was helping them out, one last time.

If Darius wasn't still overcome with a sense of danger, he might have been sad. As they turned a corner and followed another path marked by Saul's bloody handprint, he glanced over at Eva. Her brown eyes were teary.

They went on like that for half an hour, but suddenly, Thorn stopped.

"*Great*," she muttered, and Darius looked over her shoulder to see what she was talking about.

A cave-in.

Massive slabs of cut stone had collapsed into the cavern. A slick of packed dirt, large rocks, and debris blocked their path. There was a tiny hole toward the top left corner, where Darius could hear something beyond. It sounded like slow-moving water. Thorn turned to him and put her phone into his palms. Her fingers felt cool against his skin.

"Hold this," she said as she turned back to the pile of rubble and pulled her hair into a ponytail at the base of her skull. "And stand back."

Then she set to work digging them out. Thorn was able to shift the large rocks with shockingly little effort. She gripped the edges with the tips of her fingers and used her body weight and powerful legs to move them around. She pulled large boulders down and into the tunnel behind her and dug through dirt and dust with her bare hands. After a few minutes, Nicholas muttered something under his breath, gave his phone to Eva, and began to help her. While Thorn was much stronger and better able to move the larger rocks, having two of them work simultaneously made their progress go more quickly. As the hole in the debris wall was forced open, the sound of water became more apparent.

And so did the smell of sewage.

"Ugh," Nicholas groaned, and he covered his nose with the crook of his elbow. Thorn kept digging. "What is *that*?"

"This tunnel must lead out into the sewers somewhere," Thorn said. She grunted and shifted another large rock. Her forehead glistened with a thin layer of sweat. Nicholas was coated in it. Beads collected at his hairline and dripped down the bridge of his nose.

Soon, they managed to get a hole just big enough for a grown man to squeeze through, and that's exactly what they did. Thorn led the way, followed by Eva, Nicholas, and Darius bringing up the rear. He wedged himself through the opening, and for a brief moment, worried what would happen if the cavern came collapsing in around him. To his relief, though, it didn't, and he came out on the other side in one piece.

But the other side was *stinking*.

Thorn had been right. Just a few dozen feet down the tunnel, it turned again and opened up into the side of a long, brick-walled passage. The stench of sewage got worse the further in they got, and Darius pulled his shirt up over his mouth and nose again. Eva, Nicholas, and Thorn did the same. It did little to help. Instead, Darius just breathed in the hot, humid smell of his own skin alongside the foul air around him. Thorn looked up and down the sewage line for a moment before she gestured toward the left and started to walk again.

It was impossible to avoid the water underfoot. Darius tried not to think of what was *in* that water as he moved through it. It was six inches deep, and quickly his socks and shoes were saturated.

Thorn took them through the tunnel and around a corner, where light filtered down from overhead. Darius glanced up to see a small, circular disk above them and a ladder leading up to it. He could sense the people up there. Hot energy, everywhere. His stomach dropped. He hadn't even stopped to think of how busy it would be in Manhattan at this time of the day.

"I wonder where it comes out," Eva said. Her voice was muffled behind her clothing.

"Near 8th and Avenue B," Thorn said. Nicholas's brows furrowed, and he threw Darius a look, but Darius just shrugged. Thorn turned to them. "That hole is going to lead out into the middle of the street. I'll hold the cars off until you all climb out. Then, head to a sidewalk and *stick together*. The Sins are on high alert. They'll be looking for us. Try to keep your heads down and your faces covered. Got it?"

They nodded, and with a final, resolute look, Thorn started climbing the ladder. Darius gestured for Eva to follow behind her, and then he and Nicholas came up last. As they reached the manhole cover, he could hear traffic driving by.

Thorn didn't seem bothered by that or by the sensation of human beings all around them. She waited until the energies above came to a stop, and she pushed the manhole cover open. As she pulled her body out of the sewer, cars began to honk, but Thorn didn't move. She stood over the hole and helped them up. One by one, they heaved themselves onto the busy New York Street as onlookers stopped to stare, and furious drivers laid on their horns. At last, Thorn reached down and pulled Nicholas onto the asphalt.

Then she replaced the cover, and the four of them hurried to the sidewalk. Darius looked around to get his bearings and found himself in the shadow of a massive, ornate building. Saints Brigid & Emeric Church loomed overhead like a pillar of false piety. Dread thickened the air. They were less than half a mile away from the orphanage.

CHAPTER TWENTY-THREE

"What are we going to do?" Darius asked. He sped up to walk beside Thorn as she powered through the pedestrian traffic on the sidewalk. Nicholas and Eva followed quickly on their heels. All four of them kept their heads cast down, trying to watch the ground at their feet rather than the faces of the people swirling around them.

Thorn didn't respond to him as she reached into her pocket and grabbed out her phone. "Montgomery," she said, speaking loudly to be heard above the dull roar of city sound. "I know I went off the grid. I was underground and lost service. I'm sending my coordinates now. *Hurry.*" Then she hung up, typed in a few commands, and kept on moving, completely unperturbed by the stares that followed the four of them as they strode, filthy, wet, and stinking, down a busy New York sidewalk. The bustling crowd parted around them like undesirable debris in a gutter. If he wasn't so concerned with what the Sins were up to, Darius might have been self-conscious.

"Is Wrath close?" he asked. Thorn glanced his way. Her brows were furrowed, and her mouth set into a hard line.

"Closer than I like," she said. Then she threw a quick look over his shoulder, back in the direction they'd come.

Darius's teeth clenched together. His sense of impending danger had dulled as they'd gone through the tunnels, but almost as soon as they'd come aboveground again, it roared to life. Goosebumps raised along his shoulders and arms.

"We've got to get out of here," he said. He tried to speak quietly and calmly. The last thing he wanted to do was alarm Eva and Nicholas, but something in his voice caught Thorn's attention. Her expression shifted—her eyes went a little wider, her jaw a little tighter—as she looked at him. Then, she looked past him—past Eva and Nicholas—and her white face went even whiter.

"Shit."

She grabbed Darius by the shoulder and pulled them into Tompkins Square Park. They tucked behind a bike rack while a police cruiser rolled by. Thorn's fingers tightened on the skeletal remains of a picked-apart bike, still chained to the rack, until the police turned the corner. Then she leapt up, ushered the others forward, and they sped to the other side of the park. A couple of grimy, old men huddled together beside the public bathroom's graffiti-coated walls, leering at the four of them as they reached Avenue A. Thorn led the way across the street, ignoring honking traffic, and slipped inside a convenience store. They ducked behind a shelf, and people dispersed around them. Darius heard them whispering—felt them *staring*—as he and the others peered out the large glass windows onto the busy street outside.

The police cruiser appeared again. The officers inside looked out at the sidewalk as they drove slowly past.

Eva's hand wrapped around Darius's, and he glanced down at her. Her face was pale, scared, and angry. "Damn it," she muttered. "This is all my fault. If I hadn't—"

"Don't," Thorn said. Darius turned toward her, but she didn't look at either of them. She focused on the street outside. Her brow furrowed in furious thought. "It doesn't matter. We're here now, and we're getting the fuck *out*. Montgomery will be here any minute."

"How do you know?" Nicholas asked. His eyes narrowed, and Thorn threw him a hot look, but she didn't answer him. Then Darius realized he hadn't seen Sparkie since the orphanage. He must have gone to find help…

And if he was in the car with Jeremiah, Thorn knew exactly where he was.

Sure enough, a few minutes later, a black SUV pulled up in front of the convenience store. Thorn quickly led Darius, Eva, and Nicholas out of the building and onto the street, much to the relief of the anxious, young cashier who had done nothing but stare at them since they'd arrived. As Thorn opened the back, passenger-side door, Sparkie peered at them from Chris's shoulder.

"Hurry," Jeremiah said. He sat behind the wheel, watching the street behind them in the rearview mirror. "There's a heavy police presence in Lower Manhattan right now. They're looking for you."

"No shit," Thorn grumbled as she helped Eva climb into the car. Chris was sitting shotgun, and she held a rifle in her lap. Nicholas got in next, and Thorn shut the door behind him. Then she pulled Darius around the car. His sense of uneasiness began to grow again. He looked down the street as they reached the back of the vehicle.

A police cruiser turned the corner.

"They're here," he called out.

Thorn swore and opened the back hatch. Sparkie vaulted through the cab and took off into the sky. The cruiser's lights flashed, and before Darius knew what was happening, Thorn grabbed him by the shoulders and tossed him into the back of the SUV.

"Go!" she screamed as she slammed the door shut.

Jeremiah shifted the car into drive and peeled out. Darius fumbled around and managed to get up just in time to see Thorn, gun drawn, sprinting at the police cruiser as it sped toward them. She leapt onto the hood of the car, smashed her heel through the windshield, and—

Darius flew to the side. The Martyr SUV made a hard

turn, and Darius tumbled, slamming into the wall. They sped north, through tall buildings, around other cars and pedestrians and cyclists. Darius felt their energies bolt past him and disappear, only to be replaced with *more* heat, *more* people in the busy center of Soho. Darius struggled to find his footing. Every time the car jerked, he stumbled again. He was able to lift his head just enough to see a flash of red and blue dart through the air in front of them and down another side street. Jeremiah turned to follow it; Darius gripped the headrests to stay upright.

Then something came careening through the car's back window and thudded into the frame next to Nicholas's head. Darius turned to see *another* police car following them. One of the officers leaned out the window and pointed a handgun at them. His eyes looked distant, his expression like stone.

"What the fuck!" Nicholas gasped. "They're not supposed to open fire on the street like this!"

"They must be Programmed," Chris called. Then she turned around and raised her rifle to her shoulder. "Cover your ears and *get down*!" Darius jammed his fingers into his ears and flattened himself against the floor of the SUV. He felt Eva and Nicholas curling up to be as small as they could be in front of him. Then Chris pulled the trigger.

Gunfire erupted and shattered the back window. The cruiser behind them jerked violently. Darius looked up to see it smashed into a car parked on the side of the road. The officers leapt out and called for backup as Jeremiah turned them down another street again. There was a brief reprieve, but something still wasn't right. Darius could tell. Anxiety seated deep in his gut, and the twisted feeling didn't fade. He came up over the seat and looked to Nicholas; the other Virtue stared back in horrified recognition and understanding.

Then sirens deafened them. Darius covered his ears again as he turned to see three more cops pulling in at them from different directions. Jeremiah swerved, heading down another new street. Darius collapsed to the floor as Chris fired another round of shots out the window. One cruiser pulled away. Jeremiah turned…

But then the cops shot back. Darius heard the hard *thuds* of bullets against metal. Eva screamed, and Darius's heart sank into the pit of his stomach. He called out her name— tried to get to standing—but the frantic swerving made it hard for him to move. When he finally managed to pull himself over, he saw Eva gripping her chest. Blood blossomed on her blouse and seeped through her fingers. She looked at him with wide, terrified eyes.

He reached out his hands toward her, felt the energy pooling in his palms—

Then another flurry of shots rocked the vehicle. One slammed into Darius's side and took the breath right out of him. He gasped, grabbed the wound—

Another shot. Jeremiah's energy blinked out.

The car careened to the left. Across the street. Chris was screaming—for Jeremiah, for Darius, for God—as the SUV flew up onto the sidewalk and slammed into a light pole. Darius was thrown forward, through the cab, through the cracked and blood-splattered windshield. His body bounced down the road.

Away from the car.

Away from Eva.

The gritty asphalt under his ragged face lured Darius into unconsciousness as hot energy swarmed around him. The last thing he remembered was flashing red and blue lights as a police cruiser whipped around the corner and screeched to a stop. The doors opened, a cop leveled her weapon at Darius, and—

Another police cruiser came in and slammed into her, into her vehicle, and Darius's mind succumbed to darkness.

The shattered front windshield laid in pebble-like shards

around Thorn as she drove her foot onto the gas, urging the stolen police cruiser forward. She sped through the streets, following the Martyr SUV and the cops chasing it, but she was too far behind to do any good. Hopelessly, helplessly, she could only watch as shot after shot was leveled at her people.

With a sickening jolt, she felt a point of cold energy blink out, and the Martyr vehicle took a sharp turn. It veered across the oncoming lane, over the sidewalk, and crashed into the light pole at the corner.

The cops ahead of her slammed on their brakes. A woman got out and drew her gun—

And Thorn swerved left. She slammed the stolen police cruiser into the officer and her vehicle. Thorn felt the woman's cold energy extinguish immediately as the airbag exploded in her face and threw her back against the seat. A rush of debris flew through the broken windshield. Shards of glass cut against her arms and shoulders, tore open a gash in her forehead. Hot blood poured down her face. Along the bridge of her nose. In the swooping curves around her eyes.

For a moment, she was blinded. Her world was a rush of white and red as the airbag deflated and blood clouded her vision. Blinded, but not sightless. Sparkie circled overhead. The other officer in the car had survived. He clambered over the back of the cruiser and aimed his weapon at Thorn. Chris was screaming orders. Frantically trying to pull Eva out of the car while Nicholas sat in shocked silence. And Darius—

Darius lay motionless in the middle of the street.

Thorn's heart felt as though it had stopped beating. The world around her went dull and quiet as dread sank deep into her bones. That emptiness in her chest grew, threatened to overwhelm her, as she fought past the airbag and wiped the blood from her eyes. She crawled out the mangled windshield, cutting her hands and knees on jagged glass. Now she could *really* see him. Darius laid there. Silent. His face swollen and scraped to hell, his shirt red and soaking.

The unfamiliar cold rush of panic flooded through her.

She leapt to her feet. Jumped down to the asphalt. The officer behind the other car popped up and took a shot at her. The bullet crashed into her car, and without thinking—without worrying about being careful or taking chances—she drew her gun and shot back. Hers hit his throat, and his lifeless body tumbled backward. Then Thorn ran toward Darius, ignoring... everything. She ignored the chilling *cold* of more police drawing nearer, the screaming of sirens and squealing of brakes, and Wrath's *vengeful* Influence barreling toward them. She ignored everything except for Darius. Thorn lifted his limp body into her arms. His dead weight was slick in her injured, bleeding fingers as she sprinted the rest of the way to the SUV. Chris called out her name, and her voice woke Thorn. The situation came roaring at her like a storm, and she took a half-second to take it all in.

Jeremiah. Dead. A bullet hit him in the base of his neck. He was slumped over the wheel, his eyes and mouth open and gaping. Nicholas curled up behind him.

Chris was crouching beside the front tire of the SUV. She peered through the smoke furling up from the damaged engine while she trained her rifle on a new police cruiser coming at them from across Allen Street. A cut on her cheek dribbled bright red blood down to her jaw, but otherwise, she seemed unhurt. Her face was set, her teeth clenched.

Eva lay on the sidewalk by Chris's feet. Thorn put Darius down beside her. Eva was conscious but pale, and her eyes were wide with terror. Her breath came in harsh, ragged gasps as blood gurgled from a bullet hole between her ribs. Thorn grabbed her face. Her skin was cold to the touch.

She was dying.

And Darius—fuck, for all Thorn knew, he was already dead.

"Hold on. You're going to be okay," Thorn said to Eva, knowing it wasn't true—knowing damn well she was lying to a dying woman for the sake of comfort in her final moments. Eva didn't seem to hear her. Her eyes were pained and distant. Thorn gently placed her head onto the concrete and turned her attention back to Darius. She pressed her fingers against his throat—trying to find a pulse—but all she could feel was her own frantic heartbeat in her fingertips. She glanced up at Nicholas. "Wolfe, what the hell—"

But he was climbing out of the car now. His face went so white that the only color left behind was a splatter of freckles and blood spray. He wobbled on his feet, and Thorn grabbed his hand. As soon as he was on solid ground, she lowered him down, had him sit, and she asked, "Darius—is he alive?"

Nicholas looked down. At Darius. At Eva. His face, if possible, went even paler. Thorn thought he was going to pass out. She reached out and smacked him sharply on the cheek. "Nicholas! Is he alive?"

It seemed to work. He shook his head, blinked, and took a gasping breath.

"Yeah. Yes. He's alive. *Fuck.*"

Then Nicholas rushed up to Darius's side and grabbed his head in his hands. Thorn watched as the road rash tearing up Darius's face began to shrink and mold itself back together. A wave of such palpable relief washed over her that she almost stumbled backward. Life came back—her lungs filled again, her heart skipped into rhythm—and the world came into sharp focus. More vehicles pulled up in front of them. More officers got out. Wrath was closer now, and Thorn was certain she felt another horrifyingly familiar energy getting out of one of the new cars.

Thank god for the building at their backs. They couldn't be totally surrounded.

Eva coughed. Blood dribbled from the corner of her mouth. Thorn rushed over to her and grabbed her by the face again. Her lips were starting to turn blue.

"Wait—*wait!*" Thorn turned to Nicholas and tried to get his attention. The concrete beneath her feet pooled in blood. "Eva's *dying*. You've got to heal her. *Now*."

But Nicholas shook his head. "I'm almost done!" he shouted, but that wasn't true. Thorn could tell it wasn't. The wound in Darius's side still hemorrhaged blood, and his face was only now starting to look normal again. Thorn tried to reach out, but Nicholas was too far. She swore and looked back down to Eva.

Her brown eyes fluttered beneath their lids. Her breathing was coming in harsh, wheezy gasps. Thorn pressed her hand against the seeping wound in Eva's chest, and she pushed down hard. With every rapid heartbeat, more blood pulsed between Thorn's fingers.

"Hold on," she said. A gunshot went off, and Thorn glanced up to see Chris return fire. She pulled the trigger on her rifle and laid out a round of bullets into the growing line of police waiting just on the other side of the street. Thorn felt a point of cold energy disappear. She looked back to Eva. "Hold on, you hear me? Just a little longer."

But Eva just stared at Thorn. She desperately reached up. Her hand floundered around Thorn's collar until Thorn released her wound and wrapped Eva's fingers up in her own. Her fingernails were pale and dusky. Thorn held on tight.

"Hold on," she said again. "You're going to be—"

But Eva's body shuddered, and though her eyes were looking right into Thorn's, the light behind them faded.

All at once, her life blinked out.

"No!"

Nicholas dropped Darius and leapt over his unconscious body. He stumbled—his legs weak and shaking from the effort of healing—but he clambered over anyway and pressed a hand against Eva's chest. His face contorted in fear and anger and sadness, and he swore. "No, *no*! Damnit, come back!"

But it was no use. Eva's eyes were open and unseeing. Her mouth slack. Bright red with blood. The flame in Thorn's stomach flickered, then it roared. She gently laid

Eva back down on the ground and grabbed Nicholas by the shoulders.

"Finish healing Darius," she said. Stern. Unyielding. Nicholas stared back at her, and Thorn shook him once. "Wolfe, did you hear me? *Finish healing Darius.*" At last, he nodded, and she made her way over to Chris.

Chris hadn't moved. She sat in position, poised professionally and patiently, as she shot round after round of quick, bursting warning shots to keep the line of police away. Thorn crouched beside her and grabbed her pistol from the ground where she'd dropped it when she laid Darius down. A huge figure stood in the center of the line of officers. Gluttony. He was covered in armor, blocked by a massive riot shield. He held up a megaphone and called out to them.

"Lay your weapons down."

His voice made Thorn's stomach writhe in fury. Her lips curled up as she tightened her grip around her gun.

There was a smug smile across Terrance Moore's broad lips. Ten heavily armed and armored cops flanked him. All their firearms pointed right at the battered Martyr vehicle. "Come out with your hands up, and nobody gets hurt."

Thorn knew it was a lie, and she knew Gluttony didn't think they'd fall for it. It was a formality. A cover. Justification for mowing them down in cold blood when they inevitably "resisted arrest."

She'd be damned if they went down without a fight.

"Backup?" Thorn asked Chris quietly. The police stopped shooting, so Chris had done the same. Thorn's hand tightened around her weapon. She watched as the expressions on every single officer simultaneously shifted. Their eyes became disconnected—mechanical and deadly.

"We have six units closing in," Chris said. A hint of anger tinted her strong voice. Thorn rarely saw Chris get angry. In the momentary ceasefire, she took the opportunity to reload her rifle. Thorn watched as she flung her blood-stained ponytail behind her shoulder and swapped her empty magazine out for a fresh one. There was a cold look in her bright green eyes. "Or *trying* to. There are police blockades all around the neighborhood. Holly's working on scrambling their communication. Why hasn't Gluttony attacked? We're outnumbered. He could take us all down in no time…"

"Because of *them*," Thorn growled, and she cast a look back at Nicholas. He was almost done healing Darius now, but for some reason, Darius still hadn't woken up. Thorn's stomach flipped uncomfortably, and she turned back to Chris. "He knows we have *two* Virtues here, but he doesn't know which two. For all he knows, one of them is Temperance. He doesn't want to take that chance."

Chris nodded slowly, but she didn't speak because Moore had lifted his megaphone again.

"Come on, Rose. Be reasonable… A lot of people have died because of you tonight. How many more are you going to kill?"

Thorn's rage mounted. It bubbled up in her chest and her throat, and it kept on bubbling until it had nowhere else to go except to explode…

And Thorn jumped to her feet and fired round after round into Terrance Moore.

Her bullets slammed against him. She heard them thunk uselessly against his armor, again and again. One slipped in the gap between his shoulder pad and chest plate, and he swore and grabbed his arm. A couple of Puppets collapsed. Thorn shot until her clip was empty and the ones still standing returned fire. They aimed low. Into the vehicle, making sure *not* to kill Thorn, but the shards of metal thrown up by the bullets splattered against her face and sliced into her skin.

She ducked back down again. Swapped her spent clip for a new one.

"I fucking *warned you*!"

Moore's voice was followed by a barrage. His line of Puppets opened fire in an unending wave of gunshots. They were tearing the car to shreds, making it impossible for Thorn or Chris to get up and return fire. Thorn felt Wrath arrive. Her energy came in, just behind the line of officers. A cold weight fell into the pit of Thorn's stomach.

Then Wrath's Puppets began to swarm them. A dozen people—unarmed and unprotected civilians—clawed their way through the line of police. Thorn shifted focus. As soon as they were close enough, she began to cut them off from Wrath, but there were too many of them. She couldn't get them all—

Suddenly, a gunshot went off beside her. Nicholas had crawled over and reached into the Martyr car to grab Jeremiah's gun from its holster. He was shooting through the shattered windows of the vehicle. His aim was sloppy, his form awful, but his pale face was set in a determined rage. One of the Puppets went down with a bullet in his leg. Nicholas kept shooting.

And he'd given Thorn an idea.

Jeremiah's body was still laid out in the front of the SUV. Fully armed. Ready to go. Like he always was. While Thorn used her gun and her Influence to fend off more Puppets— while Chris blindly shot her rifle at the oncoming swarm and Nicholas kept firing round after round with reckless urgency—Sparkie dove down from the sky and climbed into the car. The lizard dug around in Jeremiah's pockets.

He emerged seconds later with a grenade.

"Jeremiah, you sweet son of a bitch," Thorn breathed as Sparkie dropped the grenade into her lap. A woman rounded the edge of the SUV—one of Wrath's Puppets. Nicholas raised his gun and shot her in the chest. She collapsed, dead, on top of Eva and Darius. Thorn pulled the pin from the grenade and threw it into the air.

Sparkie dove to catch it and carried it—over the heads of the Puppets desperately sprinting through enemy gunfire—over the line of police in heavy armor—over the Sins—

And he dropped it.

"Grenade!" Gluttony screamed. Thorn felt Wrath's Influence falter. Felt her energy leap out of the way—

An explosion rocked the street.

The Puppets around them collapsed. A handful of their cold energies snapped and disappeared. The gunfire stopped, and instead, it was replaced with rabid, furious screaming. Thorn looked over the hood to see Autumn Hunt desperately crawling toward an unconscious officer. She grabbed his rifle and rolled behind one of the remaining cars. Her legs were bloodied and damaged. Thorn couldn't see Gluttony, but she could feel his energy out there. Somewhere. Laying low.

"*You fucking bitch!*" Wrath screamed. Her voice carried across the space like a haunted echo. Now that the gunfire had stopped, the New York street was eerily quiet. "*I will tear them to pieces, Rose! Every fucking one of them! And you're going to watch!*"

Sparkie circled again and spotted a dark vehicle moving through the crowded streets—past pedestrians hovering around the blockades and rows of confused officers trying to keep the area secure. Thorn hurried to Darius and heaved the Puppet Nicholas had killed off of him. He looked good as new. His skin was mended, his body put back into shape, but he was still unconscious. A nervous flicker made her chest constrict.

"Get him," she said to Nicholas, who just nodded. "Chris, grab Torres. Hurry."

As Chris and Nicholas went to work, Thorn came back to the Martyr SUV. She felt Wrath shifting behind the car, and Thorn pulled Jeremiah's dead body out of the front seat as a blast of bullets slammed into the ground. Chunks of asphalt flew up.

"*Don't fucking move!*"

Wrath's voice was high and wild. Thorn looked to Chris with a frown. Chris shared the same dark expression.

How the fuck were they going to keep Wrath from just shooting the hell out of their backup?

Thorn laid Jeremiah onto the ground and rushed over to Chris. She grabbed the rifle off the other woman's shoulder and propped it up in her hands.

"I'm almost out of rounds," Chris said. "The rest are in the back of the car."

There was no way they were getting to those now.

"I got this," Thorn said. She slowly eased up behind the bumper and looked over at the cruiser where Wrath was hiding. She could see the Sin peeking her head around the hood. "As soon as our backup arrives, I'll just fucking shoot at her. Keep her too busy to shoot back. You two, get Darius and the others into the car—"

"Why don't we just leave Eva and—" Nicholas started to say, but Thorn cut him off.

"Get them into the car," she snarled. Nicholas gawked at her, and she went on. "I won't leave *anyone* behind. As soon as you're all in, I'll follow you. Now *go*."

Because their backup had turned the corner and was coming in behind them. Thorn could feel Liz Wright and Conrad Carter now…

And so could Wrath.

Autumn Hunt moved to come up and start shooting, but Thorn beat her to it. She tapped on the trigger—sending pulsing waves of gunfire into the front of the police cruiser. Every time Hunt shifted, Thorn shot. She felt Carter slam to a stop, and she was vaguely aware of movement behind her as Nicholas and Chris pulled Darius and Eva across the sidewalk and into the back of the SUV. Wrath tried to rise up and shoot again; Thorn quieted her with another round of bullets.

Then Chris came back for Jeremiah—

And Thorn's gun ran out of ammo.

She pulled the trigger; it clicked uselessly in her hands.

Autumn Hunt came up shooting.

Thorn threw her rifle to the side and grabbed Jeremiah under his shoulder. As she hoisted him onto her back, Chris ducked under the car. Thorn pulled her back to her feet.

"Just run!" she screamed.

Run and pray.

As they sprinted the short distance to the new Martyr SUV, Sparkie descended from the sky and attached himself to Wrath's face. The Sin screamed an animalistic, visceral snarl and clawed at him. Her nails raked against Sparkie's wings and sent torrents of pain down Thorn's spine, but she kept running. They got to the car and threw Jeremiah's life-less body into the far back. Chris hopped into the center seat as Thorn jumped through the rear door. Carter took off driving before she'd even shut the hatch.

Sparkie disengaged, avoiding Hunt's long fingers as she tried to grab him, and flew high into the sky. By the time Wrath looked back over the vehicle, the Martyrs were gone.

Thorn ran a hand over her face. Carter drove them ex-pertly through the streets of Manhattan, his expression steely and cold. Chris and Nicholas tended to Darius in the center seat. For some reason, he hadn't woken up. Nicholas kept trying to heal him, but it wasn't working. Thorn's stom-ach twisted uncomfortably.

Then she looked down at Eva and Jeremiah. Empty and lifeless. Their eyes were wide open and dull. Thorn reached out and, with one hand, closed them. Her fingers lingered a little longer on Eva's cheeks. The familiar sense of fury flooded through her chest, but this time, it was paired with something more—a sense of loss she hadn't felt in years.

Not for herself, but because Darius Jones had just lost the last part of his family he had left, and he didn't even know it yet.

CHAPTER TWENTY-FOUR

Thorn strode through the doors to the hospital ward. Raquel was treating the injured TAC operatives halfway down the hall, and Chris glanced up to Thorn. The anger had faded in her expression, instead leaving her looking pale and defeated underneath the harsh, fluorescent lights. Thorn's heart grew heavy, and her jaw tightened.

Anger was better. Somehow. Thorn knew what to do with anger. She wanted to stop—to talk to Chris and guide her through yet *another* loss of someone she had loved dearly—but she didn't have time. There were more pressing matters to attend to.

Like why the hell Darius was still unconscious.

Raquel asked something, and Chris turned back around to answer her. Sparkie shifted restlessly before he vaulted from Thorn's shoulder and glided across the ward. He landed deftly on the sheet beside Chris's hand and butted his head against her knuckles. She didn't look up again as Thorn kept walking, but she did accept Sparkie into her lap gratefully. It would have to do for now.

Thorn came up beside Darius's bed and swiped a wisp of damp, clean hair behind her ear. Her mouth set into a firm frown as she looked the Virtue over. His tawny skin was smooth and flawless—a sharp contrast to the rough, minced state it had been in when Thorn picked him up off the street just hours ago. Now he looked peaceful. Calm. If she wanted to lie to herself, she could have believed he was just sleeping. The muscles on his face were relaxed. His eyelids soft. Lips parted, just slightly. His hair clung to his forehead with dried blood and dirt. Part of Thorn ached to push it away from his face, to grab his head in her hands and scream his name until those bright, optimistic green eyes finally snapped open.

But she knew it was more complicated than that. A nervous bubble made her stomach feel uneasy. She looked up to Elijah. He and Alan stood on the other side of Darius's bed, and they considered her quietly.

"Why the hell hasn't he woken up?" she asked.

Elijah sighed, passing Alan a look that made it clear they had *just* been discussing this very thing before Thorn had come into the room. That pissed her off. If Elijah had let her in the hospital ward when they got there, instead of *insisting* she go and get herself cleaned up first, he wouldn't have to repeat himself now.

The glower on her face must have made that clear because Elijah shook his head and said, "I don't know. All my tests came back normal. There's nothing wrong with him—nothing my machines can see, at least. I can only assume that either Mr. Wolfe didn't completely heal him—"

"He did," Thorn cut in. Her brows furrowed deeper.

"—*or*," Elijah went on with a pointed look in Thorn's direction, "that even a Virtue's healing power can't override the brain's innate need to protect itself. From what I've heard about the crash and Darius's injuries, he sustained some *serious* head trauma. Healed or not, his brain shut down, and it's not ready to come back on again."

"Can you do anything about it?" Thorn asked.

Elijah barked one cold chuckle and crossed his arms. His thick brows pinched together skeptically. "Can I do anyth—what do you think I *am*, Thorn? He's already been treated by the best medical techniques we have at our disposal. I'm just a *doctor*. If a Virtue's healing magic can't wake him up, I sure as hell can't, and I wouldn't anyway. All his tests are normal. I say we let the poor guy rest. He's in for hell when he wakes up…"

Thorn's chest constricted around her heart, and she looked back down at Darius again. That was right… Fuck, maybe he was better off unconscious. She heard Alan breathe a sigh—felt him watching her from across the bed.

"You *are* certain he does not know about Miss Torres?" he asked quietly. The door to the hospital opened, and Alan cast a glance up toward it. Thorn didn't need to look. She knew by his distinct lack of energy it had to be Nicholas. When Alan looked back at her, she nodded her head.

"Yes," Thorn said. As Nicholas came up to the foot of the bed and looked down at Darius, Thorn turned to him with what she hoped was an understanding expression across her face. "Eva died after Darius was thrown from the car."

Nicholas blanched. He was clean now, too. Elijah had issued the same orders to Nicholas he had to Thorn: no sewage-stinking filth in his hospital ward. But while he was freshly washed, he still reeked—of pain, guilt, and failure. The confidence in his eyes had faded. The creases lining his face were deep and anguished.

Thorn recognized this expression—this feeling. Nothing was harder than the first time you fucked up—the first time a decision you made led to losing someone. It had been nine decades since Thorn's first big mistake, and she still remembered everything about the night Donovan's father had died. She hadn't been able to get to both him *and* the baby, so she'd had to make a choice.

After all these years, she'd never been able to forget the look on his face when Wrath sunk a blade into his chest—the sound he made as he drowned in his own blood.

"That's on me," Nicholas said. His voice cracked a little with an emotion Thorn hadn't seen in him before. He shook his head. "I should have healed her first. Thorn was right." Then he looked up at her, and their eyes met. He swallowed hard. "God *damn it*."

Thorn walked around the bed and grabbed Nicholas by the shoulder. "Come on," she murmured, gently leading him away from Darius's bedside. The last thing they fucking needed was him waking up to *this*. Elijah's office was open, and Thorn steered Nicholas toward it.

"You did what you could with what you had," she said. "That's all *any* of us can do. We just… follow our gut and hope we get it right. Sometimes we don't."

"My gut fucked me over," Nicholas said. He pulled his shoulder out of Thorn's grip, just inside Elijah's door. They were alone now. Mostly alone. Alan had followed them, but he stopped outside, standing with his back against the door frame. Nicholas didn't seem to notice. Or care. He groaned and ran his hands through his hair as he went on. "It fucked *Eva* over! She's dead because of me. I'm a Virtue. I'm supposed to just *know* these things. God, I was so fucking *stupid—*"

"Stop it," Thorn cut in. Her sharp voice shattered the mood of the room, and Nicholas froze in place. She took a step toward him, and this time, she grabbed him by both shoulders and held on tight. "Stop punishing yourself for being *human*."

Nicholas's mouth dropped open, then closed again, and he swallowed hard. His face filled with a strange blend of self-contempt and recognition, like he couldn't *believe* she didn't hate him as much as he hated himself, but fuck, he was glad she didn't. For the first time since she'd broken his nose back in that hotel room in Spokane, Thorn felt like she was finally seeing her as more than a corrupted, broken vessel.

"Thorn is right," Alan said. She released Nicholas's shoulders as Alan turned into the room and considered him. His dark, half-empty eyes were compassionate and understanding. "We will accomplish nothing if we sit here assigning blame. You saved Darius's life today, Mr. Wolfe. Don't overlook that."

If Nicholas was touched, he did a good job of hiding it. A deep frown settled onto his face. Then an approaching energy made them all pause. Elijah popped his head into the room and cleared his throat.

"I hate to interrupt," he said. "But I have injured Martyrs on my hands, and with my *usual* healer out of commission, I was wondering if you would care to help?"

The doctor raised his eyebrows at Nicholas as he gestured back into the ward, where Chris and the other Tactical Unit members were waiting for medical attention. Nicholas glanced over to them and nodded.

"Oh. Yeah. Of course."

As he and Elijah began to head away, Thorn called them back. "Harris," she said, and the doctor turned. "Let me know the *second* Jones wakes up. I want to be the one to tell him about Eva."

Elijah nodded, and a visible relief flooded over his face. "Gladly," he said through a heavy sigh. "God knows I've given him enough bad news this week."

He headed off again, and Thorn made to leave the hospital ward. Sparkie unfurled himself from Chris's lap, leapt to his feet, and vaulted across the room. With a single flap of his massive, leathery wings, he landed on Thorn's shoulder. Before she got through the doors, Alan was beside her.

"You took a big risk today," he said as they walked into the waiting room. Thorn frowned and looked over her shoulder. He was watching her with a tempered, paternal admonishment. Thorn stopped dead and spun on her heels to face him. He crossed his arms and glared down his long, prominent nose, his black eyes a mirror of her own. "This could have ended *much* differently. You are lucky you are alive."

Thorn scoffed and propped her hands on her hips. "*I* took a big risk? You were in on the plan!"

"I thought it was too dangerous from the start," Alan

hissed, and he swept a long arm in an arc beside him to accent the point. "To assume the Sins would abandon the orphanage was foolish and unbecoming."

"I didn't assume they'd abandoned the orphanage," Thorn shot back. She was yelling now, and she felt her voice drawing attention. The cold energies in the hospital beyond them paused, hedging a little closer to the door. Thorn tried to temper her volume, but it was hard. Sparkie's wings opened up and quavered. He glared back at Alan with beady, little eyes as Thorn kept on yelling.

"We have units patrolling the area every single week. Holly has installed cameras and targeted satellite images in the neighborhood. I went down and *walked the streets* looking for anyone Programmed to recognize me. We did everything right, but none of it fucking mattered, and you think now's the time to say, 'I told you so?' You think I don't *know* what we lost here? Jeremiah and Eva are *dead*."

Alan was quiet. His jaw was set tight—his mouth a thin line behind his black goatee. His hands gripped his biceps so tightly Thorn could see the outline of his bones against his knuckles. For a moment, she was reminded just how alike she and her uncle could be. Sometimes it was easy to forget, if not for his long life and the *Peccostium* seared onto the back of his neck, that he'd been possessed by Wrath once, too.

And then they shared moments like this.

But unlike Thorn, Alan was able to find his balance much more quickly. He stared at her for a few seconds longer, and then his facade fractured. His shoulders sloped back toward the ground, his teeth unclenched, and the fire in his irises faded. Thorn was left staring back into those void-like eyes, and she saw a glimpse of panic there.

"We could have lost so much more," Alan said, more evenly. More honestly. "You must be more careful. The Sins have become scared and desperate. You cannot rely on luck and a fragile armor that Wrath wants you alive. She may change her mind, or the other Sins may work against her. I cannot stand the thought of losing you."

Then Alan put his hands on her shoulders. They were warm against her bare skin. She took a deep breath to soothe the beast clawing in her chest, but it had little effect. Her fingers ached for a cigarette to hold—or a face to punch.

But instead, she reached up and placed her palm over the back of one of Alan's hands. She focused on relaxing the muscles in her face and tried to give him a sympathetic smile, but she knew it came off forced. It would have to be good enough.

"Don't worry about me," she said, but she knew he would. He *always* would. She was the last person he had—the only person who could stand by his side forever. Thorn knew the feeling. When you watched everyone else you knew pass away, either violently and painfully or with the creeping, slow death of age, you grew most attached to those who didn't leave you.

For Thorn and Alan, that meant each other... and only each other.

"Then don't *make* me worry," Alan said. Thorn forced another half-smile.

Because they both knew she couldn't promise that.

Ink flowed from the tip of Thorn's pen and onto the page in smooth, tight script—a long-abandoned writing style she just couldn't seem to give up. The same way she couldn't abandon good, old-fashioned pen and paper for the convenience of typing. There was something almost cathartic about writing her reports by hand. Meditative. It forced her to stop. Slow down. Really focus on what had happened and digest every single detail.

Every *gruesome* detail.

She paused, her hand hovering over the notebook, the pen tip a centimeter or so above the next line. This was always her least favorite part about these reports. The inevitable moment when things went from bad to worse, or from worse to worse still. She hated reliving the chaos. The trauma. The deaths. Sparkie curled himself around her throat and held tightly to her. She took a deep breath, rolled her shoulders, and continued.

I disabled the two officers in the cruiser, Thorn wrote. Her left hand glided across the paper, her fingerless glove providing a barrier against smudges as she worked. *I rendered them unconscious with quick blows to the head. I didn't want to use my Influence and draw Wrath to our exact location, and I had to make sure they could not call for backup. I stole their cruiser, and I followed after the Martyr vehicle. I was hoping to run interference and allow Montgomery to escape. That did not happen. The officers must have been Programmed, and they were shooting into the SUV. Montgomery, Jones, and Torres were hit in the attack. Montgomery was shot at the base of his skull and died instantly. Jones was shot in the side and Torres in the chest. With Montgomery dead, the vehicle lost control and crashed into a light pole on the corner of Broome and Allen Street. Jones was thrown from the vehicle on impact. He went through the windshield and rolled into the middle of Broome. When I came onto the scene, he was laying in the street. I thought—*

Thorn paused again, closed her eyes, and Sparkie let out a low, sharp hum. She was struck again with that unfamiliar feeling—remembering the dread, the sinking and overwhelming sense of *not knowing*. She didn't like it. It made her heart feel tight. Her breathing, shallow. For the greater part of one hundred and twenty years, Thorn had always been able to rely on her Sin senses to know whether or not the people around her were dead or alive. She had never realized how much she took it for granted until she didn't have it anymore.

Seeing Darius laying there, wondering if he was okay, had been one of the most agonizing moments Thorn had experienced in a long, long time.

She put her pen back to the page.

I thought he was dead.

A rapping at her office door made Thorn jump. She swore under her breath. This was another thing she hadn't noticed she took for granted—not being caught off guard. Before Darius came to the Underground, Alan was the only person who could surprise her. Everyone else was betrayed by their cool, human energy.

Now, she felt surrounded by the lack thereof.

The rapping came again. Thorn sighed, closed her notebook, and got to her feet.

And though she couldn't sense him, Thorn knew who it was. Darius was unconscious, and Alan didn't *rap* on doors with quick and impatient taps. He *knocked*. Properly. Three loud, slow, and almost rhythmic beats.

So when Thorn opened it to see Nicholas standing there, with his laptop under his arm, she wasn't surprised.

"Oh good, you're here," he said before Thorn had a chance to speak. He took a deep breath. "I need to ask you for a favor. A *big* favor."

That did surprise Thorn. She raised a single eyebrow and stepped to the side, sweeping one arm into her office. Nicholas stepped over the threshold, and she shut the door behind him.

"What kind of favor?" Thorn asked.

Nicholas's bright eyes were hard. "I'm going to destroy Sloth," he said plainly. "And I want you to come with me."

Sparkie perked up on Thorn's shoulder; she just stared at Nicholas. The implications of what he was saying rolled around in her head. She crossed her arms and frowned.

"What the fuck are you talking about? You'd have to know where he is."

And the look—the gleaming, proud look—returned to Nicholas's face, and Thorn felt her jaw fall open.

"You *found* him?"

Nicholas nodded.

"*How*? Holly hasn't given us any updates—"

"She wouldn't be able to," Nicholas said. "I didn't find him using her system."

He let that sit in the air between them for a moment. At last, Thorn threw her hands out and said, "Well?"

"I looked at his behavior," Nicholas said. He headed to Thorn's desk, pushed aside the notebook she had been writing in, and set his computer down. Thorn followed behind him. "Holly's system works on facial recognition, which is basically what the Sins' Programming does. If he's smart, he'll be hiding his face. I bet he's wearing some kind of mask when he's out in public, and I'm pretty sure the only reason we got footage of him last time was because he was inside. He took off his protection, whatever it was."

"Right," Thorn pressed.

"If that's true, Holly's system won't work. Neither will the Sins'. So, I started looking at what we know about Sloth." Nicholas turned to Thorn and raised a hand, counting the items off on his fingers as he listed them. "We know he works with street vices—prostitution, drugs, human trafficking, that sort of thing. We know he doesn't have a real home and he moves around a lot, and we know, right now, he's on the run from the Sins *and* the Martyrs, and to keep himself safe, he's attaching his bombs to people who will then *blow themselves up* when they see someone dangerous.

"That last one was actually my biggest clue," Nicholas said, and he turned back to his computer, hit a few keys, and navigated through his research. Sparkie peered down at the Virtue, tilting his head, as he kept talking. "Programming isn't the same as Puppetting. He's not completely in control of them at all times, so he *has* to attach bombs to people who aren't going to fucking freak out about it. That's why he used druggies. These people are high as fuck anyway. He probably keeps them high."

"You think he's in another drug den?" Thorn asked.

But Nicholas turned to her with a bright, self-indulgent glint in his eyes. "*No.* He got caught last time. Holly added all the local drug dens she could find to our files, so we've been keeping an eye on them. He hasn't shown up. He probably knows that's where we'll look for him."

"Damnit, Wolfe, get to the fucking point," Thorn snapped. "*Where is he?*"

"The *point*," Nicholas said, and his jaw tightened. The exasperation in his voice was evident, but he took a deep breath and went on. "Is that I've narrowed down a few places Sloth could be hiding out—where the Martyrs and Sins wouldn't think of looking for him, and he'd have enough addicts around to carry his bombs. I've been looking into this for months, and I planned to go to each of them… I was rereading the list today and, I can't explain why… but now I'm pretty fucking sure he's *here*."

Nicholas opened a map on his screen, navigated to Lower Manhattan, and pointed to where the Manhattan Bridge crossed through Chinatown.

"Why here?" Thorn asked with a frown.

"It's a big homeless encampment," Nicholas said. He zoomed closer on a narrow street that followed the bridge above it, right beside an old playground. "It goes underneath the overpass and stretches for about half a mile. Over a hundred people live there, and I'd bet plenty of them are drugged up enough not to notice they're carrying a bomb around. I'm telling you, he's here."

Thorn stared at the map. It was less than two miles south of Alphabet City—too close for comfort. She shook her head.

"This area will still be swarming with Sin activity," she said. "And TAC is scrambling after—"

"No," Nicholas said sharply, and Thorn looked up to him. The pride had faded from his face. Now it was set in grim resolution. "Just us. He knows to look out for an armed force. He'll be expecting it."

"That's reckless," Thorn argued, and her mind went back to Alan. "We can go undercover, bring a team in street clothes—"

"I can't bring anyone else," Nicholas cut in, and his jaw tightened. "I *won't*. I already let one person die. I can't take the chance someone else will, too."

Thorn looked him over and took a slow, calculated breath. An Initiated Virtue's instincts were well documented. Thorn had no reason to doubt them.

But she *did* have reasons to doubt Nicholas.

She crossed her arms.

"Why do you want my help?" she asked. "You said you were planning on doing this alone."

A dark flash crossed Nicholas's face again—a flash that reminded Thorn vividly of the way he'd looked down at Darius in the hospital ward. A potent blend of failure and shame. "If today taught me anything, it's that I *can't* do it alone," he said. "Sloth needs to go. One way or another. If I fuck it up again, I need to know that son of a bitch is dead. You're the *only* person I can count on to make sure that happens."

Thorn considered him for a moment. Then she turned and looked at the far wall of her office. Maps stretched across it, covering the beige paint in brighter, wilder colors. Thumbtacks and bright red thread set out the boundaries of the Sins' standard territories. She looked at one of them in particular. Gregory Witham. She took him in. His dilated, blue eyes. His greasy hair. His waxy skin and chapped lips.

The rage in her chest roared to life. Alight and eager for another chance to wring the mother fucker's throat. If Nicholas was right—if Gregory Witham *was* at that encampment—they stood a good chance of catching him off guard.

"Okay," she said. "But this time, we do things right."

CHAPTER TWENTY-FIVE

Dusk sat on the horizon. Hours ago, massive skyscrapers and buildings blocked out the sun, casting the streets in long, gray shadows. Thorn walked along the pedestrian path underneath Manhattan Bridge, an old pair of sneakers crunching on the gravel while the first hint of a fall breeze swept through her baggy sweatshirt. She glanced around the neighborhood with a frown. Sparkie circled high above, and Thorn could see the beginning of the homeless encampment in the distance. Ramshackle huts of plywood and PVC pipe leaned up against old chain link fences. They stretched for several blocks beneath the bridge. The pedestrian path passed right through it—but the pedestrians didn't. Thorn watched as other citizens—people who *didn't* live in the encampment and liked to pretend this kind of problem didn't exist in New York City—turned from the footpath and crossed the street instead.

Too many people functioned this way, working under the convenient mindset that if they ignored a problem long enough, it would just go away. From Thorn's experience, it never fucking worked. She stopped walking, and Nicholas came up beside her.

"There it is," he said as they watched the tent city in the

419

distance. He was more put together now than he had been before their first attempt to come for Sloth—and more comfortable. She worried their clothing lulled him into a false sense of security. Full body armor had a way of forcing you to think in terms of combat, but now, she and Nicholas had dressed down. Thorn looked over his outfit—loose jeans and a hoodie, much like hers. If Sloth were in there, this would hardly keep them safe. She'd managed to convince Nicholas they *at least* needed to wear kevlar vests under their sweatshirts, and she'd brought along her pocket-knife and a handgun strapped into a holster at the small of her back. It didn't feel like enough.

Not when they were hunting a Sin.

"Can you sense him?" Nicholas asked. He didn't look at her. His attention centered on the encampment. Thorn focused on it, too. It was a bluster of cool energy—moving pieces pushing against and blending into one another in a way that made it hard to differentiate one being from another. She took a deep breath and shook her head.

"No," she said.

"Doesn't mean he's not here," Nicholas responded almost defensively. He cast Thorn a hot look before jamming his hand into his hoodie's front pocket and pulling out a light blue scarf. "Mask up."

He wrapped his scarf around the lower part of his face, covering his nose and mouth, before lifting his hood over his head. Thorn did the same. This had been Nicholas's idea. If Sloth hid his face to avoid Programming, there was no reason to think they couldn't do the same.

Thorn had to admit, it was smart. It felt strange—her hot breath got caught up in the deep red fabric—and she knew it would be more challenging to fight if she had to, but the temporary inconvenience of covering most of her face was well worth it if it meant she didn't get herself blown to pieces again.

"You clear on the plan?" Thorn asked as she started walking. Her voice was muffled, and she turned to look at

Nicholas. She couldn't make out his expression. "We're in and out, as quickly as possible. Pay attention to anyone who's acting high and *avoid* them. If Witham is here, his Indirect Influence will probably make these people more agitated than normal. If we don't find him in an hour, we're out."

Because an hour was all they had. Thorn set up an automatic alert on her phone, which she'd left behind in the car a couple of blocks away. If she didn't make it back to her vehicle in time to shut it off, the alert would send out an emergency signal to all the Martyr leadership, explaining exactly where Thorn was and what she was trying to do.

Alan had asked her not to make him worry… so she wouldn't. Not unless she had to.

"We'll find him," Nicholas said confidently. They walked into the bustling encampment, and Thorn wished she shared his certainty.

They were quickly submerged in human energy. People crammed into every available space in the long, narrow tent city wedged underneath Manhattan Bridge. As far as Thorn could see, there were more people, more make-shift structures, and just more *shit*. The whole place reeked—of refuse, of sweat, and of human waste. The unsheltered who took up residence here, people who had *nothing*, had gathered whatever belongings they could and crammed them into shopping carts. Strollers. Trashcans with rolling wheels. Old camping tents, poked full of holes and covered with dusty tarps, functioned as homes. Some people didn't even have that. Thorn saw families, mothers with young children, huddled underneath cardboard boxes. She took a deep breath and shook her head.

Human beings were not meant to live like this.

But Thorn didn't have the time to focus on that—or the emotional energy. She pushed forward, holding one hand against her scarf to make sure it remained securely in place, and she tried to pay close attention to the individual human energies around her. It was tedious work. The further away people were from Thorn, the more their energies blurred together. Separating one from another was a challenge in close quarters like this, but it was also critical in identifying Gregory Witham.

If he was even here.

They were soon struck with another problem. As they quietly pushed their way through the makeshift houses, they drew attention. Thorn was acutely aware of the whispers following them—and the people attached to those whispers—as they trekked down the path.

Despite their attempts to "dress down," Thorn and Nicholas still stuck out here. They were too clean. Too fresh. Too *unfamiliar*. As much as the outside world tried to pretend like this were lawless and disconnected, these people were a community, and communities stuck together. They knew their own, and they looked out for them.

Damnit, Thorn wished Eva was still around. She could have blended in here seamlessly.

As Thorn moved further down the path, a sudden movement of energy to the side caught her attention. Someone reached out for her, muttering incoherently as they grabbed at the hem of her sweatshirt. She deftly twisted away, and the frail, jittery man stumbled forward. He lost his footing, tripped over his oversized clothes, and fell onto the pavement. Nicholas bent down to help him up.

But before he could, someone else shoved him away. An older man hoisted the jittery guy up off the ground and shot Nicholas a nasty look. "Pick on someone else, huh?" he growled. Then he reached out and pushed Nicholas again.

Nicholas's scarf slipped down.

"What's your problem?" he said, "I was trying to—"

But he stopped dead as the jittery man's eyes glazed over. He looked at Nicholas and reached into his pocket…

Thorn moved quickly. She forced the other man to the side as she grabbed for the Sentry's wrist and pulled it away from his jacket. A cheap burner phone sat in his palm. He cried out as Thorn knocked it away and went for his other hand. Suddenly, a swarm of angry people was upon her. They filled in the space between her and the Sentry—pushing her back, screaming and spitting at her face as they pulled the addict away to protect *him* from *her*. Thorn's heart skipped a beat as he reached into his pocket a second time. She went to grab her gun—

Nicholas lunged through the crowd. He elbowed his way past people and leapt for the Sentry, managing to wrap his fingers around the man's hand as they fell to the ground. A flare of rage built up in Thorn's stomach, and she ripped through the mass, shoving men and women aside so aggressively that they toppled over one another like dominos. They thinned out just in time for Thorn to see the Sentry's eyes blink, and he uttered a simple word:

"Clear."

He opened his hand, palm up, and gave Nicholas the detonator.

"Thank fucking god," Nicholas muttered as he grabbed the device, ripped it open, and tore the battery out.

Thorn stared at him.

"What the fuck—"

She didn't have the chance to finish her question. The throng of transients swarmed again, screaming at her—and at Nicholas.

"Thieves!" a woman yelled, snatching the broken detonator from Nicholas's hands. "They're thieves!"

The crowd started screaming at them—accusing them of theft, of violence, of worse things in a chorus of fevered, angry voices. They pushed in around Thorn and Nicholas again, and their hands grappled with them. Tore at their clothing and their faces. Their closeness was suffocating—almost blinding. Thorn's senses drowned in a sea of hot bodies and cold energy. It made it impossible for her to make sense of where she was—and where she needed to go. As a set of fingers raked against her cheek and threatened to tear her scarf from her face, she turned and jammed the heel of her hand into a young man's mouth. He stumbled backward, blood dripping over his lips, and he spat out a tooth. The crowd roared.

"Get *out!*" they cried, disjointed and stuttered. "*Get out!*"

"We need to go," Thorn said as she grabbed Nicholas under the arm and tried to pull him back the way they'd come, but he ripped out of her hands.

"We can't," Nicholas yelled over the noise, wrapping his scarf around his face again. "He's here! We *know* he's here! This could be our only chance!"

A sinking dread dropped into Thorn's gut. He was right. She knew he was right. Thorn roared and cinched her scarf tighter around her head. "Fuck—FUCK. Okay. Let's move." Then she turned back, headed deeper into the encampment, and fought her way through the mess. They were surrounded, angry chants and jeers and swears calling after them as they pushed into the tent city. The further in they got, the angrier and larger the crowd became. The people who lived here were suddenly full of a violent, unrelenting energy—like hornets defending their nest.

And they viewed Thorn and Nicholas as a threat. She couldn't fucking blame them.

The two of them kept pushing through. Thorn fought off the urge to Influence the crowd away, and she relied on her brute strength alone to keep them back. She shoved. Punched. Threw people out and into the oncoming hordes. Soon, they learned to keep their distance, standing at the edges instead—throwing bricks and debris and spoiled food onto Thorn and Nicholas from every angle. With the crowd further back, Thorn could see a little more clearly to find openings in the path.

Nicholas pressed ahead of her. He dove right into the crowd and reached out to touch anyone he could. He grabbed people by the hands, the throats, whatever skin-to-skin contact he could manage. He got punched. Spat on. Screamed at. At one point, a woman wielding a massive slab of plywood took a swing at him and caught him in the side of the head. A cut opened up in his eyebrow and dribbled blood onto his scarf.

Thorn came up to stop him—to force him to get behind her where she could protect him—but then he reached out for another man, and the man's eyes glazed over. He said, "Clear," and handed Nicholas a tiny, cylindrical item.

Another detonator.

Nicholas opened it, tore out the battery, and threw it into the crowd. Then he kept moving. Kept touching. Thorn gawked after him. Her dark eyes went wide as it all clicked into place.

That mother fucking Virtue had learned how to *Deprogram* the Sentries.

She rushed up to Nicholas's side again and helped him push through the crowd. "Hurry," she screamed over the roar of protest as she ducked to avoid more thrown debris. "We don't have much time!"

She worked to clear a path in front of him now—to get the people he'd already tested out of the way so he could latch onto more. As more items flew their way, Thorn moved in to take the brunt of the attack while Nicholas continued his work—his *critical* work.

But hurrying was difficult. Sparkie swooped overhead, coming in closer as the light grew dimmer and the crowd became more distracted. They were too busy berating Thorn and Nicholas to notice the tiny shadow in the sky. His vantage helped Thorn navigate the mass and find less obstructed routes with fewer people.

So they kept *pushing*—Nicholas trying to Deprogram anyone who came too close, and Thorn feeling out, desperately, to catch a sense of Sloth in this buzzing hive of human coldness. It was hard. Impossible. Energy blurred together so tightly in this packed space Thorn could hardly make one out from another. As Nicholas worked his fucking Virtue magic on another Sentry—disabled *another* detonator—Thorn called to him from over the noise.

"It's no use," she said. "I can't feel him anywhere—"

But then she froze, her breath caught in her throat, as

Sparkie spotted a hunched, hooded figure moving through the crowd—past where Thorn and Nicholas were—toward the exit.

Gregory fucking Witham.

He was rushing down the narrow alley between the shacks and tents, away from the loud, boisterous crowd. They had probably spooked him—the uprising of energy making him nervous enough to look for a new hiding spot but not *so* nervous that he had to blow the place up and risk hurting himself.

An onslaught of violent, desperate emotion roared to life in Thorn's chest, like a monster awoke in the pit of her gut and started clawing its way toward the surface, ripping her to shreds as it looked for an escape. She grabbed Nicholas and dragged him toward where Sloth was slinking off.

The Sin cut through the encampment like a serpent, his long, lanky figure moving with all the grace of a blind rodent. Sparkie glided above him, watching as he wrung his hands and threw a nervous look over his shoulder. Every so often, a flat tongue darted out to wet his chapped lips. When he searched the crowd, Thorn knew he couldn't spot her. Knew he couldn't feel her.

Knew he had no idea how close she was to wrapping her hands around his throat again.

Thorn and Nicholas sprinted along the far fence and off the main path. They leapt over debris and sleeping bodies—through makeshift houses and toilets. Thorn was swift and graceful, and Nicholas struggled to keep up. She could hear him stumbling behind her—knocking things over—but she didn't slow down. The chants and jeers still followed them, but less violently now. Less intense. There was a sense of angry relief in the air as the *intruders* started heading back to the exit—back where they belonged.

Thorn tore through a small shelter and ducked down behind another. She could feel Witham now—could see him out of the corner of her eye as he neared the edge of the settlement. Nicholas had been right; he was covering his face. It was hidden behind a thick pair of tinted ski goggles and a huge beanie, which he had pulled down over his ears. His oversized coat hung loose on him like a second skin. He could be hiding anything underneath it. The uncertainty made the anger in Thorn's gut swell.

He looked ridiculous, demented, and every bit as dangerous as she knew him to be. She couldn't let him get away. Not again. He shuffled toward the exit—he was less than twenty feet from it now.

Thorn veered to the left, vaulted over a pile of pallets, and tackled Witham from behind.

The two of them rolled onto the filthy pavement and slammed into the chain-link fence edged up along the Hudson. She wrapped her arm around his neck, reaching for the base of his skull as he flung himself in a desperate, backward circle. Thorn slipped, her grip moving up to his face, and suddenly his teeth sank in deep around her wrist. She screamed as pain shot from her *Peccostium* and into her muscles, weakening her hold. He shrugged her off, spun, and plunged a knife into her thigh. Thorn roared and threw an uppercut into his jaw, stunning him for a moment.

Then his eyes met hers, and he was caught so off guard that he just stared, slack-jawed. Thorn pried the blade from her leg as he dipped his hand into his pocket. Drew out a detonator—

Before he had the chance to strike it, Thorn kicked him. Her heel collided with his fingertips, and the device flew backward. Witham turned to run, but Thorn was too quick for him. She leapt onto him again, this time catching him by the throat, and the two of them crashed onto the asphalt together. In a swift, seamless motion, Thorn wrapped her fingers around the back of Witham's neck. He screamed obscenities into the dusk as her nails raked against his *Peccostium* and dug into it—deeply, *vengefully*. Thorn forced him around and knelt against his sternum as she tore the mask from his face. His bright blue eyes frantically looked her over, wild with a primal, hateful fear.

Thorn wanted to see that fear as he died—wanted to *watch* the life fade from his eyes—as she tightened her hand around his windpipe. His face started to go red. He gasped for a breath he couldn't take. Thorn toyed with the knife in her other hand.

But she paused, relaxed a little, and took a deep breath. The minute her grip loosened, Witham started to scream.

"Fuck—*fuck*!" he hissed, his voice full of pain. He weakly tried to reach into his pockets, but Thorn slapped his fingers away with the hilt of the blade. "You *bitch*! He's *here*, isn't he? Your fucking *Virtue*! I can tell. I can tell he's here! He's doing it again—you *fucking bitch, let me out!*"

Thorn ignored him as she dug her nails deeper into the mark of the Sins at the base of his neck. The crowd had caught up to them—screaming at her. Thorn took a chance and forced her Influence out to make her and Sloth look like nothing more than two beggars fighting over a scrap of fresh food. The crowd averted their gaze. Shamed. Almost embarrassed. All except one in the distance, pushing its way toward Thorn and the others with a mechanical urgency. Sloth's Puppet. He managed to hold onto one.

Thorn's heart leapt into her throat. It didn't matter that Wrath was too injured to come for them now—not if that Puppet reached them and hit the fucking detonator.

With one hand still pressed firmly against Witham's *Peccostium*, Thorn dropped the blade and started searching his pockets. She pulled out cash, a plastic baggy full of indistinct white pills, loose bullets, a mint tin full of weed, a half-eaten sandwich wrapped up in gas station towels, and a loaded handgun. Witham continued to rage as she set the safety and tucked it into the waistband of her leggings.

"—*get the fuck off of me! You cunt! You piece of shit, angry bitch! You little—No. NO! Get him the fuck away from me!*"

Nicholas rushed up to Thorn's side. His breathing was harsh, his mask loose around his chin, and he stared down at Sloth. Thorn glanced up to him. A bitter resentment rose into her chest, boiling through the tightening muscles in her throat, but she swallowed it down.

"Are you ready?"

Nicholas didn't say anything right away. He just watched the Sin with a bemused, almost pitying expression. He took a deep breath and looked down at his hand. Then he looked to Thorn.

"I need to touch his *Peccostium*," Nicholas said.

Thorn frowned. "*What?*"

"I don't know what to tell you," Nicholas said. He was almost yelling to be heard over the constant stream of threats and curses coming from Witham's mouth. "I just... I'm doing what Diligence wants, and it's telling me... it's telling me that it's time to join with him—to get *into* Sloth. That's what the *Peccostium* is, right? A way in?"

Thorn shook her head. "I don't fucking know," she snapped, and she turned to look down at the twisting, writhing monster in her hands. She was afraid to let go of the mark—afraid he'd slip out of Nicholas's hands and escape *again*.

But she didn't have much of a choice. Sloth's Puppet was getting closer. She faced Nicholas and took a deep breath.

"All right, come here!"

She moved around Sloth's head without losing her grip against the *Peccostium* on his neck. It was hard. His filthy, greasy skin was slick under her nails. Nicholas wedged himself between them and slid his fingers underneath Thorn's. For a moment, they held onto the Sin together. Nicholas glanced over his shoulder, and he passed her a soft smile.

"*GET OFF. STOP TOUCHING ME, YOU FILTHY MOTHER FUCKER.*"

"Tell Darius I'm sorry," Nicholas said.

Thorn's mouth set, and her brows furrowed. She felt Nicholas's fingers underneath her own, warm and strong. She tightened her grip around them once before she nodded and pulled her hand away.

As soon as she released the Sin, he tried to break free.

He twisted again, but Nicholas grabbed him with his other hand and held on tight. Witham's mouth opened, and he screamed.

"I'LL FUCKING KILL YO—"

But his words morphed into an animalistic howl. A wild wind rushed through the encampment and swirled around Nicholas and Sloth. It pulled debris and trash into the air, twisted Thorn's face covering around her throat, and tore her hair from the hood over her head. Sparkie tumbled through the gale. His tiny body lurched from side to side, disorienting both him and Thorn, until he managed to twist around and slam into her shoulder. He crawled inside her sweatshirt, and Thorn fought to see through the chaos.

Bright light radiated from Nicholas's hands and illuminated him from underneath. The gust ripped off his scarf and sent it flying into the sky. In the dusky light, Thorn could see nothing but the wide, awestruck look on Nicholas's face as he stared down at Gregory Witham.

And Witham *shrieked.* Just one word. Repeated over and over again.

"No!" His voice was desperate. Broken. Inhuman. *"No, no, NO!"*

The word became thick and garbled as heavy smoke poured from his gaping mouth. He gagged on it, choked it out, as it overwhelmed him. It collected around his prone body as his skin began to glow a low, deep orange. Thorn could see the outlines of blood vessels and bone through Witham's flesh as he burned from the inside out.

Then he let out a final, manic scream—a scream so loud, so piercing, Thorn had to cover her ears and close her eyes—as his body dissolved and his energy disappeared. All at once, the wind stopped. Paper and garbage fluttered down around Thorn's head like falling snow.

Nicholas Wolfe collapsed. Motionless and empty.

And the world was silent.

Thorn stood at the entrance to the encampment. In the commotion, her Influence had faltered. People filtered back, peeking their heads out from behind toppled tents and destroyed lean-tos. They hovered around her but kept a distance—a boundary between Thorn and the rest of the world.

A boundary within which there was no human energy.

She took a deep breath—she hadn't noticed she'd been holding it in for so long—and a careful step forward. The smoke had been whisked away, but the ashes which had once been Gregory Witham lay in an almost-human shape on the concrete beneath her feet. Part of Thorn was exhilarated, but it was bittersweet and tainted.

Nicholas's body curled up on the ground, his back to her. Gray, dusty, and still. Thorn reached his side, knelt by his hip, and moved to turn him over so she could more easily lift him.

As soon as she touched his shoulder, Nicholas shot up and gasped.

"Fuck!"

Thorn's heart leapt into her throat, and a jolt of shock shot down her spine. Sparkie became agitated. He twisted and turned inside Thorn's sweatshirt, against her skin, as she stared at Nicholas's face. It was filthy, coated in ash and dirt and blood, but there was no doubt about it.

Nicholas was *alive*.

But something was wrong. Something was *missing*…

"I—I can't breathe," Nicholas choked out. His brows were high on his head, his eyes wide and panicked as he took short, rapid breaths. He tore his sweatshirt open—ripped the zipper apart—and his fingers fumbled with the straps of his bulletproof vest. "Thorn, *I can't breathe. My heart. There's something wrong with my heart.*"

Thorn just stared at him, watching in shocked silence as he clawed at the space right between his lungs—the exact spot where Thorn and others like her felt a deep, aching emptiness.

And suddenly, she felt like she had been dunked in cold water. Wild water. Over her head, in her lungs, filling her up in a way that her soul didn't anymore.

Just like it had the night she had escaped Wrath.

"Oh, *no*..."

Nicholas's eyes searched her face—darted from her eyes to her mouth to her eyes again. "What? A-am I dying? Is my heart giving out?"

Thorn shook her head and sat down beside Nicholas. His hands quaked as they continued to desperately grope at the empty spot in his chest—the spot where his Virtue had once lived.

It didn't anymore.

Thorn took a deep breath and grabbed Nicholas by either side of his face. She held him firmly and forced him to look into her eyes. His irises were pin-tight, full of an animalistic terror Thorn knew all too well.

"There's nothing wrong with your heart," she whispered. "There's something wrong with your *soul*."

"My-my soul?" Nicholas stammered.

Thorn nodded slowly, and a look of dawning realization warped Nicholas's expression. He stared at her with a mounting sense of loss and pain and fear.

Until the numbness set in.

Thorn didn't wait for him to recover. She helped him to his feet and draped his arm over her shoulder. Then she headed back toward the car, toward the Underground, with the shell of a Virtue holding onto her like a lost child.

CHAPTER TWENTY-SIX

Darius wished he'd never woken up.

It had been five days since the crash, and he couldn't escape it. It replayed over and over in his head, every waking hour. He saw it when he closed his eyes at night and in the slow moments during the day when he paused enough to breathe deep and sigh. It came at him in vivid, brutal flashes that made his legs feel weak and his heart hurt.

Deafening gunshots.

Red blossoms opening up in the pale green fabric of Eva's shirt.

Jeremiah's energy blinking out, like someone had reached inside him and cut a wire.

But mostly, he remembered Thorn.

He remembered opening his eyes to see her sitting by his bedside. He remembered the look—the relieved and *grateful* look—on her slender face when she saw he was awake. And he remembered how that look fell apart when he asked her one simple question:

"Where is Eva?"

Darius knew the answer before she said anything. It was written out in her dark, empty eyes and the soft, repentant frown tugging at the corners of her lips. She reached out, took his hand up in hers, and squeezed his fingers tight.

"Eva didn't make it."

That was it. Those four words fell around him, on top of him, like debris from a broken building. They knocked the wind from his lungs, concussed and confused him, to the point where all he did—all he could *think* to do—was stare at her. Through her. At the world out and beyond her. A world without Eva.

And he still hadn't snapped out of it. He felt buried. Suffocated. Floating and detached, like he was living in a nightmare, and he just *couldn't* wake up.

He didn't want to.

Darius stepped into the courtyard from the hallway that led to his room in the western wing of the Underground. He'd been drawn out here for... something. He wasn't sure what. Maybe he was hungry, or maybe he craved company after spending so many days alone. Whatever it was, it wasn't enough to keep him moving forward. He paused in the entrance and stared across the vast, cavernous room.

The dining area outside the kitchens bustled with Martyrs. Their voices carried over to him, echoing off the concrete walls and tiled floors, bouncing back and forth in a jubilant dance that only added to the tenor of the conversation. This was the most packed the courtyard had ever been. A hundred people sat together, talking and joking and laughing while they enjoyed personal pizzas and calzones. Kenia happily refilled toppings at the ingredient station on one end of the counter while Abraham walked through the tables, handing off fresh-cooked pies to members of the Gray Unit, the Tactical Unit, even the tech team. Holly sat with Raquel and Skylar, talking through a mouthful of food while she covered her lips with the back of her hand. A few tables away, Alan shared a table with Lina. He stood out— a tall and dark contrast to the men and women who worked for him—but even he had a soft smile on his lips.

Darius stood by the hallway, his throat tight and almost *angry*, or maybe just *sad*—the line between the two was blurring so much that Darius had a hard time telling them apart anymore. He felt so broken, so isolated, that he couldn't imagine how anyone here felt any differently. They had all lost someone, too. Jeremiah Montgomery had been in the ground for less than three days. How could the Martyrs be this... *happy?*

But he knew. In his gut, his heart, his *soul*, he knew.

Because Gregory Witham was dead, and Nicholas Wolfe was not.

The news of the Sin's defeat and Nicholas's survival hardly had the weight to really sink in for Darius. While the Martyrs were inspired by the destruction of yet *another* Sin— something which had once seemed impossible but had now happened twice in less than twelve months—Darius just couldn't find it in himself to commemorate it. And somehow? *Somehow* Nicholas's survival didn't make him feel better. In a strange, haunting way, it made Darius feel *worse.*

He'd been so convinced this was his purpose—so *sure* he would die taking down Envy or die trying—that he'd gotten comfortable with the idea of it. He stopped looking too far toward the future because he didn't think he had one.

But now he did. A future *without* Eva.

A surge of emotion bubbled up Darius's throat, and a wave of tears filled his eyes. He grabbed the nearby wall, looked up, and blinked them away. Why the hell had he even bothered coming out here? He wasn't ready for this...

"Hey." A voice behind him caught Darius off guard. He startled a little and turned to see Nicholas standing in the hallway. Empty. Painfully so. This was the first time Darius had seen him since he'd destroyed Sloth, and it was disconcerting. The magnetic pull was gone—along with the Virtue once nestled inside Nicholas's soul. Now he felt just as barren, just as blank, as Alan and Thorn always had.

It showed on his face. His bright eyes had dulled, and when he smiled, it didn't feel real. Darius wasn't sure if he was imagining it, but even the color of Nicholas's skin seemed to have lost its shine, and his freckles were dusty and gray. He felt older. Sadder. He cleared his throat and stepped beside Darius.

"Why aren't you out there?" Nicholas asked, jutting his chin toward where the rest of the Underground was still laughing and chatting on the far end of the courtyard. "It's been a pretty big week for the Martyrs."

His voice carried an unfamiliar tone. Nicholas watched Darius with an intensity that hadn't diminished with the loss of his Virtue. It was focused, driven, but this time, a little sad. Regretful. Darius shook his head again and turned his attention back across the room.

"I don't really feel like celebrating," he said.

He wasn't the only one. Darius couldn't help but notice that not *every* Martyr was present at the big group dinner. He didn't see Thorn, which was hardly a surprise. The only time Thorn made an appearance in the courtyard was when she came and went from the gym or to her sleeping quarters. But many members of the Tactical Unit hadn't shown, either. Most notably, Chris. Darius knew that she, like him, hadn't left her room much in the last few days.

For some, mourning was a very private matter.

"People've been asking about you," Nicholas said. "They want to make sure you're okay."

Darius glanced at Nicholas—his brows furrowed, his mouth set into a brusque frown. Make sure he was *okay*? He had no idea how to respond to that. It had taken seven days—just *seven days*—for Darius to lose not just Saul, Juniper, and Lindsey, but Eva, too. It was like losing the orphanage again. The last link to his old life—to the man he was before he became a Virtue.

Darius's lack of a response seemed to tell Nicholas enough. He cleared his throat and cast a look across the courtyard. Darius followed his gaze. More people had gathered. The elevator doors opened, and even *more* Martyrs poured out. Elijah and his wife. Their two sons.

Thorn—

A small wave of surprise broke over Darius.

She and Mackenzie walked along the far side of the dining area, talking casually as they made their way through the crowd outside the kitchen. Before they slipped behind the counter to where the pizza station was set up, though, Thorn's head lifted. She quickly surveyed the Martyrs gathered there, her dark eyes piercing and aware. They took in every face with a sharp, attentive focus before sweeping through the courtyard. When she saw Darius and Nicholas standing across the room, she paused.

Then she nodded, just once, before allowing Mackenzie to draw her back into the conversation and lead her in to make their food.

Darius had never seen Thorn eat a meal in the courtyard with the rest of the Martyrs.

Nicholas seemed to know what Darius was thinking. He took a deep breath, and on the exhale, he said, "She's been coming down a lot. I think she's trying to check on you without, you know, *checking* on you."

Heat rushed to Darius's cheeks. He felt a little ashamed he hadn't realized just how many people would be this concerned about him. Nicholas was one of those people.

Though Darius didn't turn to look at him again, he could see from the periphery that Nicholas hadn't stopped watching him. The other Virtue—*former* Virtue—just stared at the side of his face.

At last, Nicholas said, "I'm sorry about Eva."

Darius's heart skipped a painful beat as it fell into the pit of his stomach. Just the mention of Eva's name was enough to make his throat tighten and his hands ball into desperate fists at his sides. His fingernails dug painfully against his palms. He went to clear his throat, but he felt the pressure of trying push against his aching chest, so instead, he sighed.

"It's not your fault," Darius said. His voice cracked at the last word. Nicholas shook his head.

"It is," he said. "I should have healed her first. If I would have—"

"Stop," Darius said. He closed his eyes and raised a

437

hand. "Please. I know what happened. I don't need to hear it again."

Hearing it once had been hard enough.

Nicholas coughed a little and shifted uncomfortably. He looked deflated—like he was trying to keep himself afloat but just didn't have the breath anymore.

A guilty pang rocked through Darius's gut. It occurred to him that he wasn't the only one who lost something important—something that had been an integral and intimate part of his life. Even though *he* didn't want to talk about it... maybe Nicholas *did*. Maybe he had to.

"How are *you*?" Darius asked. Nicholas glanced up at him, and Darius continued. "How do you feel?"

"Hah!" The sound came out a little strangled, and Nicholas raised a hand to scratch the back of his head. "It's weird. I thought I was having a heart attack, couldn't sleep for two days straight, and I kinda get why Thorn is such a bitch all the time now, but I'll manage."

Darius tried to smile, even though he knew it would look forced. "Still, it's got to feel pretty great to have destroyed Sloth. Good job, man. That's incredible."

Then Nicholas's expression faltered. His mouth tightened, and his brows furrowed a little bit. "You'd think, huh? But no. Not really." He looked back up to Darius, and seeing the frown settled onto his face, he sighed. "I mean, it *is* a good thing. I know it is. But it doesn't *feel* good. It doesn't feel much like anything. It just feels like... like I'm done. It's done. And now... fuck, I don't know where to go from here."

A tense silence fell between them—a pause full of loss and doubt and instability. Nicholas's eyes cast down at the ground, unfocused and distant as he thought. Darius watched him. He hadn't noticed before, but Nicholas had placed a hand over his chest, almost absent-mindedly. His palm was flat against a spot just between his lungs.

It was the same exact space where Darius felt the aching emptiness of Eva's death.

But the pain of loss was different. Darius knew firsthand that this void would heal. Maybe imperfectly, with cracks and chips to show what he had gone through, but eventually, this feeling would go away. Nicholas's would not. What he had given up ran deeper.

Darius took a slow breath. "Why do you need to go anywhere?"

Nicholas looked up at him. His frown deepened. "What do you mean?"

"There's a lot you can do for the Martyrs," Darius said. "You only took out one of the Sins. We've still got five more. Help us bring them down."

For a moment, Nicholas considered Darius. He finally dropped his hand from his chest and shoved it into the front pocket of his slacks. "You sure you want me to stay? I was a total dick."

"Maybe, but we need you," Darius said, and he smirked. "You're driven, smart—hell, you figured out how to *Deprogram* Sloths' Sentries."

For the first time since he'd come to join Darius, a sign of light and laughter returned to Nicholas's face. He leaned back and waved off the compliment with a lazy hand. "Ah, that wasn't really me. Skylar did most of the heavy lifting."

"Skylar?"

"Yeah," Nicholas said. "I remembered you telling me she taught you *how* to Program, and I needed some expert help. All I did was go through the footage from the attacks to figure out what the triggers and rules were. Skylar wrote the script to undo the Programming Sloth did. She deserves the credit."

Darius shook his head. "Don't cop out—you know what you did was impressive. Even Alan has a hard time with it, and he's been Programming for over a century."

Nicholas shrugged. "I'm just glad it worked. Otherwise, I'd probably be dead."

Darius's mouth fell open. "What? You didn't test it?"

"How the fuck was I supposed to test it? Ask Sloth to

Program some poor asshole for me so I could get some practice in?" Nicholas asked with a laugh. A real laugh. Seeing a genuine smile light up his face made Darius feel a little better. Despite his sorrow—despite the deep, aching loss—he felt his mood start to lighten.

"God," he said, and he shook his head with a soft chuckle. "Does Thorn know? She'll be *pissed* you took that kind of risk."

"What's she going to do about it now?" Nicholas asked, and he raised his eyebrows. "Break my nose?"

Then he laughed again, and Darius couldn't help it. He did, too.

"Man... I forgot she did that," he said.

"Eh." Nicholas shrugged, but his expression softened. For a brief moment, he seemed lost in thought. "She did what she had to do."

Then the laughter faded, and the two of them shared another silence. Darius watched the side of Nicholas's face as his eyes disconnected again. Darius could only imagine what was going through his head—how he felt now with that vacuum inside his soul.

"I meant what I said." Darius's voice sounded stronger than he felt himself, and Nicholas turned to look at him. "The Martyrs need your help. *I* need your help."

Nicholas stared at him for several seconds. His resolve began to break again. The hint of emotions he was trying to stamp down—of fear, sadness, and loneliness—crept into the creases of his face and the emptiness behind his eyes.

"Thanks," he said. His voice caught up, so he swallowed and shook his head. It was awkward, like he was embarrassed at his show of vulnerability. Nicholas held out a hand. "Now, let's go find us some god damned Virtues."

Darius smiled. He grabbed Nicholas's outstretched fingers with a firm grip. "Let's do it."

Nicholas nodded. When he released Darius's hand, he quickly took off through the courtyard, past the bustling Martyr crowd gathered at the kitchen, and toward the elevator. Darius knew he was headed up to the R&D headquarters to start on more research, but he marveled at how strange it was to watch him leave without being able to feel it.

Without half of his soul, Nicholas was practically invisible now. The elevator doors closed behind him, and he disappeared entirely.

Darius stared for a moment, his eyes unfocused, his mind wandering. He took a deep breath and gently raised his hand to his chest. He laid his palm flat against his sternum—felt the beating of his heart; the slow, rhythmic expanding and collapsing of his lungs; and the dead weight nestled between them.

It wasn't permanent. He would eventually recover from losing Eva. This ache would fade. This time. One day, though, he would be just an empty vessel—a has-been Virtue—with a void pulling him into the dark. His stomach knotted into an uncomfortable ball. He couldn't imagine living that way.

But he knew he could. He knew it was possible. He had proof.

His eyes focused again, and he slowly looked over to the Martyrs. They were still talking. Still laughing. Still celebrating. Darius took them in. Each face was full of life and purpose they'd been missing a year ago.

Even in the throes of loss, they were able to find joy. Maybe it was because loss was all they'd had for so long. Loss was old. Familiar. *Normal.*

But joy was new. So much of what they were going through now was *new.*

At last, Darius found who he was looking for. Thorn. She was sitting at the counter with Mackenzie. The Irishwoman's back was turned to him, but Thorn sat sideways on her stool so Darius could see her face. Even she looked more at peace than she usually did. Her dark, half-empty eyes were more open, more relaxed. She whipped her black hair behind her ear with one half-gloved hand, and she nodded along as Mackenzie spoke, but Darius could see she was distracted. Her eyes kept darting toward him. As soon as she saw that he was watching her, her focus shifted. She looked right at him.

And Darius was relieved to see her expression was not the same canvas of happiness the rest of the Martyrs shared. There was an understanding there—an empathy at what Darius was going through, and not just with losing Eva.

But at what he *would* go through when Envy was finally destroyed.

The tightness in Darius's gut started to relax. There was a comfort in knowing he wouldn't be going through it alone.

He wasn't really alone, though, was he? He didn't just have Thorn, Alan, and now Nicholas to help him navigate the eventuality of losing half of his soul. He had the Martyrs. Darius started walking through the courtyard. Eyes moved to him. Faces lit up, full of relief and gratitude at seeing him out in the open again. He realized the emptiness he was feeling now—and the emptiness that would someday be just as much a part of him as his Virtue was today—was etched into every single one of these faces. As people came up to him and slapped him on the back, or hugged him, or told him how glad they were to see him, Darius saw that they were all vessels. Just like him. Empty vessels who had lost *so much* in this war against the Sins that they had forgotten what it was to feel happy.

"Darius," Raquel said. She and Skylar got to their feet, and Raquel wrapped her arms around Darius's shoulders. He felt a few hot tears fall from her eyes and onto his neck as he hugged her back. She took a deep breath and pulled herself together. "We've missed you!"

He smiled against her hair and looked up. Skylar was watching him with a sympathetic half-smile. Holly hadn't gotten to her feet, but she caught his eye and nodded.

"Sorry I've been so distant," he started to say, but Raquel didn't let him finish.

"*Don't,*" she said. She came back and pointed a finger at

Darius's chest. "Don't be sorry. It's okay to need some space."

"Yeah," Skylar said, reaching out and gently patting Darius on the shoulder. "You don't owe us an appearance out here to make *us* feel better. We're just happy to see you."

Darius was overcome with a sense of gratitude. He felt it chipping away at the stone in his chest, filling in the hole little by little.

"Thanks," he said, but the word sounded strangled through the emotion tightening around his throat. He cleared it and tried again. "I'm gonna go grab something to eat."

He went to walk past, but before he did, Raquel grabbed him up in another affectionate embrace. "If you need to talk, you know where to find me," she said quietly. Her words twisted at a sensitive spot in his heart. He felt a wave of tears spring up just behind his eyelashes, and he blinked them away.

"Thank you."

Then she squeezed him once, and he was on his way. He gently pushed through the throng of people, receiving more kind looks and warm touches. Parker Boseman threw him an eager wave and compassionate smile. Her father, Marcus, just nodded in his direction. Darius nodded back. As he neared, Alan got to his feet and grabbed him firmly by the shoulder. That was it. Nothing but a steady grip and a focused look that made Darius feel secure. Then he moved on. John shook his hand. Elijah and his family raised their glasses. More touches. More *love* as Darius moved through the crowd.

The Martyrs' warmth enveloped him in a comfortable blanket of human energy—human *life*. They moved as one, their auras blurring at the edges, giving the illusion that they were more than their individual selves. They were one force, one power, and they were *strong*.

At last, Darius came out on the other side. The heat ebbed as he walked by the last table and came up to the counter where Thorn and Mackenzie were waiting. Thorn had watched him the entire time he'd been crossing the courtyard, and she was still watching him now. Her dark eyes were pointed and alert but softer than Darius was used to. All of Thorn was a little softer. The muscles along her jaw were more relaxed, the line of her neck less rigid. Even her thin lips weren't pressed so tightly together.

Mackenzie had been watching him, too. Her bright eyes went wide, her toothy grin somehow wider. As soon as he was within earshot, her hands shot into the air.

"Jones!"

The Irishwoman hopped off her stool with an almost childlike fervor, and she threw herself into Darius's arms. He wasn't prepared for it. Mackenzie was small, but her momentum sent him stumbling backward. He barely managed to hold onto her and stay on his feet. Thorn laughed. The sound caught Darius off guard. He looked up at her from over the top of Mackenzie's bright, electric blue pixie cut. She wore a bemused smile, and her brows rose on her head.

He smiled, too.

"Hey, Mackenzie," Darius said, and he let out a laughing groan as she squeezed him uncomfortably tight and lifted her feet from the ground.

Then she let go, flopped back down, turned to Thorn with a victorious smile. "And *you*!" She stomped back over to the counter and brandished a palm-up hand to the Forgotten Sin sitting there. "You owe me ten bucks!"

Thorn rolled her eyes. "Just saying, 'I betcha ten bucks' doesn't mean any of us has ever actually agreed to your ten-buck-bets, McKay." But a smirk still tugged at the corner of her mouth, and Thorn dipped into her satchel, drew out her wallet, and handed Mackenzie a crisp ten-dollar bill all the same.

Darius frowned curiously. "What bet?"

Thorn tried to wave the question off, but Mackenzie jumped right in. She folded the money and shoved it into the front pocket of her jeans as she said, "Thorn thought it would take you a week to leave your room."

"That's *not* what I said."

"Okay, *fine*," Mackenzie said with a dramatic shrug. "*I* said I wondered when you'd leave your room, and *she* said you needed time to process everything that went down and to give it a week before worrying about it, and *I* bet her ten bucks it would be sooner. *Better*?" She cast Thorn a sly look and winked.

Thorn just watched her with a cool expression. "Yes."

"Anyway," Mackenzie said, thumping Darius on the shoulder while she rushed behind him and into the kitchen. She called over her shoulder as she walked along the other side of the counter. "Ya hungry? I can whip you up a quick pizza."

"Oh, I can get it."

"No, no," she said, and she waved him off. "Sit down. Relax. I hope you like anchovies."

Mackenzie raised her eyebrows, bit her lower lip, and disappeared into the walk-in refrigerator. Darius chuckled as he took the abandoned stool she'd been occupying before and turned to Thorn.

"So, you're taking bets on me now?" he asked, but he asked it with a smile and a lighthearted note to his voice. Thorn arched a brow as he continued. "And you gave me a *week*? You have *no* faith…"

His smile stretched a little wider. Thorn shrugged and lifted a glass of water to her lips.

"If anything, it shows how much faith I have in you," she said. "My personal record is three months."

She passed him a small, comforting smile over the rim of her glass. There was a dark humor behind her eyes. Darius chuckled.

Then, as Thorn placed her water back on the countertop, she turned to him with a more serious expression. "How are you?"

She spoke more quietly than Darius was expecting— more intimately. A somber tone to the way she asked it let

Darius know she wasn't asking for courtesy's sake. He looked up at her. Her eyebrows had shifted, just a little, into concern as she leaned toward him. For a moment, he thought about that question.

How *was* he?

His heart ached. His body felt exhausted. His mind was reeling—from Eva's death and Nicholas's soul being divided and destroyed.

Darius shook his head. "Not too good, to tell you the truth."

Silence fell between them, but a patient and perceptive silence. Thorn didn't look away from Darius's face. Her soul-piercing eyes just looked deep into his, and she slowly nodded. Darius took in a deep breath, and then he tried to smile.

"But I will be."

A bit of the tension faded. The grim air between them shifted. For the first time, Darius saw a little bit of the joy he'd seen in the rest of the Martyrs reflected in Thorn's expression. Her smile was small but *real*.

"Don't rush it," she said. "You have plenty of time."

Her voice carried an air of relief—of alleviated guilt. Darius remembered when Teresa had destroyed Pride and how *furious* Thorn had been when they thought destroying the Sin meant sacrificing the Virtue's life. She'd gone so far as to tell Darius to leave. She had never been happy asking him to die for this war.

But even if he didn't lose his life, he wasn't coming out of it in one piece.

"I actually wanted to ask you something," Darius said, and he turned more fully toward her. "You know what it's like—what Nicholas is going through. Can you *honestly* say it's better than dying?"

Thorn considered him for a few long, thoughtful seconds. Her lips slowly came together in a light frown.

"Yes," she said at last. "At first, he won't think so. At first, he will *wish* for the release… He'll dream about it. He may even consider doing it himself." Her voice briefly broke, and Darius noticed she pulled her scarred arm in and put it in her lap. "But death is a *cop-out*. It's an easy way out of a shitty situation. Nicholas isn't less of a person without that half of his soul. He's just a different person. Learning to be that person—to *accept* him? That's his challenge now, but it's worth it. He's more than his Virtue. He always has been."

From the intense, driven look in Thorn's eye and the *ardent* way she'd spoken, Darius got the feeling that she wasn't really talking about *Nicholas*...

Which was fine. Darius hadn't really been asking about him.

Instead, he was trying to navigate this new realization— this new *truth*—he was going to have to come to terms with.

A future. Without Eva, without Kindness, and without a soul.

ABOUT THE AUTHOR

MC Hunton is a bright personality with a shockingly dark taste in the stories she writes. She has been obsessed with storytelling since she was a child and has been honing her craft for over two decades. MC graduated with a bachelor's degree in Creative Writing in 2010 and has been working on her debut series, *The Martyr Series*, since 2005. She has a penchant for fast-paced action, deeply-rooted sociopolitical and spiritual themes, and emotionally driven plot and character development.

Check out what she's up to by visiting her website:
www.MCHunton.com

CPSIA information can be obtained
at www.ICGtesting.com
Printed in the USA
JSHW032202110622
26970JS00002B/12